Dealer

By

Eric T. Stiller, Jr.

Text Copyright © 2015 by Eric T. Stiller, Jr.
Cover Illustrations © 2015 by Rick Stiller
All rights reserved.
Published by House of the Four Seasons Publishing

ISBN 978-0-9892702-1-2

Visit: rickstiller.com

For dear friends,
Long gone

Dealer

By

Eric T. Stiller

On the third day, Bernie kicked over the last jug of water. In a frenzy to escape the sweltering heat, he clamored over the stern, delirium driving his desperation across an endless sea of slow syrupy swells to a frosty mirage on the horizon. Augie and Ruck lunged to wrestle him back into the lifeboat, as two gray dorsal fins sliced the surface inches below his chin.

"What? Are you nuts?" yelled Ruck.

"We're gonna die out here," moaned Bernie, tucking into a fetal position, in the bilge water sloshing around the hull of the tiny dingy.

"If you wanna be fish food, have at it," said Augie. "Just swim away from the boat, so the sharks don't come lookin' for more."

"You said we'd be rich not dead!"

"If you guys had checked the sump, we'd be sippin' Sunrises in Key West by now," snapped Augie, pulling a grungy green Jets tee-shirt over his head, scant protection against a blazing tropical sun oozing into the horizon, as he curled his lanky frame into a shadow in the shallow curve of the bow.

"I checked it," said Ruck. "No way to know we were going to get hammered by that storm. We got swamped by twenty foot waves and even two of them couldn't keep up."

"So, we lost the boat and a half a ton of primo weed," whimpered Bernie. "Even if we do survive, how're we going to pay everyone back? They're gonna kill us."

"We'll do it again, only this time we'll use boats we can trust," said Augie. "Three days stranded is long enough to realize that we've gotta get organized. We'll succeed because there's too much demand and too much money. We just need to learn the rules of the game."

The blast of a horn interrupted his ramblings, as a Cuban gunboat approached out of a scalding sunset. A sailor, manning a machine gun mounted on the foredeck, eyed the three desperately sunburned young men in the tiny skiff with a smirk, "Gringos!"

An officer stepped out of the bridge and yelled, with the barest hint of sarcasm, "Hola! Are you in distress?"

The boys sat up, hands above their heads.

Augie called out, "Our boat went down in that storm three days ago. We sure could use some food, water, and a lift to dry land."

"You realize that you are violating the sovereign territory of the Republic of Cuba and you will be detained by the authorities as spies or illegal aliens, at the very least. If convicted, the minimum penalty is three years hard labor. Considering the tension between our two countries, diplomatic arrangements might be difficult and expensive."

Bernie yelled, "So, you're suggesting we can float around out here without food or water, until we die, or surrender to you?"

"Si, Senor."

Ruck quipped, "I'm votin' for terra firma, myself."

"Permission to board?" shouted Augie.

～

La Cabana, a heavily fortified 18th-century bastion perched on a rocky outcrop guarding the harbor entrance, served as a military prison during the Batista regime, a dungeon where prisoners disappeared without a trace. After the rebellion, Che Guevara administered ruthless trials and executions for the remnants of the defeated establishment, with brutal efficiency, but most patrons of the government fled long before the revolutionaries stormed Havana. Currently, the crumbling garrison housed enemies of the state and criminal detainees, separated from the general criminal population in the city jail for political expediency.

A squad of guards in tattered uniforms removed the handcuffs and shoved the boys into a dank overcrowded cell in the bowels of the complex. Rats scurried and roaches flitted around a light bulb in the ceiling above a hole in the floor that served as a toilet, flushed by a stream of gray water dripping from a broken faucet.

Undeterred by the new arrivals, a small crowd huddled at the back of the cell for a boisterous game of dice, while most sat on the six cots lined up against the walls or leaned passively, staring at the Yankees. Two stout thugs started towards the new meat, grinning like starving mongrels stalking easy prey.

Bernie backed against the wall of rusted iron bars, "Fuck, this doesn't look like a Tupperware party to me."

Augie brushed Ruck out of harm's way and, without warning, punched the first hulking boar squarely on the nose with a straight right, toppling the giant in a heap. He spun to batter the smaller goon with a flurry of four quick shots. He scanned the pack of potential muggers, motionless with mouths agape, but no one made a sound or moved to tend to the two fools on the floor for a long moment...before the tiny cell erupted into chaos and they morphed into a raging mob, closing on the boys in slow motion.

Keys rattled at the door and a guard burst in, discharging a pistol into the ceiling. He surveyed the moaning bodies on the floor and motioned for the boys to exit the cell.

Thirty minutes later, they were admitted to the Commandant's office, a sparsely furnished room with piles of paper stacked on every surface. The guard saluted and closed the door, as the warden stood and pointed to a wooden bench with a riding crop, "Sit!"

The boys sat obediently, as each had so many times in the Monsignor's office at Sebastian Academy.

The sweaty man, clothed in a rumpled uniform and worn boots, strode back and forth beneath a ceiling fan that barely moved the sultry blue haze of a stale cigar, thumping the crop against his boot. Finally, he stopped, tapping several times, and said in mildly accented English, "If these walls could speak, they would tell tales of torture and horrific deaths wrought at the hands of desperate despots, defending a fleeting moment of power. Today, we house enemies of the State and the most dangerous criminals in absolute security. You three arrive and cause chaos in the first five minutes of your incarceration and you haven't even been charged yet!"

"We didn't start it," said Ruck.

"Silence!" yelled the officer. "It would be easy enough to make you disappear, as if you'd never been found floating around in the Gulf, and, I'm sure, your cellmates would relish a rematch."

Augie stood, "These guys didn't have anything to do with it. I took them out."

"I might have suspected. Sit!" He turned back to his desk, "I fought alongside Fidel and Che but, now, I have become an administrator, merely a cog in the revolutionary machine. Even in this insignificant role, I realize that we must be seen in the foreign press as benevolent, if we are to expand the fight for the freedom of our brothers and sisters throughout the region. Public sympathy is a powerful weapon."

"What does that have to do with us?" asked Bernie.

"Arrangements have been made for the Red Cross to

evacuate you to the Swiss Embassy, where you will await the court's decision. I can not predict the outcome, but I would hope that the authorities see the practical benefits of your repatriation, rather than internment where you would surely die." He leaned on the edge of the desk, with the slightest smile, "Besides, there is no honor in the senseless deaths of the three stupid young Americans. That is counter-revolutionary!"

"What you're really saying is that you don't want the responsibility, if we happen to die on your watch," smirked Ruck.

"You do have a point, young man." He waved his hand around the stacks of paper, "I have more important things to worry about than filling endless forms with fiction."

~

Bernie slumped into a chaise in a tepid breeze wafting through open French doors and turned to Augie, who was flipping through an aged National Geographic, "Not that I'm complaining, this sure beats the hell outta that rat-infested hellhole, but that General guy didn't spring us out of the goodness of his heart. '

Augie held up a double page spread of topless African natives and smiled, "Someday, we're gonna have to go on safari!" He tossed the magazine on the table, "Think about it, they have nothing to gain by holding us, we're a bureaucrat's nightmare, and they sure don't want the parents of damaged American youngsters spouting off to the press. Besides, they've got crucial things to worry about, like whether an armada of Yankees is going to appear on the horizon or how they're gonna feed their people. As far as they're concerned, we're a bunch of spoiled kids, who were lucky to survive our own ignorance."

"Yeah, but there's more to it than that," added Ruck.

"I'm guessin' the Red Cross got in touch with our parents and the old man is making sure that we're well cared for with a generous donation…and you can bet he's pissed."

"Makes sense," said Bernie. "He's definitely got connections in all the right places."

Augie smirked, "Asshole owns the right people."

"I'm thinkin' we should have taken up boxing or judo or something, back in junior high, when you did."

"I'm thinkin' you're right," replied Augie.

"So, when are we getting out of here?" asked Ruck, who looked absolutely tropical with his dark hair slicked back, a white linen shirt opened two buttons down from the collar, loose beige pants, and sandals.

"Relax, the wheels are turning and we're just along for the ride. In the meantime, we're safe and well fed until things get worked out." He handed out long, fragrant cigars, "We might not have dope but these are pretty sweet."

The boys puffed, "Speaking of sweet, did you check out our 'minder'? She can't be any older than we are."

"Yeah, and she's built too, even under that baggy uniform," laughed Bernie. "First one to get her in the sack wins the title of 'The Man'!"

Augie grinned, "You guys already lost."

~

Diffused by a fog of blue smoke, the warm cast of a green glass desk lamp framed the orange glow of a cigar clamped in his father's mouth. "You okay?"

Reluctantly, Augie stepped into the darkened study, "Yeah."

"Sit."

His butt barely touched the chair, when his father leaned his massive girth across the imposing desk, screaming, "Augustus Constantine, what the fuck did you think you were doing? You punks cost me a bundle and more than a few favors."

"Trying to make a buck."

"How does a screw-up, with a lifetime on the sea, get caught in a squall, sink a yacht in Cuban waters, and paddle around in a lifeboat without supplies for three days?"

"Profit potential. It's simple math. We bought the boat for twenty grand and the load of pot for twenty-five. We should have spent more on a better boat but the storm that got us was a killer, so I'm not sure it would've made any difference. If we'd completed the trip, we would have cleared two-hundred grand, after expenses."

Julius sat back, "That's a lot of money." He took a deep drag on his stogie, "Where'd you get the dough?"

"A bunch of people pitched in."

"And they'll be wanting repayment, at the very least, if not a piece of your ass."

"I'll find a way to pay everyone back with interest," snapped Augie.

"Damned right, because no LaGuerre ever welched on a debt and you won't be the first!" He rocked back, puffing on the cigar, "You've putzed around the factory and you've had offers for some pretty good jobs, so why are you doing this?"

The son rested his elbows on the edge of the desk, "First, because every job I've ever had taught me how not to run a business. Everyone I worked for survived in spite of their own stupidity and a complete lack of imagination. Everything was done the way it had always been done, so there was no potential to make more than a salary, unless I figured out how to buy the company and fire the entire management staff. Second, because this is a brand new market and supply is spotty at best. No one's organized a system to import and distribute the product efficiently. The demand is phenomenal and the profits are unbelievable."

"What about these other drugs...the hallucinogens and junk?"

"I don't mess with them, they're bad karma. Grass is

different. It's a natural plant that grows from the earth and it's been used as a sacrament for thousands of years all over the world. And I'm pretty sure that no one ever died from smoking a joint. The only people with a problem are the cops and the politicians, and even that was conjured up by the government to control the Mexicans and the Blacks back in the Thirties."

Julius stared at his son, no longer a gangly kid, rather, a tall handsome graduate who still bore that mischievous glint in his intense dark eyes. No doubt anxious to begin his own quest to conquer the world, yet too naïve to comprehend the toll that ambition drains from the soul. "So, you're trying to imitate the old man, eh?"

"No, I'm trying to create my own capital to do what I want, instead of having to depend on you."

"You want for nothing! Nothing!"

"True…but it's yours and, like it or else, there are always strings attached. I want to earn my own."

"My son the drug dealer!"

"Hey, I know you're involved in a lot of deals that can't possibly qualify as kosher, so don't give me that crap! I count fifty-eight different checkbooks in the office and those are only the ones that aren't locked up."

"I came up from the streets and I've busted my ass for forty years to provide for my family!"

"And so will I!" screamed Augie. "And by 'family' are we talking Mom and the kids or Carlito and Uncle Vinnie and all the rest of the clan?"

The old man leaned forward, his eyes blazing, "I wanted a better life for my children, including you."

"The old ways are changing. Look around, all these long-haired kids are smokin' dope and they're perfectly willing to pay for it."

"In the old days, a few of the smaller families handled the

drugs but it was considered a dirty business. It was not a trade to be respected."

"But prostitution and gambling and jamming every union in the city was any different?"

Julius' eyes glared through a swirl of blue smoke, "You're a grown man and I can't direct your life, in spite of my misgivings, but I'll make two demands. Do not disgrace the family name and keep your little brother out of this,"

Augie stood, "I'll be discreet."

The old man rested his heels on the desk and leaned back, "Damned right! You and your little buddies owe me fifty grand for the ransom and I expect to be paid."

"Fine, I'll have you paid off in ninety days."

"If you don't, I'll take it out of your ass with interest!" laughed the old man, groaning, as he hauled himself out of the chair to lean on the desk. "The Lollipop is in Charlotte Amalie and needs to be brought up for servicing before winter sets in. Cappy's got a dry dock for us in two weeks. You supply the crew."

Incredulous, Augie just stared, "But...?"

"If you sink my boat, make sure you drown, because I won't be bailing your butt out of jail, I'll be lookin' to grind you into chum."

~

The glass door groaned and slammed as Augie pushed through the foyer of the old graystone and trudged up five flights to the flat, thinking, *"If I cashed the trust, I could just about pay everyone off and be done with it...or, I could use it as seed money. Basic economics — research, plan, prepare, and make your move. When you succeed, expand into the next opportunity. When you lose, you learn, you find the mistakes in the business plan, and, if the premise is still valid, you continue."*

The frosted transom above the door was dark, as he reached to insert his key into the lock, but the door creaked open. The apartment was dim, save the faint glow of streetlights creeping through the blinds and a sliver of amber firing across the planked floor from his bedroom door. He tiptoed down the hall and peaked through the gap to spy Abby, beautifully naked, nestled back into the pillows on the king-size mattress, thrusting a giant vibrator between her legs.

She looked up without interrupting the rhythm, "Come 'ere big guy, you've got just what I need."

Augie sauntered over, dropped his bag, and leaned over for a kiss. Abby unbuckled his belt, popped the button on his jeans, and pulled down the zipper to grab his cock. "Still work?" smirked the little blond, squatting on the vibrator, as her tongue flicked from stem to head and her lips parted.

~

Abby was leaning on an elbow, blowing smoke in his face, when he opened his eyes, "So, ya' wanna fuck or are ya' gonna tell me the story or what?"

He slowly focused on her blue eyes peeking through a veil of thin blond hair, tan skin, button nose, and perfectly round little everything, "Mind if I wake up?"

"Wanna smoke a joint?"

"How 'bout coffee?"

She stood up and sauntered into the kitchen.

"Nice butt," said Augie, pulling a pillow over his head.

The little blond padded into the bedroom to deliver two mugs and a tray of bagels, cream cheese, and Welch's jelly. Her eyes squinted through the smoky trail of a Marlboro, with a two-inch ash, clamped in the corner of her mouth, "Coffee and food."

"Thanks," said Augie, sitting up and ruffling his dirty blond curls.

Abby poked his ribs, "You don't look like you lost any

weight."

"I've been eating Cuban steaks for a month."

"How'd you manage that?"

He took a sip of coffee, "Look, I'll tell you about the interesting stuff but I think you'd be safer, if I left out the business side of things."

"What do you mean?"

"I don't want you to be in a position where you might be forced to testify against me or be suspected of being involved."

"So you went off to buy some pot and you came back paranoid about the Federalies?"

"Importing is a different game than just buying a pound and dealing it out to your friends. If someone's going to succeed at this, they're going to have run it like a business."

"Fine, Prince Charming protecting my honor!" laughed Abby. "All you want is my pussy."

"That too," smirked Augie through a mouthful of bagel.

"So…the steaks?"

"Oh, we got swamped in a storm, sank the boat, and lost the load. We floated around in a dingy for three days with no food and a couple of little jars of water before a Cuban gunboat picked us up. The authorities dumped us in the kind of dank, ancient, rat-infested jail cells you see in creepy old movies, jammed with Cuban criminals, who didn't like Yankees much. With some prodding from my father, the Red Cross got us out and put us up in the Swiss embassy. They took care of us until we finally got cleared to fly out to Mexico City."

"Sounds like quite an adventure," said Abby, stretching out on the pillows. "I'm sure you didn't find time for any ass, while you were gone?"

"Well, there was our beautiful Cuban minder, who followed us around whenever we left the embassy."

"You asshole!" shouted the ferocious little dynamo, swinging a pillow at his head. "C'mere, I want some of that."

A banging at the door interrupted. Abby sat up, disappointed, "I'll get it." Her tight buns bounced in perfect rhythm as she trotted down the hall and stood on tiptoe to peer through the peephole, "Shit, it's your buddies from Cuba."

"Let 'em in."

The little blond unlatched the bolts and pulled the door open to give Ruck and Bernie a hug, "I'm glad you two survived."

"Us too," laughed Bernie, trying not to stare at her pert nipples or the tiny puff of blond hair between her legs.

"There's coffee on the stove. Augie'll be out in a minute." She turned and strolled back into the bedroom, swinging her hips, with a big smile. "Well, their day started better than yours."

"How come?"

"They both had hard-ons before I finished hugging them."

"Put some clothes on," smirked Augie, dragging on a pair of bell-bottoms and a burgundy shirt. He grabbed his cup and a cigarette and headed for the living room at the front of the flat.

"You guys okay?"

Ruck grinned sheepishly, "My folks weren't too happy about any of it. Lots of yelling and screaming about how I disgraced the family and being disowned and stuff."

"Heck, my ol' man said it was too bad we didn't drown," said Bernie, "and meant it."

"Well, are you up for getting this right?"

Both nodded.

"Fine. Let's break this up, so the tasks suit the talents. Bernie, you're the scholar, so, transform yourself into a hip college professor and go see this PR guy."

"What do we need advertising for?" asked Bernie.

"We don't. We need research. You're writing a thesis on the history of smuggling - including slaves, liquor, weapons, and any kind of contraband during the wars – from the revolution right through Vietnam, and the current exportation of guns and importation of drugs and humans to and from South America and the Caribbean. To shore up the research, you're specifically interested in how the fortifications around the borders of the United States and Canada have moved and changed in relation to the threat. If he gets inquisitive, simply tell him that you've got a publisher lined up who doesn't want you talking about the project, because you're taking a different perspective on the whole thing, sort of outside looking in."

Bernie rubbed his sparse moustache, "Makes sense to know your adversary's strengths. I can do this."

"Great," said Augie, turning to Ruck. "Now, the ol' man wants the Lollipop brought up from Charlotte Amelia."

"How'd you manage that? I thought he'd skin you alive."

"We had a...confrontation and he was pissed but...I'm not really sure how it ended up this way. Anyway, you head down to St. Thomas and get her ready."

He turned to Bernie, "After you set up the research, catch a flight to Montego and hook up with Wilfred. No doubt, he'll be hangin' at that record shop off Market Street. I'll have it set up but you've gotta make sure we get quality product, none of that soggy moldy crap he tried to pass off on us the last time. If we're buying a half-ton at a time, it'd better be primo, weighed and packaged, or we'll go find another source. Make sure he understands that, if he acts like a pro, we'll be steady customers. You good with that?"

"No problem, I can handle him, but I think his mother, Nell, is the brains behind their deal. What are you going to do?"

"I'm going to do some research on other sources and get our scratch together, then meet up with Ruck on Wednesday, so we can connect with you by Sunday. We should have the wind with us all the way and storm season's pretty much over, so maybe the old tub with the broad beam might make good time."

Bernie looked up, "We better not screw this one up or

everyone from your ol' man and our parents to the Cuban government are gonna be lookin' for a piece of our asses."

~

Landing on the runway at Cyril E. King Airport in Charlotte Amelia, a jetty extending a thousand feet into the sea, created the illusion that the craft was certainly going to belly flop into the drink until tires bumped on pavement and the knot in Augie's stomach released. He marched down the stairs from the 707, slimed by a blast of soggy tropical air, and strolled across the tarmac with a beige linen sports coat draped over his left arm and an expensive leather briefcase in his right hand. His long curls were shorn to just below the collar of a touristy Hawaiian shirt he wore over crisply pressed khakis and shiny penny-loafers with mercury dimes in the slits.

He grabbed his bag, got his passport stamped, and, yes, he was certainly visiting as a tourist. Within minutes of departing the plane, his body was crushed into back seat of a small taxi-van tearing down Route 30 for the marina in Long Bay. The driver leaned over the seat at sixty miles an hour, with total disregard for lanes or other traffic, to offer a warm welcome. His bloodshot eyes left little doubt about his mental state and Augie suspected that his brains were swaddled inside a swirling rainbow knitted cap, pulled down to his eyebrows, which surely contained at least a bushel of dreadlocks in a pouch at the back.

Augie started to scream but the driver turned back to the road, "Relax Mon, the Jah is watching over us and, if you believe, we will come to no harm."

"Turn around and watch where we're going, so we don't run over this Jah guy."

The driver burst out laughing, "You Americans just don't understand."

"What?"

"The Rastaman inhales the sacrament to be close to God or Jah. He is the shepherd and we are his flock, his ignorant children seeking illumination. The sacred herb soothes the mind and opens the soul to purity and truth." He laughed, "Yankees just want to get high on the whacky weed but they don't want to take time to follow the righteous path to enlightenment."

"Why are you telling me this?"

"So that you don't make a grave mistake."

"What's that?"

He turned around again, his bloodshot eyes hypnotic, his voice a melody, "The herb is not a commodity, it is a sacrament. If you treat it with respect and honor, use it as the gods who provided it intended, you will reach understanding and equilibrium with the natural world around us. You'll find balance and purpose and Jah will watch over you."

Augie curled into the back of the plastic-covered seat, as the van swerved between two slower cars, spun hard right and screeched to a stop on the street above the docks. He exhaled slowly, feeling the blood beginning to rise back into his brain. "What do I owe you?"

"Ten dollars."

"Ten? The sign said six!"

"You didn't scream, so that's extra," laughed the slender man with an enormous smile of perfect pearly teeth. "And the information that I provided is certainly worthy of the investment, if you're as smart as I think you are, Mon."

Augie handed him a twenty and dragged his suitcase, briefcase, and coat out of the cab, as tires screeched and the car sped away. He piled his stuff on the curb and extended his arms to stretch an aching back. Long distance travel aggravated an old football injury and his spine was twisted for days after a flight unless he could find a good masseuse.

He grabbed his bags and lumbered down the steps to find the Lollipop, docked at the third pier, taking on fuel and water. Ruck popped out of the bridge, "'bout time you showed. I was gonna leave without you!"

"Yeah, right," laughed Augie, hugging his slender friend. His dark hair was slicked straight back and he was sporting starched blue shorts and a dress white shirt with epaulettes and little golden anchors on the collar, knee socks and deck shoes. "Do you always have to look like you stepped out of a Saks ad?"

Ruck looked down at his clothes, "What's wrong with this?"

"You're way too...yachting mod."

"Mod, I'm not a mod, I just like nice clothes. Besides, this is perfect for the skipper of a fine vessel like this."

"Shit, whoever marries you is going to have competition in front of the mirror!"

"You asshole! Have you looked in the your own mirror lately. You look like some business guy trying desperately to be hip."

"That's exactly how I want to be perceived. The cops are looking for hippies. We don't look like hippies."

"Good point."

"So, how's she check out?"

"All systems are go. Pumped the bilge, changed the oil in both engines and the generators, got supplies for three weeks, charted our course, and checked in with the harbormaster. There are no storms between here and Africa, so we're cleared to make way tonight," said Ruck. "How'd it go on your end?"

Augie grinned, "I just needed to check some things out."

"Like what?"

"Well, Jamaica is one source for fine weed but there are plenty of others. The more I think about this enterprise that we're building, the more I see it from a different perspective. I know that doesn't make any sense but look at it this way, we've been focused on a specific little piece of the market in our own backyard. If you zoom out a little, you notice that there are other backyards and neighborhoods and cities that all want pot. It's enormous. So, how do you supply customers in different parts of the country?"

"You've either gotta create an overland network or find the source closest to the market," mused Ruck, smiling. "Columbia's known for growing fine weed and, that kid from the neighborhood, Antonio's whole family is from Bogotá or someplace. I bet we could learn a lot from him."

Augie smirked, "Already did. If we pull this off, we'll split our profits between another round of this and one on the West Coast. I've got people waiting."

"This could get out of hand real quick."

"Yeah, I know."

The old cruiser eased into the docks of the marina in Montego Bay, just as the sun was setting in a blaze of red and yellow streaks fanning across the sky behind the bluffs to the west. Bernie staggered out of the clubhouse bar, meandering along the wharf until he lurched into a piling and leaned over the stern of the Lollipop, stammering, "Perr-rmisss-sion to commmme a-bord"

Ruck tossed a line and the drunk dropped his beer in the drink, fumbling to catch the rope. "How long have you been hangin' in that bar?"

"Oh, since...uh...'bout noon."

"Great, just what we need, you fucked up. I sure hope you've got your shit together."

"Yes, sir, captain, I do. It's all been arrrrrangged for Monday, yeah, that's tomorrow," said Bernie, now hopelessly tangled in the line between the boat, a pylon, and a cleat.

Ruck jumped onto the quay and snatched the rope, lashing it neatly on the tie-down. He stood up to grab Bernie by the collar of his plaid shirt and slam him against the piling, "We've got work to do. You can get fucked up at home but not on our time. You got it?"

"But you guys were late and I was bored," moaned a listless Bernie.

"You could always chase some pussy or just hang out at the beach and smoke a little weed but, no, you've gotta get shit-faced. We've been rotating watches for days and I'm definitely too tired for your shit, man."

"Alright, alright, I'll get it together, I promise. Besides, I've had things ready to roll for a couple of days now, so this is just a tiny little dimple on an otherwise smooooooth road ahead."

"You better be right about that," said Augie from the stern. "We haven't got time to screw around. Get on board and we'll make some coffee, then we're going to eat a big steak, because I'm sick of boat food already."

Bernie sat precariously on a stool in the galley, sipping black coffee and trying desperately not to puke.

"So, how'd it work out?" asked Augie.

"You were right, Wilfred's a cool kid but he's a gofer for his mom. Nell's got a finger in every brick of weed that moves through this town and she isn't afraid to let you know about it either. She's one tough dame and big enough to back it up."

Ruck chuckled, "Your kind of girl."

Bernie couldn't hold back and heaved in the sink. He turned on the water to rinse his mouth and wash his face. He brushed his sandy hair back as he settled on the stool and picked up his coffee cup, "That feels better."

"You're a dumbshit, you know that?" said Ruck. "Tell me about your girlfriend."

"I'd guess she weighs in at about two-fifty, minimum, and you could pick her voice out of the cheering crowd in a soccer stadium. She's real bright, right up front about everything, and seems like she's talkin' straight but, I'll tell you what, I sure wouldn't want to get on her wrong side."

"Yeah, but what's the product like and how's it gonna go down?" asked Augie.

"The weed is primo. I've got a brick in the rental but you'll approve. Deal's gonna go down in Tom Piper's Bay, down the coast, tomorrow night. She claims her family's been fishing out of that cove for generations."

"Sounds like we'll be playin' on her turf," said Ruck. "Not sure I like that."

Bernie shrugged, "I have no reason to believe that this whole thing isn't going to go down as agreed. I just feel like they're real folk, who want to sell to customers they can trust."

"Then, I guess, we have no choice, but we'll be prepared in case things head south. Now, are you sober enough so we can get something to eat?"

~

The Lollipop motored west along the rugged northern coast into dusk and idled through the mouth of Tom Piper's Bay, heading for the lights in Elgin Town. Three battered skiffs, with outboards that whined like angry insects, pulled along side and a voice, akin to melodious cannon fire, called out, "Is my Bernie aboard?"

Ruck cut the engines and Bernie leaned over the rail, "Lovely to see you on a beautiful night like this!"

"You're an old charmer, that's what you are!" laughed the huge woman. "Now get your skinny butt in gear and help me up there!"

Bernie opened the gate at the stern and lowered the diving platform to grab her hand. Augie took the other as Wilfred and another boy pushed from behind. With concerted effort, she stumbled on deck and straightened up, "Thank you, gentleman. I appreciate your help. Now, can we get down to business?"

"Could I offer you something cool to drink," offered Ruck, guiding her into the salon.

"Two fingers of dark rum on the rocks, if you have it?"

"Coming right up."

She took a seat in an armchair facing the door and Augie sat down opposite. "Bernie tells me that this relationship might be true romance, if we all get along."

"That's what we're hoping. We have an anxious audience and it's expanding geometrically."

"Then I want to make sure you're satisfied with the product and with our service."

"Show me what we're buying."

She put two fingers in her mouth and whistled. Wilfred appeared with a kilo brick wrapped in red cellophane and handed it to his mother, then stepped back to the doorway. A large fishing knife flashed in her chubby hand and sliced open the binding.

Augie broke the slab in half and inhaled, then held it up to the table lamp. Finally, he tossed the brick back onto the table, "It's fresh-picked, hasn't been cured, and it's moldy."

Bernie leaned back on the coach and reached behind a pillow, which meant Wilfred had a gun. Ruck walked over from the bar to offer their guest her drink on a silver tray with a Beretta underneath.

Augie raised his hands, "Before this gets out of hand, let's back up a minute. It seems to me that, if you're trying to export the teachings and sacrament of Jah, and making a tidy profit on the side, then you probably want the help of people like us. You provide the best of your harvest, we provide cash to expand your enterprise and spread the word across the whole country. We all win."

Nell smiled and winked at Wilfred, who pocketed the pistol. "You might not understand Jah but you feel it, don't you? It is a warmth in your soul, an assurance that there is someone looking out for you, an Almighty, an energy binding all of us with the cosmos of living things."

"And that's something that everyone should understand."

She snapped her fingers and a kilo wrapped in blue foil sailed across the cabin. "You are a very bright young man and honest in your heart. I think I will like you." She slit the foil and smiled, presenting the package like an offering. "I think you will find this to your approval."

The scent was fresh and minty, the texture of the plump six-inch manicured buds was firm with just a little suppleness when squeezed. Too wet and the product will mold, two dry and potency is diminished, water weight lost, and it burns like lint. He pulled several buds from each half and inspected them. "No seeds."

"The female plants are segregated from the males, so all their energy is focused into making flowers and resin in a desperate quest to be fertilized."

"The potency increases."

"By more than fifty percent. We do have our own chemists and agricultural consultants working to create a sustainable orchard, rather than dealing with amateurs hacking clearings out of the jungle, trying to make a few bucks."

"That's the spirit I was talking about. I'd like to see your grow the next time."

Wilfred said, "You'll be impressed and surprised."

"So, is this really the product you're selling us or are we going to play games?" asked Bernie, sniffing a bud.

"We can load you now, if you have the cash?"

"Then why did we have to go through this deadly little drama?" asked Ruck, tucking the Beretta in the back of his waistband.

The fat woman laughed, "Because I wanted to make sure you guys weren't trouble, first, and that you actually know what you're doing. I don't have time for amateurs or pirates."

Augie smiled, "We're just hippie businessmen who want to spread joy across our sad, sad land."

"Amen to that," said Ruck.

～

Ruck eased the Lollipop around the north end of Gardiners Island in the darkness of a moonless night, then south through Cherry Bay to nestle in the protection of a long curving spit of sand. Before the old cruiser's anchor dropped, a trawler, with a long flat aft deck for the tourist anglers, idled alongside. "Ahoy mates!" yelled the bearded skipper. "Can we see your papers?"

Augie leaned over the rail and smiled, "Right on time but screw you anyway!"

"Safe journey?" called Teddy Parsons, a gregarious bull with dark flashing eyes, framed by a thatch of black curls and a bushy moustache. His old man owned half of Manhattan but he and Ashton ran a little guided-fishing business over the summers, then headed to the Caribbean for the winter months.

"Smooth and calm," said Bernie as he tossed lines to tie off fore and aft.

"Worthy of the effort?" yelled Ashton Lambert, son of a Wall Street Banker.

A mischievous grin crinkled Augie's eyes to slits, "Heh, heh, I'm pretty sure you're gonna like this, if we can offload it without you guys dumping it in the drink."

Teddy stepped out of the little wheelhouse, "We've got nets!"

"Great!" yelled Ruck, rolling a dolly of boxes onto the aft deck. "Let's get busy."

They transferred more than fifty boxes in less than an hour but all five were dripping with sweat. "We've gotta get some labor to help out," laughed Ashton. "Call the union!"

"Yeah, just what we need," moaned Augie, stretching his back. "Inspectors!"

"That's far out," said Teddy.

"Are you trippin' again?" asked Ruck.

"Naw, just flashin', man, just flashin'. I can handle this."

"You better!" said Augie quietly. "They're dredging out Napeaque Harbor and they've installed a utility dock at the north end of the bay. Donny and Hank'll meet you there with the vans in thirty minutes. Easy in, easy out."

"You guys be safe," yelled Bernie, as the trawler cast off and turned south. "We'll catch you tomorrow."

Abby awoke to a knock at the door and padded, naked, down the hallway to peer through the peephole. Donny and Hank were leaning on a stack of brown cardboard boxes. She opened the door, "Don't you guys ever show up at a reasonable hour? I was actually asleep!"

"Shhh, keep it down," said Donny, with a peck on the cheek. "We're just delivery boys but there's a lot to bring up, so why don't you go put some clothes on?"

Hank added, "Yeah, you're definitely a serious distraction."

"You wish," smiled Abby, strolling down the hallway, swinging her hips.

"Bet she's a handful," said Hank, lugging a stack of boxes to the dining room.

"I'm bettin' she'd hurt you so good, you'd be begging for more," laughed Donny.

"Or mercy, one!"

"Next load."

After nearly two hours of creeping up five flights from the alley behind the building, daylight glowed under the window shades.

Abby brought a tray of coffee and Danish, "Thought you might need a little boost after working so hard all night."

"Thanks," said Hank, grabbing a sweet-roll and a mug.

Abby tossed a packet of rolling papers on the table and flicked a switchblade to slice open one of the boxes, "I'm thinkin' we ought to test this out, just to make sure."

She pulled out a kilo brick bound in blue foil and knelt beside the table to slice the wrapper. The sweet fresh aroma wafted from the packing and she grabbed a large pinch, stripping good bud from the stems. The little blond placed a paper between two fingers of her left hand and filled it with crumpled pot. The paper disappeared with a flick of her digits and she licked the gum to seal a perfectly cylindrical joint.

"That's amazing!" said Hank. "How'd you do that?"

"My ol' man rolled his own and taught me how to do it for him when I was just a little kid." She popped a kitchen match with the nail on her thumb and lit the joint, inhaling deeply. "Oh yeah, that's what I'm talkin' about."

Donny took a drag and coughed, "Sweet."

Hank grabbed the reefer, "I could get to likin' this."

Abby laughed, waving her hand at the wall of boxes, "I think we might finally have enough!"

The latch clicked in the door and Augie sauntered in, spying the brick on the table, "So, what'd ya' think?"

Abby exhaled a huge cloud of smoke, wheezing, "Dynamite!"

"You guys have any trouble?"

"Naw, just haulin' all this shit up five flights."

"So, how'd you feel about taking some of it back down?"

Abby stood up on tiptoes to French-kiss him, making sure the boys had a nice view of her ass as she rubbed her crotch up and down his thigh, "How long since you slept?"

He laughed, "Not quite as long as it's been since I had any

good lovin'.""

"Nothin' slowin' you down," said Abby, grabbing a paper to roll another joint.

"We've got customers waiting for product. The sooner we get it out there, the sooner we finish the deal." He pointed to the stack in the dining room, "That's all gotta be gone in a day or two at most."

"No rest for the weary," said Donny. "What needs to go where?"

"Five boxes to Ned's garage, over in the Bronx. He said he'd be in around nine and it's Sunday morning, so you can take your time getting there."

"Yeah, I know where he's at," said Hank. "Let's get crankin'."

"Get some rest and come by tonight. I'll have another delivery ready to go," said Augie.

"Right," said Donny, stacking up three boxes and heading for the door.

Augie put a briefcase on the table and opened it, removing a blue file. He grabbed a cup of coffee and settled back on the leather sofa, "Jets don't start until noon."

"I bet I can find something to do in the meantime," said Abby, slipping off her robe and snuggling against him. "I'm cold."

Augie laughed and wrapped a wool throw around her supple body, "Give me a few minutes to read this report and I'll fill your order, Ma'am."

"What's in the report?"

"We had a PR firm look into where the border patrol is most active and where they're lax. Bernie dressed up like a college professor and claimed to be doing research for a book. They only charged us three hundred bucks," he said, holding up a thick volume. "This is golden."

"Yeah, if you're planning to bring in more than a boatload

once in a while."

"Hey, I told you that I would not and could not talk about the business part of this for your own protection and that's the way it's gotta be, okay?"

"Fine!" she said, stomping off to the bedroom and slamming the door.

Augie leaned back and turned on the table lamp, "Welcome home."

He scanned the summary, which indicated that the government's current primary concerns were illegal immigrants arriving from Cuba and the Caribbean, Eastern block countries slipping spies across the Canadian and Mexican borders, and illicit arms shipments heading for Latin American mercenaries, or, at least, those working for our enemies. The seizure of drug shipments was a miniscule eighth on the list of priorities.

Other than normal patrols by the Coast Guard and Customs Control around the major ports, there was no systemic security from northern Georgia to North Carolina or from Los Angeles north to Oregon, with the exception of San Francisco. The press reinforced public awareness of the presence of Soviet submarines along our coasts, just as our own monitored the movements of their fleets and radio traffic in the Barents Sea in the north and the Bering Sea along the Pacific Rim, but there was no threat of invasion by sea. The central coastlines were open to leisure and commercial traffic with limited monitoring.

He dropped the booklet on the table and snatched a Marlboro, "They can't be making it that fucking easy, can they?"

He leaned back and puffed, thinking. The trip from Charlotte Amalie to Jamaica to Bahia Mar in Ft. Lauderdale was a breeze and the inspector took one look at the familiar old yacht and stamped their papers with a wave of the hand and a C-note for his troubles. They motored into traffic through the Inter-coastal Waterway to St. Augustine, then north along the coast, just as they had, year in and year out, since he was a kid.

"That's it, isn't it? If you look like you're going about normal business, nobody pays any attention. That's one of the secrets. High noon is better than midnight and a businessman is less conspicuous than a hippie."

Chapter 2

Augie sauntered through the employee's entrance at the old dairy warehouse on Waterbury Street in the South Bronx, since transformed into a steel fabrication shop that trembled with a mind-altering din. He greeted Nate, the foreman, with a shout and wave and trudged up the steel staircase to the offices on the second floor.

Miss Patton, who always wore a tiny flowered hat tipping precariously from a towering hive of chestnut curls, as if she was just on her way to church or a formal picnic in the park, stood to greet him. "Why Augustus, how nice to see you. You've grown into such a handsome man and I'm sure you have plenty of girlfriends. Is your father expecting you?"

"It's nice to see you too," replied the reluctant heir apparent. "I was just in the neighborhood and thought I'd see if he was in."

"He is. Let me ring Miss Krieger and see if he has time in his schedule."

Miss Krieger was the old man's personal secretary, a woman who could be mistaken for a hulking fullback in a shapeless dress, with mannerisms to match. She ran the office with military precision, as the quartet of bookkeepers, occupying a line of desks that faced away from the windows to avoid distractions, might attest. She also knew where most of the skeletons were hidden.

Miss Patton said, "Thank you," and hung up the telephone. "Miss Krieger will be right down to escort you to his office."

"I know where his office is," replied Augie impatiently.

"Ah, here she is now."

He turned to the charge of a gray-haired bull in a baggy gray dress, black stockings, black tie shoes with block heels, and a scowl that conveyed her irritation at unnecessary interruptions in her duties. The corners of her thin lips barely creased as she extended a cold firm hand, "It's so nice to see you again, Augustus. Your father will see you now, if that's alright."

"I won't take much of his time," said Augie, following, as she stomped down the hallway and up the back stairs to the third level. She returned to her desk in a windowless alcove and he turned into his father's office at the back of the building. The floor and walls of the long room were tiled in black and white, which felt cold and barren and echoed every sound, in spite of stacks of heavy drapes flanking a wall of sheet glass that provided a view over the buildings to Eastchester Bay and City Island beyond. Julius LaGuerre was a man of the sea and every spare moment, aside from business, was spent on the water.

His father stood in a wash of sunlight, his feet spread and field glasses at his eyes, following an orange freighter motoring east through the sound. Without turning around he asked, "Why do we waste time on land, when we could be out there?"

"Because it's the time on land that allows you the freedom to cruise the seas and you're too old to sign on as a bilge-boy on one of those tubs."

Julius laughed and walked over to a rather ordinary desk to light a cigar, "So, you got the Lollipop back safe and sound. I knew you could do it."

Augie blushed at the sarcasm, "She's in dry-dock and Cappy said they'd have her out in two weeks. Maybe just enough time to take her back down before winter sets in."

"We'll see." said the burly man, bald on top and gray at the temples above a ruddy complexion, weathered by his days at sea and too many shots of good whiskey. His jowls reminded Augie of an aging bulldog with dark piercing eyes that could burn a hole in your soul without the slightest snarl. He wore the scars to prove it.

The son placed a black leather briefcase on the desk and grinned, "I believe our accounts are now even."

"You're not saying that…?"

"There's fifty-grand in hundreds. I believe that was the figure you mentioned as payment for saving my ass."

Julius picked up the satchel and placed it on the floor behind the desk without inspecting the contents. He glanced up without smiling, pointing the tip of the cigar, "I don't want to know, but I do want to know whether your little brother is mixed up in this?"

"He doesn't know anything, other than I gave him some pot to share with his buddies."

"You keep it that way. He adores you and he's always imitated everything that you've done so easily…but he's not you, even if he'll never stop trying to match his perception of your success. You need to look out for him."

"I try to look out for all of 'em."

He waved at the money, "Family is more important than anything else. Just you remember that."

"How could I ever forget?" smirked the son. "You've been commanding me to honor the family and take care of my siblings and do all the right things since I could walk. Well, that's what I'm trying to do. It might be different from how you went about it but, in the end, it really isn't that different…other than I think this business can be carried out with a handshake instead of a gun."

The old man sat back in the black leather office chair and puffed on his cigar, "Where there's money, there's always some asshole who believes, truly believes, that they deserve a piece of the action, whether they've contributed a drop of sweat or not. No business is pristine and the guys who made it didn't get there by being mister nice guy. They all stepped on toes and moved the competition out of the way, when they had to. That's how things get done."

"That's how things used to get done. I won't ignore your advice but I think I can make this happen in a different way."

"I guess we'll find out just how smart you are, wiseguy. Just don't fuck up."

~

Augie and Ruck climbed out of a cab at the marina in Chula Vista and started up the path to the clubhouse. Ruck said, "I've been talking to this guy for a couple of weeks and this might be the one. He said he'd be here by two o'clock."

"Think that little runt with the dark hair and beady eyes, pacing back and forth sucking on a butt, might be our guy?" smirked Augie. "If this was the City, I'd guess he's a speedfreak."

"The gods can be cruel sometimes," muttered Ruck, walking directly to the kid in a loose yellow-striped surfer shirt, green baggies, and aqua flops that made him look like a wilted daisy. "You wouldn't happen to be Maurie, Maurie Giles?"

"Yeah, man, that's me, and you must be Ruck," said Maurie, tossing the butt on the manicured lawn to extend a hand.

"This is my partner, Augie LaGuerre."

They shook hands, "That's some moniker you've got there."

Augie didn't smile, "Yeah, it gets translated as 'the war'…but, in my family, it's 'the warrior'."

"Awesome!"

"You got a boat to show us?"

"Oh, yeah, right this way," he said, pointing down a long gangway that split off to access a parking lot of slips with every imaginable size and shape of craft from runabouts to sea-going mansions. The masts in a cluster of sailboats, nestled in the center docks nearest the jetty, waved like a field of Kansas wheat.

Augie and Ruck followed Maurie past hundreds of classic yachts, from weekenders to a black schooner, easily more than two hundred feet long, with teak decks and gleaming brass fittings. "What'd you think that would cost?"

Maurie laughed, "That's beyond our reality, dudes, but I think you're gonna like the one we've been talking about. She's a beaut."

"You never did tell me her name," said Ruck.

"Oh, it's *Whisper* and here she is."

She was stern in to her berth, with a broad white hull amidships tapering to a piercing arrow at the bowsprit, the teak decking was freshly sealed and polished, the sails and wheel covered in bright blue canvas, and the mast, tall and straight as a redwood, was topped out with a radar dome.

"She's one hundred and sixteen feet long, twenty-five at the beam," said Maurie, walking around to leap onto the boat.

"What's she draft," asked Augie.

"Twelve feet fully loaded. Sleeps eight comfortably and twelve to fourteen, if you double 'em up in the fo'c'sle. She's got double freezers, a full cook top and oven, communications, entertainment center, all the comforts of home."

"How 'bout the tanks?"

"Oh, six-hundred gallons, fuel and water. She's got a single diesel and a full-time generator but she's not going to use much gas under sail. She could make an ocean crossing, if you wanted."

"Why's she for sale," asked Augie.

"First owner died and his young wife doesn't sail. She just wants to cash it out as fast as possible."

"How come no one's stepped up locally?"

"The guy had a certain…reputation for being tied up with some shady people and that just starts an endless wave of rumors about murder and dirty money. Besides, San Diego's doin' okay but I don't see a lot of folks throwing big dollars around these days."

"Can we check her out?" asked Ruck.

"Sure, have at it," said Maurie, unlocking the hatch to the main cabin.

Augie walked through the salon, furnished with functional but beautifully finished cabinetry and furniture, past a full galley, to the chart table and communications bay. He inspected the electronic gear and clicked the button on the light over the map table. A course was charted to Tumaco, a small fishing village on an island along the northwestern coast of Columbia. Augie grinned, "And those cruel gods can also guide you through the muck."

Ruck appeared from inspecting the engine room, "I don't think I've ever been on any boat as a clean as this. This guy was obsessive."

"Yeah, I agree. Check out the electronics. He's got everything you could want."

"Have you checked out the stern?"

"Not yet, take a look."

He returned a few minutes later, "Nice, master and captain's cabins with private heads. The beds have six-hundred count Egyptian cotton sheets and the galley's fully stocked. They didn't miss a trick."

"What about the bilge?"

"When's the last time you saw a hull that was completely dry?"

"Never."

"Have now."

"What's he want for this?"

"A smooth hundred."

"Let's offer fifty in cash."

"You want to piss him off or what?"

"He said the lady just wanted the cash. Let's see how much."

"Alright but I've got some doubts."

"Fine, I'll do it," snapped Augie, climbing the ladder to the quarterdeck, where Maurie was lounging in the shade of the boom. "My friend tells me you're asking a hundred grand?"

"Yeah, that's what she wants," said the greasy surfer, standing.

"How 'bout fifty grand, cash?"

"Are you trying to insult the lady?"

"No, I'm trying to save her the forty-eight-percent tax she's gonna pay to the state and Uncle Sam. This way everyone wins."

"I don't know," said Maurie, "but I'll make a call and see what she says."

"Great. I want to see how she goes on the open water, so we'll rig her for a test drive, while you're gone, if that's alright with you."

"You bet, I'll run up to the clubhouse and find a phone."

"See you in a few minutes."

~

The diesel purred and *Whisper* motored north through the bay, past aircraft carriers, destroyers, cruisers, supply ships, and subs docked at the Naval Station, around North Island and Point Loma to open water. Augie turned her into a blustery northwest wind and Ruck volunteered Maurie to help raise the mainsail, then the jib. The surfer had no experience on a sailboat but he was strong and willing, if unstable, as the deck rose and dipped in the chop.

Augie leaned the bow to port, the sails billowed, and Whisper gathered speed, cutting smoothly across the wind. The crew winched down the lines and Ruck tied them off to gleaming chocks. Maurie might be comfortable on a surfboard but he stumbled back to the quarterdeck.

"Haven't spent much time on a sailboat, huh?"

"Naw, I've got my board, it's perfect 'cause you only ride downhill."

Augie laughed, "This is less work!"

"Wind power," added Ruck, taking the wheel.

"So, what'd your lady say?" asked Augie, leaning on the starboard rail.

"She was pissed, at first, but I pointed out that she'd end up paying almost half in taxes, so she's calling her accountant. She'll have an answer by the time we get back."

"Fair enough." He put on a pair of polarized aviator glasses and called to Ruck, "How d'you like her?"

"She's really smooth, even in a strong wind. Probably because she's got wide hips to balance the keel."

"I agree but I want to see the bilge while she's underway." He padded down the ladder to the galley and then into the engine room, which was spotless and quiet, save the hum of the generator. Pulling up a floorboard hatch, he peered inside the clean dry hull. "That's amazing."

He checked all the outboard fittings, hoses, clamps, grease leaks on the engine or the generator, but everything was as if it had just been delivered from the factory.

Augie climbed out of the hatch and Ruck asked, "Well?"

"Clean and dry."

"That's fantastic." He looked over at Maurie, whose face was decidedly green. "If she wants to sell, we want to buy. We can have the cash within twenty-four hours."

The surfer leaned over the rail and puked. He rinsed his face with salt water and crumbled to the deck, "If she feels the way I feel, I understand why she wants to sell this ol' tub."

Augie and Ruck burst out laughing, "That could be one reason."

Whisper eased into the docks at Tumaco after midnight, where a dozen fishing trawlers were tied up but not a single yacht. A few streetlights dotted the wharf and the village beyond but the only person in sight was a boy, of about eight, sitting on the edge of the planking with a fishing rod and pail of bait.

Ruck walked up to him, "Do you speak any English?"

"A little, from Yankee fishermen."

"Can we tie up there until morning."

The boy shrugged his slight shoulders, "I'm not the dock master."

"Will the boat be safe?"

The boy held out his palm and looked up at him with wide dark eyes and a big smile, "I will look after it for you until daylight."

"How much?"

"Twenty bucks."

"How do I know you'll stick around all night?"

"I don't have a home, so I fish tonight to eat tomorrow."

"No one looks after you?"

The boy's eyes teared up, "Well, my mother died in childbirth and my father was murdered by paramilitary pigs, who stormed the village when I was five. I've got an aunt and uncle but they don't like me much, say I'm a bastard, that I should be someone else's problem."

Ruck handed the kid fifty dollars, "That's one hell of a story kid. You look after my boat and I'll give you another one of those."

"Big spender," muttered the boy, turning back to his rod.

Augie locked up the hatch and they wandered up the dirt road into the village. "Antonio's dad said to meet his cousin, Felix, at the Ritz."

"I'm thinkin' that this Ritz might not quite be up to its namesake in Madrid. I got to stay there for a couple of days with my folks, when I was a kid. King Alfonzo had it built to welcome the aristocracy and dignitaries, who were coming for his coronation. It was also the jumping off point for the Orient Express."

"I'm bettin' you're right," laughed Augie, spying a sign under a single light bulb with 'Ritz' scrawled in hand lettering. The 'z' resembled the slash of Zorro. They entered a plank door into a dim hallway with a counter along one side and a staircase on the other. A young girl in an aqua blouse popped up from behind the desk, "Buenas noches."

Ruck walked over and smiled, "We're looking for Felix

Hernandez."

"You'll find him in the bar," said the girl, pointing to a doorway beneath the stairs.

Augie peered around the corner to find a heavy-set man with long dark hair in a loose ponytail and a bushy moustache, wearing a beautifully embroidered poncho, sitting alone at the dusky bar in a haze of cigar smoke with a half-empty bottle of tequila and a shot glass. From the three butts under his stool, he had been waiting for a while.

Ruck walked up to him, "Excuse me, are you Felix Hernandez?"

His eyes were droopy and bloodshot but he spoke distinctly, "'bout time you Yankees showed up."

The boys took stools on either side and Augie placed a hand on his shoulder, "Giermo sends his regards and his ol' man, Padeo, too."

Hernandez smiled broadly, "I went to visit them in that stinking rat's nest and I still don't understand why anyone prefers living like rodents in a polluted maze to the freedoms of the countryside and the ocean. I felt like I might have to climb one of those tall buildings just to get a glimpse of sky and a breath of fresh air."

Ruck laughed, "Actually, in some ways, the city's just a condensed version of all the conveniences you have here. You just have to know how to get around and where to find what you need."

"I love all my brothers but I prefer the company of birds and animals and fish."

"My father's said almost exactly the same thing," said Augie. "His greatest love is the sea."

"He's a wise man," replied Felix. "Wise men are hard to find."

"That's true," said Ruck. "And, from what I've seen, wisdom comes at a price most dear."

"You're very smart for someone so young."

"Both of my grandfathers repeated the family wisdoms and histories endlessly. I actually paid attention to most of it."

"Never stop learning," said the Columbian, "that's the secret. It doesn't matter what you're learning, as long as it makes you reach a little farther than you have before. It makes you grow."

"But, even wise men don't have all the answers, otherwise we'd be basking in a utopia surrounded by the wonders of plenty," said Augie. "I think there's a balance in the world between good and evil that forces us to figure out what we believe in, what we'll defend or destroy, change or rebuild to justify our place in the grand scheme of things. We have to choose who we are, before we become who we're supposed to be, if that makes any sense."

Hernandez grinned, "You boys need a drink."

Ruck walked around the end of the bar and wiped out two relatively clean shot glasses and the big man poured. He lifted his glass, "To our children's children's children!"

"Amen to that," said Ruck, downing the smooth amber liquid in one swallow. "Oooo, that's very nice."

"It should be, my cousin, Heidi, runs the plantation and the distillery. It's an old family recipe."

"Cheers to her artistry!" said Ruck.

Felix poured another round and turned to Augie, "So, my cousin in America tells me that you'd like to do some business."

"Yes, we're in the market for top grade marijuana."

"There's pot growing all over the country. You could just go out with a machete and hack some down."

Augie laughed, "What I'd like to do is form a relationship with someone who knows how to grow, cure, and package their finest produce, someone I can trust. I don't know whether you're that person or not, but I'd like to find out."

"What kind of quantity are you seeking?"

"We could handle a thousand pounds, if you can supply it."

The Columbian did a rough calculation in his head, "That's four-hundred and fifty kilos. That's a lot of money."

"What kind of price can you offer in that quantity?"

He paused again, "One hundred and thirty-five dollars a key. Best quality, delivered by noon."

Augie didn't hesitate, "A hundred a key. There's plenty of room for your profit in that."

"Setting up a deal like this costs money."

"Yeah, I know, everyone's palm has to be greased " said Ruck, "but, on the other hand, if we can find a way to work together, not just on this load but dozens, you're gonna make a lot of money."

"So, you want to do business or not?" asked Augie.

Hernandez struggled to his feet and shook their hands, before stumbling towards the door. "I'll make arrangements and meet you here for coffee at nine o'clock."

The young girl from the previous evening wore a bright yellow blouse, bare at the shoulders, and leaned low to reveal ample cleavage as she poured thick coffee into Augie's mug. She stood and cocked her hip, as she filled Ruck's cup, and placed a small platter of cream, brown sugar, and lemon slices on the table, "Try a little lemon, it cuts the bitter."

Ruck looked up, "Do you ever sleep?"

"Oh, I have a cot behind the front desk."

"You have a house full of beds but you sleep on a cot?" asked Augie.

"Greeting our guests and accommodating their needs is my job. I don't get to choose when they arrive or leave."

Ruck laughed, "It makes perfect sense, but still...?"

"It's fine, I'm used to it. Can I get you gringos anything

else?"

Augie scanned her curves and grinned, "We're good for the moment."

The girl turned and sashayed away, glancing over her shoulder seductively.

"Gotta get her name," said Ruck.

"Juanita."

"How'd you know that?"

"I asked her when we walked in."

"You don't miss a trick, do you?"

Augie started laughing, "If it's the right shape, I can't help myself."

"You do help yourself a lot, actually, and what's the deal with Abby?"

"She's just a fucking buddy."

"Does she know that? I mean she's pretty much living in your place."

"She's more like a horny cousin, who just wants lots of kinky sex."

"You're weird, she's weird, and it's all gonna blow up on you, if you're not careful."

"Aw, we're fine."

"And she doesn't mind you screwing every willing female you can find?"

"Just as long as I save enough for her."

"You're in deep do-do, you know that?"

Felix strode into the bar, standing tall and sober, "Buenos Dias, muchachos. Como esta?"

Ruck looked up with bloodshot eyes and lifted his cup, "Top of the morning to ya'."

The huge man sat down heavily and leaned his elbows on the table. Juanita arrived with an earthenware mug and a pot of steaming coffee. He nodded gratefully, "Gracias."

She brushed past Augie's chair and ambled around the counter.

"How we doin'?" asked Ruck.

"I believe everything is in order. My cousins are assembling the shipment, as we speak, and I'll deliver it to your boat at one o'clock."

"Why one o'clock," asked Ruck.

"Because everyone leaves for supper and a siesta."

"Makes sense to me."

"Will you have the payment?"

"Will we see a genuine sample of the product before delivery?"

"Oh, of course," said the Columbian, reaching beneath his poncho to lay a brick wrapped in pink cellophane on the table.

Ruck glanced around at the people seated at the two other tables but no one seemed to be paying any attention, "What are you nuts?"

"Everyone in our village knows everything about everything. It is completely impossible to keep a secret and, besides, do you honestly think that anyone didn't know exactly why you were here, when you arrived on that beautiful yacht in the middle of the night?"

"That kid!" stammered Ruck.

"That kid is my nephew, Paulo, and he did exactly what you asked of him. No one touched your boat."

"But everyone knew we were here immediately."

"It's like a telegraph, especially between the women," laughed Hernandez. "Another way to look at it is this…if things go smoothly, you go away with your pot but the narco-dollars sift down through the village to benefit the entire population and we all realize that. My neighbors are my security."

"My old man always says, 'Keep it in the family,' and there is wisdom in that," said Augie.

"I think I'd like your ol' man," said Felix, stabbing the pink wrapper with a thin fishing knife. He plucked some buds and handed them to the boys. "I think you'll approve. It's the fall harvest, cured to just under twenty percent moisture, no mold or fungus. The aroma is sweet and fragrant and the potency is very high."

Augie crumpled a bud, finding three plump seeds sheathed in red tendrils glistening with resin. He held it to his nose and inhaled a deep rich intoxicating fragrance. He smiled, "You almost don't even need to light this up."

Felix laughed and patted him on the back, "I think we'll enjoy doing business together."

"Is it all like this?"

He raised his right hand, "On my mother's grave, every brick."

Ruck lifted his cup, "Here's to many more glasses of wonderful tequila and this rich coffee."

"Here's to our children's children's children," said the Columbian. "It is for them, we do the things we must."

"Amen," said Ruck.

Augie and Ruck removed the interior paneling in the salon and the master berth, before Hernandez arrived in an open truck with three teenagers in shorts and vibrant bandanas riding in the back. He pulled up along the wharf and stopped next to Whisper, "Buenos Dias! Que pasa?"

The harbor was completely deserted, as Felix promised, when Ruck popped out of the hatch behind the mast, "Right on time! Come aboard."

The huge man leapt and landed lightly on the deck, "This is a magnificent vessel. Does she run as smoothly as a knife through butter?"

"Better," said Ruck, as Augie appeared out of the rear hatch. "Can we offer you a beer?"

"No, we probably want to get on with business before the telegraph system arises from its siesta."

Augie motioned for him to follow down to the main salon. The panels were neatly stacked against the dining table and the rough fiberglass of the inside of the hull showed between the struts. He pulled out a black leather satchel, placed it on the counter, and opened it to reveal neatly bound stacks of hundreds. "I believe we agreed on fifty. Feel free to count it, if you like, but it's all there."

Felix picked up three bundles arbitrarily and flicked through the stacks, "I believe you but our agreement was actually for forty-five five."

"Fine, donate the balance to the children's school," said Augie. "Let's load this puppy, so we can all be on our way."

"You just hang on to the money until we finish. I don't want these youngsters getting any stupid ideas."

Ruck stashed the case in the galley as the three boys ferried a stream of brown boxes through the rear hatch. Augie opened the sixth box and extracted a pink brick. He peeled back the cellophane and stuck his nose in the weed, inhaling deeply. "Yup. Start packin'."

He grabbed another box and repeated the inspection several times. Felix sat on the couch, shouting obscenities at the boys to hurry them along. He looked up at Ruck, "Your friend is a cautious man."

"We've been burned before and we'd much rather have many happy endings than disappointment for either side."

"As you wish, but it's all primo. If you find any that doesn't meet your satisfaction, when you get to your destination, I'll be happy to replace them."

Augie and Ruck lined the inner hull with more than four hundred pink slabs, the weight distributed evenly fore and aft, and replaced the wall panels.

Felix stood, "She won't be quite as quick across the wind but she'll get you home." He shook hands, picked up the briefcase, and climbed the steps to the quarterdeck. "Adios amigos. I look forward to seeing you again very soon."

"Thanks for everything," said Ruck, following him into the sunshine.

"Remember, keep it in the family," said the huge Columbian, hopping onto the quay and sauntering back to the old truck.

~

Whisper docked in Acapulco to top off the tanks and find a fine meal for the crew, before tacking west, then north for the long haul paralleling the coast in international waters. They headed northeast at Morro Bay and hugged the rugged beauty of Big Sur to put in at Monterey.

Ruck tugged at the wheel to trim the sails and Augie leaned against the rail, "We've been lucky so far."

"Yeah, we've made the right connections."

"It isn't always going to go right because people are greedy, looking for the quick buck, instead of a thriving enterprise," said Augie. "We've got to refine our methods."

"We got burned on the first try, so we learn as we go, that's the best we can do."

"Naw, we can do better than that. This is still little stuff. Easy in, easy out, but there's bigger scores to be made and more efficient transportation. We need to move up to the big leagues."

"Well, at least we know this batch is gonna disappear fast."

"Bernie's got it set up with his cousins. This shit's gonna be in five or six states before sundown tomorrow."

They eased around Carmel and Pebble Beach. Augie pointed, "See the house nestled into that bluff over there?"

Ruck pulled out the binoculars, "Yeah, what about it?"

"My old man rented that place for a month, one summer, so he could play golf on the Pebble Beach courses and he rented a yacht, over in Monterey, so he could go boating when he wasn't playing golf. He and mom brought all the kids and we had a blast. You get up in the morning and it's all foggy and quiet. We'd find deer, foraging in the front yard and they weren't even spooked by noisy kids. I could see spending some time here."

"Yeah, I've been out here too. Best part is that you can pick your weather…foggy and cool on the peninsula, seventy and sunny over the mountain in Monterey, or hot in Carmel Valley. Plus, Big Sur is a couple hundred miles of magical wonder."

"After talking with our friends in Jamaica about Jah and the energy that binds the Earth with every living creature, you have to believe that there are places all over the world, where those forces are stronger or closer or more powerful. This has gotta be one of them."

Whisper heeled over as she tacked across the current between the jetties to enter the harbor. Ruck turned her bow upwind, while Augie pulled down the headsail and then the main, and motored in to dock along side the fuel tanks at the end of the wharf.

A slender boy with long blond hair in a thick ponytail, dressed in a pair of cutoffs and a bronze tan, appeared on the wharf, "You'll be needin' some fuel?"

Ruck tossed him a line, "Not much but we'd like to top her off and the water tank too, if your water is good."

"Good as it gets," laughed the boy, as he tied her off fore and aft. He grabbed a hose from the gas pump and jumped onto the mid-deck.

Augie brought the key to open the lid and the boy inserted the nozzle, "Probably won't take much 'cause we just picked her up in San Diego."

The kid inspected the long sweeping curves of the deck, "I bet she's a willing filly on the open water."

"Yeah, we took her for a trial run and she's graceful, even in heavy winds."

The nozzle clicked and the kid looked up at the tank, "You're right, only took twenty-six gallons."

"We've been under sail most of the way, so the only drain is the generator," said Ruck. "Can you top up the water too?"

"Sure," said the boy replacing the hose and hauling another onto the deck. "This is city water, so you don't have to worry about it, like you do when you head south of the border."

"Well, as far as we know, this girl's only had American-made in her tanks and we'll probably keep it that way," laughed Ruck, eyeing Augie.

The boy withdrew the hose from the water tank and pointed the stream over the side, as he reached up to grasp a slender shredded leaf from the sail track on the boom. He held it close, then looked up with quizzical eyes.

"What's that?" asked Augie.

"It's a little piece of palm frond but this palm doesn't grow in California."

"How do you know that?"

"The guy who builds my boards always works a piece of palm into the design. It's his signature and he collects them from all over. See the lime green lines running across the leaf? I'm guessin' it came from Central America someplace."

Ruck piped up without hesitating, "Well, now we know why Wifey was in such a hurry to sell the boat."

Augie picked up the story, "Wow, he really did sail down to Columbia."

"And died while he was there, so the wife had to haul his corpse back to the States to make things kosher." He turned to the boy, "The wife of the previous owner was in a hurry to sell this boat, so my friend's father bought it. When we picked it up, there was a chart on the map table with a course along the Central American Coast. So we're guessin' he probably made that trip. He just didn't make it back."

"Yeah but getting a dead body all the way back to San Diego wouldn't have been easy," said the kid.

"There's a huge freezer in the galley and I'm bettin' they had at least a basic crew along, so she would've had help," said Ruck.

"Amazing that you picked that up from a palm frond," said Augie.

"I'm a surfer, man. Surfing is all about riding as close to the power of nature as you can get. She's running the show, we're not."

Augie bowed, "I'll agree with that. That magic is all around us."

"Yeah, especially here," laughed the kid.

"What do we owe you?" asked Ruck.

The boy looked up at the tank, "Fourteen eighty-five."

Augie handed him a twenty, "Keep it kid, we appreciate your help."

"Thanks."

"Hey, is there somewhere we can tie up, until we find out what my ol' man's got planned for this girl?"

"Yeah, down by the warehouse at the other end, there're a couple of slips for temporary stowage. If she's moved out by tomorrow, shouldn't be a problem."

"Cool. Thanks again," said Ruck, as the boy tossed the lines back on deck and Whisper eased away from the dock.

"Let's get her tied up, then we'll call Bernie and see whether he's got his shit together," said Augie.

"Roger that," replied Ruck, shaking his head.

"Then we'll rent a slip in the marina."

An hour later, Augie sat down at the table in the Crab Shack, eyeing the waitress who delivered two platters of steaming claws,

"Man, those smell absolutely wonderful!"

The brunette smiled, "I had 'em steamed special just for you, Honey."

Ruck looked across the table at Augie and chuckled, "Will you turn that thing off, just this once? I'm trying to enjoy my meal!"

The waitress giggled and scurried away. Augie opened a claw, dipped it in drawn butter, and pulled the meat out of the shell in one bite. He dabbed his chin with a napkin, "Wow, these are great."

"Boat food is pretty good but it just can't be this fine."

"Agreed." He leaned closer, "I talked to Bernie. He's sober and he'll be here within the hour, with a truck and a couple of guys. He says it's all outta here tonight and he's trying to open things up with his cousin, Taylor, up at the University of Wisconsin. That's like fifty-thousand hippies!"

"Outta sight!"

"I keep saying the demand is huge and we're only filling a tiny little piece of the action."

Ruck calculated, "This will be cleaned up by the weekend and we'll have the investment in the boat and the product paid off, with...at least another three hundred in the kitty."

"See, it's starting to mount up."

"In a hurry," said Ruck, slurping a claw and a chug of ice-cold Olympia.

Chapter 3

Bright morning sunshine glistened off the snow, as Taylor strolled up the sidewalk along Langdon Street and across Henry, for her first meeting with a dealer that her boyfriend, Randy, set up for her.

Freddie, a rotund bear of a man, agreed to meet at the Plaza for burgers at eleven, after the fans cleared out to head for Camp Randall Stadium to watch the Badgers get trounced by Michigan again. Unfortunately, the home team had not won more than the occasional game, in an embarrassingly long time, and most of the athletes spent more time partying than attending classes. Victory was not even a consideration and a loss would not inhibit unrestrained revelry in any way whatsoever.

She pushed through the glass-paneled door and gazed around the room, from a bar along one wall, booths and tables behind, to a kitchen at the back. A fat hippie, dressed completely in denim, squeezed out of a booth and walked over to greet the tall curvy blond, "I'm intrigued by your invitation to have lunch together."

"Well, don't get your pecker all out of whack, this is about business."

He extended a ham of a hand and led her to a corner booth, "I hope this is the beginning of something special."

She sat and pulled the table to make room for Freddie's girth, "I think that depends on whether I end up seeing you as a gentleman and a businessman or a cad and a thief."

"You're right up front aren't you?"

"I understand what the word 'professional' means. I'm looking for a business associate who can respect and protect my position."

"I'm glad we agree. I like to keep my agreements straightforward, a simple handshake will suffice."

"I'm guessin' that you have the enviable dilemma of too little supply for too much demand."

When he smiled, his eyes crinkled and the tips of his scruffy moustache curled up, "There are fifty-thousand hippies on campus, probably another fifty hanging out on State Street every night, and we're the only organized operation in the city."

"What can you handle?"

"As much as you can supply lady, as long as it's primo or better."

"How about a hundred pounds, Columbian?"

Fat Freddie's jowls jiggled when he chuckled, "That'd be a start."

"There's a logistical problem."

"What's that?"

"It's being delivered in California."

"No problem! My guys came up with a brilliant solution."

"What's that?"

"We've got another supplier in northern California, so we came up with this scheme and it works."

A long white Cadillac limousine pulled to the curb, as Taylor, Freddie, and a posse of five gorgeous freshmen emerged from the airport into a dense San Francisco fog. Linda, a tall lanky redhead, whined, "The least you could do is provide some decent weather. We can be cold in Madison!"

A driver stepped out and opened the rear door, "Step right this way, ladies."

Taylor looked up, as she was about to step into the car,

"Bernie! But…how'd you?"

"You needed a limo, so I rented one. Besides, how often do we actually get to see each other?"

She hugged him, knocking his little black hat to the pavement, "I'm so glad to see you!"

Freddie was staring quizzically, as she turned, "Oh, I'm sorry, Freddie, this is my cousin, Bernie. Bernie, Freddie."

They shook and Freddie looked him in the eye, "It's a pleasure, man."

Bernie picked up his hat, "Where too, Ma'am?"

"We need a clothing store that sells hip but professional suits for these ladies and then we need to find a restaurant."

"Can do. We'll head down the Embarcadero to the wharf, I'm sure we can find what you need somewhere along the way."

"Great, let's go."

Bernie pulled the limousine into the Paisley Frog and Freddie escorted the girls on a shopping spree.

Taylor called after him, "Dress them so they could walk into any office in a big corporation and fit right in."

Freddie made a point of checking out the five lean asses strutting into the shop, then turned around and grinned, "You betcha!"

She opened the door and slid into the front seat, "This worked out better than I might have hoped. All I asked for was five Samsonites with twenty pounds in each, plus a spare for the girls' clothes, and a limo. I didn't expect you to personally deliver my shit."

"It's better this way. I wanted to get a feel for your guy and first impressions seem real. The cases are in the trunk, packed, so all we have to do is feed you and deliver you back to the airport for the two-thirty flight."

"You're awesome!"

"Just take care of business and we'll be fine."

"If all of this works as planned, I'll have full payment in two weeks, actually sooner. I've got projects due, so I've gotta be finished by then."

"I can send a courier."

"I think Lydia's coming in for a few days."

Bernie smiled, "Your sister's carried money for me before."

Taylor smirked, "I knew she wasn't just acting off Broadway."

"No actor in New York, besides the stars, can afford to be an actor. Everyone's got something going on the side to finance their stage habit."

"She already looks like a rich bitch, so she doesn't have to play the part."

"She is a rich bitch and so are you!" laughed Bernie.

"You asshole! I don't get any money until I'm twenty-five."

"Yeah, so how are you financing all of this?"

"Well, I do get an allowance."

"Yeah, probably enough to feed half the homeless in San Francisco."

She looked down at her nails, flexing long graceful fingers, "I don't want to be just anything. I want to be everything, experience everything, and the only way to do that is to have enough money to make my own decisions."

"That sounds really familiar, actually...oughta be a song. Just make sure those are the right choices before you leap. This business ain't for stupid sissies."

She laughed, "Bet I can still kick your ass!"

He turned to her, "I bet you could but you've turned into a beautiful woman and I don't want to see you screw things up."

"I'll be careful. I'm starting to collect some friends I can trust."

"It's the family we choose, darlin'."

Freddie followed a gaggle of giggling girls out to the car,

each dressed in gorgeous pantsuits or long flowing skirts under vibrant blouses and tailored jackets. Freddie piled in and settled into the lounge at the back, "How'd we do?"

Bernie and Taylor leaned over the back of the seat. "You all look fabulous!" said Taylor, "Well, except for your chaperone!"

Freddie blushed, as all the girls snuggled in around him. "Thank you Uncle Freddie."

"Uncle Freddie? You pervert!"

"They're just expressing their appreciation for our generosity!"

"This is business, so all of you behave yourselves until we're finished!"

A chorus sang out, "Yes, Ma'am!"

Bernie drove them to an unobtrusive warehouse along the wharf with a small black and white sign that read, 'Cass's Crab Café'. "I hope everyone likes seafood, because you won't find it better than here."

The parade of beauties trooped through a plain side door into a massive room with a huge window overlooking the pier and the water. A squatty man approached, in a waiter's white shirt and black bow tie beneath a tiny moustache that curled above a grin, "Master Bernie! I'm so glad to see you with so many beautiful ladies. I hope that you've come to spoil them on our finest!"

Bernie hugged the little man, "It's good to see you too, Vincenti, your cousins send their greetings."

"Please extend my warmest regards to your parents. How many of you are there? Eight, yes? Please follow me." He guided the guests to a long smooth redwood table, angled to the view. The boys took chairs at either end, while Vincenti seated the ladies and handed out menus, "Our specials today include fresh tuna, seared on the outside, rare in the middle, with a medley of vegetables from our own gardens; a lobster bisque with a salad of fresh greens, sweet red onions, and orange cherry tomatoes; and, finally, fried calamari with sweet and sour sauce. Of course, everything on the menu's available. May I order drinks for you?"

"I think we'll keep this one dry, thank you," said Bernie. "How 'bout some of your herbal tea all around?"

"Coming right up."

The girls started chattering and Freddie moved around the table to sit across from Taylor, "What needs to be done to get things in order."

"Enjoy a wonderful lunch and I'll deliver you to the airport. Everything's been taken care of," said Taylor's cousin.

Freddie settled back into the chair, "I sure do enjoy working with people who have their shit together."

Bernie leaned on his elbows, his eyes drilling into Freddie's skull, "You just keep your shit wound tight, brother, and we'll make another opportunity to have lunch together. I'm trusting you to do right by my little cousin, here. Don't disappoint me."

Freddie grinned, "I'm a student-businessman. I want to make a lot of money in a hurry, so I can get on with the rest of my life, and I don't need to screw anyone in the process. Simple as that."

Bernie extended his hand, "I think we understand each other. Now, can we get on with ordering? I'm starving."

~

Freddie's buddies, Dave, Corey, and Billy, were waiting to collect the luggage, when the travelers finally arrived on a puddle jumper from Chicago. Freddie escorted six hot chicks through the lobby, "You girls look beautiful. You should get this guy to take you on the road more often."

Sophia, a tall curvy surfer from L.A., smiled, "If he wants to take us shopping again, we'll be glad to help out."

They piled into a rented van and rolled through a mild

blizzard to the dorms on West Johnson, where they deposited four of the girls, with two hundred dollars each for their troubles and a brand new Samsonite full of their own clothes. The van motored around to Landon House and Taylor hugged Sophia as she got out. "Thanks for helping out."

"It was a blast," smiled her friend.

Freddie turned to Taylor, "We've got a house where we can stash this stuff but no one, outside the four of us, knows anything about it. As far as everyone else is concerned, we live in the dorms just like every other freshman. I want to weigh this out tonight, so we both agree on the exact count."

"Fine. Let's go."

The van headed up Gorham to Sherman before turning into a tiny cottage, on Lakewood Avenue, that was surrounded by trees and backed up to the lake. Taylor got out and looked around, "How'd you guys find this place? It's beautiful and almost secluded."

"We just got lucky," said Billy. "My brothers lived here before Sammy, the next oldest, graduated last year, so I just took over the lease. C'mon in, they fixed it up nice enough to entertain girls once in a while."

"I'm bettin' more than once in a while."

A sun porch at the back opened into a small but efficient kitchen stocked with every utensil a cook might need. A round dining table sat next to the windows and a long living room stretched to the front. The furniture was well used but the whole house was immaculate. Corey pointed to the stairs, "There're are two bedrooms and a bath upstairs and a half bath 'round the corner here."

"This is really nice. You're lucky to have it."

"Yeah, we can move at least a couple of us in here next year."

Freddie interrupted, "If you guys'll haul those cases to the basement, we can get to work."

"Can do," said Dave, heading out the door.

Freddie led Taylor down a wooden staircase to a tiny basement with metal storage lockers along one wall and two long worktables in front of a giant brass scale in a glass box. She walked up and touched the case, "That's beautiful."

"And accurate," said Freddie. "We all chipped in to buy it from an antiques dealer in Oshkosh, who collects weird stuff, when we first got into selling weed."

"Good investment."

Dave, Corey, and Billy clomped down the stairs and laid the suitcases on the tables. Freddie produced a key and the boys opened each case to find nine neatly packed pink bricks. They opened the glass case and measured out the first kilo.

Dave adjusted the counter-weight and whistled, "This one's right on the money with three grams to spare for the wrapper."

"That's what I like to see," said Fat Freddie. "If they're all like this, we'll have everything taken care of in ten days or less."

"Less," said Dave, breaking open a brick to stick his nose in the weed and extracting a bud to roll a joint. "This'll go fast. There's nothing else this sweet in town, we can charge a premium."

"I'm all for you guys making your profits but you take care of my share first, then I don't have to wait around until you're finished tying up loose ends. You should break even in four or five days. I want to turn this in a hurry, so we can go again."

Freddie exhaled a cloud of sweet blue smoke, "Great minds think alike."

~

A slender crescent moon chased into a raging orange sunset behind the glow of the Capitol building as Freddie guided the long white Caddy down East Washington. He turned to Taylor, "By the way, everything's lined up and ready to roll."

"Good, I've gotta be on the morning flight. Deadlines."

The fat man smiled, "I think we're gonna have a beautiful relationship."

"You take care of your part, I'll take care of mine, and we'll both be ready to retire when we graduate."

"That's the plan. Hey, d'you hear about the riots?"

"What riots?"

"Bunch of protesters are staging a sit-in up at the Commerce building and the cops are going crazy lobbing tear gas and beating people up. It's nuts!"

"I had to make a quick trip home, so I'm clueless. What are they protesting?"

"Dow Chemical is recruiting engineers to help make more napalm and fun stuff like that."

"The war doesn't make any sense to anyone, especially the guys who are dyin'. I've got a cousin over there, who's a medic, flying around in helicopters picking up the dead and wounded, so I'm thinkin' that's probably worth protesting."

"Damned right! Madison is one of those cities, where weird but brainy people gather together and bizarre things happen. I've got a feeling that it won't be long before this whole thing will escalate into something much bigger than anyone can imagine."

"Sort of like Columbia and Berkeley."

"Yeah, we're about to witness it all but there is a plus side," laughed Freddie.

"What's that?"

"Protesters'll keep the cops occupied. Besides, we don't look like subversives. I'm too fat and you're too...collegiate in that getup."

"It wouldn't surprise you to know it was on purpose?" asked Taylor with a smirk.

"You learn quick." He checked his watch and turned on the radio, "There's this new DJ on the student station. The guy always plays dynamite music and isn't afraid to rap about his opinions."

The car filled with the Beatles' opus, "A Day in the Life."

"That's apropos," said Taylor. "My ol' man owns a couple of radio stations."

"Really? What kind of music?"

"One station is old-timey country singers and regional sports. The other is an underground station that's just getting started."

"That's cool, do you get to hang out at the station?"

"Yeah, but it's basically pretty boring. DJ keeps up the patter and spins the platters, while an engineer makes sure the signal's going out into the cosmos."

The song ended and a soft resonant voice said, "Good evening. I'm Rick on the Radio and I'm glad you're with me tonight...but I've got a question. How come you're sitting on your asses listening to me, instead of supporting our friends up on Bascom Hill? Take your transistor radio and head out the door, folks, and I'll let you know what's happening as we learn it. The time for talkin's done. It's time to fight back." The opening version of "Sgt. Pepper's Lonely Heart's Club Band," blasted through the airwaves to rally the troops.

"That guy could get his ass in a whole bunch of trouble, if he's not careful."

"Yeah, but who's gonna bother with some kid broadcasting on a tiny station within the confines of the university? That's more trouble than it's worth."

"DJ's have to pass an exam to get their license and abide by strict rules, even on a student station. You can't say anything you want on the air, no matter how right it is."

"He's not inciting to riot. He asked the listeners to support those people who are protesting. If they decide to get involved, that's their decision."

She grinned, "I'm going to like living here.

"Even when it's ridiculously cold. Hey, you wanna go see what's happening?"

"Naw, let's just ease through this and make sure we get it right." She smiled, "I'd hate to run into my minder, Shirley, from the dorm. She just wouldn't understand."

"You could always say it was a guy."

She laughed, "Or a girl!"

Freddie's plump belly jiggled against the steering wheel when he laughed. "Fine, I'll just take you to the cottage."

"Oh, that's a great idea. Can we order one of those delivery pizzas, while we get this sorted out? I'm starving."

"Sure, I wish I'd thought up that one."

"You make more in a week than they make in a year, what are you complainin' about?"

"I just admire people who follow through on clever ideas. I hope lots of folks from our generation contribute to what the world might be one day."

"Then our clever idea is to keep them supplied with inspiration," suggested Taylor.

"It's a mission!" said Freddie, turning into the driveway of the little house on the lake. The warm amber radiance of the porch light washed over the steps, spilling down onto the cobbles, glistening like a carpet of gemstones in the darkness. He grabbed her small case and toddled around to unlock the kitchen door and flip on the lights.

"I love this little house," said Taylor wandering through to turn on a table lamp in the living room.

Freddie grabbed the wall phone and dialed, "Hey, can you get me a extra-large sausage and mushroom? Cool, on Lakewood, just north of the park. Yeah, that's it."

"Pizza'll be here in thirty. You want to check out the score?"

"Sure," she said, following him down the narrow stairs to the basement. He walked across the room and wheeled a cabinet away from the wall to reveal a large safe. Squatting, he twirled the silver dial back and forth, until a tiny click released the latch, and opened the heavy door to reveal stacks of neatly wrapped bundles of bills. Making no attempt to conceal the bounty, he peeled a handful from the pile.

Groaning as he stood, he laid them out on the worktable, "I believe you'll find each of these contains one hundred one-hundred dollar bills - used, faced, and non-sequential. The odd one is five thousand. You can count it if you like."

Taylor picked up a stack and flicked through the bills as if shuffling a deck of cards, noting the condition of the bills and scanning for any sequence in the serial numbers. She picked another and counted rapidly. "I believe you but there's the small matter of my share of the expenses for our little excursion to the coast."

"Tell you what, I'll eat it this time but you get to pay for the next one…and the pizza."

"Deal," smiled Taylor, collecting her loot.

He sealed the safe and followed her up the stairs. "Actually, I was kind of hoping we could set up another batch. People are burnin' through this stuff like it's a weed."

"It is!" replied Taylor, stashing the cash in her bag. "I'll know more when I get back from payin' our bill."

"Great, lemme know. Gotta give those customers a reliable source!"

Chapter 4

Detective Silas Sejnowski, a burly career cop, who followed in his father's footsteps as his father before him, trudged through a cold wet snow into the Tenth Precinct on West 20th, dropped his coat on the back of his chair, un-strapped his shoulder holster and placed it reverently in the top drawer of his desk, and sat down with a groan.

His partner, Jimmy McElroy, Irish, educated, and irreverent, peered over the top of his wire-rim glasses, "It's fucking miserable out there."

"Yeah, but that don't stop them hookers and johns from screwin', thieves from thievin', the drunks killin' each other, or those stinkin' hippies dealin' drugs on the street down in the Village. The only difference is that it's a bigger hassle to get the bad guys out in the open."

"I've got a couple of longhairs who trade information for food money, now and then."

"So what's happenin' now?"

"Big shipment of high-grade Jamaican pot just blew in like this damned blizzard. Blue foil bricks are turning up everywhere and demanding top dollar."

"So how's that shit get from Jamaica to the streets?"

"Figure that one out and we'll get a commendation."

"Fuck the commendation, I want to put these commie pricks behind bars, where they belong, and I don't care what we have to bust 'em for…but it sure would be nice to work our way up to the supplier."

"If they're smart, they're insulated behind layers and layers of gofers. I agree, we should start working on it, but wading through all those losers is gonna take years. Maybe there's a better way?"

"How's that?"

"We find someone close to the target and turn 'em."

"Yeah, like that's gonna fall in your lap," grunted Sejnowski.

"We gotta get some other folks involved with this, spread a wide net to find a string of little fish that feed bigger fish and bigger until we see the pattern. We need all the snitches to sniff around on this thing and see what we come up with."

"Fine, you set it up with the other guys but let's keep this away from the Captain. He'll want to set up some damned task force to work out the logistics or some nonsense. Let's just get some good cops to do what we do, until we have something to take upstairs."

"I agree."

"Fine, get on with it. I've got a ton of reports to finish or the boss is going to put me on rations."

McElroy grinned, "That wouldn't hurt you one bit."

"Fuck you! Asshole!"

~

Antonio knocked on the apartment door. He rarely stopped by unannounced but Augie had been distant or invisible for weeks and he was worried that he might be pissed off.

Abby peaked through the peephole, "Oh, it's Tony!"

She unlatched the bolt to throw the door open for the lanky little brother. A sheepish grin curled at the corners of his mouth, under a mop of dark hair masking timid black eyes and most of his face. She reached up to hug him, "How ya' doin'? Where ya' been, we haven't seen in you a while? How's school?"

Antonio blushed, "I'm fine. School's a drag but I'm getting' through it."

"Hey, you've got one year and you're done. Even I could do

that!" They walked through the dining room to the kitchen, dark green Formica counters under old wood cabinets on pale sea-green walls over a black and white tiled floor. "Can I get you some coffee?"

"Sure," he replied, sitting with his back to the wall behind a round table in the corner to watch her tight butt move, as she wandered from the sink to the stove and back. "How's Augie? I haven't seen him in weeks and I just wanted to make sure he wasn't pissed at me or somethin'?"

"Naw, he's just busy trying to put something together," she said, carrying two cups to the table. "Hell, I don't see him for weeks at a time, either."

"What's he up to?"

"Got me. He won't talk about it."

"I thought you knew everything."

"I only know what I'm supposed to know and nothing more," said Abby. "On the one hand, I understand how your brother gets when he's trying to accomplish something - full throttle, no distractions – but, on the other hand, I kinda resent not knowing when he's leaving, let alone, when he's gonna show up again."

"That's not like him," said Tony. "He cares about you."

"He cares about all of us like a big brother but I don't believe our thing is love forever after or any of that."

Tony blushed.

"I know he's a horny rat but I love him just the same."

"You're a brave and tolerant woman, Abby. You deserve better."

"He might be a lot of things but underneath it all, he's a good person, a caring person who helps everyone. I can't clip his wings and, so far, he always comes back."

"You two are just horny!"

"Well, yeah, there's that!" cackled Abby, grabbing a shallow cookie tin from the shelf. "Wanna smoke a joint?"

"Sure, is that the same Jamaican stuff?"

"Yeah."

"That stuff's everywhere. Other kids are even selling it at school."

"Really? Maybe some college kids brought it in."

"Naw, some guy tried to sell me a bag at a concert in the Village last weekend. It's bigger than that." He took a puff on the joint. "Augie gave me a pound of this shit a few weeks ago, you think it was his?"

"I have no idea but I kinda wish it was true," smirked Abby, as a huge hit exploded into a coughing fit. "Then we wouldn't have to worry about where the next joint was comin' from!"

"Or the next pound."

"Look, you know him even better than I do, so, whatever he's up to, he'll let us in on it when he's ready and not a second before."

Tony toked, "I wanna be a part of it."

"You haven't even graduated high school yet, you numbskull! Dealing isn't some glamorous gig for amateurs to fuck around with, it's dangerous."

"What are the cops gonna do to me, I'm underage?"

"You really are an idiot. They'd break you down until you whine like a baby and turn on your source. You wouldn't last five minutes in interrogation. And, oh yeah, get busted, lose your stash, you've still gotta pay for it. You fuck up and they've got you comin' and goin' and, believe me, you definitely aren't ready for prime time, kiddo."

"I don't think they offer courses in the basics of dealing at college."

"Wanna bet? It's happening on every campus in the country. Kids are selling to each other, learning about chemistry and commerce and contracts and trust...and...criminal law and emergency room procedures and what happens in a morgue. Yeah, you can sell to your friends, that's one thing, but the next level is a whole different ballgame and the level after that's even more intense."

"How do you mean?"

"Well, say you buy a pound from someone, who bought it from a local guy, who got ten from another guy, who received a shipment of a hundred out of a load some other guy brought into the city, and he's a courier for a major distributor who paid an importer to bring in tons from South America or the Caribbean. It's a long chain of people, who have to depend on those before and after them, and there's a whole lotta money floatin' around." She paused for a last hit on the roach, her blue eyes squinting in the smoke, "You can bet that everyone in the queue knows where every penny is and who owes who what."

Tony lit a Kool, "I guess I never thought about it like that."

"I'm not sayin' whether Augie's dealing or not, I don't know. What I am saying is that a punk high-school kid from a good family doesn't need to get mixed up in all of that. You've got time to do some cool things, don't rush it."

"I know you're right but, sometimes, I'd do just about anything to be more than Augie's kid brother."

Abby laughed and lit a Boro, "Hey, he loves you a lot and he wants you to grow up to be your own person. You're not him and he's not you. Just because he does something, doesn't mean that you have to do the same thing. Do what's in your own heart and you'll find your own happiness."

He stubbed out his cigarette and stared at her pert nipples pressing through a tight purple sweater, "He's a fool."

"I get to say that, you don't."

"He oughta do right by you, you're smart and funny and gorgeous."

"You're dreaming and I'm not gettin' between you two.

Don't even go there, you've just got a big hard-on in your pants."

"Can't I get you to help me out here?"

"Honey, I'm bettin' you can find all the help you want from that little Puerto Rican girl you've been datin'."

"She's a girl, you're a...woman."

"Now you're embarrassing me."

He scooted his chair next to hers and placed her hand on his crotch, "I'm in pain and you have the cure."

"Okay," she said, unzipping his fly to yank his dick through the zipper and squeeze his balls until his jaw dropped open. "You just wanna get off, right?"

"Oh, yeah," moaned Tony leaning back.

She wrapped her hand around him and stroked violently three times before he groaned and a spurt of semen arced across the table. She let go and walked over to the sink to rinse a rag in cold water, returning to clean him and wipe up the mess.

He winced as he tucked himself back in, "Thanks."

Abby leaned over and kissed him on the forehead, "Don't ever say I didn't do anything for you, kid. Now, clean up your act, pay attention to what you're supposed to be doing, and get the fuck out of this apartment before I beat you with a broom!"

~

Augie and Ruck traipsed through the din of traffic, headlights streaking through a dense gray fog, past cafes and shops along Damrak heading for Amsterdam Centraal. Ruck stopped at one of the espresso bars, "C'mon, let's have a coffee. We've got a half-hour and it's a ten minute walk at most."

They took chairs and a waiter appeared carrying a tiny tray. Before he could ask, Ruck held up two fingers, "Two espressos and cream, please."

The waiter bowed and disappeared. Ruck pulled a New York

Times from under his arm and Augie asked, "Where the hell d'you get that?"

"At the newsstand by the hotel while you were fiddle-fartin' around."

"That's like gold."

"I know, but I've gotta read you this opening paragraph of a front page story and we'll save the rest for after our meeting. And I quote, 'The problems facing the country over the use of Marijuana continue to grow with new figures released showing more US Servicemen have been court-martialed for smoking Marijuana than any other offense and police officials in San Francisco, California estimate that one quarter of all high school students currently smoke Marijuana'."

Augie grinned, "Like I keep saying, the market's getting bigger every day. I sure hope Bernie's got things lined up with this guy."

"Hey, they were bunkies while he was here for his junior year, so he has ties."

"I thought my family was huge."

"Italian heritage ain't got nothing on a Jewish family from the old country and the same's probably true for a Muslim family too," laughed Ruck, watching headlights and taillights appear and disappear in and out of the mist. "I only got to spend one summer bummin' around the Continent and there's so much left to see."

"That's 'cause you were fiddle-fartin' around," smirked Augie, gazing up and down the misty boulevard. "It's amazing how your perspective on history gets skewed, when you're out of the country. Schools don't teach kids that America is a mere pup compared to cultures that evolved into these great cities and nations over thousands of years."

"And how many wars?"

"Too many."

The waiter brought two small steaming cups, a little pitcher of cream, and sugar rolled in brown paper funnels that looked like miniature versions of the giant spliffs they smoked in Jamaica. Ruck smiled and handed him five Guilders, "Ah, thank you."

He sniffed the aroma, added a spot of cream, and took a sip, "While I was out looking for a paper, I called home to check up on things."

"And."

"We've got shipments enroute on both coasts and distribution is ready and waiting."

"Makes me nervous until it's on dry land."

"Yeah, me too, but we've known all these guys since we were kids and they're all competent sailors. Hell, they're almost family."

"Family presents its own weirdisms."

"Every sibling is unique."

"And some are smarter than others."

"Being an only child, I got the best and worst of both."

"That's why you're so screwed up."

"Fuck you!" laughed Ruck. "I've got my shit strapped on tight."

"That's why your dick's so small, it's starved for oxygen!"

"You asshole!" smirked Ruck, checking his watch. "Drink up or we'll be late."

"Hey, this was your idea."

"Seemed like a good idea at the time," he said, checking his watch, "but, now, we gotta scoot."

They arrived on the platform as the train rumbled into the station and a drowsy Bernie jumped off amid clouds of steam from hissing brakes. "This is my ol' roommate, Fasal," he said, as a slight man with pale chocolate skin and flowing black hair hopped off the last step and extended his hand.

"Fasal, these are my friends, Augie and Ruck. Guys, this is Fasal."

Everyone shook and started to the exit. Ruck walked next to

Fasal, "So, where're you from?"

"Lebanon, actually, although I was educated on the Continent, where I met Bernie, and attended university at Cambridge."

"I'm impressed," said Ruck. "Is it difficult to go back and forth from one culture to the other?"

"At first, it was, because, like all young people, I tried to compare the customs and beliefs, as if I might pick and choose. A great uncle cautioned me that I was following the wrong course. He made me see that those things most sacred in each society are to be treasured, because they could not exist where people have a different belief system. At the same time, we are all the same because, at the very root of our social nature, we all need the same basic things to function and survive."

"I finally learned to appreciate that each culture develops ways of dealing with similar problems in the manner that best suits their particular situation. People in the mountains have to survive different challenges than those who depend on the sea. Reality for those on the plains or the desert has no meaning for the populations of large cities."

"Yeah, I get it. There is beauty in the truth of every culture."

"Well put!" laughed Fasal. "You'd be a prime candidate for conversion to Islam."

"I'm betting that growing up Catholic is just as mind-bending as being born a Muslim."

Bernie chimed in, "So, where we goin'?"

"I was hoping we could swing by the Rijksmuseum," said Augie. "There's a painting I want to see."

Fasal smiled, "I've spent hours in front of 'The Night Watch'. It's a mesmerizing painting and, I might add, far more inspiring than strolling through the red light district."

Ruck chuckled, "We made a pass through there last night. The presentation is way better than the hookers on the streets of

New York."

"One has to admire the cultural determination to bring all the secrets to the surface, where everyone can see and there's nothing to hide."

"Is that the big draw for the gallery?" asked Ruck.

"No, the museum is enormous, but it's the most famous and, perhaps, the most baffling. You'll see."

They caught a cab that turned off the grand boulevard to follow Singel in a long arc along a canal, lined with every configuration of boats and barges, most converted to floating homes decorated in garish colors, docked across the street from blocks of tall slender interconnected buildings housing shops and homes behind traditional facades. The cabbie turned onto Liedsestraaf and screeched to a stop at the entrance to the museum, a heavy Gothic edifice to a million works by history's greatest artists.

Ruck paid the cabbie and caught up with the group. Fasal was saying, "There's a cool little restaurant just down the street, if we're hungry after this."

"Sounds good to me," said Bernie. "I'm starving."

They contributed Guilders to admissions and passed through massive galleries until they found a relatively small, dimly lit room built to feature enormous canvases on each wall. The group stopped before "The Nightwatch", with more than thirty formally dressed figures crammed into what appeared to be a tiny tavern. Originally titled, "The Shooting Company of Frans Banning Cocq and Lieutenant Willem van Ruytenburch Preparing to March Out," the figures are loading weapons to the drill of a drummer, some talking quietly or gazing off canvas expectantly, but there is not one pair of eyes looking directly at the viewer.

The boys walked quietly, respectfully, from one side to the other but there was no eye contact. Bernie whispered, "Now, I know why you wanted to see this. It's mysterious and magical, filled with a sullen sense of balance between anticipation of a hurt or a shooting contest and the interaction between the characters. I can't believe you didn't turn me on to this years ago."

Fasal smiled, "It's actually a rather whimsical portrait of a militia guild that Rembrandt finished in 1642, probably commissioned for their own vane posterity. This was the height of the Dutch Golden Era, so militias were more concerned with social interaction than defending the realm. He made quite a commission, these guys were the rising merchant class, each one paid one-hundred Guilders to be included in the painting and that was a princely sum."

"That's fascinating. He's caught each character and combined them into something that's so much more…powerful. It's like the first page of a great novel."

"That's why we and a million other people come to stand here dumbfounded."

Bernie said, "Have you seen enough, Augie, I'm hungry."

"Didn't you eat on the train?"

"No, he fell asleep and wouldn't wake up until the trainman hit the brakes."

"Fine," said Augie, staring at the huge painting. "It's as magnificent as they said it would be."

"And thought provoking too," added Ruck. "In a way, it's too bad the guild system evolved into unions. In spite of the hardships on the apprentice, there was a certain elegance in passing a craft or a trade down from one generation to the next."

Augie smiled, "The one thing that hasn't changed is a son's obligation to atone for the sins of his father."

"That applies to generations too," added Fasal. "We are the keepers of the future and we must do better than our predecessors."

"That's huge," said Bernie, "especially with Viet Nam and Civil Rights and social revolution and East and West and all the rest of it. It's all happening right now."

"Your country has a chance to make a giant leap forward but the biggest problem with any revolution is who's going to decide what's going to happen, if they actually take power. Usually, they don't have a clue. Anarchists are good at creating a movement and rallying a hodge-podge of fighters but they've never run a business in their lives, let alone have any idea about which levers to pull to make the system work. China's revolution has nearly destroyed the country because they're persecuting intellectuals, scientists, and the managers who know how to keep things running. Their fanaticism has resulted in chaos and starvation for millions of citizens and it will take at least a generation to rebuild their economy. It's up to our generation to find a middle path."

Augie leaned over to the Lebanese, as they walked through the entry into a frigid blast of north wind, "That's why we're trying to put together a very small group of like-minded people to serve our clientele and make some money along the way. All straight up, no bullshit, gentleman's agreement, and everyone benefits."

"It is my custom to withhold a portion of my profits to be donated anonymously to provide for needy children in my country. I believe they call it tithing in the West. I will only work with you, if you adopt a similar philosophy."

Augie stopped in mid-stride, "That's exactly what I've been trying to do, transform this deal into a means of helping people who have no where else to turn."

Fasal's perfect white teeth glistened, in spite of the gloomy skies, "As they say in your country, 'Power to the People!' I believe we have much to discuss."

"I certainly hope so."

They turned into a little pub that reeked of beer, stale cigarette smoke, and good sausages. A pudgy man in a white apron beamed, as he stepped from behind the bar to hug Fasal, "It has been a very long time since you were last here. What's happened to Sasha?"

Fasal bowed his head, "I'm afraid I let her get away."

"You're a foolish young man but we're all guilty of faux-pas in matters of the heart."

"Of that, I am guilty," smiled the young Lebanese. "She decided to go back to her village in Sweden, after she got her nursing degree."

"Some young man will be very lucky to catch her. Now, I assume that you and your friends have not come here to discuss the sad details of your miserable love life but rather to enjoy a fine meal. I also assume that you'd like your usual booth? Yes? Follow me."

They slid into a round corner booth in the shadows at the rear with a view of the entire room and Fasal said, "We don't need menus, just bring us your best and a round of Grolsch."

The little man smiled and backed away, "As you wish."

Ruck said, "This Sasha lady must have been something."

"She was gorgeous," said Bernie. "I was always jealous of you two."

"We used to dine here a lot. It was one of the warm comfortable hideaways that we shared." He paused, "Sometimes, we're not intelligent enough to realize what we have until it's gone. Unfortunately, I doubt that she will be my final gaffe."

Augie chuckled, "All of us succumb to temptation and lust."

"Of this, he knows what he speaks!" laughed Ruck, as a waiter appeared with four chilled mugs, golden with beer, and warm bread and butter on a cutting board.

"So, what have you and Bernie worked out?" asked Augie, as the waiter walked away.

Fasal smiled, "We all come from large families that encompass many people with unique talents and connections. In the Arab World, divisions are not established by political boundaries or lines on a map, so much as where different families have lived for hundreds or thousands of years. Beirut is as cosmopolitan as Paris or Rome and the local joke is that the Americans go to Europe on holiday and the Europeans come to Beirut, the Switzerland of the Middle East. It is truly a beautiful place. It's also a convenient transit point for commerce between the East and the West."

"And the product?"

Fasal smiled, "We do not smoke the leaf of the plant. Rather, the pollens and oils are made into hashish by hand in the mountains from Lebanon to Afghanistan and along the Himalayan chain. The high is far more intense and a kilo brick is about the size of a hardback novel, which makes it convenient for shipping."

"The quality is truly mind-bending," added Bernie.

"What kind of price are we talkin' for the best quality?" asked Ruck.

"One hundred a kilo in batches of one thousand kilos."

"Where?" asked Augie.

Fasal smiled, "That is, if you pick it up in my home town. The biggest problem with that option is that you probably wouldn't make it out of the country with the product or your lives. As in all civilized countries, not everything is as peaceful and honorable as it seems on the surface and commerce has its price."

"Then how does this work?"

"For two hundred, I can have it delivered anywhere in Europe. For three, I'll have it on the dock in New York within sixty days of your order."

"And how much do you expect up front?"

"Half, in cash, preferably American dollars."

Ruck asked, "Do you have a sample?"

"Actually, I do. There's a little wooded park just up the way."

~

The rusting hulk of the old Norwegian freighter, Westanfald, docked just after midnight on Sunday morning, bearing goods loaded in Beirut, Catania, Marseille, Cartagena, and Sines, in Portugal. Within two hours, the paperwork cleared customs and heavy cranes began offloading crates and pallets that were carted away to the warehouse for sorting.

Bernie and Augie appeared at the dispatcher's office with a shipping order shortly after dawn. An old man sat behind the cluttered desk, shielded by a cage of steel mesh with a little slot for passing documents, under a bank of fluorescents that tinged his gray pallor a sickly green. "We're here to pick up a shipment for A&R Steel Company," said Bernie, who was wearing a beat-up Mets cap and a grimy windbreaker.

The clerk took the yellow receipt with a gnarled hand to inspect the shipping number. He flipped open a heavy log and pawed through several pages, "Ah, here it is. You guys are Johnny on the spot. This just offloaded a couple of hours ago."

"Boss said to be down here bright and early," said Augie.

"You got a truck?"

"Yeah," replied Bernie, "company flatbed."

"Looks like that's what you're gonna need 'cause this is a fairly hefty crate. Pull around over on that first dock in the number two building across the way and I'll have 'em haul it out for you."

"Gee, thanks," said Bernie with a smile, grabbing the shipping order and heading for the door.

The front-loader slipped the container onto the bed of the truck, that Augie borrowed from his old man's company for the night, with a gentle touch. Ruck saluted the driver and rigged the tie-downs. He jumped into the passenger seat, "Man, that guy was talented. D'you see how he settled that box like it was fine china on a formal mahogany table."

"Gotta admire talent, no matter what it happens to be," replied Augie, heading north on a deserted FDR. "We'll hop onto the Bruckner."

"A warehouse in the Bronx is perfect, the cops don't want to go in there, it's too dangerous. Kinda looks like they've decided to let the gangs have at it, until there isn't anything left to fight over." said Ruck. "What are we doing about security?"

"Well, I've got a pair of Dobermans in training and a local kid came around to warn me about all the arson that's been going down and how, if I could help him out with some of his products, he could pretty well guarantee that our building would remain unmolested. Oh, and his name is Jesus."

"Sophisticated talk for a street kid. Think he can back it up? And, oh yeah, what'd you have to buy?"

Augie laughed, "A big Sony television, brand new in the box, at fifteen cents on the dollar."

"Think he's got any more of those?"

"Sure...he'll show up again and ask what we're looking for. Then he goes out and steals it, brings it back, gets his cash, and he's good."

"Only in the city!"

"We'll see. If he works out, it's a cheap bribe." He pointed, "Kid said he was looking after the gas station next door too. Guess they need fuel to start the fires."

Ruck looked around the once thriving neighborhood, now block after block of brick and concrete skeletons. The warehouse and the gas station were the only buildings still intact within sight.

Augie backed the old truck into the bay and the rolling steel door rumbled closed behind it. The warehouse was littered with bits and pieces of hot cars and cabinets full of tools. The landlord said that it used to be an auto-body shop but it looked more like they were tearing down stolen cars for parts and left in a hurry.

At the very rear of the building, the former tenants constructed a steel reinforced parts-room surrounded by two layers of hardened rods implanted from floor to ceiling, broken only by facing gates of the same construction. They rolled the crate out of the bed of the truck and across the shop on a dolly.

"We'll never get it up the ramp," said Ruck. "We're gonna have to unpack it."

"We'd better hurry, I've gotta have this truck back in less than an hour or I'm screwed. 'Ol Paulie comes in on Sundays to clean up and he's sure to notice it's missing."

They pried the planks from the top, then the sides, to reveal a pallet stacked with forty-eight gray boxes, secured with metal packing tape. With handcarts, they muscled four boxes a trip and, sweating profusely, finished in a little less than twenty minutes.

Augie mopped his forehead with his sleeve and rubbed his back, "Damn those things are heavy, my back's killing me. Bust open one of those boxes and grab a brick before you lock up. We've gotta hit the road."

"And we've gotta get this shit sold, if we're gonna come up with the other half of the bread for Fasal by next week."

"I'm guessin' we're not going to get much sleep."

Abby was curled up in a chair near the window, staring through a gap in the buildings at the long shadows crawling across Riverside Drive and the Hudson Parkway to sweep along the river like undulating serpents. She started, as Augie's key clicked the latch, but she didn't get up.

He walked over and kissed her on the forehead, "Good morning."

Her eyes were red and her cheeks damp with tears, "Where the fuck have you been on a Sunday morning? It's our morning to stay in bed and fuck!"

"Business, but I'm here now. I've gotta meet some people later but the Jets are playing the Dolphins on TV this afternoon, so I'll try to be back for the second half."

Abby took a sip of coffee, "There's hot coffee and Danish

on the stove, if you want some."

Augie wandered back to the bedroom to deposit his jacket, then through the kitchen to present her with a little block of hashish and a pipe, "See if this might cheer you up."

She sat up, warmed the hash over her Zippo, crumbled some into the pipe, and lit it. Her eyes opened wide and she coughed, "Wow, that's strong shit."

Augie smiled, "Thought you'd like that."

She offered the pipe but he passed, so, she nestled back into the overstuffed leather chair to toke until only glowing ash remained in the bowl. "There's something we need to talk about."

"Yeah, what's that?"

"I'm pregnant."

He stared, dumbfounded, "But I thought you were on the pill."

"I was but the doctor told me to stop for three months."

"And you didn't bother to tell me?"

Tears filled her eyes, "I meant to but…I guess I didn't think it could happen in the first month off the pill."

"So, what now?"

She curled tighter, "I've never felt like this before, like I'm bonding with a little us, living inside of me. I can sense its life and it scares the shit out of me. I know we're too young, but other people have had kids before they were ready, but it's a huge responsibility and I'm not sure either of us is ready. Unless you want to be a daddy?"

He sat up, "You know I love you but we don't have that kind of relationship and, you're right, neither of us is ready to settle down and raise a family."

She burst into tears, "I knew you'd say that…"

He tried to wrap his arms around her but she pushed him away, "Go away, I need to be alone."

"I'll call my uncle, Dr. Andriotti, to see when he can

schedule you."

"Get the fuck outta here!" screamed Abby.

Bernie honked twice and the rolling door lifted just enough for the black limousine to slip into the warehouse before it clanked down into a steel trough in the floor. He hopped out and opened the trunk to pull out six Samsonites in different colors, as Augie wheeled a dolly loaded with gray boxes. "These for your cousin from Madison?"

"Yeah, Taylor, she's got things set up, so, I figured we'd let her have sixty keys, just shy of a hundred grand. Her people are turning this shit in a hurry."

"So, ten bricks per case and we can use some of that packing material to keep 'em from banging around."

Ruck walked up with a clipboard, "If this keeps up, we'll have our payment covered by tonight."

"That's cool, 'cause we definitely want to set this up again," said Augie.

"I told you my connections are good," said Bernie. "You just gotta believe, man."

"Oh, I believe, believe me, I believe. Have you guys done the math on this deal?"

Ruck smiled, "Yeah, when this one's finished, we'll have two million dollars to work with."

"We're developing networks on the west coast, the Midwest, and the northeast and they all want more product," said Bernie

"And we've got people we can trust moving the loads around the country," added Ruck.

"We need some vehicles with big secret compartments to connect the points of entry with the distribution network."

"That's easy," said Bernie. "My cousin, Sal, owns a body

shop. He's been customizing cars for years. I'm positive he has the talent and know he could use the bucks."

"Check it out," said Augie. "I'm also thinkin' we could use a winter vacation in Florida in January."

"Of course, there's more," laughed Ruck.

"Well, we've all spent time on the Gold Coast but, the last couple of times I was down there with the family, I took off and went exploring. There's a stretch of keys up by Port St. Lucie that's fairly deserted, the reefs are deep, and there's a long sheltered inlet that parallels a secluded road."

"Okay, so you could bring speed boats right in to shore," said Bernie, "but where are they coming from?"

Augie smiled, "What if we had the guys bring Guinevere up for us to enjoy for a couple of weeks. We can use speedboats to offload the product into the beach, before she comes in to dock. When we're done, the guys can head south for another run. Hell, we know enough people, between us, to off one load through Florida."

"What about the Coast Guard?"

"If we believe the research in our report, they're primarily concerned with immigrants floating in from Haiti and Cuba. With overcrowded crappy boats, they're taking the shortest route, Key West if possible, to seek asylum. The Coast Guard isn't paying much attention to pleasure yachts farther north."

"We need to get this scouted and worked out before we pull the trigger. It's logistics, man, logistics!" said Bernie.

"Fine, you get with Sal and see what his recommendations are to carry and conceal heavy loads," said Augie. "Ruck, you're in charge of finding us a couple of fast boats, someplace to keep them, and a house on the beach. And, I'll set up the delivery and distribution."

Bernie held up his index finger, "My cousin, who's coming in to get this load, said something about having a thing with some band guy from Georgia. I wonder whether he's got connections?"

Augie smiled, "Well, we can be pretty sure that he's not a narc, if he's playin' Rock-n-Roll. Most of those guys are bandits."

"I'm going to pick her up in an hour, I'll ask her about it."

"Great."

Chapter 5

Abby jumped as the latch clicked and Augie appeared with that little grin, "Are you decent?"

"I've never been fucking decent in my entire life. That's why you keep comin' back for more."

He closed the door and sat down on the old sofa, "Actually, I just wanted to check up on you and to apologize for not being with you, when you went to the clinic. If I could have, I would have, but you have every right to be pissed off. I'm sorry for making you go through all of this."

She started crying, "You're a first-class bastard, you know that? You fucking move out in the middle of all of this? What's with that?"

"You're right…"

Abby interrupted, "I don't want to hear your lame excuses. I fucked you because I used to think that you were my best friend and I never asked much in return. Just…be my friend back."

He leaned over to wipe the tears from her cheeks and place a gentle kiss on her forehead. "I took you for granted and abused our relationship and left you in the lurch. Even if it's not forever, you deserve better."

"I agree, asshole."

"I've taken care of the bills at the clinic and the rent and utilities are paid for the apartment through the end of June. How you doin' on groceries?"

"I'm still cramping and haven't been able to get out much, so I've been eating through the larder and it's getting' kinda thin."

"I'll take care of it. Have you been back to see the doctor?"

"No, I'm scheduled for Tuesday."

"I'm thinkin' you need to call the office, at least. I don't know shit about this but you shouldn't be having pain this long after the procedure."

"Procedure? There's a fairly insensitive word," said Abby, tears running down her cheeks. "They took your baby out of me and killed it."

"I know…and…I'm sorry, but let's not sacrifice you to obstinacy or my screw-ups. Call the doctor."

"Fine. Go buy food and bring back a pound of pot. I'll call while you're gone."

He kissed her again and walked out the door.

Thirty minutes later, he stumbled into the apartment, struggling to haul four overflowing grocery bags to the kitchen. He glanced over at an ashen Abby and stopped in mid-step, "Did you call?"

"Yeah. They said I should come right in…and I'm bleeding." She lifted her leg to reveal a white towel stained with blood.

He dropped the sacks, wrapped her in a blanket, carried her down the five flights of stairs to his black Fifty-Seven Chevy, double-parked just outside the door, and settled her in the passenger seat.

Abby cracked, "Fancy car, where'd you get this, asshole?"

"Guy owed me some money and gave me the car instead."

"Good thing it's fast, 'cause I think you need to get me there quick," she moaned, curling into a ball.

The rear tires squealed as two-hundred-and-eighty-three horses pushed the Chevy past sixty before the end of the block.

Augie looked up from a ragged magazine, that he had pawed through at least a dozen times, as his sister, Mary, sat down next to him. "How'd you know?"

"Word travels fast." Her full red lips smiled, accentuated by a pale complexion under dark auburn curls trailing past her shoulders and probing dark eyes that could see through any fool.

Augie was envious of her intelligence, her intellect, and her determination, and he was proud that she'd decided to attend law school, after she graduated next spring.

"How's Abby?"

"She's out of surgery but they haven't been back to tell me anymore and that was, like, four hours ago."

She took his hand, "She's gonna be okay. You've just gotta believe."

"I haven't said this many Hail Mary's since we went through Confirmation together."

"Sometimes, those old habits help."

"Yeah, along with a gallon of coffee and a couple of packs of 'Boro's."

"Think food might help?"

"Can't leave until they come back," said Augie, leaning back on a bright orange Naugahyde chair. "How're you doin'?"

"I'm getting through my final classes and I really enjoy beating the crap out of arrogant third-year guys, who think they're God's gift in debate."

He chuckled, "You kick some ass, girl. Haven't you been applying to law schools?"

"Yeah, I've got six applications out, but first choice is Yale."

"I'm impressed. You'll get in."

"I'm hoping." Mary leaned close, "You need to spend some time with your little brother. I get the feeling that he's gonna screw up big time, unless you rein him in."

"What the fuck's he doin' now?"

"Partyin' too much, tryin' to be the coolest guy on campus by always having the best drugs. We know and he knows that he's just a goofy putz but, when he goes down, he's gonna go down hard. I've tried to talk with him but he just blows me off."

"I take it you mentioned the legal ramifications?"

"Oh yeah, and New York is not lenient. Speaking of which, I don't know what you're up to but I worry about you too."

Augie smirked, "The bad influence that doomed Tony."

"He told me that he's pretty sure you're behind all the wonderful smoke that's available everywhere. Is it true?"

"I don't want to reinforce his fantasies. It's a dangerous world out there."

"And, knowing you, you're right in the middle of it. So, you're not denying it."

"I'd rather we keep this to ourselves. The ol' man's already pissed but, when I showed him the numbers, he backed off."

"It's always about profit with him. I thought I'd spend the summer getting his crap organized, so the IRS doesn't throw his ass in jail. Now it looks like I'll have to take care your shit too." She paused, "I'm guessin' you're already seeing the problem of having too much cash."

His eyes twinkled behind that little impish grin, "There does seem to be a problem of mass."

Mary laughed, "Crap, you're in way deeper than I thought."

"I've been thinking about buying a business that deals mostly in cash."

"Grocery stores," said Mary, without hesitating. "Straight up cash business that provides a most basic commodity that everyone needs to replenish every day. I'm assuming a mom and pop on the corner isn't going to offer enough flexibility."

"Maybe two or three of them."

"Shit! How big is this?"

He stared for a long moment, "Well, I've already cleared more than three million in profit."

She whistled a long descending tone, "That's incredible."

"And it's just getting cranked up. At this rate, we'll make ten times that in the next year."

"I sure hope you're covering your tracks. The Federalies would love put you away for conspiracy for a very long time, especially if you fail to pay taxes on it."

"That's why I need something legit as a front."

"Tell you what, I haven't taken my first class in law yet, but I'll look into it for you. You're gonna owe me big."

"I already do. You're here, aren't you?"

"Yeah, 'cause you're my only big brother."

They looked up as a young doctor, with wavy black hair, bloodshot eyes, and two days of stubble, shuffled into the waiting room. "How is she?"

"She'll live."

"But is she gonna be okay?" asked Augie.

"She's lost a lot of blood and we've given her several transfusions. She'll be weak for a few days, so we're going to keep her. We had to do another D&C and…well, I'm not sure she'll ever bear children. It will depend on how she heals."

"Oh, no!" gasped Mary.

Augie slumped into a chair and held his head in his hands, to mask the tears running down his cheeks.

~

A heavy wet snow was falling horizontally in an easterly gale, as Taylor disembarked at LaGuardia airport. She hustled into the terminal to find Bernie leaning against a post with a stony smile, "I just came from this, couldn't you have ordered up a warm day?"

"Hey, it wasn't this bad until you showed up!" He hugged her between an oversized purse and a leather attaché, "You need a hand with any of this?"

"Yeah," she said, offering the briefcase. "You are now in charge of that."

He took the valise, "Everything go okay?"

"Not a problem, other than Lydia flaking out on me. We're ready to go again, if you've got the product."

"I think that can be arranged. Do you have any bags?"

"Just one overnight bag."

"C'mon, we'll pick it up. I've got a car right outside."

They piled into a sleek Buick Electra and headed out of the parking lot. Bernie said, "Well, we've got three choices. We can head into the city and stay at my apartment, we can drop by to see my parents, which probably doesn't qualify as one of our better options, or we can head up to a friend of mine's place on the water, south of New Rochelle."

"I'm for nature over crowds," said Taylor, gathering long blond hair into a thick ponytail. "Peace and quiet are hard to come by, in a girl's dorm on a campus with fifty-thousand students and probably that many more just hanging around taking up space."

"How long do you have to put up with that?"

"Technically, fall semester, but I'm spending the summer and I've already got my eye on a place by the lake."

"So, are your people gonna work out okay?"

"Yeah, they're typical loutish freshmen in every way, except when it comes to business, and then it's deadly serious."

"You said you were looking into a Southern connection?"

"I'm dating a bass player from Macon and he's looking into it. He's pretty well hooked up in Georgia and Florida but, knowing him, he won't move until everything feels right."

"Sixth sense?"

"Maybe. Onstage, he's a driving force but, when he's not with the band, he's quiet, observant, and probing in a laid-back, matter-of-fact kinda way. He just seems to grasp things, even when nothing's been said."

"So you trust him completely?"

She laughed, "He's one of those guys that you wouldn't

think twice about leaving your most precious possession with, because you know it will be there when you come back for it."

"One of those guys!"

"Yeah."

"And, I can tell, you're sweet on him."

"It's just so comfortable with him, like I've always known him. Hell, I slept with him the first night I met him and I don't fuck anyone on a first date."

"Sounds heavy to me."

"It's casual and his drummer told me that he's got a live-in Southern honey. So, when we're together, we're together and, when we're not, we're not."

"He's a lucky hippie."

"Did you ever have one of those relationships where you knew that, even if it fell apart, you wouldn't regret one minute of it?"

"Nope, never got that lucky."

"Well, this is one of those."

Bernie drove the Electra down a winding gravel path to a little white cottage, with a slate roof and green shutters, tucked into a dense cluster of trees facing out on the Sound. Taylor hopped out of the car and pulled the hood of her coat over her head, "I want to see the water."

Bernie took her hand and they trudged through the snow around the house into a gale piling whitecaps across the bay. A dozen seagulls struggled across the wind, skimming through clouds of icy foam tossed up by the breakers. Taylor pulled her coat around her body and turned into the wind. She leaned over to Bernie, "I do this on Lake Mendota when it's freezing. All the girls in the dorm think I'm nuts but I don't care. It just makes me feel so alive."

"It makes me feel cold," said Bernie. "I'm votin' for a big fire and a hot dinner."

"And, maybe, a glass of wine in there too?"

"Knowing Augie, you could probably name your vineyard and vintage and he'd have it."

"I'm likin' your friend," said Taylor, taking his arm. "How come he's not here?"

"Oh, he had to move a boat to the Caribbean for his dad. He'll be back next week. You'd like him and I can guarantee, he'd like you."

"That sounds dangerous."

"Knowing him as well as I do, I'd suggest running in the opposite direction before shaking hands. He bought this place but left his girlfriend, who just had an abortion, with the apartment in the city until the lease runs out."

"That's better than kicking her out on the street but it's still cold."

"Weird part is that they'll jump back in the sack, first chance they get." He unlocked the door and dropped her bag in a bedroom off the hall. "There's a bathroom through there and plenty of blankets in the closet, if you need 'em."

"C'mon, I'll show you around and start a fire." He walked down the hallway into a large room with a kitchen along the back wall facing a bank of windows overlooking the water. Comfortable furniture was arranged around a fireplace and a large Sony television. Bernie wadded up some newspaper and stuffed it under a pile of dry logs. "This should be hot in a jiffy."

Taylor found a bottle of Chardonnay in the fridge and Bernie produced a bag with two steaks, potatoes, and salad makings, "I'm thinkin' this ought to be enough."

"Those are beautiful steaks," she said, handing him a glass. "Here's to good business."

"Here's to family!"

Their glasses clinked and he said, "Think you can handle the same amount again?"

"Sure."

He placed the briefcase on the counter and opened it, flipping through the stacks of bills."

"Ninety-eight thousand on the penny."

"Great!" replied Bernie, closing the case. "I've got sixty-four keys for you but we're working on a better delivery system. We'll send it by car to arrive wherever you want three days after you say, 'Go'."

"Aren't you afraid of cops on the road?"

"We're having some vehicles reconfigured for our needs. Even if they searched, they'd never find the secret compartments or the air-jacks that keep it level."

"James Bond!" laughed Taylor.

"Probably more along the lines of Dr. No."

The phone line crackled, "Randy? It's Taylor."

"How are you?"

"Tired, just back from a fast trip to see my cousin in New York."

"New York's exhausting."

"Actually, I never got into the city. We stayed out on the Sound."

"I'm jealous, it's beautiful out there," laughed the lanky bass player. "Everything go okay?"

"Yeah, no problem and we're lined up for more."

"Cool."

"He was asking whether you've learned anything yet?"

"Yeah, I've got a couple of things cookin'. Does he have anyone working Chicago?"

"I don't know, but I'll find out."

"Y'know, I'd like to meet this guy. I understand that you're dealing with family but, just as he wants to protect his end, we need to do the same for the people we work with."

"I can see your point," said Taylor. "It's like a chain of dominos."

"Yeah, going in two directions and we don't need to get caught in the middle, if they all come tumbling down."

"How's this gonna work?"

"We're doing some frat party and a concert at the University in Princeton in a couple of weeks. Don't ask me how we got the gig but it might prove convenient for everyone."

"Get me the dates and the place and I'll see what I can do. Oh, and Princeton doesn't have frats, they have eating clubs."

"Eating clubs? That's weird."

"Long story."

"I'll get 'em from Travis and call you back. Heck, bring 'em to the show and we can have dinner after."

"You expect me to waste a perfectly good night with you?" laughed Taylor.

"It's business. We can sleep in."

The crowd was still cheering when Peachtree finally marched off stage and Taylor wrapped Randy in a hug, "That was fantastic!"

"We're cookin' tonight!" said Randy, high-fiving Danny, the guitarist, and Ronnie, the drummer, as they headed for the private lounge to pack guitars and collect their gear. "Did you bring your cousin?"

"Yeah, and his partner. Bernie and Augie. You'll like 'em."

"Great. I've gotta go get cleaned up, so meet me at Le Harve over on Witherspoon in thirty. We've got reservations."

The deep aroma of garlic and onions wafted from sizzling dishes on a tray, balanced by a waiter in formal black and white cruising gracefully through the narrow room, illuminated by sconces on mustard walls and candles on formally set tables. The bass-player, with muttonchops and waves past his shoulder blades, unbuttoned his leather jacket, to reveal a burgundy paisley shirt over gray hip-hugger bells and Beatle boots, and walked to the back.

The tall blond stood to hug him, "Randy, I'd like you to meet Bernie and Augie."

He sized them up, as they shook hands all around. Bernie was short, fair, and slender, sandy hair and green eyes, genial but definitely not the alpha in the pair. Augie was tall with broad shoulders and curly brown hair cut short enough to pass as a hip businessman. Intense probing eyes crinkled with an affable glint and a crooked grin tweaked the corners of his mouth. Both were wearing expensive tweeds and sporting Rolex watches.

Augie said, "Your band is hot, man. When ya' gonna play the city?"

"We're just starting to make contacts and get some bookings. We've played all over the South and Midwest but we're just gettin' started up here."

"I'll put you in touch with some people who can help."

"Cool," said Randy. "We've got a manager, Travis, and I'll pass it on to him."

"Is all your material original?" asked Augie.

"Yeah, we all write and contribute. Most of our stuff starts with a riff or an idea and just grows from there."

"You doin' any recording?" asked Augie.

"Not yet, just two-track demos that we send to the clubs."

"I'd like to help with that too."

"Sure," said Randy. "What ya' got in mind?"

"Studio time's expensive, so maybe your manager and I can work something out, to get things moving."

"I'll give you his number."

The waiter arrived and Bernie ordered a bottle of Rothschild, "If that's alright with you?"

Randy smirked, "Hell, wasn't too long ago, we were praising the merits of a bottle of Ripple."

"I'm glad you approve," smiled Bernie. The waiter handed Randy a menu and disappeared. "Taylor tells us that you might be able to help us expand into the South?"

"Right to it, huh?"

"I like your music and your professionalism on stage. I've got a feeling it carries over in your character. Especially if my cousin is sweet on you."

"I'll vouch for him," laughed Taylor.

"I've got a couple of contacts that are reliable and solid, organized and honest. Not the kind of folk who would take a bunch of acid and zone out on our profits. One in Lauderdale and another in Chicago, if you don't already have that covered."

Augie took a sip of water and wiped his mouth with a napkin, "Detroit, yes, Chicago, no."

"Then I have two clients capable of building their networks to turn your supply," said Randy, leaning back in his chair.

"That's what we were hoping for," said Bernie. "The demand is expanding exponentially and someone's gotta provide the product."

"We'll have to work out deliveries to these guys, because I'm on the road too much to meet other people's schedules."

The waiter appeared and handed the bottle to Bernie, who inspected the label and nodded his approval. A rapid twist of the corkscrew and a gentle tug produced a plump cork, which the waiter offered to Bernie for a sniff. He smiled, "Ah, that's wonderful."

A tiny splash in a glass whirled around and around, as Bernie inhaled the scent, inspected the color and clarity, and, finally, tasted the ruby vintage, sucking air through pursed lips to enhance the flavor. He raised the glass in approval and the waiter poured the other three glasses and finally his.

"Are you ready to order?" inquired the waiter, a waif of a

man with black slicked-back hair, a pencil thin moustache, and a soft French accent.

"If you'll give me a minute to scan the menu," said Randy.

"Well, let me offer two specials this evening. The first is a succulent Beef Wellington with Béarnaise and a marvelous filet of sole meuniere, both with pommes frites and sautéed vegetables. I will return in a moment."

"Thank you," said Randy, scanning the menu. He looked up at Taylor, "What're you having?"

"That filet of sole sounds good."

"Likewise the Wellington. What about you guys?"

"I'm with her," said Bernie.

"I'm going to try the scampi, that's as close to Italian as they offer." said Augie, folding the menu. He looked up, "No problem on the deliveries, we can take care of that. If you'll get the information to Taylor, we'll figure out scheduling."

"That works. What about quantity and price?"

Augie leaned back, that little grin tweaking the edges of his lips, "I'll tell you what, I'll make you a deal."

"That sounds dangerous," laughed Randy.

"Let's start your folks out with fifty kilos each and we'll wave the deposit. If they come through and everything works out hunky-dory, we'll up the quantity on the second round. The price will remain the same, plus a dime a pound shipping."

"I wasn't expecting you guys to be so generous," said Taylor. "We'll set it up."

"Let's call it family," smiled Bernie, raising his glass and squeezing her right hand, as her left slid up Randy's thigh under the tablecloth.

~

Taylor rolled on her back, sighing, "What a way to start the day."

Randy snickered, "Too bad we don't get more than a day or two together at a time."

"Maybe it's good in a way. Gives us something to look forward to."

He tickled her. "It's never enough!"

"God, I wish I didn't have to go back to school."

"You're living two lives."

"Yeah, trouble is I like 'em both. There's just not enough time."

"We're heading back to Georgia for a week off to practice. Then we head out for four nights in Lauderdale."

"That's like going home for you."

He smiled, "I'll stay with my mom, the rest of the guys can find enough trouble without me."

"That's good. Are you going to set things up, while you're down there."

"Yeah. I'll see my friend and get all his info."

"Who's the other contact?"

"Jason, our roadie. He was dealin' when I met him and he's the only one who put two and two together about my coming to see you in Madison. He's from Chicago and has connections in Milwaukee too."

"So, nobody else in the band knows?"

"Nope."

"Not even your secret sweetie in Macon?"

Randy blushed and licked her nipple, "She's a nice lady but it's not like...this...with her. And, no, she doesn't know anything."

"You've gotta be the luckiest guy on the planet, having two ladies who love you enough to tolerate you having the other!"

He leaned up to kiss her, "I'm thinkin' you and I are just gettin' started."

She wrapped her arms around his neck, "I sure hope so."

He laughed, "You're givin' me shit about Sunshine but you

had to notice that Augie couldn't take his eyes off of you."

"Sunshine? Really, Sunshine?"

"Scout's honor."

"How'd she get a name like that?"

"That actually reflects her personality perfectly. She's just always up and smiling and sweet, like she's walking around in a meadow full of flowers and butterflies on a warm sunny day. It's infectious."

"Mother-earth-hippie-girl?"

"Definitely, but clean and tidy."

"And very sexy!" roared Taylor. "But I'm bettin' she's no intellectual challenge to you."

"Oh, she's intelligent, no doubt about that, and she's lived all over the world. She might play the Southern belle for effect but there's a whole lot more going on behind those pale blue eyes than she's ever going to let on." He started laughing, "My mom used to ask, sometimes, in jest, 'What are you going to talk about when you get out of bed?' and the proper response was that, with some women, you never want to get out of bed long enough to find out."

"Ooooh, that sounds like a challenge to me!" She giggled, rolling to pin his arms and legs, while she nibbled on his nipples.

~

Augie scanned the interior of Bernie's new Porsche, "This is some ride, brother."

Bernie grinned, "Yeah, I just couldn't help myself. The deal was too good to pass up."

"You know this thing's a shark."

"What do you mean?"

"It can never stop moving in the City. You park it for two minutes and, I guarantee, it's gone."

"Ah, I'll be careful, it's my new best love.

He rolled down the window and leaned back with his arm out, "First glimpse of spring."

Bernie gunned the engine and dropped into third, as an Oldsmobile plowed across his lane, "'bout time, it's been colder than a witch's tit for most of the winter and we're still not done."

"A few days in the tropics always cures the winter blues."

"What's cookin'?"

"Ruck's down in St. Thomas, checking out a new boat."

"How big?"

"Ocean worthy, hundred and twenty foot trawler with all the gear. We'll be able to move tons at a time outside territorial waters and look like we're just out there fishin'."

"Sweet. Anyone spoken to Nell or Wilfred?"

"Yeah, I need you to go down and set this up. We'll start with two tons for a trial run and, if everything works out, we'll double it on the rebound. I want to get our guys checked out on the boat."

"And there's another shipment coming in from Fasal next month."

"Gotta hope those hippies'll be ready for a summer of love," laughed Augie.

"This whole thing has turned into a spider web, stretching across half the country. Think maybe we're growing too fast?"

"We've gotta move while we can, 'cause there are other bright guys out there, who are gonna set up their own systems. This isn't going to remain a gentleman's game for long."

"You've gotta know there's a cop someplace, who's wondering where all the good dope suddenly appeared from."

"That's why a long chain of connections through loyal people is the best protection we can get."

"I hope you're right," said Bernie.

"What'd ya' think of the new guy."

"My cousin's take wasn't far off the mark. He's intelligent, calm, deliberate, and creative."

"The question is whether he's snowed her or is he really honest? And, oh by the way, she's gorgeous, intelligent, ballsy, and way too sexy."

"You keep your grimy mitts off her and, oh by the way, he asked to meet us to protect his people, remember? That's a good start."

"Yeah, you've got a point," said Augie. "And we need a path to the South. That's huge."

"Guess we'll know for sure, when this one's done."

"Fifty kilos? They oughta have it finished up in a couple of weeks, if they've really got the market."

"If it's anything like Taylor's people, they'll be clamoring for more in half that."

"We'll have the smoke."

~

Tony knocked on the door of the white bungalow nervously. Augie opened it with a grin and wrapped him a bear hug, "C'mon in. Glad you could come by. Wanna beer?"

"Sure," replied Tony, following him down the hallway to the great room at the back. He walked directly to the windows, "Wow, this is beautiful. I can see why you moved out here."

"Better than watchin' the whores struttin' up and down the streets in the City." He handed him a cold brew and put an arm around his shoulders, "How ya' doin', kid?"

"I'm okay."

"Still datin' that Puerto Rican chick?"

Tony blushed, "Well, her and a couple of others."

Augie laughed, "I can tell you from experience, the ladies always win, so watch out. How's school?"

"Boring. I can't wait to get out of there."

"Hey, it's better than getting drafted, so stick with it You need to go to college or they're gonna grab your scrawny ass and ship you off to Nam…and family connections aren't going to get you out of that one." He dropped his arm, "How's the scene out there?"

"It's hot, man. Everybody's groovin' on good music and plenty of fine drugs."

"Yeah, I hear you're hot shit on campus."

"What do you mean?"

"Word has it that you're the go-to guy, if anyone wants some good dope."

"Well, yeah, I guess that's true. Why fuck around with shitty pot."

"And what else?"

Tony hesitated, "Oh, you know…acid, 'shrooms. ups, downs, the usual stuff."

"What else?"

"Well, some of the older guys are always after junk and coke and meth."

"And you know a guy, who knows a guy, right?"

"Yeah."

"That's how to get your ass busted or worse, you dumbshit. People doing that shit are dodgy, they get strung out and violent. Are you snortin'?"

"I've tried most of it."

"And what'd you think?"

"It'd be real easy to get strung out, so I only do coke once in a while and I've only tried junk a couple of times."

"Look, the Jamaicans treat Ganja with respect, like a sacrament. That's how we should look at all mind-altering drugs. Under the right circumstances, maybe, but if you're buyin' and sellin', then stick to the one that isn't going to kill you or anyone else."

"You oughta know," said Tony.

"What's that mean?"

"It's pretty obvious that you're not just screwin' around with this, you're in it up to your ass."

Augie snapped, "You're a privileged high school brat, who doesn't have a clue about what's really goin' on out there."

"I'm your brother and I can see what's happening. Do you honestly think anyone, who isn't completely blind, doesn't know?"

"Like who?"

"The whole fucking family knows!"

"Great."

"So cut me in, I can sell a bunch."

"You don't need to be involved in anything other than graduating from school. When you've got your own education, we'll talk."

"What do you know that I don't?"

"Well, I got a degree in economics and an MBA, for one thing. I've made a lot of stupid mistakes that I hope you don't have to go through, because I want better for you."

"Better than what? Livin' fat and traveling all over the world?"

"How'd you know I've been traveling?"

"I stopped by to see Abby, a while back, because I was worried about you. She finally admitted that she didn't have a clue about where you were but that you'd been gone a lot."

"Can't trust anyone."

"From what I hear, that goes both ways."

"What's that supposed to mean?"

"It's no secret that she had an abortion and you didn't even bother to show up. Then you moved out and left her with the apartment? What's the deal with that?"

Augie slumped on the leather couch, "Like I said, I've made a lot of mistakes. It's complicated."

"But you look like a guilty asshole to me."

"Believe me, I am, but she and I both agreed that we don't have the forever-after kind of love and neither of us was ready to start a family. I'll know when I find the right one."

"She's a special lady. She deserves better."

"You're right about that." He clicked the television on and Walter Cronkite's grave jowly face appeared on the screen.

"Dr. Martin Luther King was shot and killed on a balcony at the Lorraine Motel in Memphis, Tennessee this afternoon. Police are searching for the assassin."

"Holy Shit! The world's starting to heat up with stuff like the massacre in Orangeburg by a bunch of crazed Highway Patrol thugs, protests and riots at Columbia, and now this," said Tony. "There's gonna be rioting in the streets tonight."

"This might be a good time for you to be home," said Augie. "Go directly to the house and stay there."

"But...?"

"No 'buts', this could get real bad, real quick. Now go!"

Tony chugged his beer, ambled down the hall, and out the front door. He jumped into the old man's Lincoln and peeled down the driveway.

Augie picked up the phone, "Ruck, have you seen the news? Yeah, well, I'd say we should lock down the stash and guard it. Things are gonna get hairy and we don't need our stuff getting caught up in the riots. I'll meet you there."

He turned the sound up and Cronkite said, *"We'd like to play a small and tragically profound piece of Dr. King's final speech, given last night at the Ebenezer Baptist Church."*

The familiar reassuring baritone rose from gentle prophetic premonition to a rousing crescendo of promise and hope,

"Like anybody, I would like to live a long life.
Longevity has its place. But I'm not concerned about that now.
I just want to do God's will. And He's allowed me to go up to

the mountain. And I've looked over. And I've seen the Promised Land. I may not get there with you. But I want you to know tonight, that we, as a people, will get to the promised land!"

Augie flopped on the couch, "He had to know. He saw it coming."

~

A hammering on the steel door echoed around the warehouse and Ruck grabbed a Forty-five, before peering through the peephole. "It's that kid, Jesus."

"Let him in," yelled Augie.

A wisp of a boy with long black hair falling from an orange leather headband, huge dark eyes, and an angelic face, stepped inside, "You guys don't have to worry. All the crazies have already burned out everything around here."

"Yeah, but they'll be looking for gasoline," said Bernie.

"No problem, the pumps are turned off and locked up, so all they could do is trash the place. I pointed them in another direction."

"Are you kidding me?" asked Ruck. "How much is this service going to cost?"

"Pass me a couple hundred for my troubles and I'll make sure the crazies pass right by your door."

"Done," said Augie, handing over two crisp hundreds. "We're staying put, just in case you screw this up."

"I don't blame you, but you're losing sleep over nothing. Oh, you got any spray paint?"

"Yeah," said Ruck, pointing, "there's a can of gold over on that shelf."

"Thanks!" Jesus smiled, grabbed the paint, and let himself out into the night.

"Do you believe that?" asked Bernie.

"Wouldn't surprise me if he didn't pull it off," said Augie. "Let's get comfy. We're not going anywhere for a while."

"Think he knows?" asked Bernie.

"With all the gas and oil stink, I doubt he could smell anything, even if there is a ton and a half of product in the cooler."

At dawn, the streets were quiet and empty of traffic but the air was thick with smoke and soot, as Ruck opened the door and stepped outside. "Hey, you guys've gotta see this."

Augie and Bernie stumbled into first light and followed his pointed finger to the huge steel door and a rippling gold Puerto Rican flag, artistically painted across the entire width.

"I'll be damned," said Bernie. "The kid's a genius."

"Smart enough to take our money and laugh at us," said Ruck.

"Naw, that was a good investment all the way around," said Augie, admiring the banner. "Kid shows spunk and originality and, besides, he's got some talent."

"Yeah, but it's the blacks who're pissed off," said Bernie.

"Dr. King was talking about the dignity of man for all people of color, hell, for all of us. Wasn't that long ago that Wops and Spics and Paddys and Jews were in the same boat," said Ruck.

"Maybe his death will bring people together but, considering how fucked up this country is, that might be wishful thinking."

"It's all about everyone doing their part and, seein's as you two have your heads up your asses, I've been making donations to the soup kitchen down in the Village since the first of the year."

"Sort of giving back a little of the food money that those fools spend on our dope?" asked Bernie.

"Yeah, there's a little bit of guilt in there...but not much," laughed Ruck. "They're all paid out of an account for one Joannie Appleseed."

"That's great!" laughed Augie, settling back on the rear seat out of a Fifty-four Fairlane that was braced against the wall.

"Shoulda' called it High Co."

"That's too obvious and lacks imagination. We're spreading good vibes across the country, planting the seeds of social revolution!"

Augie smirked, "Actually, we've also been buying blankets and pillows and coats for the homeless shelter since last fall."

~

Tony pulled to a stop behind the darkened baseball field at Sebastian Academy next to classmate Mitchell O'Brien's white Corvette and got out. He slid into the passenger seat, "How's it goin'?"

Mitch looked pale and jittery, "I'm needin' my meds man. You got what I need?"

Tony pulled a dime bag out of his pocket, "That's all I could get but the guy says he'll have more in a couple of days."

"Guess that'll have to do," said O'Brien. His hair was damp from sweat and his eyes darted from one side of the windshield to the other, as he handed over the money and snatched the bag. "Thanks, man, I gotta find someplace private to do this."

Tony jumped out, as the car squealed away and stadium lights flooded the field, casting long shadows that snaked closer and closer as a covey of blue police uniforms converged with guns drawn.

"Turn around and place your hands on the hood of the car!" said the first cop, smacking Tony in the face with the butt of his gun.

~

Augie stood, as a guard escorted Tony into the visitor's room. His tousled bangs drooped over a large bruise around a swollen left eye, his right arm was clamped to his chest, and his clothes were torn and dirty. The policeman closed the door as he left.

"You look like shit."

"Yeah, they roughed me up a little bit, before they brought me in," said Tony, dropping onto a chair and placing his cuffed wrists on the table.

"You okay?"

"If they don't kill me, Dad will."

"Not if I get your ass first, you little punk. What they fuck were you doing?"

"Doin' a guy a favor."

"Heroin? We talked about all of this! It's bad karma."

"Yeah, I know."

Augie sat down next to a man in an impeccably tailored black pinstripe suit, a red tie, and perfectly round wire rim glasses framing dark probing eyes under a kinky gray Afro, the color and texture of wire wool, "Don't know whether you remember our cousin, Rudy Feinman. He's the only Italian-Jew lawyer in the family and he's yours."

"Glad to meet ya'," said Tony, extending a shackled hand with a grimace.

"So, Anthony, you sold some heroin to one of your friends, who turned out to be a junky snitch and traded you to get off on his own charges."

"That son of a bitch!"

"What's Dad's first rule?" asked Augie.

"Keep your mouth shut."

"Right, so what did you tell the cops, while they were beating the crap out of you?"

"Nothin', man. I told 'em I got the smack from some dude on the street in the Village. Just tryin' to do a guy a favor."

The lawyer cleared his throat. "According to the records, you're coming up on your eighteenth birthday in a few weeks?"

"Yes."

"Between the obvious physical abuse and the fact that you're still a minor. We might be able to get you off on this. I'll see what I can do."

"Can you get me out of here?"

"Not until you're arraigned this afternoon and the judge sets bail. I'll see if I can get the charges dropped, in the meantime." He dropped the file in a gunmetal gray briefcase and popped open a Polaroid camera. He snapped three shots, with a flash and a whir, and left the room.

Augie leaned over, "Are you out of your mind?"

"Just trying to live in the shadow of those who came before."

Augie's fist slammed the table, "You dumb sonofabitch! I'm not worthy of emulation and you've wasted years trying to imitate my life. You have a life of your own! Be who you're supposed to be, because you're a total failure at impersonating me."

"I've spent my whole life hearing everyone say, 'Oh, Augie did this or accomplished that,' but they never spent much time talking about your fuckups or anyone else's homeruns or touchdowns. Hell, everyone got better grades than you, even me."

"That's the point, you can be anything you want to be. All you have to do is work at it. You're smart enough to accomplish your own wonders, instead of hanging around waiting for a big bag of cash to fall into your lap, so you can goof off for the rest of your life. And, oh, by the way, this business definitely isn't for you. Stop pretending before something really bad happens and there's no going back. There's no way anyone else can save you from your own stupidity. The first one's free, kid, but don't expect me to bail your ass out the next time."

Tony started crying, "I'm sorry, but I like having people like me."

Augie put an arm around his shoulders, "Those people only want what you've got and they'll vanish the moment you don't have it anymore. They aren't friends, they're leaches and they'll suck you dry without a second thought."

"Yeah, I guess I already knew that." He looked up, "Fuck! I'm definitely kicked out of school and the old man's gonna be pissed."

"Yeah, you're gonna have to face that one on your own. I've been through that persecution often enough to say, it ain't pretty."

Tony snorted, "Guess catchin' a bunch of shit from him is better than spending years in the slammer."

"Are you finally getting the point?"

"I don't want to go to jail."

"You're already in jail and you better hope that Cousin Rudy's as good as he claims."

"I hope you're right," said Tony, slumping on the table. "I didn't mean to fuck up."

"Nobody means to screw up but, most of the time, they forget to solve the problem before it occurs. You can't just blindly walk into a situation that might be dangerous. You have to scope it out, know your people, and have a plan, if things go off the edge."

"I guess that's real life."

"That doesn't have to be your real life. You can make up whatever you want, getting it right is a matter of diligence and patience."

"God, you sound philosophical. I can talk to Father D'Angelo about saving my soul."

"Hey, I'm still learning about life but I finally understand that when things go south, you've gotta do two things, solve the problem and learn from the mistake. Doesn't do any good if you just repeat the blunder."

Tony looked up, "Speaking of screwups, did you ever get things squared away with Abby?"

"Not that it's any of your business but, yeah, we're cool."

The door creaked and Rudy Feinman strode into the room,

placing his briefcase on the table, "I've spoken with the judge and the city attorney, raising questions about your age and your physical condition, let alone indisputable entrapment and the credibility of the only witness, considering the only evidence is a small plastic bag with minute quantities of residue inside. Evidently, your friend consumed the entire contents before he wrecked his car. He's been taken to the hospital with a critical overdose."

"Oh, shit!" said Tony. "Is he alive?"

"The last report indicated that he was in critical condition, beyond that, I don't know anything further. As a result of their failure to intercept the evidence, a young man might very well die, and there's no way we'll let them get away with bringing charges of manslaughter or attempted murder for their ineptitude. After the prosecutors considered the options, all charges have been dropped. You are free to go but the judge said that, if he ever sees your name come up on the docket, you will spend seven years in a deep dark place." He pulled a form from the case, "You will sign, where I have marked, and your brother will witness."

Tony scribbled his signature on four sheets of paper and pushed them across the table, "Get me outta these fucking manacles."

Augie pushed the papers back, "First, this isn't Perry Mason, your ass is on the line here, so, you read and understand every word, every sentence, and every thought in these documents. They'll be filed with the court forever and you, sure as hell, better understand what you've just signed!"

Tony turned the pages and started to read, "Holy shit! You weren't kidding, if I'm brought up on anything worse than a parking ticket, I go to jail. That sucks!"

"That, my young cousin, is reality. In this reality, I saved your ass. Don't let there be a next time."

"Yes, sir," said Tony, passing the sheets back to Augie. "I'll do my damnedest to stay out of trouble."

Augie signed the forms and handed them to Rudy. He also placed a thin metal briefcase on the table. "Thank you for your troubles."

Rudy nodded, took the two cases and left the room without a word.

~

Detective Sejnowski clamped down on the butt of his stogie, his eyes scanning a folder. The chair creaked as he leaned back, "So, did your snitches ever come up with anything on where all that pot came from?"

"Naw, just petty stuff, hippies dealin' on the street and high-school kids sellin' to their friends. We haven't moved up the ladder one rung," said McElroy. "We've seen two more waves come through. The first was different, street claimed it was Columbian. Then green hash from the Middle East showed up everywhere."

"These assholes have more than one source. This is bigger than some schmo haulin' in a load from Jamaica. This shit's coming from all over the world!"

"Fuck, do you really think it's all coming from one group?" asked the Irishman.

"Why not? We've seen little flurries of this or that blow through town but never anything like this. Three different importers spreading it all over the city, like honey on sliced bread, in rapid succession? I don't think so."

"We need someone to keep an eye on who's bein' busted for what in Records. We'll see if anyone got popped for these three brands and figure out whether there's a pattern."

"That's a start," said Sejnowski. "Damned hippies think they're so smart and the cops are all ignorant brutal bigots."

"Well," laughed McElroy, "Most of 'em are."

"Speak for yourself, asshole!"

"At least, I'm Anglo-Saxon," said the Irishman, ducking a

stapler tossed overhand across the desk. "I'll just make that call and see if we can get some help on this."

"Damned right!"

~

Augie placed a platter of bruschetta and an icebucket full of Coors on the table on the patio as Ruck and Bernie settled in.

Bernie said, "Fuck! Coors? Where did you get that?"

Augie grinned, "You're never gonna believe it."

"Who?"

"Jesus!"

"That kid from the warehouse?" asked Ruck.

"Yeah. He came by last week and said that some guy hijacked a semi full of cold Coors and he could get it for me for twenty bucks a case, so I bought five."

"Far out!" said Bernie, popping a can.

"Actually, compared to European beers, this stuff is like Rocky Mountain piss-water but that doesn't mean I won't drink one or three." Ruck turned to the windows, "This sure is a beautiful view."

"I just needed out of the city and got lucky finding this place, a little space from humanity."

"So, what's cookin'?" asked Ruck.

"You guys heard about Tony getting popped for smack? He plays stupid and the old man grounds him for the rest of his life but blames it on me. They dropped the charges and he only got kicked out of school for four months, four months! He's charged with heroin distribution and a kid almost dies, something doesn't make sense in here somewhere."

"We should be so lucky, if they ever caught us," said Bernie.

"The ol' man's hired a full-time tutor to make sure he graduates on time."

"Fastest way to get him out of the house," laughed Ruck.

"Right on!" smirked Augie. "I've been thinking that we've been lucky, so far, but it's a little too close to home. Maybe, it's time to take a break."

"What do you mean, we're just getting fired up," said Bernie.

"I mean, we've got enough in the pipeline to keep the troops supplied for a couple of months, which will get us closer to harvest with fresher quality and better prices. If anybody's looking at us, it's time to be doing nothing but goofin' off."

"We've got full loads on the way on Whisper and Guinevere and we offloaded the trawler a couple of weeks ago, so we should be stocked up for a while." smirked Bernie.

"Exactly. So, how are the accounts doing?"

"If we put imports on hold," said Ruck, "the working fund will have eight million, which leaves profits on the last series of deliveries of six and a half million!"

"I'd suggest we all do our damnedest at maintaining a low profile. Don't go flashin' money around or someone's gonna notice."

"Like you're stayin' under the radar," said Bernie. "Partying with hot actresses at the Twenty-One or hot cars or this place. Hell, there was even a shot of you in a tux with two blonds that made the society page in the Times for some charity ball."

"Guilty as charged but, if we get caught, the biggest penalty's gonna be tax evasion," said Augie, "so each of us has to find a way to launder the money, so it's legit, and then pay Uncle his share like model citizens."

"What are you going to do?" asked Ruck.

"I've started a corporation called, 'ACLG Management'."

Bernie started laughing, "I know you've got that MBA but what are you going to manage?"

"Actually, I'm looking at a grocery store in Paramus."

"No shit?"

"Yeah, seems logical, everybody spends cash in a grocery.

There are lots of businesses that turn cash. Look around."

"You know, he's right, " said Ruck. "Dry cleaners, hardware stores, lumber yards, gas stations…it's endless."

"I'd suggest you guys use this time to check some things out for your own benefit and future security. This isn't going to last forever," said Augie. "Meantime, let's finish what we've got cookin' and start up again in September."

"I'm cool with that," said Bernie. "This is turnin' into a real job."

"Nothin's for free, brother, nothin'," said Ruck.

"You headin' out for Jamaica tomorrow?" asked Augie.

"Yeah, we'll get Nell squared away and negotiate a series of shipments for the fall."

"Okay, Ruck can coordinate what's coming in and out for the next couple of days," said Augie. "If that's alright with you?"

"Sure, no problem, but what are you doing?"

"You heard that Mary got accepted to Yale Law School last week?"

"No shit! Congratulations, she's brilliant!" said Ruck.

"Wish the rest of us were that smart," added Bernie.

"Well, I found a little guest house right on the water south of Milford, which is only about twenty minutes from the campus, and I'm takin' her up there to see it tomorrow. It's a surprise."

Ruck laughed, "I'd call that incentive."

Chapter 6

Taylor walked out of LaGuardia Airport, shielding her eyes against the setting sun glittering off the Manhattan skyline, to spy Augie leaning against a gleaming black Fifty-Seven Chevy. "I thought Bernie was picking me up?"

"He had to run down to Jamaica for a few days, so I'm your next best choice." He smiled and opened the door for her.

"I can't refuse a gentleman," smirked Taylor, tossing her thick blond ponytail over her shoulder.

Augie climbed in and asked, "Are you hungry?"

"Yes, I'm famished. Haven't had anything but airplane food since this morning."

"Great. You like Italian?"

"Sure."

"I'll take you to a real Italian restaurant. My uncle Manny's place makes bread and pasta by hand every day and the sauce, according to the recipes from the old country, with fresh ingredients. You'll like it."

"Let's go," said Taylor, leaning into the back seat to retrieve a very feminine purple briefcase. "I thought Bernie'd look stylish carrying this around but giving it to you is even more fun."

"It's all there?"

"Every penny. Well, there aren't actually any pennies. Oh shit, you know what I mean," laughed the beauty.

"I have no doubt," smiled Augie. "When do you fly out?"

"First thing in the morning. I've still got classes in my other reality."

"So you're doing all this and going to school?"

"Yeah, I'm only taking fifteen hours but I'll probably take

eighteen in the fall."

"What major?"

"Marketing and Communications. My ol' man owns a couple of radio stations, so I've kind of grown up in that...realm."

"What kind of stations?"

"Oh, I call one the country bumpkin snoozer, because the programming is targeted to folks who live on farms and work in factories and like hillbilly music and local sports and prayer meetings and all that. The other one's the complete yin, for the first station's yang, and just started up, playing underground music and sponsoring hippie concerts."

"The second one sounds more fun than the first but I'd be willing to bet the country station is the breadwinner."

"You're right about that. How'd you know?"

"Simple business, it's a huge stable market, loyal to the local community. Oh, and I have an MBA."

"I'm impressed. I figured you guys just stumbled into this whole thing."

Augie laughed, "Well, we actually paddled into it but that's a long story. In a way, you're right but we've taken a professional approach, working up business plans and projections, goals and deadlines, supply chains and distribution networks, just like any other business. The one thing we don't seem to have to invest in is marketing or I'd hire you."

Taylor blushed, "I'm only a freshman and I know I don't know shit...but I will."

"You're really somethin', you know?"

"I could take that either way."

"No, you're gorgeous, intelligent, smart, driven to experience life, and you don't seem afraid of much."

"I'm not. I have a black belt in judo." Her blue eyes crinkled when she smiled and she laughed from her gut. "My older brother made me take classes when I was a kid, so he wouldn't have to protect me all the time."

"Smart brother. Dangerous sister." He pulled into a large parking lot and parked next to a white stucco building with exposed beams surrounded by junipers shimmering with sparkling white lights. He walked around to lock the briefcase in the trunk and opened her door, "C'mon, you'll enjoy this."

Uncle Romano, a rotund, balding man with a smile to match his girth, appeared out of an enormous dining room with white plastered walls, beamed ceilings, dim chandeliers, and candles flickering on white table clothes with black napkins folded to resemble swans. "Ah, Augie, how nice to see you! I'm so glad you brought your beautiful friend for real food, instead of that crap they're trying to peddle in those fancy-shmancy restaurants uptown!"

Augie hugged him and turned to Taylor, "Taylor, this is my Uncle Manny Romano. As you can see, there is no lack of pride in his house."

"I'm very pleased to meet you," said Taylor with a radiant smile.

He took her hand and kissed it, "It is my pleasure, Madame, but I truly do not understand what you see in this guy."

"We're just friends," laughed the blond.

"He's never been just friends with any female I know of, other than aunts and grandmothers and even they are suspect."

"I'll watch out for him."

"And I'll enjoy watching out for you, young lady. Please follow me." He grabbed two menus and toddled through the tables to a private booth in the far corner that offered a view into the kitchen garden outside French doors. He offered menus, "You should read through our offerings but, if I know my nephew, I'll just bring a little of this and a little of that."

"That sounds wonderful," said Taylor, handing the menu back.

"Could I offer you something to drink?"

"I'd love a glass of Chardonnay, if you have it?"

"Absolutely. And Augie?"

"I'd like a malt Scotch, with a little ice on the side."

"Are you acquiring those uptown tastes?"

"Naw, this habit came from my ol' man. He drinks whiskey with his buddies, but Scotch when he's alone."

"Ah, family secrets," laughed Romano. "I'll remember that one!"

"And get my ass in more trouble than I'm always in, no thank you."

"I'll be right back with your drinks," said the chef, as he tottered to the bar.

"He's a lovely man," said Taylor.

"Yeah, I like him but I know he's an asshole, because I had a job here, one summer, and he worked my ass off for not much money."

"Bet you learned a few lessons there."

He laughed, "Don't do business with family."

"I guess Bernie and I've broken rule number one."

"He's proud and protective of you but he also believes that you're going to turn all of this into something incredible, if you don't screw it up."

"I won't," replied Taylor, casting her eyes down to a flickering candle on the table.

He stared for a long moment. "You had some trouble on this last batch, didn't you?"

"Why do you ask?"

"Because of the way you responded. It was too abrupt."

She smiled, "Guess I'm not very good at hiding secrets from people I like."

"So?"

"So...one of our guys in South Florida got jumped by a

couple of thugs and cut up pretty bad. He ended up in the hospital and they got away with his stash and his money."

"Is he okay?"

"He's a drummer and they sliced up his palms, so it'll be a while before he can play with his band."

"That sucks," said Augie, "but I get the feeling there's more to the story."

Romano appeared with a tray and served warm bread, a bowl with balsamic vinegar dribbled into thick olive oil, a chilled glass of wine and a tumbler of amber malt Scotch with ice in a glass. "Enjoy!"

"Thank you," said Taylor lifting her glass to toast. "We don't have any confirmation but word has it that those guys won't be hijacking anyone's load again."

"That's not good business. Once the violence starts, it escalates, and there's no stopping it until it's finished."

"You sound like you know what you're talking about."

He hooked a thumb towards the door, "We're in New York and, here, Italian family allegiances can save your life or mark your doom."

Taylor stared for a moment, "Is all of this part of that?"

Augie laughed, "No, they're completely separate on purpose. We've tried to put this together with people we know and trust and people they know and trust. We make deals on a handshake and everybody does their bit to make it happen the right way. Maybe I just wanted to prove that it could be done without gangs or guns or violence. Bad shit's gonna happen, you know it and I know it, but life is worth more than money. We can always do another deal to make up our losses. We can't stitch a life back together, once it's gone."

"I'm glad we agree but there's always the question of what to do if someone just out-and-out screws you?"

"Know your partners and you won't have that problem.

Trust a friend of a friend and you're already in trouble."

"I see your point," said Taylor, long fingers gracefully dipping warm soft bread into the oil.

"I should warn you that you'll be getting three more shipments and then we're gonna shut it down for a couple of months to let things cool off."

"That ought to keep the troops happy through the summer. Things'll slow down on campus but we've still got Chicago, Milwaukee, and South Florida, so we'll spread it around."

"That works for me," said Augie raising his glass. "From our evening in Princeton, I'm guessin' you've got a thing going with Randy. Is it serious?"

"There's a round about come-on, if I ever heard one," laughed Taylor.

"I'm serious."

"Oh, I'm a girl, so I can tell that you're thinkin' with your dick. Put it back in your pants, I'm taken."

"Fair enough," smiled Augie, "but, if you ever get bored, just let me know."

"We'll see," said Taylor, "but don't hold your breath."

"For you, honey, I'd learn patience."

"Small chance! I know trouble when I see it."

At precisely eight o'clock, a black 1964 Lincoln backed into the gravel drive and rolled to a stop at the back door of the little house on Lake Mendota. Freddie waddled out the back door, as a tall muscular guy with a neatly trimmed moustache and dark greasy slicked back hair climbed out. "Hey, man, they call me Fat Freddie."

The guy laughed, "I can see why, you're a big boy. I'm Victor. You sure got some weird stuff going on in this town. Been listening to the news reports about the anti-war riots all night on the radio."

"Yeah, it got pretty crazy on State Street last night, lots of teargas and people getting beat-up. We couldn't get out of there until after two this morning and, even then, we got gassed on the way home. It was a fucking police riot."

Victor walked around the car to open the rear doors, "Guess we can help with the attitude around here."

"Cool, there's a big festival starting today. Peachtree's playin'."

He pulled the seat forward and flipped up the back to reveal a dozen boxes buried in a custom well. Freddie whistled, "That's about as clean as I've ever seen. D'you do the work?"

"Naw, we've got a guy who works wonders with metal. He's done three other cars for us and I think there's a couple more on the way. There's more side panels around the trunk and hydraulic shocks to even things out. Where do you want this stuff?"

"Oh, downstairs...through the kitchen."

Vic stacked up three boxes and headed for the back door.

Freddie asked, "D'you ever play ball?"

"Yeah, why?"

"I used to be an all-star center, State champs."

"I was a left guard and linebacker. Playin' defense was more fun, beating the crap outta little runners."

Taylor opened the door to the staircase and followed Randy out to pick up a couple of boxes. "We're supposed to be getting half hash and half weed."

He peeled back the tape and stuck his nose in the corner of a carton, "Hmmm, this one's hash for sure."

Ten minutes later, they were sitting in the parlor sipping coffee and downing hot bagels and crème cheese.

Freddie asked, "How long you been on the road?"

"Oh, I stopped to drop a load the first night but went straight through last night, so I'd get here on time."

"You want to rest up?" asked Taylor. "We've got an extra bed upstairs."

"Naw, thank you. I'd best be heading out. Supposed to trade out cars in Cleveland tonight, then head for Florida tomorrow."

Randy asked, "You going to see Jacob in Lauderdale?"

"Yeah, why?"

"Good guy, straight shooter, no bullshit, you'll like him."

"I'd just as soon slide right by the bullshit and get on with what I need to be doin'," said Vic, standing. "I appreciate your hospitality but I'd best hit the road."

Taylor reached up to hug him, "You be safe and watch out for the cops. Tell the guys, I'll be in touch next week."

The Lincoln eased onto the street and disappeared. Randy said, "That was smooth."

"So far, we've never had a problem getting the product into town," said Freddie.

"Yeah, but I think, for the moment, we should just sit on this. Trying to move it around, with all the pigs on the street, is asking for trouble," said Taylor.

"But we've got people waiting," said Freddie.

"They're just going to have to wait until things chill out. It's too big a risk."

"Okay, fine. Have it your way," said Freddie.

"She's right you know? Think long term, what's the goal?" asked Randy.

"Okay, I get it, but we've gotta get some of this into the festival and that starts this afternoon."

"No, actually, we're not," said Taylor, quietly. "This is too big to screw up. When things quiet down a little, we'll get to work."

"But…" stammered Freddie.

"No 'buts', we're gonna do this right. That's why it works, because we don't get greedy and we act like professionals."

"Fine."

"And, now that the delivery's been made and safely stashed away, you get to go away and don't come back until I call you."

"But..."

"That was the deal. I'm the cute sorority chick, who lives in the cottage that now has flower boxes under the windows, and you guys get to stay the fuck away, so we don't draw attention to the stash. Now, go on and we'll see you at the festival!"

Randy couldn't stifle the grin, "Sorry, man, but you know she's right."

"Yeah, I do. I just see instant profits going up in smoke!" said Freddie, pulling on his jacket.

Taylor walked over and kissed him on the cheek, "And we're going to keep making lovely profits for the next three years and we're not going to get stupid, even for one tiny moment. You guys have the big party house, where you can get into all the trouble you want. Now, go."

Chapter 7

Augie settled into a comfortable deck chair on the terrace at the Lodge in Pebble Beach. He marveled at the view, across the eighteenth green and over the sixth to the beaches along Carmel, softened by a gentle fog rolling off the surf and drifting up into the forest.

"*I could get used to this,*" he mused, as a wave of jet black hair blocked his view and Sidney Chui leaned over to kiss his cheek.

"It's been a few years but I wasn't surprised to hear from you," said the tall Thai tigress with green eyes and a dancer's grace, taking a seat. "Once study-buddies, always study-buddies?"

"Something like that," laughed Augie, looking around. "I'm guessin', if you can afford to hang out here, you must be doing alright."

A waiter approached, "What may I get you?"

"Just some hot coffee with cream on the side, if you please."

"And you, sir?"

"I'll have the same, thank you."

The waiter marched away and she smirked, "I wish I could say that I own a membership here but it's my dad's and we use it for business and family."

"My ol' man had a guest membership, one summer, and we stayed in a house up on the ridge, where he could see the golf course and the ocean."

"Then you know how special the forest really is, it's magical."

He gazed around at the beauty, "This is the place where capturing a little piece of paradise requires a huge investment."

"I'm almost sorry I dragged you through the finals for your

damned MBA. Your brain cells are stuck in analytic mode."

"So, what are you doing?"

"Well, we have an import-export business that goes back more than a dozen generations."

"What do you bring in and from where?"

"Why do you ask?"

"Well, I'm curious about importing products from Thailand, in particular."

Sidney smirked, "Gateway to the Golden Triangle?"

"That obvious?" smiled Augie.

"Well, at least you found a business perfectly suited to your weird sense of gamesmanship and adventure."

"You don't know the half of it!" laughed Augie. "Your knowledge could save me from a whole heap of hassles."

"And our connections might smooth your path." The smile in her green eyes vanished, "My family name literally means 'hammer' or a weapon with a heavy round metal ball on the end of a handle. They were used in pairs to rout an opponent with brutal efficiency. Our company logo is a pair of crossed hammers and with good reason. In the East, your manner, your aura of authority is only slightly more important than your connections."

"So, what are the pitfalls of dealing in Thailand?"

"Bribing the best sources directly rather than getting tangled up with the Tongs."

"Tongs?"

"Yeah, they're sort of merchant associations, some with direct gang affiliations, sort of like our Mafia, controlling different industries."

"I know about that."

"With your last name, I bet you do. Tell me what you need and I'll tell you if I can help, okay?"

"An intro to the used freighter market and a reliable shipyard."

"That I can do. What else?"

"That's it for now."

"Don't you need a connection for your…product?"

"No, I've got that covered."

"Who?"

Augie started laughing, "If I tell you, I'll have to kill you."

"Aw, C'mon!"

"Okay, do you remember that skinny English kid with the thick glasses, dark bushy hair hanging in his pimply face, kind of quite and shy, but a mischievous brainiac, when you got to know him?"

"Yeah, Stoney Montgomery. He had a sexy British accent but he was from Hong Kong instead of jolly ol'."

"One in the same."

"So how's he hooked into all of this?"

"I'm guessin' he decided to go out and earn his own fortune, to one-up his father's success. Whatever, he's got a thing going from Thailand to the Continent and he's looking to expand to the Americas."

"So what are you after? I'm guessing pot. Somehow, dealing heroin doesn't seem your style and you wouldn't need a freighter."

He smiled, "You are so in tune with my psyche. How come you never let me get past first base?"

"Because I watched you march through the entire register of females in the school."

"Not everyone, I did have some standards."

"Yeah, like that icky Sarah Flannigan with the droopy tits?"

Augie smirked, "She shaved her pussy."

"Really? No shit! Well, whatever, I wasn't going to become another notch on your pecker. I liked you too much to waste that much energy getting emotionally involved with a juvenile, who'd get bored and wander off to find a new conquest. No thank you, Mister."

"That bad, huh?"

"Pretty much. Hell, if we'd gotten involved, you wouldn't be sitting here today."

"Naw, I really liked you."

"Bullshit. You stuck around because I was smarter than you and willing to kick your ass across the finish line."

"I am forever in your debt."

"More than you know, buster." She paused, "Tell you what, I've got to go to Hong Kong and Bangkok next week. Why don't you come with me and I'll introduce you to some people who can help."

"You'd really do that?"

"Yeah, but I want a cut of the first shipment."

"How much?"

"Five percent."

"A one-time fee?"

"Yes, unless you find that I'm so useful, you want to make it a permanent arrangement."

"We'll see how this plays out."

"Fine, I'll arrange your passage, you take care of making capital available when it's needed."

"Done. Now do you want to fuck?"

The green eyes flashed as she burst out laughing, "You never quit, do you? Go home and pack your bag...and don't waste time fantasizing about what isn't going to happen."

Stewardesses handed out surgical masks, as the passengers departed the plane, after a polite but firm warning, "Ladies and gentlemen, Hong Kong is recovering from a major influenza epidemic. So, for your own protection and as a courtesy to those you encounter, you are requested to wear a mask at all times, while you are in public. Thank you for your cooperation."

"Shit, you brought me all this way to make sure I suffer before I die a gruesome death?" groaned Augie, untangling his gangly frame from the seat. "Fifteen-hour flights kill my back. The first thing we need to do is find me a masseuse."

"You probably strained it screwing all those girls in school. There's a great massage waiting for you at the hotel." She looked up at him, "This is a different world and you'll stand out like a gleaming white beacon in a land of wary midgets. Keep your eyes open and your mouth shut."

"Yes, Ma'am!"

Sidney's high-heels clicked a confident cadence, as she marched up to Customs and presented her passport to the clerk. He looked at her photograph and then the name, smiled respectfully, stamped the page and handed it back to her with a slight bow. She pointed to Augie and said something in Chinese. The agent took his book and stamped it without looking, handing it back to him with a polite smile and a respectful nod.

They walked out into morning sunshine and a waiting Jaguar, "What'd you do to that guy, slip him a twenty?"

"As I told you, we've been trading in and out of Hong Kong for hundreds of years. We're a local family held in high esteem and worthy of his courtesy."

"I've got a lot to learn."

The car peeled away from the curb and Sidney jabbered a few rapid-fire commands. The driver nodded and headed into the bustling city at top speed. Dozens of construction cranes rose above concrete and glass towers sprouting out of a cramped metropolis bristling with humanity. The driver eased through an interweaving stream of rickshaws, scooters, and bicycles coursing through the streets with automobiles and buses flowing along like so much driftwood in a gushing stream.

Augie gazed in wonder at the passing scenes, "This is surreal.

It feels like the future is sprouting right out of the past."

Sidney sighed, "And they call it progress. I would prefer they invest more effort to ensure the preservation of the symbols of our culture and the monuments to our history."

"Just like New York, tear down a treasure to build a parking lot."

"Profits have more immediate value than history."

"Unfortunately."

The Jag turned south across the bridge to follow Gloucester Road to Victoria Park, then zig-zagged through a neighborhood, screeching to a stop in front of a white building with a blue tiled roof that swept down into broad eves with a column of sculpted figures riding the arch. Augie pointed as the driver opened the door and offered Sidney a hand.

"Oh, those are roof charms to ward off evil spirits. At the top is the wind and storm summoning fish, then the bull who casts away evil, the brave goat-bull, a mythical lion, heavenly horse, auspicious seahorse, and at the very tip, the chiwen, who is the son of a dragon and ready to defend the realm with fire and water. Our culture believes in spirits, in luck, and omens. If the signs are not aligned, a business deal or a romance can fall apart in moments."

"So keep your mouth shut, right?"

"You're learning, now come along."

The driver carried the bags up the steps through a heavy paneled door into a light, airy atrium. Before he could place the cases on the floor, a tiny woman with an enormous smile shrieked, "Sidney, Sidney!"

Two small children raced into the courtyard and wrapped their arms around her legs. "How long can we keep you?" asked the girl.

"I've only just arrived, sweetheart, but I'll make time for you."

The little woman turned and bowed to Augie, then leaned

over to Sidney, whispering.

"No, no," laughed Sidney. "He's just a friend and he'll need a room of his own, thank you."

She bowed again to Augie, "The children call me Beabea and you may too."

"Thank you," said Augie, as she chided the children, who grabbed the suitcases and dragged them away.

The tiny woman beamed, "So, how do you know my niece?"

Augie smiled, "She was my tutor in graduate school. I wouldn't have graduated without her help."

"You young people have such big dreams but, sometimes, humble ambitions are the foundation for attaining worthy aspirations."

"In this day and age, we might hope that any dream is possible."

"Confucius could not have said it better," smiled Sidney. "Whenever my parents aren't staying at the house here, I stay with my aunt and three generations of cousins.

She pointed to Augie and said something in Chinese. Beabea walked behind his back to prod with a boney finger until his knees buckled. She, "Tisk-tisked" a couple of times, then stood on tiptoe and sniffed, scrunching her nose in mock revulsion, "Your Qui is feeble and your body's out of balance. You're crooked, I fix."

She led them to small adjoining rooms and offered Augie a white robe. "Take off your clothes."

He peeled off his suit and pushed his hands through the narrow arms of the gown, which was far too short for his long legs, then followed her down a narrow flight of stairs to a room in the cellar, paneled in cedar, with a flat wooden rack suspended over steaming coals. She handed him a towel and pointed to a round tiled tub in the floor. Wrapping the towel around his hips, he draped his robe from a hook on a post, and knelt in the center. Without warning, she dumped a bucket of cold water over his head and handed him a bar of gray soap, "Wash."

When he was lathered up, she dumped another bucket over his head. He stood and dried himself off. She pointed and he climbed onto the platform to lie face down, shivering, until the hot vapors, reeking with eucalyptus, cleared his sinuses and tore open every pore on his body, to release a flood of toxins.

BeaBea held up a kettle filled with scalding stones and placed them, one by one, down his spine. He stifled a scream but within moments the muscles began to relax and the pain eased. "That's magic."

"No, that's just to get you relaxed enough to adjust your spine."

"You're going to what?"

She smiled and walked away, only to return a few minutes later to remove each stone, one by one, and wash his back with a cold wet towel that made his muscles flex in spasms.

"Now we can begin," said the tiny tyrant, climbing the stand to sit on his butt. She pressed boney fingers into the muscles in the curve of his spine and slowly slogged up his back, like the blade of a sturdy plow, until she hit the raw spot between his shoulder blades. He bucked but she kept pushing until her knuckles lifted his skull away from his vertebrae. Then, she started at the bottom and dug her way through the tension again and again, until he stopped resisting.

"Now you are ready."

Dripping sweat hissed on the coals below the rack. "Ready for what?"

"To feel relief," she said quietly, kneeling on his back with her shins pressing on either side of his spine, her knees tucked between his shoulder blades. Without warning, she pumped her legs and his spine cracked with the bark of broken timber.

"What the fuck did you do to me?" shouted Augie, before he realized that his pain was completely gone.

The little woman climbed down, adjusted her skirt, and stepped into his line of view. "When you are ready, there is a warm pool just outside this door. Wash the poisons from your skin and give your muscles time to absorb the heat, so they might learn to hold your bones in place again."

"I don't know what you did but thank you very much. I feel much better."

"You should take better care of your body young man, it will have to support your spirit for many years to come."

"I appreciate your advice." He placed his hands together reverently.

She turned and climbed the stairs.

~

A sleek glass elevator rose up through a fifty-story atrium, sunlight pouring shimmering slashes of luminous mercury into a geometric forest of ficus trees in the courtyard. Golden doors opened to a single desk sitting before a wall of windows overlooking Victoria Harbor bustling with countless junks, sporting triangular sails and riding favorable winds to their anchorage, while dodging heavy traffic of great freighters and container ships.

A tall, raven-haired woman with sea-green eyes in an emerald silk dress, that clung to her pale skin like wet tissue, stood and said, in a refined British accent, "You must be Mr. LaGuerre."

"I am."

"Mr. Montgomery has been unexpectedly delayed for a few minutes and instructed me to make you comfortable until he can return. Would you care for a drink?"

"Malt Scotch?"

"Neat or on the rocks?" She inquired, pressing a button on her desk to open a panel in a blank wall revealing a well-stocked bar.

"Neat would be fine," said Augie, setting his briefcase on the burnished teak floor. "And who are you?"

"I'm Sarah Fine, Mr. Montgomery's secretary," she said, pouring two fingers of amber Scotch into a tumbler from a tall square crystal decanter. She handed him the glass with a cocktail napkin, embossed with the company logo – a crystal dragon, and gestured to a pair of Eames chairs, "Make yourself comfortable."

The lanky brunette's hips swayed hypnotically, as she strode to her desk and pressed another button. The latch in the elevator doors clicked and she walked over to stand over him with the bright red talon of her index finger touching the corner of full lips, "Could I interest you in a nice blow job while we wait?"

Twenty minutes later, a once shy, frumpish Stoney appeared wearing a Mod silver suit with a slender black tie, coiffed hair, and no tortoiseshell glasses. He walked over to shake Augie's hand, "I'm so sorry to keep you waiting and I do hope that Sarah took good care of you, as I instructed."

"She is a gracious hostess," smirked Augie.

"Please, come into my office," said Stoney, walking to a pair of tall brushed aluminum doors that parted, opening into a starkly modern office with a massive slab of polished redwood, rough around the edges, supported by chrome sawhorses as his desk in front of the same panoramic view into the harbor, tall palms at the corners, and a massive Andy Warhol painting behind two facing pairs of Barcelona chairs and a simple glass table centered on an oval carpet that spiraled out from a sunrise center into a rainbow.

"This is pretty swanky," said Augie. "You must be doing well."

"That's what we went to school for, right? To learn how to make gobs of money and that's exactly what I'm doing."

"Looks like research pointed us in the same direction and I like your logo."

"Got to have a little bit of humor hiding under the corporate façade, now don't we?" laughed Stoney. "How much you coin' in the States, mate?"

"We've been up for a over year and we've got a network that runs from Florida to Chicago, New York to L.A. Good people, good product, good profits for everyone."

"It's different here, tricky. Everybody's into everybody's business, making sure they all get a piece of the action...but, as I've proven, it can be done. I act as a partner, with my associates, to make sure that the product is top quality, properly packaged for shipment, and that it clears customs for delivery onto the ship of your choice."

"We'll be buying one in Thailand."

"Buying a ship can be a complicated business."

"Not if you have the right acquaintances," smiled Augie.

"Like who?"

"Like Sidney Chui."

"Not that gorgeous slanteye from school?" He pointed to the harbor, "Shit, her old man's family controls half of everything cruising through that pond out there. What's she fucking around with you for?"

"I think she wants to jump my ass."

"I think you're daft, Romeo. She's way too classy for you."

"Well, at least she's got the connections to set up the contracts on the ship, so, for that, I'm thankful and not asking the 'why' question until it seems appropriate."

"You're still an asshole but I always liked your bravado, your cool."

"Looks like you've made some changes, yourself."

Stoney brushed a tiny piece of lint from the sleeve of his jacket, "We're chameleons who transform into different persona, to suit the tasks in each new phase of life. Our time together was student life, scruffy and loose, but this is business. When I'm finished with this, I'll become someone else."

"I like the transition."

"We were primed to enjoy the finer things in life."

Augie laughed, "Yeah, so much pussy, so little time."

"Fuck, I figured having Sarah take care of your libido would provide us at least an hour to bang out a deal!"

"I came here specifically to see you, bub. She was your idea, not that I'm complainin'."

"Fine, then, what are you after and in what quantities?"

"High grade bud or hash, probably five tons for this first run."

"I usually don't deal in less than ten but, for an old friend, I'm willing to let you have either for two hundred a key. The harvest is just finished for the golden happy weed."

"I can get primo Columbian for half that and it's a shorter transport."

"In small quantities," laughed Smokey. "Fine, one fifty but not a penny less."

"I'll pay half up front, the balance in ninety days."

"I'd prefer sixty days, payable in greenbacks, but, coincidentally, I'll be in New York over the holidays. I'll be staying at the Waldorf."

"Done."

"So, have you got time to hang out or is your leash too short?"

"We're leaving for Bangkok in the morning and I think I'm expected for the family dinner tonight."

Stoney smiled, "Right then, we'll catch up in Bangkok. I've got something I want to share with you. I'll be at the Ocean Marina down the coast in Pattaya the first of next week. Look me up, when you've got your schedule worked out."

Tea was served in delicate porcelain cups, decorated with

tiny lotus flowers, on a terrace shaded by palms and surrounded by a wash of purple bougainvillea at the Four Seasons, just across from the Royal Bangkok Sports Club. Sidney smiled, "While Hong Kong is racing into the modern world, as the economic and political touchstone between East and West, Bangkok grew from a tiny trading village that sprouted up, where the Chao Phraya River splays into a web of canals and rivulets, before dumping into the Gulf of Thailand. It's called the Venice of the East, with good reason, because almost any point in the city can be accessed by water. The population is more than than five million and reflects every facet of Asian culture, from the most delicate temples to glass high-rises, but there are definite traces from the colonial powers, the French to the east and the British to the west. My family grew out from this city but I did get to spend a few years here as a young girl and, someday, I'd like to come back to stay for a bit longer." She paused, "With Ying there must be Yang, so, this is also a place where, if you have the money, you can buy pretty much anything you can imagine."

"New York's like that," said Augie, trying to sip black tea from the tiny cup without slurping it all over his shirt.

"No, there are things you can buy here that are not available anywhere else," smiled Sidney.

"Like what?"

"You're the horny toad. You can have sex with a chicken or a goat or young boys or girls or the world's most beautiful women or anything else you could ever want to poke that weenie in."

"I've heard stories…"

"They're probably all true but what they don't tell you is that some people go into the red light districts and never come out. There's everything from rotgut whiskey to the finest Scotch and champagne, pot and hallucinogens, cocaine and cheap heroin, sex in every form, and violence to back up every scam ever run on the naïve. Some people can't resist realizing their own fantasies at any price, including their own sanity."

"The same goes for business. We're meeting Bing Watt down near Pattaya tomorrow to check out several ships that might be of interest. He knows his boats, or my father wouldn't have employed his services over so many years, but watch your ass and your mouth. Pride is worth far more than greenbacks to my people and he's kind of cantankerous to begin with."

"Respect."

"Yes, respect and face and station are central to the Eastern psyche," she smiled. "In many ways, there is a certain...assurance in knowing how to act in relation to those around you."

"On the other hand, you're allowing society, or whoever, to judge and direct you on so many different levels. It's a convenience for organizing a class system but I'm bettin' it doesn't foster creative thinking."

"I disagree, wouldn't you feel freer to create, if social awkwardness was eliminated and communication could flow efficiently?"

Augie smirked, "It'd probably help to be on the upper tier of that heap to reap the benefits."

"You came from a privileged family and I'm absolutely sure you benefited, considering you weren't even close to MBA material when you applied to school but you got in anyway. The point is that those tenets are at the very root of this society and, to understand the mindset, you must comprehend our belief system."

"Every place I go, I find that I'm ill-prepared to absorb all that I want to learn about the places and the people and the customs that make this city so different from the Venice in Italy." He smiled, "I've traveled a lot but I think my awakening started during the wildest cab ride through Charlotte Amelia with a stoned-out cabbie hanging over the back of the seat, lecturing me on the sacred sacrament and how Jah looks after the faithful, weaving blindly through traffic at sixty miles an hour. Maybe, when I'm finished with this, I'll study anthropology."

Sidney laughed, "Knowing you, you'd find a way to make it dangerous."

He sipped a second cup of tea, "If we find the right boat, my friend will fly in from Hawaii to do a thorough inspection. I hope that won't show disrespect, rather good business."

"I'm sure that would be acceptable."

"So, think we might find some time to relax on a beach someplace, when all of this comes together?"

She cocked her head, "Don't get hung up in your fantasies. We're business partners, first, and friends, second. You don't have to make this complicated. You dominate in your world, I'll dominate in mine, if that's alright with you?"

Augie grinned, "Fine, just be that way."

"I will, you can count on it."

~

Bing Watt was a slender waif with black eyes that crinkled when he smiled, a long spindly salt and pepper ponytail, and a tiny spit of beard on his chin. He wore a bright yellow linen shirt over soiled cut-off khakis and worn sandals and bowed formally. "I am pleased to see you again, Miss Chui, and to meet your friend, Mister Augustus Constantine LaGuerre."

Sidney bowed and Augie reached to shake his rough calloused hand, "I'm impressed that you know my full name."

"I must know many things about prospective associates before I agree to meet. In these times, one can never be too careful."

"Unfortunately, I must agree, but having mutual friends offers some assurance to both sides in any venture."

"And so it must be," said the tiny Thai entrepreneur, as he guided them along a wharf surrounding a fleet of rusting ships, in various states of restoration, crammed gunnel to gunnel and spilling out into the bay. "Miss Chui tells me that you are looking for a seaworthy ship, capable of making the Pacific crossing, with deck access and sufficient space and integrity to haul a delicate cargo. I might also assume that you would be interested in employing my firm for custom restorations to suit your requirements."

Before Augie could answer, Sidney said, "Chui Antiques will be shipping a full load of Chinese treasures on the first voyage, so integrity is everything."

Bing Watt smiled, "Most of these ships are far too large, let me show you something unusual." He scurried along the quay and stopped next to a white ship, her bridge aforedeck and a long flat steel deck stretching back to a bulbous stern. She was broad at the beam and high at the bow and, other than patchy rust and chipped paint, appeared in prime condition.

"This was a research vessel for the Canadians before things cranked up in Vietnam. Whatever their project was, it got canceled, and I happened to make them an offer they couldn't refuse, before anyone else knew it was for sale. She's got huge tanks, twin diesels and generators, a ton of navigation gear, and a surprisingly large cargo hold considering she's just over forty-five meters long. The Canadians claimed that she's engineered so that, even if she keels over, she'll right herself."

Augie walked along the dock, surveying the lines, inspecting the hull, and pondering the physical dimensions of five tons of hash and weed. He wandered back, "Let's take a look inside."

Bing Watt rolled a gangplank across the pavement and they climbed aboard. The bridge was equipped with state of the art radar and communications, gauges and dials to monitor all the ship's functions, and a two-hundred-and-ninety degree view with rear-facing portals port and starboard.

Augie walked over to sit in the captain's chair, raised for a clear view from the center of the cabin, and surveyed the instruments, "It would only take a skeleton crew to run everything."

Bing Watt smiled, "Probably three minimum, four or five for a long haul. Follow me and I'll show you the rest."

He bounded down a narrow flight of stairs to a large white cabin dissected by a long table with sinks down the middle, flanked by a dozen research stations that lacked only the equipment.

Augie peaked into two giant freezers on either side of a tight hallway to cramped but comfortable crew quarters at the bow, ahead of a full galley. "They were set up."

Sidney said, "I'd love to see all the gear they took with them. Someday, maybe I'll get to study the seas."

"Wrong profession?"

"Next lifetime!"

Bing Watt opened a hatch and climbed down a ladder into an enormous open hold. He pointed to the ceiling, "There are two loading hatches and I'm convinced that this space has never had any water in it.

He walked across the steel deck, pulled up a panel, and produced a flashlight to illuminate the hull between twin fuel tanks running parallel the length of the hold. "See, no sloshing water. It's dry as ash."

Augie and Sidney peered down inside, "That's fairly amazing. How old is the ship?"

"Commissioned in Nineteen-fifty-nine. The diesels and drivetrain still have another year on warranty!"

"What do you think?" asked Sidney.

"Is it big enough to carry your cargo?"

"Yes, I think it's perfect."

"The obvious question is how much do you want for her?"

The tiny Thai stroked his little beard pensively, eyeing Augie, "Because you are the friend of my friend, I'll let you have her for eight hundred thousand...dollars, American."

Augie walked away without responding and stepped into the engine compartment at the stern. Twin diesels nestled behind twin generators and coupled by a pair of stainless steel shafts that pierced the hull through stout sealed bearings. The room appeared to have been cleared out in a hurry but there was not a spot of grease or evidence of water. After a few minutes, he walked back to Sidney and Bing Watt, "Tell you what, I've got an expert who's flying in tomorrow to check her out. If he's approves, I'll give you five, cash."

"Seven-fifty."

Augie gazed around the cabin. "Six."

"Fine, I'll come down to seven."

"Six-fifty, you have her in tip top shape and I'll pay for the additional improvements we'll need."

The little man smiled, "As Miss Chui can attest, no ship leaves this yard until she's fully worthy."

"I'm trusting lives and cargo to your expertise, my friend," said Augie. "Make sure you keep your part of the bargain."

Sidney smiled, "Another successful negotiation! I think you should christen her the Maple Dragon!"

A Rolls Royce Silver Cloud pulled to the curb and a husky driver in a black tuxedo stepped around to open the door for Augie, with a stiff bow and a tip of the hat. Stoney Montgomery offered a flute of cold Dom Perignon, "Lovely you could make it! Shall we start the evening off with a little bubbly?"

Augie settled back into plush leather, as the car accelerated north along the coast road, and sipped, "Nice ride. When'd you give up driving yourself?"

"Oh, I employ this luxury when I know I'm going to get hammered, a much more civilized outcome to an evening of revelry than ending up in the slammer. Thai jails make the Tower of London look tame."

"I'll take your word on it. So where are we going?"

"Oh, I thought we'd take in an exotic dinner and then I'd like to introduce you to what all this wealth can really buy, the lifestyle it can provide."

"What?"

Stoney laughed, "Pretty much anything you could imagine and then some."

An hour and several glasses of champagne later, the Rolls wheeled onto Thanon Surawong, turned into a side street and stopped before a recessed entry framing two immense slabs of Tigerwood with forged dragon handles and a pair of large modern sconces on either side, casting a warm glow down the steps.

"Ah, finally," laughed Stoney, as the driver opened the door and bowed. "Pick us up at three."

Augie watched the Thai driver move the car thirty paces along the street and park. "Is he going to hang out?"

"Aye, he feels responsible for my security, especially in a neighborhood like this," he said, pointing. Here and there, professional girls, dressed in tiny miniskirts, fishnet stockings, spiky heels, and ready for a night hustling tourists in the discos, smiled invitingly at passing pairs of shy boys or made kissing sounds to European drunks stumbling from one Go-Go club to the next.

"The Thai people are all beautiful," said Augie.

Stoney smiled, "That's why horny people from all over the world come here to fulfill their fantasies."

He opened the door and stepped inside a warm, dim room with intricately woven rattan furniture covered in pastel pillows, weeping palms and splays of delicate orchids, and a diminutive and strikingly beautiful Thai woman with coal black eyes that glimmered in the light of a bank of candles climbing floor to ceiling between two pairs of French doors.

"Mr. Montgomery, what a pleasure to see you again."

"It is my privilege," said Stoney kissing her hand.

"Kylee, I'd like you to meet my friend, Augie LaGuerre. Augie, this is Kylee."

"I am very pleased to meet you," said the tiny woman, with a slight but formal bow.

"I'm sure the pleasure is all mine," said Augie.

"I will be disappointed, if it is not," smiled Kylee, turning to Stoney. "Would you like your usual suite?"

"That would be lovely."

"Please follow me," said the tiny woman, dressed in a tight orange sarong and stiletto heals that accentuated the hypnotic rhythm of her hips, as she strolled through the doors on the left, along a quiet hallway lined with surrealistic erotic paintings, to stand before a doorway on the right. "This way, please."

A round table, graced with white linens and two settings of silver and crystal, occupied the center of an amber room under a glistening chandelier. Banks of flickering candles surrounded plush chaises, upholstered with a glittering golden fabric, sprouting from each corner under ceiling fans and huge palms. Stoney stretched out on one of the divans and pointed to another, "Might as well get comfortable, enduring this much pleasure can be arduous."

Augie sat down and leaned back into a pile of pillows, as the doors opened and a tall shapely woman with blazing green eyes, long black hair and longer legs in extremely high platform heels, strode into the room followed by twin girls pushing a small cart. She was completely naked under a sheer gown and walked over to bow to each of the men. She dropped her robe and Augie gaped as he scanned her perfect shape. She ran her hands across smooth, creamy brown skin, unblemished by a hair anywhere on her body, except shimmering tresses that flashed blue as she bowed and stretched out on the table.

The girls filled champagne glasses for each of the men, then trotted over to carefully arrange sliced fruits, vegetables, and edible flowers with tiny shrimp, mussels, caviar, cabbage rolls, tiny sausages, and sweet jams, until her torso was covered with an intricate floral arrangement.

Stoney took a chair, "The thoroughly delectable edible woman!"

Augie sat down opposite and leaned on his elbows to inspect the living feast, "This is so incredible, you almost hate to destroy the composition."

The woman started laughing and little rings of intertwined shrimp fluttered around her nipples, "I can promise that every inch of me is delicious."

Stoney laughed, "So, start in the middle and work our way out?"

"Sure," said Augie, scraping some fish eggs out of the center of a bloom around her navel and savoring tiny sausage stalks that crawled across her belly to a burst of pink shrimp on her left breast.

"I can promise you the dessert's to die for, there's a pudding of white chocolate between her legs, mate."

"I guess we'll have to eat our way there."

Stoney took another long swig of champagne and one of the girls offered to refill Augie's, "Certainly, something to clear the palette. Every bite explodes with a new combination of flavors and there are so many possibilities."

The Brit plucked a tiny crab from between her breasts, "This is bonding, mate. We're brothers bound by an insatiable appetite for extravagance and pleasure."

"And business."

"That makes it all possible, doesn't it?"

Finally, Augie ran a finger between the beautiful woman's legs and leaned back in his chair to inspect a wondrous glob of white chocolate cream, "I think I've had my fill. I might be Italian but the idea of a vomitorium is a little too far out there."

"That's what it's all about, mate, knowing your limitations. We don't pay attention to what other people think because we know, precisely, where our margins lie. If you're like me, you've always lived on the edge, taking on different personas to realize your most immediate goals, but you always knew exactly how far to push it, before it would turn like a serpent and bite you in the ass "

Augie grinned, "We learned where those boundaries are because we pushed it past the limit and suffered the consequences."

Stoney roared, "Yeah, well, philosophizing is all well and good but you've got to scrape your knee a few times, before you learn to take a corner flat out!"

"Something like that."

The Brit rose and leaned over to kiss the woman passionately, "Would you mind if I finished off that chocolate before you leave?"

The beauty smiled and parted her legs. Stoney leaned over, fluted champagne glass in hand, and took long slow slurps, pausing to savor the luscious chocolate. He licked harder and faster, until the woman arched her back and whimpered.

Stoney wiped his nose and mouth with a napkin, "My compliments to the chef and to you for such a marvelous presentation."

The beautiful lady stood, wiped off most of the food, wrapped herself in the gauzy gown, and bowed. "It has been my pleasure as well as yours." She strode through the double doors and disappeared.

The tiny twin Thai girls in gauzy green robes reappeared, one carrying two crystal glasses and an ice bucket with yet another bottle of Dom Perignon, the other bearing a golden tray with several tiny urns and two long slender pipes, carved into serpents rearing up with fangs extended.

The first woman-child poured two glasses expertly, while the other walked over to Augie and pushed him gently into the cushions, loosening his tie and unbuttoning his shirt. "You should be relaxed. May I remove your shoes?"

"Absolutely."

The girl pulled off his boots and massaged the soles of his feet. The second girl handed him a bubbling glass of pale ocher. He smiled, "Ah, this is heaven."

Stoney started laughing, puffing on the slim gray pipe, "We've only just begun."

The woman-child handed him a pipe, struck a match, and leaned to light the tiny bowl, revealing small perfectly round breasts beneath a mist of emerald silk. Dark eyes smiled knowingly, as he inhaled deeply and coughed violently. "What the fuck is this shit?"

"Opium," said the girl, smiling as she leaned close to light the pipe again and again, until Augie settled into the cushions, his brain soft and pudgy, his limp extremities swathed in cotton candy. "That's intense."

"Yeah, the first one's always the best," laughed Stoney.

The two girls stood on either side of the chaise, dropped their sheer veils to the floor, and climbed into his arms.

"Do you ladies have names?"

"I am Li," said the one on the left, "and this is my twin sister, Lia."

"That could get confusing."

"Only to you," said Lia, opening his shirt to rub his chest.

The girls kissed around his eyes, across his temples into his ears, then down his cheeks to French kiss in perfect rhythm. They crawled higher, offering four pert nipples to suckle, while they unbuckled his belt, loosened his pants, and Li giggled, "Americans have big ones."

The twins kissed their way down his chest, nibbling on his nipples, probing his belly button, and flicking their tongues to arouse fleeting tremors quivering through his extremities. He groaned during a momentary hesitation in the synchronization, as slippery fingers probed and eager lips fluttered like tiny fishtails trembling in expectation. A flight of delicate digits slithered and writhing tongues tangled, until their passionate persistence pitched his pretentious pride over a crushing cascade, his carnal cravings crashing through the fog in his brain to ignite waves of primal bliss.

"I think I could get accustomed this," moaned Augie, through drooping eyes, as Lia cleaned him with a warm cloth and Li buttoned up his clothes. "Thank you ladies."

They gathered their gauzy gowns and bowed, "You're welcome."

Augie sank into the pillows, toking on the tiny pipe and admiring their beautiful asses as they trotted out. His arms and legs went limp, his mouth was dry, and he felt as if he was observing everything around him through a murky haze, without emotion or attachment.

A barefoot boy, certainly as beautiful as the girls, walked in, dressed in loose black linen pants and an open silk shirt. He bowed formally to Stoney, then Augie, emptied the remains of the champagne in Stoney's flute into the bucket and refilled both glasses, handing one to Augie, "Might there be anything else, Sir?"

Augie struggled to focus, "Actually, I'm a little too fine, thank you."

"Very well," said the boy, dropping his clothes to the floor next to Stoney's lounge. "Do I please you, Master?"

He gazed up and down at the smooth unblemished skin and the little potbelly above a crouch that had yet to sprout even a shadow. He motioned for the boy to turn around to display the curve of his spine, strong thighs, and a tight round butt. "Oh, you'll do nicely, won't you?"

"I am your pleasure," whispered the boy, leaning to kiss Stoney delicately on the mouth, while unbuttoning his shirt and pants.

"You are a beautiful boy," said Stoney, reaching both hands to caress his ass. "I'm sure you know how to please me."

Augie grunted, unsure whether he was hallucinating or

reliving a nightmare. His brain was completely disengaged, concerned only with maintaining this tranquil haze, while ignoring any stimulus that might interfere with the moment. He nodded in and out of consciousness, dredging up murky, long repressed memories of being taken to the Monsignor's office, in the first grade at St. John's School, where he was left alone in the cold wood-paneled room with the principal.

Father Mulhanney, a slight but intense weasel of a man, with beady eyes peering through little rimless glasses, pursed his thin colorless lips to contain the scent of alter wine on his breath, while intoning the sins of the flesh and how the devil captivates little boys.

He asked whether Augie's little penis ever got hard. Embarrassed, the youngster admitted that sometimes it did.

"That's the devil at work, young man. I'll have to inspect you."

"But…?"

"Embarrassed are we? Well, just so you don't feel that this is so unusual, I will show you mine and then we'll examine yours. Is that fair?"

Before Augie could reply, the priest unbuckled his pants and dropped them to his ankles, then picked the boy up and sat him on the edge of the desk. He lifted his robes to expose a fat drooping organ and large hairy balls that hung low in his sack.

"The devil temps even the most pious."

The priest took Augie's hand and wrapped his little fingers around the soft member, which started to grow. "Rub up and down a little and you'll see the true beast that lives within all men."

Augie stroked a few times until it grew long and thick, throbbing in his small hand.

"More! More!"

He pulled it twice more, before the priest groaned and trembled, as a squirt of fluid erupted across the desk.

The Monsignor pulled up his pants and dropped his robes. "So you see, even I fall victim to his evil and that's why I must protect you. Now open your pants."

Augie unbuttoned his fly and the Monsignor cupped his dick and balls. "It doesn't seem to be hard now. When does it grow?"

"When I sneak out my father's girlie magazines."

"Pornography at your age? That's disgusting!"

Augie tried to cover himself but the priest pulled his hands away. "We'll just have to see whether we can cure this problem."

Without hesitating, he leaned over and took Augie's little dick and balls in his mouth, slurping his tongue around and around, until the boy was aroused. Terrified, Augie reared back, balled up his little fist, and slugged the priest in the temple. His tiny glasses shattered and flew across the room, as the principal staggered back, crashing into the desk chair. "How dare you strike a priest!"

Augie cowered, "I'm sorry…I was scared you were going to bite it off."

The Monsignor fumbled around on the floor for the mangled remains of his glasses, before standing to straighten his robes. He turned and squinted at the boy for a long moment. His hallow cheeks glowed fiery red and there was a trickle of blood dripping down his ear. He cleared his throat and said, calmly, "I'm pleased that you resist the devil's work! When your penis gets hard, slap it until it withers, and do not look at those filthy pictures or spy on your naked sisters either."

Augie tucked his shirt and fastened his pants.

"Now, we won't tell anyone of your sin, it will remain our secret, but you will say one-hundred Our Fathers and one-hundred Hail Marys before the day's end. Am I understood?"

A voice interrupted the nightmare, "Augie! Hey man, are you in there?"

He opened his eyes to find Stoney leaning close to his face, "Are you okay, man?"

His brain struggled to abandon the long-buried memory, "Revelations, man, revelations."

The Brit laughed, "Yeah, that's the splendor of it, you drift off into your own world. Stay with me here, we need to talk a little business. Are you up to that?"

"Sure, man, I'm together…"

"When's the boat going to be ready?"

"Thirty days."

"Great, I'll have your order ready when you are."

Augie struggled to sit, rubbing his bloodshot eyes. "That's heavy shit, man."

"Is this your first time?"

"Yeah. I've snorted a little doojee before but it wasn't this intense."

"That's because this is the real shit, man," laughed Stoney. "The crap you get on the street was stepped on at least a dozen times, before it went up your nose. We need to proceed carefully, the whole point of indulging in opiates is to push your soul as close to the serenity of death as possible, without actually tumbling off the cliff. Even a little too much can be fatal, so you're done for the night. I'll have my driver take you back to your hotel."

"What about you?"

"I'm a heavyweight, mate, I'm just getting started."

Chapter 8

The crowd was still cheering as Peachtree marched off the stage at the Café Au-Go-Go after a second encore. An ebullient Danny hugged his bandmates, "You guys were fantastic and that keyboard solo was amazing!"

Tanner slapped him on the back, "That's hitting the note, brother."

"We kicked their asses!" yelled Ethan.

Ronnie grabbed Randy, "I hate to rain on your parade, man, but did you notice Sunny and Taylor sitting together?"

"Yeah, they both insisted on being here and they were holding hands."

"You're in deep shit."

"Think they'd notice if I just slipped out the back and hid in the hotel?"

"I don't think you've got a chance of getting away clean, man, 'cause here they come."

Sunny dragged Taylor through the crowded hallway with Augie, Bernie, and Ruck in tow. The little blond jumped into Randy's arms, wrapped her legs around his waist, and planted a passionate kiss on his lips. "You guys were great!"

Taylor walked over and kissed him too.

He blushed, "Am I in trouble here?"

The girls giggled. "More than you know but we'll figure that out later," said Sunny. "Augie's just introduced Travis to Stanton Tosh, the booking agent."

"Cool. I know they've talked on the phone but he's never heard the band live."

"From the smile on his face, I'd say you're gonna be busy,"

said Taylor. "Bernie told me that guy's got his fingers in all the big festivals this year and most of the clubs in the Northeast."

"I'm up for that," said Randy.

"You're up for anything," laughed Sunny, grinning at Taylor.

"You two look like two cats who shared the canary. Did you take some love drug together or what?"

"I thought I'd feel resentment," said Sunny.

"Me too," added Taylor, "but after checking each other out, we decided that you have good taste in women."

"So, no clawing cat fights?"

The girls laughed, "Quite the opposite."

"Bummer. Do I get to participate?"

Taylor smirked, "We'll see. But first, Augie's invited the whole crew for a real Italian dinner and it's impolite to refuse."

"I'm game," said Randy, an arm around each of his ladies.

"So, let's get the rest of the crew together and head out," said Taylor, latching on to Danny's arm. "Want a hot date and some good food?"

"Why, yes Ma'am, I believe I might be interested in your proposition."

Sunny grabbed Tanner and Ethan, "Hey, our friend Augie wants to introduce you to real Italian food. Wanna come."

"You always make me wanna come, darlin', but I'll take good food as a second choice," laughed Ethan, wiping down his flute.

Terry wandered over, "Union says we can't drag the gear out 'til their guys show up in the morning, so we're in."

"Great, get the rest of the guys."

"We've even got two limos waiting outside!" added Bernie, as five gorgeous girls in thigh-high white boots and tiny mini-skirts appeared. "Ah, a few more friends to spice the brew. This is Callista, Siena, Heather, Mackenzie, and the lovely Ann."

The roadies collected Travis and Stanton Tosh and steered the party into two black stretch Cadillacs at the curb. Terry looked around, as they pushed through a huge gaggle of fans, and turned to Danny, "Are you diggin' this? There are so many people out here it could turn into 'A Hard Day's Night' in a flash."

Danny laughed, "I've got my spiky track shoes on, man. I'm ready!"

Augie nestled into the back seat next to Taylor, Randy, and Sunny and said, "I'm glad everyone could join us, I know you're going to love my uncle's restaurant. The food is wonderful and I can guarantee that everything is fresh."

"How can you guarantee that?" smirked Sunny.

"Because he worked my ass off for a summer and he only has one way of doing things, the old way!"

"Gee, that sounds like my mom!" laughed Randy.

"Mine too," yelled Ethan who was casually caressing a bare patch on Callista's long legs, between her skimpy skirt and shiny boots.

Ruck turned around from the passenger seat in the front, "You guys were really hot tonight. The crowd loved it."

"We call that hittin' the note, brother," said Tanner.

"How's the album coming?" asked Augie.

"It's gonna be great," said Ethan. "We've finished most of the tracks and our producer is working on the final mix. We've got some reel-to-reels at the hotel, if you want to hear the rough mix, but we can't let go of 'em until we're ready to release. Sort of listen but don't touch."

"When we play live, I can't always hear every note the other guys are playin' but, in the studio, everything jumps right out at you. Onstage, it's a frenzy but we're learning to underplay stuff on the album," said Danny. "Sometimes, hittin' that one note means more than a high speed riff."

"Yeah, it's different than the live sound," said Ronnie, "but it's really good."

"Sure looks like Travis and Stanton are in a groove," said

Ethan, cocking a thumb to the second car. "Thanks for setting up that connection for us. Hell, thanks for all your help."

Augie smirked, "You guys kicked the shit out of him tonight and he knows money when he hears it. They'll work something out, just watch."

He leaned over to Taylor and whispered, "Is this the home girl?"

"Yeah, bright, sexy, and brimming with Southern charm. That's a dangerous combination."

"How's that workin' for ya'?"

"Better than you might imagine," she replied coyly.

"What's he got that I haven't?"

"Magic!"

"A giant schlong or what?"

"Just know that he's a lucky man," laughed Taylor, "and I can absolutely guarantee that you're already well cared for."

"Well, if that doesn't work out so well, you just let me know."

"As I said the last time, you're dreamin' and we're better off being business associates. Nice and clean and profitable for both of us."

"Can't argue with that, although I'd love to try."

"Bernie tells me you're getting into grocery stores."

"Yeah, I bought the first one down in Paramus, spiffed the place up, replaced most of the big suppliers with locals, but kept every one of the employees and added a few more. It's a gold mine."

"A cash business."

Augie grinned, "I'm looking at two more, one in Westfield and another in Watchung. People use the little local store when they need something in a hurry but they'll drive for thirty minutes to a larger store that has everything they need, to save a few cents. So, why not transform those small groceries into what the customers want? The investment's nothing and refitting isn't that bad a hit. We made it all back in ninety days and I didn't even spike the punch."

"That's incredible but you're back to the same problem."

"Only more so," laughed Augie.

"Good problem to have."

"There are all sorts of opportunities like that. Ruck's buyin' up little chunks of land just outside the suburbs, estates mostly, and all he has to do is maintain the property for a few years, it'll be worth a fortune."

"Bernie told me he's looking into a bar, an Irish bar at that, even though he doesn't have a single drop of Gaelic blood in his body."

"I think he's onto something, because he showed me some research and realized that there are a whole slew of folks with deep pockets that need a watering hole near the office. If he fails, it won't be because he didn't pick the right location."

"He's always been a graciously gregarious kind of guy. He'll make a go of it," smiled Taylor. "Thanks for the advice."

The cars turned into the parking lot and the guests piled out and followed Augie and Taylor to the front door.

Manny Romano was waiting, "Ah, Augie, I'm glad your friends could join you, especially Miss Taylor." He took her hand and kissed her fingers. "You're always welcome here, my dear. Him, on the other hand, maybe not so much!"

"Think you can handle twenty of us, Uncle Manny?"

"Certainly, we'll put you in the Venetian room, where your guests can watch the lights, and I'll warn the kitchen to expect trouble."

"And your other guests will be protected from the ruckus," laughed Augie.

His uncle grabbed an armload of menus, "Well, that too. Please follow me."

The party settled around a long candlelit table, under

flickering chandeliers, before a wall of glass and the lights of the city. Waiters poured wine for each of the guests and Augie stood up, "I'd like to propose a toast to Peachtree. You guys put on one hell of a show tonight and, if I'm readin' the vibes right, Travis and Stanton seem to have developed a mutual interest…seeing you guys go to the top!"

Everyone cheered, although the manager and the agent smiled and continued a muffled conversation.

"My Uncle Manny's brought menus but I usually just ask him to bring the best dishes he's serving tonight and we can all share, if that's alright with you?"

"Sure," yelled the group.

The guys were chatting up the local girls and Taylor turned to Randy, "So, Sunny tells me you won't divulge our secrets."

"That's what I promised, when all of this started."

"And you almost kept your word."

"Well, she knows in a general sense but nothing specific."

"She's way brighter than you give her credit for. She wants to open up Alabama and Mississippi."

Randy turned to Sunny, who was wearing her most enchanting Southern belle grin, and back to Taylor. "I'm thinkin' that no matter how this works out, I'm in trouble."

Sunny squeezed his arm, "I brought it up to her, simple business. I know people who can help expand this thing even further, if you'll let me."

"I'm all for everyone making money on this but the closer to home it gets, the more dangerous it becomes and I sure don't want it screwin' up things with the band."

"I know how to keep my mouth shut and, besides, you forget, I've lived all over the world and I've seen every trick in the book. Hell, I was smokin' Afghani hash in Turkey when I was twelve."

"No denyin' you're a heavyweight," laughed Randy. "I still

can't keep up with you."

"You're snorin' before I even get a good buzz going."

"You're a cruel girl, you know that?"

"That's why you like both of us, we're smarter than you!" laughed Taylor.

"We'll talk about this when we're alone, okay?"

"Okay," said the girls in unison, running their hands up the inside of his thighs. "If we remember."

Travis stood up and offered his glass, "I want each of you guys to make time to personally introduce yourselves to our new booking agent for the Northeast, Stanton Tosh. If this works out, we have Augie to thank for making the connection for us."

Augie smiled and raised his glass, as a slender man in a fine black suit with a skinny old-school striped tie stood. "I was truly impressed by what I saw and heard tonight. You played for a sophisticated crowd, people who have seen the best of the best, and you kicked some ass. If your album was ready, we could have sold a thousand copies tonight."

Cheers all around.

"From what Travis told me, the tapes are incredible, so we'll build a tour to introduce you and the album in all the right places. I've had some dealings with Blossom Booking in Atlanta, and they're good people, so, no problem there. And, your producer, Hal Nelson might be just starting his own shop but he's got some fans in the industry."

Everyone clapped and cheered.

He paused and smiled, "What really knocked me out tonight was your presence, the power, the energy flowing off that stage like a flood that sucked the crowd right into the groove and wouldn't let go until the last note faded away. Hell, they weren't even satisfied with two encores!"

Danny piped up, "That's all well and good, governor, but what're you gonna do for us?"

"I like working with people who are straight forward. I'm going to make a great band famous and we'll all make a lot of money in the process. How's that?"

"We want to read the contract before anything gets signed," added Tanner.

"Yeah, we ain't a bunch of Southern hicks slingin' guitars out the back of a pick-up. We've all got degrees," said Ethan.

"Fair enough," said Stanton. "I'll get together with Travis tomorrow morning and we'll work out the details. If all of you approve, we've got a deal."

"Right on!" shouted Ronnie.

~

Randy staggered down the hallway, "This has got to be heaven or, maybe, purgatory, considering I've got my two favorite women for the night and I can't stand up."

"You've had a little too much vino, buster," laughed Taylor. "Gimme the key."

The bass player fumbled the key from his jeans and kissed Sunny, who said, "I'm thinkin' you might not be up to taking care of two of us."

"I'll manage."

"We'll see," said Taylor, as they guided him into the room and shed their coats.

The girls kissed him passionately, Taylor unbuttoning his shirt and Sunny unfastening his pants. The little blond pushed him onto the bed, pulled off his boots and socks, and heaved him into the pillows, "Let's just make you comfortable, Sugar."

Taylor pulled off her belt, Sunny grabbed the belt from his pants, and they tied his hands to the headboard.

"This is getting interesting," said Randy, gaping in wonder at long, lanky Taylor with full breasts and hips, womanly, elegant, and graceful, next to Sunny, who was short, perfectly round in all the right places, and radiated an irresistible innocent heat. Both were beautiful, sexy, intelligent, worldly, and his...at least for the moment, if he could just sober up enough to get his eyes to focus.

"That's just to keep you out of our way, Honey, until you're ready to join the fun," said Sunny, reaching up to kiss Taylor, who wrapped her arms around the little blond and slowly unzipped her dress.

Chapter 9

Augie followed a small crowd beneath a giant 'Corner Market' sign and through swinging glass doors into the aroma of freshly baked bread and pastries in the bakery next to the entry. A rainbow of fresh fruits and vegetables invited customers into the flow around the outer circumference of the store to the dairy section, a butcher and fish market, a deli, a pharmacy, a florist, and an ice cream parlor, all high-markup services.

He let himself into the offices, which had been expanded and modernized, and found the secretary, Monica Harvey, typing furiously.

She looked up, "Oh, Hi, Mr. LaGuerre. I didn't hear you come in."

"That's fine, I don't mean to interrupt. You look like you're on a roll."

"Well, I'm still trying to consolidate all the old files, so they can be put into storage."

"Just so we know what they are and where they went, we're good," smiled Augie. "Is Chester in?"

"Yeah, go right in."

He sauntered back to the rear office and knocked lightly. Chester Walsh, a beefy fifty with a stout cigar stub planted firmly in his craw and a horde of retail and marketing experience in his head, put down the financial section of the New York Times and chuckled, "Well, shit, the boss's boss shows up!"

"Sorry, I've been on the road. How are things here?"

Chester heaved his girth out of the chair and cleared a pile of invoices off the only other chair in the room, "Have a seat. I don't like that putz we just elected. Nixon's a bad guy."

Augie sat down, "Yeah, he's a snake but maybe he'll put an end to the war, so, even though I can't stand him, I might give him a chance to undo the mess that Johnson made. Besides, Republicans are good for business."

"Yeah, I keep thinking it can't get any worse but then it does." The manager groaned as he sat down and waved his cigar over reams of paper. "I've got two bookkeepers working overtime and two more coming on next week. Our success is going to be the death of me, if I don't get this shit under control and fast."

Augie grinned, "So how'd you feel about opening up two more?"

"Stores? Are you shitting me? No, you're just trying to kill me!"

"No shit, I've got one in Westfield and another in Watchung and there are more out there."

"Hold on to your ass, bucko, we've gotta get a handle on this one first."

"You'll have it whipped into shape in nothin' flat. We're going to make a lot of money for our little corporation. Hell, this is your retirement!"

"Retirement my ass. Don't do me no good if I'm dead and gone!"

"C'mon, I'll take you to see them on Thursday and, if you don't think they're both gold mines, you can nix the deal on the spot. Fair enough?"

"Alright, but you're buying lunch and it better be fantastic, none of that spaghetti and meatball shit."

"Fair enough, I know a really nice French restaurant, La Maison, with white table clothes, waiters in tuxedos, and a French Maitre'D, named Victor, who'll charm your ass off."

"Deal."

Augie picked up a large valise and placed it on the desk, "Here's the next contribution to our expansion. Run it through like all the rest."

Chester smiled and placed the case on the floor next to his chair, "How much?"

"Half a mil. I'll have another for you next month."

"Gotcha. The store's doing very well on its own, this makes it excessive!"

Augie stood up, "I'll pick you up at ten on Thursday."

"You make it hard to say no, fine French cuisine? Of course! I'll even wear a clean shirt."

Bernie was minding deliveries in California and Ruck was coordinating the next shipment out of Jamaica, so Augie sat at the curb in the Chevy, humming along to 'Hey Jude' while he scanned the exits at LaGuardia for Taylor's girlfriend, Sophia.

Taylor's phone call was intriguing, "I'm sorry I can't make it. I've got a team project due next week, so I've gotta be here, but Sophia's trustworthy and positively gorgeous! Think surfer girl with Veruschka's legs and Jean Shrimpton's mug...and, oh yeah, try being a gentleman instead of a letch!"

Augie grinned as a lanky blond with a large shoulder bag and an aluminum briefcase burst from the entrance in a whirlwind of style. The stack heals of her leather boots clacked across the pavement in long strides that swept charcoal elephant bells along like a wake behind a cruiser. A tight leather jacket, unzipped to reveal ample cleavage bouncing hypnotically beneath a vibrant hot pink blouse, trailed an ocean-green scarf that glimmered in the dull gray light. She lifted oversized shades and walked straight to the car to let herself into the passenger seat. "I'm hopin' you're Augie?"

He grinned like a Cheshire cat and reached to shake her hand, "The car's a dead giveaway."

A deep laugh bubbled up from her core, "Taylor said to watch out for you, her description of you was an Adonis who wears testosterone like cologne."

"I've never damaged a lady in my life!"

"I'll bet there are mobs of thwarted maidens strewn in your path," smirked Sophia, pulling a pack of Lucky's out of her bag. "Mind if I smoke?"

"Nope, I smoke Boro's," replied Augie, wheeling the car into traffic. "She must have a lot of faith in your character to hand you a bag full of cash, to deliver to some guy you've never met."

"Trust works both ways, right? She's helped me out, when I needed a hand, and I don't have any problem returning the kindness, especially when I'm being well paid," said the leggy blond, stretching out across the seat. "Don't mind me, those fucking airplane seats are torture."

"I have to see a masseuse after a long flight or I'm crippled."

She reached behind the seat and heaved the valise into view, "Taylor said to give you this. I have no idea of how much is there but it's fucking heavy."

"Is that all you brought with you?"

"Like that's not enough, asshole?"

"No, I mean clothes and stuff girls need when they travel."

"Shit, I've got everything I need in my bag for one night. You're in charge of getting me on the plane in the morning."

"Fine, I've got a stop to make and then we'll find some dinner. What do you like?"

"I'm from California, so I'll eat almost anything."

"Adventurous, independent, beautiful...I'll bet you make all the boys crazy."

She reached over and grabbed his erection, "Yup, happens pretty much all the time, since I grew all these curves. I was a late bloomer."

"Fresh off the vine," moaned Augie, as he pulled into the drive in front of a small industrial warehouse, with a small sign that read 'Analytic Autobody', next to a closed gas station, the only two undamaged buildings within sight.

He grabbed the metal case and said, "Lock the doors, I'll be back in five minutes."

"Gee, that makes a girl feel secure, especially in the middle of a war zone."

He grinned, "Good thing it's daylight, 'cause the really bad shit doesn't crank up until after dark."

"Taylor warned me that you're an asshole. Hurry up."

Augie banged on a large metal garage door, emblazoned with a stylized gold Puerto Rican flag painted across its width. It rolled up, as he ambled into the building, and closed immediately.

Sophia gazed around at the burned and demolished buildings, once home to families with hopes and dreams, businesses vying for success, kids riding bikes and playing ball in the street. A mangy brown dog, rummaging through a trashcan tipped over next to the pumps at the gas station, was the only living creature in sight.

Augie reappeared and climbed into the car, "You okay?"

"Yeah, but this place sure is a creepy. I've heard bad shit about New York but this has got to be the worst of it."

The shiny Chevy motored toward civilization. "Yeah, this is about as bad as it gets. How 'bout we make a run past the stores along Fifth Avenue. The first Christmas decorations are going up and I need some shoes."

"What's wrong with the ones you're wearing?"

"I need business shoes, wingtips."

"Oh, you play dress up too?" laughed Sophia.

"To tell you truth, I hate shopping. If I find something comfortable, I usually buy a bunch, so I won't have to go through the hassle for at least a couple of years."

"Shoes?"

"Yeah, I'll get two black, two brown and I'm good for a while."

"Taylor warned me that you're weird."

"How 'bout efficient?"

"Okay, shoes then food!"

~

Sophia stood, silhouetted in the moonlight, gazing at glittering ripples on the water. Augie rubbed her shoulders and kissed her neck. "Are you okay?"

"Yeah, I'm fine. Perfectly satiated, thank you very much." She stared at the reflections, "There's something soothing and hypnotic about light on the water. That was one of the first things I shared with Taylor, the two of us braving a frigid gale just to watch the waves. We're both water creatures, she's Pisces and I'm an Aquarian."

"Openness, spirituality, and creative independence. .and, usually, very right-brained."

"I'm an art major but she's majoring in marketing communications, so she's got a bit more left brain stuff going on than I do."

"What kind of art?"

"Oils, sculpture, and jewelry. Actually, I really like working with metals and gems a lot, so maybe that's where I'll end up."

"I'd like to see your work."

She held up a silver ring with delicate leaves grasping a large amethyst, "This is my only sample but I'll bring some photos. next time I get to travel."

"I'll request your exclusive services from Taylor," laughed Augie, examining the ring as he wrapped his arms around her. "You made that? It's beautiful."

She took the ring and slipped it on her finger. "You have a gorgeous view."

"Yeah, but I want a house where you can look out and see ocean stretching to the horizon. Someplace completely removed from the city. A place with a dock, where boats can sail off to anyplace on the planet, and room for lots of friends and animals and kids, someday."

"Gee, you sound like you're ready to settle down."

"It doesn't hurt to find the place, while I'm waiting for the queen to show up."

"Long-term planning. I love it and I sure hope that, whoever she is, she loves your Shangri-la as much as you do."

He looked into her eyes, "Could you hang out for an extra day?"

"Why?"

"Because I've got something that I'd like your aesthetic opinion on." He grinned that little Paul Newman smirk, "How 'bout we make a deal?"

"What deal? The fucking airline will probably screw me on the ticket anyway," said Sophia.

"I'll take care of your ticket and reservations, so you'll be back in time for study hall."

"You asshole! I'm startin' to feel like you're some ol' codger robbin' the cradle with that attitude!" She stuck out her chest, "Am I too immature for you?"

Augie stepped back to inspect her body from slender feet, up long legs to ample hips, a narrow waist, and voluptuous breasts, and grinned, "No, actually, I think you might be perfect."

She kissed him hungrily and pulled back, "But now you've got my curiosity up. What do you want my opinion about?"

"That'll be a surprise, now won't it?"

~

The BelAir purred down the Garden State Parkway to Five-Twenty, across the Shrewsbury River Bridge to Sea Bright, then south a few miles to a gravel drive that meandered through a thin pine forest to an enormous log house on the lee side of the long spit of land straddling Ocean Avenue from the beach to the bay.

Sophia jumped out and turned around and around, "What is this place? It's amazing!"

"I'm thinking about buying it," grinned Augie, padding across the gravel drive to a breezeway between a four-car garage and the kitchen. "C'mon, let's start inside and then we can walk around the grounds."

She followed him down a short hallway to a big open kitchen with a walk-in fireplace dominating the log walls of a dining cove, double refrigerators, stoves, and ovens, two work counters with sinks and dishwashers under walls of glass that overlooked the forest to the Atlantic beyond. The lanky blond wandered over and leaned on the edge of an oversized sink to stare out the window, "I'm a pretty good cook but I'd be even better, if I had that view to look at every day and someplace to grow fresh veggies."

"There's more," said Augie pushing through a swinging door into a formal dining room, extended out from the structure to provide a panoramic sweep of the bay. He stopped in the middle of the living room, open to a balcony running around the circumference of the second floor, and then walked over to rub the smooth polished surface of one of the giant logs stacked into walls. "This was originally built as a hunting lodge in New Hampshire and it was dismantled, trucked down here, and reassembled. They even made the nails, hinges, door latches, and all the other hardware on the property, carved the banisters and balustrades from saplings growing in the forest across the bay, and the chimneys are made of local rock. It's like this house was supposed to be here but it got built in the wrong place."

"There's magic in that," smiled Sophia, as she walked through another hallway into a giant game room with a private apartment beyond. "Does this go on forever?"

"Well, it is more than two hundred feet long, with a full

basement, four bedrooms upstairs, plus this one and two more off the kitchen, and sixty acres of privacy."

"That sounds like heaven to me," said Sophia. "Let's go see the outside."

"One thing you've gotta see first." He took her hand and clambered up the stairs, through the master suite to a balcony that looked out over the forest to the sea. "I'd like to wake up to that view every day."

She cuddled close, "Yup, that's magic, isn't it? I'll bet it's intense when storms come rolling in."

"I've had my real estate guy checking it out and this stretch has never been swamped."

"Well, the house does sit on a rise that's probably fifteen or twenty feet above high tide."

"Twenty-two, to be exact, and the basement actually raises the first floor another ten feet. People, who ply the sea, understand that sailors are always at the mercy of the weather gods."

"Yeah, I know what you mean. I grew up next to the Pacific and its character could change from placid to full fury in an instant. If you live by the sea, you respect it and pay attention to what's coming."

"Do you sail?"

"Sure! I grew up racing Sunfish and M-16's," smiled the California girl, "before I found surfing. You ever been on a board?"

"Naw, just body surfing but even that's a rush!"

"That rush is what it's all about, whether it's surfing or sailing or dealing. It's living on the edge that keeps people like us going in our own directions, instead of trying to be everyone else."

"Interesting, sort of them and us?"

"I don't mean it to sound snotty, it's just that some people play an instrument, while others are perfectly satisfied to pay money to listen to the result of their talent, dedication, and persistence."

Augie smiled, "That's what sets people apart, their

willingness to follow their own path, their own bliss, to wherever it leads."

"Win, lose, or draw."

"Exactly."

"I plan on being successful and comfortable. Beyond that, I haven't a clue."

He wrapped his arms around her, "You never know what you'll find behind door number three."

Tony slumped into an overstuffed beanbag chair and Augie held out a cold Coors, "How's your penance going?"

"I'm gonna graduate but I'm not ready for college and no place decent would take me anyway, so the ol' man's sayin' he wants me to go spend some time with the family in the old country."

Augie smiled, "Couldn't hurt, Sicily's winters are a sight better than here and the girls are gorgeous."

"How do you know?"

"Because he took me along, when I was eight or nine, to a beautiful little fishing village called Addaura, just beyond Palermo. The Aunties decided that I was too scrawny and stuffed me with everything they could cook and the food's incredible. The old ladies are all fat but the young women were voluptuous, just like every horny Italian boy's fantasies."

"Yeah, but I've already got girls."

"So what are you doin' besides workin' with your tutor?"

"Driving a truck for Uncle Paulie."

"Startin' at the bottom, just like I did."

"I, sure as shit, don't want to be doin' this for the rest of my life."

"Yeah, but Paulie pays you about double the going rate 'cause you're family. What about everything else?"

"I quit dealin'," said Tony, "and you keep me supplied with good smoke, so all I'm buyin' are some hallucinogens for the weekends."

"No coke or speed or downers or smack?"

Tony shook his head, "I'm trying to stay out of trouble. Shit, I thought the ol' man was going to burn my eyes out with his fucking cigar."

"Yeah, you don't want to be the guy standin' in front of that bastard when he's pissed." His grin faded, "So what's keeping you here?"

"The scene man. What could be cooler than hanging out with my buddies in the Village or the concerts in the Park listening to some of the greatest music of our time…live! Oh, and the chicks are incredible and willing."

"That doesn't get you anywhere and your friends are a bunch of spoiled losers looking for a free high."

"So, cut me in on your business. I'm cool and I'll work hard."

"You're trouble waitin' to happen, that's what you are."

"C'mon, man, lemme have just one chance."

"You don't seem to get it. You already had one chance and you blew it big-time, remember? A kid almost died."

"It was a setup and you know it."

"You should've known goin' in, not after you got busted."

"Man, I wanna be something!"

"You are someone right now, it's a question of who you want to be when you grow up and what you're willing to do to earn it?"

"Like you."

"No! You can't be like me. You have to be who you are. You have to take a chance to find out who you are, whether you can stand up, out there in the real world."

"What d'you mean?"

"I mean, I think you should take the ol' man up on his offer. Go learn about a different culture, a different life than living in this city. I guarantee that those ol' geezers will teach you everything you could ever want to know about running a business. The Patriarchs of those families have been controlling the underworld for hundreds of years. Their reach stretches across borders and oceans and they're venerated as wisemen, who maintain authority over an empire through an endless web of relatives and friends. You have nothing to lose and everything to gain. The relationships you form, while you're there, will serve you well for the rest of your life."

"Ah, man, I don't want to get stranded in some podunk burg in Sicily listening to some old codgers yammering about the good ol' days."

"Spend some time with the family, learn everything you can, and take a tour through the rest of Europe on your way home."

"Like Rome and London and Paris and Amsterdam," grinned the little brother.

"You're starting to see this as an opportunity to, not only get out from under the ol' man's wrath, but turn it into an adventure as well."

"Yeah, I think you're on to something," said Tony, swigging the last of his Coors. "So, what's happening with you, that you can tell me about?"

Augie grinned, "I bought a couple of grocery stores and met someone special. Which do you want to hear about?"

"A special lady? You?"

"I know it's out of character but I've never felt like this about any chick."

"Have you seen a doctor?" laughed Tony. "A head doctor?"

"I might consider that, if this didn't' feel so good."

"Yeah, well, your first snort of heroin is like that."

Augie smirked, "But definitely not as sweet."

"I'll bet she's gorgeous. Who is she?"

"Sophia Daniella DeRosa, a sophomore art student at the University of Wisconsin."

"How'd you meet her?"

"Through Bernie's cousin, Taylor, who's pretty hot too."

"We'll see how long this one lasts," laughed Tony. "Your last 'serious' relationship was done in a month."

Augie grinned, "Yeah, Bettie. She had an amazing body."

"And no brain!"

"Well, that too."

"So, grocery stores?"

"Oh, yeah, Mary suggested I look into common businesses that could grow over time, so I found a perfect little grocery, renovated the whole operation, and hired an ace to run the show. We're about to close on two more."

"Shit, you're gonna end up being one of those fat-cat tycoons!"

"Naw, it's just good business and I think I was lucky enough to find a little niche that no one else was paying attention to. Hell, the first one's already turning a profit."

"That's incredible. The man with the golden touch, transforming coal into gemstones, while I'm still trying to figure out who I am."

Augie clapped him on the back, "You'll get there, kid. Just don't make the journey any tougher than it has to be."

Tony glanced at his watch, "Shit, I've gotta haul ass."

"Hot date?"

"Yeah, she sizzles like bacon on a hot griddle."

"Be careful."

The kid grinned, "Always am."

"Not always enough," laughed Augie.

Tony turned from the door, "I'll think about your suggestion."

"You've gotta start someplace and Sicily during the winter

ain't a bad choice. All of this will still be here when you get back."

Augie closed the door and wandered back into the living room to gaze out over the water, thinking about Sophia. The jangling phone startled him. "Hello."

"Augie, it's Sidney."

"Hey girl, what's up?"

"I'm with Bernie and we've got a problem."

"Oh, shit."

"Worse than that. That nice dry hull wasn't so dry, when we went out to meet the guys."

Bernie grabbed the phone, "We've got a mold problem."

"How bad?"

"All of it."

Augie slumped on the couch, "Nothing retrievable?"

"Well, most of the furniture survived but the product is gunk. Evidently the bottom of the panels wasn't sealed and it acted like a wick."

He chugged a sip of beer, "What kind of shape is the boat in?"

"One of the seals on the starboard shaft sprung a leak and it's probably repairable but we've still got five tons embedded in sheet steel that's oozing resin into the bilge like maple syrup. The wrong person getting a big whiff might be a chance we don't want to take."

"So, what are you suggesting?"

"Let's offload Sidney's shipment in Monterey, then take her out and scuttle her in deep water."

"No better ideas?"

"Take the loss and carry on."

"Fuck!" The fire in the hearth hissed as the beer bottle shattered. "Do what you've gotta do. Lemme talk to Sidney."

Her voice was relatively calm, "Sorry to be the bearer of bad tidings and all that."

"Is your stuff okay?"

"Yeah, it was all sealed and the water never got to it, so we'll salvage eight-five percent and the rest is insured."

"Are you hip to Bernie's plan?"

"Yeah, I think it's the best solution. The papers lead back to our dummy corporation in Singapore, so, even if it was found, no one could ever trace it to us."

"So, better to destroy the evidence?"

"When your position is untenable, take your losses and move on to the next play, just like I coached you back in school."

"Yeah, but there's a difference between failing grades and dropping a couple of million down the drink."

"No, there isn't. Experience makes us smarter, stronger, especially bad experiences. You forget, my family has been trading for hundreds of years and not every shipment or every deal was successful. You cover your ass and remember each debt that is owed you."

~

Bernie followed the little freighter, in a classic wooden Chris Craft, as it plowed northwest into the late afternoon. He turned to Ashton, "She's ridin' really low."

"She's on her knees, brother. Knows that she's on her way to the deep."

"We'll cut her loose up near Half Moon Bay in deep water, so, even if she takes a while to sink, the currents will carry her out to sea."

"Put your faith in mother nature," replied Ashton.

"Probably better than believin' in people."

"True that!"

When the sun was low on the horizon, the Chris Craft pulled up alongside the Maple Dragon. Hank and Donny appeared on the bridge and Donny yelled, "You really wanna do this?"

"This is as good a place as any, international waters, out of the shipping lanes. Ruck said to make sure to open all the valves. Let's pull the plug and get out of here!"

"Yeah, we checked the radar, there's nothing within miles," said Hank. "We'll shut her down and open the pipes."

Ten minutes later, the shipmates scrambled onto the cabin cruiser, which circled away from the sinking freighter. The little boat bobbed in the waves for more than half an hour, as seawater filled the hull of the larger craft and she sank to her gunnels.

Ashton finally said, "She's gonna take a while to go down but she's done-for. Let's head for the barn."

"I'd feel better, if we actually watched her disappear," said Bernie.

"Hell, man, it's getting dark and, if we wait long enough, some other ship's going to stumble on us floatin' around out here. It's done, let's go."

"Fine," said Bernie, cranking up the engine and heading south.

The bridge and main cabin of the Maple Dragon resisted pounding waves, barely floating on cells of air trapped in the gap between the steel panels of the false interior and the double hull of the craft. She groaned as relentless currents dragged her north along the coast for hours, before a high tide swept her into San Francisco Bay.

～

Augie screamed into the phone, "I thought you assholes were going to take care of things!"

"What do you mean," stammered Bernie, barely conscious at six-thirty, California time.

"It's on the fucking national news. The Maple Dragon was found, half submerged in San Francisco Bay this morning by the Harbor Patrol and seized by Customs. They're calling it the biggest bust in state history!"

"Oh my god! She was almost under, when we left her and that was at least twenty miles out and a hundred miles south!"

"Well, you picked the perfect spot, dumbshit! The Feds are opening a full investigation."

"Then you better hope you covered our tracks, brother, or we're all in a big hurt."

"Win, lose, or draw, we've gotta cover seven-fifty before the holidays."

"Good thing everything else's still cookin'."

"Yeah, now we're playing catch up."

~

Silas Sejnowski hacked up a wad of flem and lit another Winston. "You got anything new on those pot punks?"

"Nothing concrete but there's a pattern developing. New product seems to show up every few weeks on the street but we still don't have any leads that'll get us closer to the source," replied McElroy. "And, oh yeah, your cough sounds like shit. Why don't you quit suckin' on those cancer sticks?"

"Ah, they ain't gonna hurt me," grunted Sejnowski. "It's a fuckin' cold."

"No, it's not! Wise up! You're my partner for what, thirteen years? I wanna keep your ugly ass around for a while longer. You actually prove useful sometimes."

"Yeah, who loves ya'?"

"You're too ugly," laughed Jimmy. "I've been looking through all the busts that come through records and there's no pattern to it, mostly stupid kids getting caught with a bag of weed or some acid or speed or whatever. There are a handful of pounds and kilos but none of it was the good stuff that's flooding the market. A few rich punks busted for harder stuff, a little heroin here, coke there, and only one was interesting and only because the plant overdosed on the evidence and almost died. The high-schooler, who provided the shit, didn't have a trace in his system."

"That's weird, once a junkie and all that."

"I don't think these kids treat it like the bums in the Bowery. They snort it on weekends, while the folks are out at the Hamptons."

"It'll still kill 'em, lights out, good night," said Sejnowski. "And where the fuck do they get that shit anyway? It's not like you can buy a dime bag on the corner in the suburbs."

McElroy flipped through a file, "Says he claimed to have picked it up in the Village, as a favor for his friend. They both went to Sebastian, so you know their folks have the pull to get these records expunged."

"So, how'd you get 'em?"

"There's always copies someplace," grinned the Irishman, "and, I've got friends in the right places."

"I'm bettin' these two will show up again for somethin' bigger."

"I'll keep the file locked up in the meantime," said McElroy. "Never know when that one little weirdism opens Pandora's box."

He picked up a newspaper article on his desk, "Oh, yeah, did you see this story about the half-submerged freighter full of pot that showed up in San Francisco Bay? Feds are investigating."

Sejnowski coughed, "Wonder whether that's the supply for our guys? How big was the load?"

"Wet or dry?" the Irishman laughed. "The official count is five tons."

"I'm bettin' it's all tied together and we need to find the asshole who's runnin' the operation."

Chapter 10

Sophia slithered from under a tangle of sheets and blankets to curl up in Taylor's arms, "You're delicious."

"So are you," whispered Taylor, kissing her hungrily. "We could spend the day in bed."

"MMMmmm, how about a cold glass of champagne in a nice warm tub for breakfast?"

"I'm for that," said Taylor, flicking her tongue across Sophia's pert nipples. "Should I be jealous of you and Augie?"

"Yeah, you probably should. He's somethin'."

"I haven't had the pleasure," laughed Taylor.

"Should have, while you had the chance, now I'd be jealous."

"Does he know about us?"

"No, silly, no one knows. You were the one who took me to New York and arranged for my abortion and, then, nursed me back to health, when I had no one else to turn to. Loving you just seems so natural. Besides, a girl's gotta do what she's gotta do to stay sane, while our men are away."

Taylor kissed her on the forehead, "So what happened?"

"First, he took me to this creepy warehouse in the middle of a war zone and made me sit in the car, while he delivered your briefcase. Then we took a ride down Fifth Avenue to see the first Christmas decorations and buy him some shoes. That guy's really weird, he finds a pair of old-guy wingtips that are comfortable and boring and buys four pairs, two black, two brown, so he won't have to go shopping again for a couple of years. Anyway, after our little shopping spree, he took me to dinner."

"At Romano's, right, and Uncle Manny's the cutest dirty old man. Then he took you to his little house on the water."

"Yeah, that's really nice and we made passionate but tender love for hours."

"Funny, he struck me as a slam-bam-thank-you-Ma'am, kinda guy."

"Anything but," giggled Sophia, stroking her thigh.

"So?"

"So, he tells me that he's got something he wants my 'artistic' opinion on and we take drive down to the Jersey Shore. You know my passion for large bodies of water, anyway, he's found this incredible, enormous log lodge on sixty acres, between the beach and the bay, surrounded by a pine forest and he wants to buy it."

"That doesn't surprise me, the guy thinks big."

"I kind of got the feeling that he wanted to see how I reacted to it."

"And?

"Are you kidding, I'd move in there in a New York minute. The fucking kitchen's got double everything and looks out over the ocean. Fuck art, I'll just cook until I weigh five hundred pounds."

"Yeah, with five kids."

"That'd be fine with me," laughed Sophia. "You gotta see this place, girl, I can see tennis courts and swimming pools and docks for boats and hellacious parties. Hell, he was even talking about a helicopter pad, so he can zoom around to his grocery stores."

"You do realize that it's all fantasy. It could all go up in smoke in a flash."

The California beauty grinned, "You take your chances on your romances."

"Just don't get too tangled up without keeping those beautiful eyes wide open. We both know he's famous for ditching girlfriends before they even have a chance to make room in a closet. Hell, Bernie told me a story about him giving a live-in girlfriend a brand new set of Gucci luggage for Christmas...packed."

"Classy, yes, capable of being tamed and trained? I guess we'll see."

"You live dangerously," groaned Taylor, as Sophia massaged her clitoris.

"I think I've got this working the other way. He's gonna have to come after me, if he wants me."

"Girl, I want you," moaned Taylor, licking her way down Sophia's stomach.

The telephone rang in the kitchen.

"Shit," said Taylor, grabbing a robe to trundle down the stairs and through the living room to grab it, "Hello."

"Taylor, it's Freddie. Listen, Corey got busted last night."

"What happened?"

"He was haulin' a pound over to some guys in the dorms, walking past the Pub on State Street and a fight comes tumbling out the front door and he's in the middle of it, when the cops showed up."

"I thought his nickname was Fleet Feet. Why didn't he haul ass?"

"I guess some guy took a swing at him and grabbed his duffle."

"What'd they catch him with?"

"Just a pound but he's in County and we can't bail him out until Monday."

"What about the house?"

"That's why I'm calling, we're on our way with everything we've got."

"You're sure you cleaned it out?"

"Nothing left but a bottle of Excedrin and a case of PBR in the fridge."

"Just make sure you're not followed."

"We're splitting up and taking three separate routes but we'll be careful. See you in thirty."

Taylor slammed the receiver in the cradle, "Fuck!"

She marched back up the stairs, "Corey got busted last night. The guys are heading over here and they definitely don't need to find you wracked out in my bed."

~

The trio appeared, one by one, to stash scales, pipes, bongs, plastic bags, and thirty pounds of hash and weed in the lockers downstairs. Taylor had coffee and bagels waiting on the kitchen table, "I think there's going to be a dry spell until the heat dies down."

"We could deal out of here," said Dave.

"Like hell you could," snapped Taylor. "We're not going to gamble the entire deal for a few week's profits. Besides, finals aren't that far off and I can guarantee that you guys could use a little study time, so you don't flunk out and really screw things up."

"She's right, you know," said Freddy. "We've been going strong since the beginning of the semester but we still gotta keep the parents happy."

Billy said, "We need to get an attorney to look after Corey. That's the first thing we need to do."

Taylor looked at Freddie, "Weren't those guys, in that apartment over the Pub, law students?"

"Yeah, Paul and Davis, and they owe me a favor. I'll truck on by there on the way back and see if they can help."

"Great," said Taylor. "Are you guys absolutely sure there's not even a roach lying around your place?"

"Yeah, we scrubbed it," said Billy.

"You know the cops or narcs are going to be watchin', so you gotta keep it clean until we know the dust has settled."

"No party this weekend," said Dave.

~

Sophia trudged down Bascom Hill through wet pelting snow driven by stiff northly winds whipping across Lake Mendota. She crossed Park and headed up State Street, past the Historical Society and the mall, where a few dozen protesters were waving signs about 'Turn in Your Draft Card Day'. She was lost in thought about a design concept to make a stone appear to float in the setting and didn't notice the Buick idling at the curb next to the library.

The window rolled down and Augie called, "Sophia."

Startled, she turned to his smile and ran to reach through the open window to hug him, "What are you doing here?"

"I'm on my way to the coast and worked in a little side trip, so I could spend a few hours with you."

"You don't fit in little side trips on a whim," said Sophia, sliding across the seat to kiss him passionately.

"Do you think we could find someplace a little more private than Main Street?"

"Sure, let's go to my place. How did you find me? There are only, like, fifty-thousand students on campus at the moment."

"I took a chance, because you always call right as I'm heading for lunch on Monday and Wednesday, so I figured you'd be walking home from class a half hour before that...I guess I got lucky, because I've only been waiting for a couple of minutes."

"How long do I get to keep you?"

"I've got to fly out of here at eight o'clock tonight."

"I guess that will have to do," replied Sophia, snuggling close. "Drive to the next stop, take a right and another right. It's only a few blocks up on West Gilman but, compared to your house, I live in a hovel."

"That's student life and, besides, property values around campus are probably out of sight."

"The landlords know there's always lots of students looking for a place to live, so they can charge way more than it's worth," said Sophia, "Pull over here, that's my building across the street. I live in the basement."

They walked down the slippery driveway hand-in-hand and through a weathered door into a small flat with a kitchen alcove to the right, a tidy workroom with a large desk stacked with books and papers, three comfortable chairs around a small dining table with a pot of yellow mums, and a workbench for her jewelry. Two large canvases leaned against the warm beige wall, one, a naked woman peering out from a tangle of white bed sheets, the second, an impressionistic placid ocean rising out of organic sand dunes with three pelicans flying across an orange sunset melting into the horizon.

Sophia wrapped her arms around his neck and kissed him slowly. "Why are you here?"

Augie pulled back, "Because, even though we've only spent a few days together, I feel something I've never felt before and I was wondering whether you felt the same way?"

She unbuttoned his shirt and rubbed her hands across his chest, "You know I do. I've been praying that you cared enough to come after me."

He reached into his pocket and held up a two-carat canary diamond set in an elegant platinum setting. "I hope this is your size and, no, I wouldn't mind if you designed a matching set of rings for us. This is just my way of saying that I want to spend the rest of my life with you."

Her eyes glistened with tears, "I can't believe this is happening. I love you."

"I've been hoping that we both feel the same magic because I know it's real."

"Me too. Do you want a real wedding?"

"Actually, I don't think we could get away with eloping, because I'm the eldest male in a very Italian family. They'll demand a celebration."

"Then that's what we'll do but I want to finish next semester before our wedding day. I'm signed up for a class with one of my jeweler idols and two other classes that will let me finish up some projects that are kind of half-baked."

"As long as we're promised to each other, I'll wait until you're damned well good and ready."

"Is there a hint of patience behind your commitment?"

"Let's just say that my priorities are beginning to shift a little bit and you're my inspiration."

~

The headlights of Augie's new Mercedes 230 swept across the drive, illuminating Abby, sitting on the front porch of the little house by the water, with a bottle of Jack Daniels in one hand and the butt of a Marlboro in the other. She gaped at the little car, oblivious to her coat barely covering a thin sweater and her pert little tits in a frigid gale, and started cackling as Augie climbed out, "How the fuck do you fit that long body into that tiny little car? And where the fuck did you find the bucks for that?"

"Nice to see you too, darlin'."

"Hey, asshole, I've seen you maybe two or three times, since the abortion, and I have to find out from your sister that you're fucking getting married? What's with that?"

"Hell, I just asked her. News sure does travel fast but I guess I should have told you first. I just didn't know how."

"Fuck, you just tell me, straight up, no bullshit. That's the trouble with you fucking men, you'd rather avoid confrontation than actually reveal what's really going on inside your cold, cold heart."

"You wanna come in?"

"Fuckin' A, it's cold out here and I've been sitting on your comfy porch, waiting for your scrawny ass to show up, for a couple of hours."

"I see you had enough antifreeze to ward off a chill."

"Hell, my pussy's hot enough to keep both of us warm at the North Pole on New Year's."

"Can't argue with that," laughed Augie, unlocking the door and flipping on some lights. "C'mon in and get warm. I'll start a fire."

"You already did," laughed Abby, staggering down the hallway to the great room. "Nice fucking view!"

"Yeah, that's why I bought this place."

"Sounds like you've been buying lots of things lately."

"Like what?"

"Well, a grocery store or seven, and property in Jersey, and new cars, and…"

"A new lady," laughed Augie, lighting some kindling in the hearth.

"I'll bet she's expensive."

"You don't even know her."

"No, but I know you and I'll bet she's got a perfect everything."

"She is good looking but really grounded."

"Where'd ya' meet her?"

"I met her through a friend."

"There's more to it than that."

"Sure there is but it wasn't like we met in a bar and chatted each other into bed. It just seemed really natural from the first minute."

"How fucking romantic," snorted Abby, taking a swig from the bottle. "Is her pussy as sweet as mine?"

"Hey, you and I will always share something special. It's always been there and it always will."

"Yeah, since the first time I let you fuck me after my Confirmation party in eighth grade."

"We had some fun together and there's no one else in my life like you."

"But...?"

"But this is different. I don't understand exactly why but I know that this is the next step, that it's right."

Abby started crying, "I always hoped you'd say that about me."

Augie put his arms around her, "I'm sorry I couldn't say what I didn't feel."

"You asshole!" shouted Abby, chucking the bottle into the fireplace. "Someday, you'll figure out what you threw away!"

Augie followed, as she stormed down the hall to the front door, "Hey, wait! How are you going to get home?"

"The same way I got here, by magic carpet," she screamed, slamming the door without looking back.

Before he could release the latch, she disappeared into a whirling flurry of snow.

"Damnit!" He turned back into the great room and stood staring out across the water. "You could have handled that better."

He jumped as the phone jangled, "Hello."

"Augie, it's Mary."

"Hey, Sis, how'ya doin'?"

"School's going great and New Haven is such a vibrant scene, lots of culture, good restaurants, and great music."

"Sounds like you've got things under control."

"Yeah, I even found a guy I like."

"Should I be the protective older brother?"

"Naw, the guy's a geek...a fascinating and good looking geek, but a geek just the same."

"Then I guess I should be disappointed."

"You smartass! He's more interesting than most of the bimbos I've seen you drooling over!"

He snickered, "Yeah, well, we're kind of getting past that."

"I think I screwed up."

"Why's that?"

"Because I told Abby about your engagement and she didn't take it too well."

"You can say that again. She just stormed out of here into a snowstorm, drunk."

"Well, she's pretty much been drunk, since you dropped out of her life."

"So, it's on me?"

"Hell, yes!" laughed Mary. "That's not to say that she was ever completely normal but definitely more grounded when she had you to lean on."

"I feel really awful about all of it but there isn't much I can do."

"Actually, I think you need to make the effort to track her down and have a real conversation, before it's too late."

He rubbed the stubble on his chin, "I know you're right."

"You're just a chicken-shit. Take control and do the right thing for a change."

"Alright. I will."

"So, how's the future Missus?"

"Terrific! She's coming in the day after Christmas for a week."

"I can't wait to meet her." She paused, "Listen, I checked through all the documents and I can't find any reason not to go through with the deal."

"That's a nice Christmas present."

"Thought you'd like that...and, we got the final papers on the third store, so we're golden on that too."

Augie smiled, "Thanks, Sis. I owe you more than one."

"Naw, I love my little house. That's enough."

"But we're just gettin' started."

"That's what I was afraid you were going to say," laughed

Mary. "Hey, I got a letter from Tony and he actually sounds like he's enjoying the old country. He even said something about how he felt the family bond from the moment he entered the village, like he wasn't visiting someplace new but someplace he's always known."

"I was going to bet on a pretty cousin, myself."

"Well, there's probably that too but, at least, he isn't whining about being homesick. I'm pretty sure he's coming home for Christmas."

"Living under Dad's dark side is not a comfortable place to be."

She giggled, "I wouldn't know. I was always his favorite."

"Yeah, like the rest of us didn't notice."

"Hey, I've gotta go, my new beau's at the door. I'll see you when I get back in a few weeks."

"Cool."

"I love you, Augie."

"I love you too."

Augie hung up the phone and wandered into the kitchen, as a gust of icy air roared down the hallway and the front door slammed against the wall. He glanced around the corner to find Abby, face down on the carpet. "Shit."

He ran to close the door and rolled her on her back. Her lips were blue but her eyes flickered, "It's fucking cold out there, you know that?"

"You dumbshit. Come in here and let's get you warmed up."

"You know what I need, cowboy."

"What you need is warmth and hot coffee and food, so shut up and do as you're told without bitchin'."

"Yes, Sir, Masta'Sa'!"

He carried her to the sofa near the fireplace, peeled off her jacket, which was covered with a crust of ice pellets, and found a towel to dry her hair. "Here, cover yourself with this blanket and I'll get some coffee."

"Fuck, I'd just as soon have another bourbon."

"You broke the bottle, remember?"

"I did? That was stupid."

"Coffee."

She wrapped herself in the blanket and curled up into a little ball, staring at the flames, "Got any dope? Never mind, that's a stupid question."

"Yeah, it is and, no, you don't need any right now."

"You're an asshole, you know that?"

"Yeah, we've established that a couple of times tonight."

"Just so we agree," moaned Abby, taking a warm cup from Augie. "I'm sorry I was such a bitch."

"I'm sorry that I haven't been fair with you."

"You're a weenie."

"Yeah, you're right, but I still care about you."

"Then, why don't you show it?"

"Because, we don't see our relationship the same way and, in the end, that hurts you."

"That's bullshit, you're just a chicken-shit!"

"True."

"So, you're really in love with this chick?"

"I think I am."

"You better be damned sure, asshole, or you're just gonna screw up someone else's life. What's her fucking name?"

"Sophia."

"No shit? Really? How come I'm getting images of Roman goddesses in gauzy flowing gowns?"

Augie grinned, "Not far off it. She's tall, blond..."

"Big jugs, tight ass, long legs, and a pert little face, right?"

"Pretty much."

"You're so fucking predictable."

"You know me best."

She sipped her coffee, "So what about the rest of it?"

Augie leaned back and rested his head on the back of the couch. "It's like everything is coming together, piece by piece, so I can move past all of this."

"You mean you actually want to go straight?"

"Sure, I want to run a real business, have a home that isn't a nut house like my parents, live a real life that's waiting for me every night."

"All you need is a fucking picket fence."

Augie roared, "No, the place I'm looking at has sixty acres with the ocean on one side and a bay on the other. All you can see from the house is nature."

"Shit, I want to see this place."

"It's not quite a done deal yet."

"When it is, I want to go."

"Okay." He looked into her bloodshot eyes, her skin was chafed but her lips were beginning to turn from bruised-blue to pale crimson and her teeth had stopped chattering. "What've you been up to?"

"Nothing as exciting as your life."

"So?"

"I got a job as a barmaid down at Bernie's place, Lucky's, in the Village four nights a week. I make good tips and he makes sure no one gives me any shit."

"Fucker never told me."

"Just because he's your friend doesn't mean he can't be my friend!"

"Never said he couldn't."

"Anyway, I'm livin' with my little brother in a dive off Second Avenue. As soon as he finds a job, we can move up to something better."

"I can help you out with that."

"I don't want hand-outs."

"Okay, fine. But I have a stash house over on the West Side

that's empty and the rent's paid up for a year. The neighbors are quiet and cool and the hookers keep things under control on the street."

"You're kidding?"

"No, I'm not. It's yours, if you need it, but it's gotta be in good condition when you move out or you pay the damages."

"That's fair. Jimmy's a slob but he doesn't tear shit up. I'll make sure."

"Cool. I'll take you over there tomorrow."

"Does that mean I get to spend the night?"

"I'll take you home, if you want."

"What an asshole. Fuck my brains out tonight and I'll never ask you again."

Augie sighed.

"You've never turned down great pussy in your life and I'm bettin' you're not going to start now."

"Fine but I'm holding you to your promise." He paused, "Are you sure you can't get pregnant?"

"I swear on my pulsing loins."

"You bitch!"

Augie walked through a light flurry, glistening in the lights and pageantry of Christmas decorations along Park Avenue, and turned under the canopy of the Waldorf Astoria, where a doorman opened a golden door and tipped his hat. He entered the classic elegance of massive carved black marble columns rising from ornate Persian carpets to an inlaid ceiling surrounded by carved friezes. A formal hush permeated the enormous colonnade, as he paced past formally dressed guests, seated in carefully arranged plush period chairs and lounges, to a clerk at an endless reception desk.

"May I help you, Sir?" The concierge's voice was polite, forceful, and barely a whisper.

"Stoney Montgomery, please."

"Would you be Mr. LaGuerre?"

"Yes."

"He's expecting you in Suite 3609. The elevators are just to the left."

"Thank you," replied Augie. His three-piece pinstriped suit, black wingtips, and a long leather overcoat, melded unnoticed into the assemblage of the privileged and influential.

Stoney answered his knock with a smile, "Ahoy, mate! Welcome aboard!"

"I see you're in fine form."

"Never too early to begin the party."

"Well, we've got some things to discuss."

"Listen, I'm sorry about your load. Bloody shame, that is."

"If the merchandise had been properly packaged, we wouldn't be having this conversation."

"I didn't promise that it would be waterproof."

"Well, we're going to hire a professional plant to process the next batch and it damned well better be sprayed for mold and sealed."

"Want a drink?" asked Stoney wandering over to the bar to pour Scotch into two crystal tumblers. "I'm assuming you've got my money?"

"You got half up front, that's more than enough to cover your ass. You don't need to be making a profit, at my expense, because your people fucked up."

"Hey, now, deal's a deal."

"Here's the deal. We're going to run this again, except this time I'm going to be on top of the final packing. I already ate my investment plus the boat, that's about all I can stomach. You want in or not? We can both walk away right now, if that's what you want, that deal's done."

Stoney stared for a long moment, then took a tiny sip of his drink, "Fine. You put half up-front and I'll run it any way you want."

"I'll put half up, when the product is properly packaged and sealed and we're both satisfied that it's ready to leave harbor."

"Why should I mess around with you when I can ship tons to the Continent with less hassle?"

"Because we represent the biggest and most organized distribution network in the States and you want in."

"Fine, then, we'll give it one more go but it's a ten-ton minimum. When do you want it here?"

"I need one shipment in February and a second in May."

"Do you have a decent craft this time?"

Augie grinned, "My good buddy, Bing Watt, and I have come to an agreement. He'll have the ship ready when we are."

"I'll set it up," said Stoney extending his hand. "You drive a hard bargain, mate. I hope you have major plans for us tonight."

"Actually, I don't."

"Did Bangkok take you over the edge?"

"Close. It's just that I'm getting married."

Stoney roared, "You're not! The original Neanderthal heartthrob is cashing in his freedom? She must be one delectable damsel."

"I'll send you an invitation to the reception."

"Hell, I should be your best man. I've got tons of awful stories about you, mate."

"That's why you're not. It'll probably be in May or June."

"Just in time to pick up my money."

"That could be arranged."

"So, you're going to leave me to my own devices?"

"Sorry, but I'm pretty sure they don't have what you're looking for in room service."

"Oh, you'd be surprised what you can order up just by picking up a telephone."

"I don't even want to know."

"Fine, then, but I, at least, brought you a peace offering."

"What's that?"

Stoney reached into the pocket of his fine wool jacket and withdrew a four-inch glass vile filed with pale brown powder, "Bit of the monkey, mate. Be careful, it's pure, just as likely to kill you, as take you where you want to go."

"I'll be careful," said Augie, accepting the bottle. "I'll be in Bangkok the first week in January. You have your shit together and we'll do some business."

"I look forward to being a better host than you've been this evening."

Augie smirked, "We only get one screw-up. Let's get this right."

"Right, then. I'll see you the first of the year," said Stoney, following Augie to the door.

He turned back into the room, a Beretta nestled in his belt at the small of his back, "You're damned lucky I didn't take it out of your hide, mate. Next time, we'll be on my turf."

Bernie and Ruck settled onto the sofa near the fire, which barely warmed the flat gray light glaring through the windows. Augie passed out beers and sat gingerly on a huge leather beanbag.

"You don't look so well," said Ruck. "You got anything contagious?"

"Naw, I got a dose."

"A dose of what?" laughed Bernie.

"The clap, asshole."

"I sure hope you didn't give it to or get it from the future Mrs. LaGuerre," said Ruck.

"No, but I went down to the clinic and got a great big hypo

of antibiotics to clear it up before she shows up for Christmas with the family."

"So you haven't quite left the field, eh?" smirked Ruck.

"Hey, just doing a lady a favor," snapped Augie.

"No shit!" yelled Bernie. "It was Abby!"

"How do you know?"

"It's just so obvious."

"Shit!" said Augie. "You guys keep this to yourselves."

"Fat chance!" laughed Ruck.

"Yeah, I own a bar, remember? That's like having a built in telegraph office. Everyone knows everything about everyone."

"I hear you've got a mutual friend working for you," said Augie.

"See, I told you it was her," smirked Bernie. "Besides, I'm just doin' an old friend a favor."

Augie blushed, "Can we get down to business?"

"Hell no, this is way more fun," said Ruck. "Did you see that three astronauts in Apollo Eight are taking off to circle the moon?"

"Yeah, that's far out, if you'll excuse a bad pun. I've always wanted to do that," said Bernie.

"You could'a, man, you had the smarts and the grades," said Ruck.

"I'm just glad we're doin' what we're doin' right now."

"Listen, I met with Stoney last night and we're going to run a load to arrive in February and another getting here in May," said Augie.

"Did he go for eating half the loss?"

"I didn't offer any money and he agreed to another shipment."

"I'd trust that motherfucker about as far as I could throw him."

"He's kinda skinny, so that's probably farther than you could trust him."

"So, how do we prevent another catastrophe?" asked Bernie.

"First, we're going to oversee the packaging. Sidney found a company that double seals the product in plastic, then applies a foil wrapper that's treated with a chemical to prevent mold."

"Is that shit going to affect the weed?" asked Ruck.

"No, because the first layer is an airtight seal," said Augie.

"Okay, so we've got it packaged. What about a boat and loading and getting the fuck out of Dodge, before your buddy double-crosses us?"

"Our boat builder has another, larger vessel that he's preparing at a seriously reduced cost."

"You're going to trust that bastard?" asked Bernie.

"In the East, face is more important than profits. Bing Watt prides himself on the quality of the work performed in his yard and he was deeply apologetic. He took complete responsibility, in spite of the fact that we both know there was no way he could predict that the seal was gonna blow, without dismantling the whole drive system. He also realizes that word of their screw-up will probably get back to Sidney's ol' man, who has lots of ships that need servicing."

"I agree. I checked everything before we bought her," said Ruck, "but you still haven't mentioned how we're going to outsmart Stoney."

"Still working on that but I'm hoping that he likes profits more than revenge."

"I wouldn't put a whole lotta trust in that theory, myself," said Bernie. "The guy's got his own people, who have guns and no reason not to use them. A bunch of drug-dealing hippies disappearing in the jungle isn't going to raise a blip on anyone's radar."

"It's a chess game and this is all about strategy," said Augie. "We'll just kidnap Stoney and take him with us, until we're out in international waters."

"And how are you going to pull that off?"

Augie grinned, holding up the vial of beige heroin, "I know his weakness."

Chapter 11

It was the LaGuerre tradition to gather in the parlor before a roaring fire, after midnight mass at the chapel, to drink a glass of champagne and open one present. Julius raised his flute in a toast, "I am thankful that all our children are here with us tonight, to celebrate this sacred day together."

"I'm sorry that Sophia can't be with us," said his wife, Maria, "but I look forward to welcoming her in a few days."

Augie grinned, "She wanted to spend Christmas with her family, because she doesn't get together with all five brothers very often, but you'll like her, she's special."

His mother smiled, "I already appreciate her devotion to family."

Mary walked over and grasped Tony's elbow, "I'm so glad you could be home for the holidays."

"I am too," said Tony, "but it was awfully hard leaving the family in Sicily. They made me feel like I belonged."

"You are the future of the family," roared Julius. "That's the whole point of your journey, to understand your heritage and the pride of being a LaGuerre."

"I'm glad I went and I'm looking forward to going back for a while. Your cousins are wise old men."

"Maybe, someday, you will be too," replied his father with a knowing smile.

Tony walked over to Augie, "Hey, before you cut out of here, I've got something for you."

"Yeah, like what?"

"Better explained when we're alone."

Augie pursed his lips, "I can wait."

Maria beamed, as she handed small boxes to each of her daughters, "It's time for gifts. Natalie, Julia, and Mary please open these."

The girls took the tiny silver packages with perfect golden bows and curtsied, "Thank you, Mama."

Natalie, the youngest, carefully slipped the ribbon from the box and lifted the lid, "Oh, Mama!" She extracted a diamond-encrusted crucifix suspended from a most delicate gold chain. "That's beautiful."

The other girls found identical necklaces.

Maria smiled, "They came directly from the Vatican, blessed by the Pope himself."

"Oh, they're lovely," said Mary, hugging her mother. 'We'll cherish them always. Thank you."

Maria presented the boys with embossed leather Bibles and her husband a book, 'A History of the Peoples of Sicily'.

He gave her a large Alexandrite, mounted on a sculpted gold ring, laughing, "It's a magical stone that changes color with the light and I'm hoping it will help predict whether your mood is cloudy or fair!"

Maria laughed, "After almost thirty years, you ought to be able to read me like a book."

After presents and warm cups of espresso, Tony followed Augie out to the car and presented a tiny package wrapped in gold foil.

"What's this?"

"Just something I picked up in Amsterdam on the way back."

Augie slipped the ribbon and tore the paper to reveal a small wooden box with flowers inlaid across the top in tiny pieces of colored glass, "That's beautiful. So, what's in it?"

He opened the hinged top to find a large wedge of chocolate hash and a small piece of blue blotter paper covered with little owls.

"It's primo, from a temple ball, which is said to be the hash-maker's hash. You'll approve." Tony smiled, "The blotter is ten hits of pure Owsley acid. Half a hit is more than enough. Thought you might enjoy the best of the best."

"Gee, thanks. That's really thoughtful of you."

"You always take care of me, it's the least I could do."

"How'd you get it home?"

Tony smirked, "I took my suitcase apart and stuffed the blotter in the lining and the temple balls in the bottom of a shaving cream can. No one even looked in customs."

"You are a dear sweet dumb son of a bitch, you know that?"

"Why?"

"Because, you're not a mule carrying this shit across borders. That's how you get busted and sent away forever. You've already got one close call under your belt. Don't go lookin' for a second, because I won't be able to help you."

"Ah, man, I just brought in a little hash and one sheet of blotter."

"They don't care whether it's a gram or a pound. You're guilty either way."

Tony hung his head, "I was just trying to do something nice for you."

"Yeah, I appreciate that, but having you free means even more to me, so how 'bout you don't do this again? You got lucky. You won't be so lucky the next time."

"Fine," said Tony, striding up the steps and into the house.

The air was cold but the sun was high in the east, as the Mercedes cruised down the New Jersey Turnpike to the property. Augie turned to Sophia, "I hope my family didn't freak you out?"

"There're sweet people and good parents."

"First impressions can be so completely wrong."

"Hey, there's the person we let other people see and there's the other identity that we keep to ourselves. I see past your father's bravado to a man who adores his children. That's good enough for me."

"I know you're right but being his eldest has not been easy for either of us."

"So what'd you expect, that he'd go easy on you? I'm absolutely positive you were a handful and he's tasked with trying to make sure that you become the best person you can be."

"Maybe so."

"No maybe. I bet you're hung up trying to top his achievements."

"Better than being jealous of his wife," laughed Augie. "I'm not Oedipus."

"He's obviously been through a tough life and paid his dues and you're the young buck, who thinks he can do better."

"I'm getting' there."

"No, you're just beginning. You've still got a lot to learn," smiled the beautiful blond.

Augie paused, "I've tried to do better in a couple of ways, like running a business on a handshake, where both parties can rely on the other. In his day, you cooperated or you ended up in the East River."

"Okay, but don't take anything away from him. He did what he had to do to provide for his family."

"That's why I want to get past this part and create something that can grow into a legitimate thriving entity. A business that will provide for our future."

"So, you're thinking about getting out?"

He grinned, "Someday. Let's just say that's the goal."

"And in the meantime?"

"I'll know when we have enough to be secure, no matter

what."

"I hope you'll let me know."

"You'll be the first and maybe the only."

She slipped her hand under his arm and leaned close, "Is this really happening?"

"I think it is. Are you sure you're ready?"

"As long as we're together."

~

The phone jangled and Augie tried to focus on the clock, "Fuck, two-thirty?" He picked up the receiver, "Hello."

"Augie, it's Bernie."

"What the fuck do you want at this hour?"

"My little red Porsche got stolen. I only left it for a minute to grab some smokes."

"You dumbshit. Where'd this happen?"

"I was just off the Bruchner at A-Hundred-Forty-Ninth heading to Pelham to see Shelley MacNamara, that redhead from school."

"Fuck, you must be hard up."

"No, man, you should see her, she grew up beautiful."

"D'you call the cops?"

"Yeah, I would've called you earlier but I've been answering questions and fillin' out forms for hours. They pretty much told me that it'll be chopped up into parts and shipped out of the country by tomorrow."

"Lemme make some calls and see what I can do."

Bernie stammered, "Really? You think there's a chance to get it back?"

"I'm not promising anything but I'll let you know what I find out when we get together tomorrow."

"Thanks for tryin'."

~

Bernie started inquiring before Augie opened the door, "So, what'd you find out about my car?"

"Nice to see you too, asshole. C'mon in." He sauntered down the hall to the great room at the back.

"So?"

"So, it's sitting in the warehouse in the Bronx."

"Really?"

"Really."

"How'd you do that?"

"Actually, it was fairly simple. I got hold of Jesus and offered him a grand, if he could get it back in one piece. He's got more connections than the families, so you owe the kid bigtime."

"I can't believe it," said Bernie. "Thank you!"

"Don't thank me, thank him," said Augie. "Like I said, it's a shark that can never rest."

"And, I'll never park it on the street again, period!"

"Amen to that," said Ruck, clapping him on the back. "Think the Jets can beat Baltimore in the Super Bowl?"

"The AFC is the future, man," said Bernie. "The Colts are a bunch of tired old men."

"I'll put a hundred on Namath," smirked Augie. "He actually believes they're gonna win."

"Guess we'll see," said Bernie.

"Speaking of nothing, can you believe they're really going swear in Tricky Dick as president in a couple of weeks?" asked Ruck.

"He's gonna turn out to be worse than Johnson," said Bernie.

"Is that really possible?" asked Augie. "I mean the guy's gonna be good for business."

"And bad for our business. No fucking doubt, he hates hippies, after all the hubbub during the campaign. He might figure out how to get us out of Vietnam but the War on Drugs is just beginning."

"I know you're right," said Augie. "We'd better start watching things a little more closely."

"Like our backs," laughed Ruck.

"So, we're outta here tomorrow," said Augie. "Is everything else wrapped up?"

"Next loads aren't due until the beginning of February," said Ruck, "Two from Jamaica, another from Columbia, and five-thousand kilos of hash from Fasal, plus another ten on this deal."

"That's a lot of product coming through all at once," said Bernie. "Any way we could space it out a little bit, even one every ten days or two weeks is pushing things pretty hard."

"Let's line up four cars on the west coast, four here, and a couple in Lauderdale." suggested Augie. "We can cover everything from New England through the Midwest with what comes through the city. We'll pull the first load of Jamaican in through Port St. Lucie, delivered directly to that market, same with the Columbian in Monterey."

"That should keep everyone happy," said Bernie. "Just so it's not all at once."

"I'll make some calls to smooth things out," said Ruck.

"Good thinkin'!"

Stoney leaned over to Augie, "Too bad you didn't bring my favorite Chinese classmate along for this episode of the adventure."

"She doesn't need to be a part of this."

"Yeah, you've got a point, mate, but she's easy on the eyes and way smarter than either of us."

"She's way beyond our pay scale," laughed Augie, as the metal door rattled open and a large truck backed in to the dock at a non-descript concrete building in an industrial block in Bang

Lamung, just up the coast from Pattaya.

Two muscular Thai workers opened the truck from the inside and started tossing bales onto a waiting forklift. Augie grabbed one at random and Stoney produced a stiletto to slice the binding, "You're going to like this load, mate."

Augie reached in and pulled out a handful of manicured bud, with few sticks and almost no seeds. He sniffed his fingers, sticky with fragrant resin, a slight minty scent without the slightest hint of mold. "Nicely done!"

"I thought you'd approve," smiled Stoney, signaling the driver to haul the first load to the hopper.

The workers dumped each bale through a vibrating shoot onto a conveyor that coursed a ribbon of evergreen buds to a scale, culling precise two-kilo lots, which disappeared inside and reappeared compressed into bricks heat-sealed in plastic. The blocks moved on to a second wrapping machine, and a third, which sprayed each brick with a fungicide, then bound them in heavy aluminum foil and secured the seams with metallic tape.

Bernie appeared at the bottom of the immense machine with a bucket of water and grabbed one of the shiny slabs off the conveyor, "Let's see how waterproof these are." He submerged it entirely, then looked up and smiled, "No bubbles!"

"Cool, it works," said Ruck.

"We'll run the hash next, so we should have the full load finished in a couple of hours," said Stoney. "We can deliver it to your ship this afternoon. I assume you'll have payment."

"It's on the boat," said Augie with that little grin, "and I've got a little surprise for you, to pay you back for the lovely gift you gave me in New York."

"And what would that be?"

"Oh, that'd spoil the surprise, now wouldn't it? But, I promise you'll enjoy every minute."

"I guess I can't argue with that," said Stoney.

The Rolls Royce arrived at the shipyard, just ahead of the truck, and pulled to a stop next to rusting hulk named the Albatross, "I wish you'd picked a better moniker for this tub. That's almost bad luck, bad taste at any rate."

"Looks can be deceiving," smiled Ruck.

The driver and Stoney's bodyguard opened the side doors and followed the four men up the gangway to the deck of the ship, then down a stairwell to the bay, which was already crammed with wooden crates marked 'Chui Antiques'.

Bing Watt installed a new sub-floor, sealed from the bilge, and boxed-in structural members along the inside of the hull that would be welded shut, once filled with aluminum bricks. Stoney whistled, "Okay, I'm impressed. Your guy's done a bang up job."

"I think this'll work," said Augie. "You could fucking sink this old girl and they'd still be watertight.

"Our guys can pack this up," said Stoney. "Where's my money and my prize?"

"Tell you what, why don't we all pitch in and make quick work of this and then we'll celebrate?"

"Fine, it shouldn't take long," said Stoney, as the first palette of silver ingots dropped through the hatch.

An hour later, Bing Watt's welders sealed the last cover and Augie whispered to Stoney, "You might not want your cronies to see what I've got for you."

"How do you mean?"

"There are some family secrets we don't share with the help."

Stoney stared inquisitively for a moment, then motioned for the driver, bodyguard, and workers to go topside, "Show me what you've got."

Ruck and Bernie followed Montgomery's men up the ladder.

Augie wandered into the forward cabins, where a pretty Thai woman offered glasses of cold Dom Perignon and slender lines of heroin. Augie toasted and produced a heavy briefcase, "It's all here, every penny, as a friend of mine likes to say."

"I believe you but we both knew this wouldn't end well, unless you soothed my anxieties with loads of cash." Stoney sat down to take a tiny hit of the pale brown powder, sputtering, "Still the best in the world."

Augie smiled, "Sharing a mutual profit, that can grow into an ongoing enterprise that will benefit both of us, is far preferable to playing games and getting people killed over money."

"It could have gotten a tad intense, there for a minute, five on five didn't give you good odds."

"You didn't notice the dozen rifles covering every move we made?"

Stoney roared, "I wouldn't put it past you, mate, but I never saw them and my guys were watching."

"Point is, we're gonna make a lot of money for each other, if we get this right, so let's not let a few not-unexpected wrinkles get in the way of making things profitable both ways."

"I'll drink to that."

"Good," said Augie, offering a hand. "C'mon, the best is yet to come."

He led a stoned Stoney forward to the master cabin, which was decorated in swags and drapes of deep red velvet. Subdued lighting focused on a spacious round bed covered with a dozen little brown boys, naked save tiny ampoules of brown powder dangling from silver chains around their necks.

They fluttered across the cabin to surround Stoney, like a flurry of anxious guppies waiting to be fed. He gasped, "Is this heaven?"

"It will be for about an hour," said Augie, as Ruck appeared and nodded.

A rumble of engines rattled through the bones of the freighter and the ship began to move, "Where the fuck are you taking me?" cried Stoney.

"We're just going for a little ride to international waters. By then, you'll have satiated your weird desires and I'll personally deliver you and these youngsters back safe and sound, so I can fly out tonight. I promise."

"Why should I believe you?"

"Because, I'm the guy who believes in making sure every partner is satisfied with the outcome of every deal, including this one. You're the one with the Beretta crammed in the back of your belt." He held out his hand, "Why don't you give that to me for the moment, so none of these boys gets hurt."

"What about my driver and bodyguard?" said Stoney, handing over the pistol, grip first with his left hand and caressing the young bodies clustered around him like a writhing skirt with his right.

"They'll probably sleep it off by the time you get back. There's plenty of Dom on the sideboard. Have fun," laughed Augie, closing the door.

Ruck followed him along the corridor, "Are those kids going to be okay?"

"Yeah," replied Augie. "First, because they're pro's. I hired them through Kylee, an acquaintance of Stoney's, who understands his weirdness. And, second, because there are too many for him to harm any one."

Chapter 12

Taylor parked the Ghia in a tiny lot behind Badger House on Langdon, late for a production class, and charged down the hill towards campus. She wrapped a heavy wool scarf around her neck against a wicked wind off Lake Mendota, as she hurried past the Union, but Park was jammed with police cars and crowds of raucous protesters covered Bascom Hill.

She marched through the cordon and found a classmate, Milly Shriver, at the edge of a swarm of students waving placards and banners about student rights and Black Power. "What's happening?"

Little Milly's coal black eyes lit up, "It's a student strike, protesting the University's lack of a Black Studies program and their racist admissions policies, and it's organized by the Black People's Alliance. Do you realize that less than one percent of the student population is black and an even smaller portion of faculty members?"

"No, but now that you mention it. We are a very white campus."

"We probably have more Middle Eastern students than Black American students. It's like a huge portion of our culture, world culture for that matter, is being systematically ignored and they want a program to define who they are and where they came from and why things are the way they are."

"Can't help but sympathize with that," said Taylor. "So what are they doing?"

"Shutting down the university," said Milly, with a triumphant smile. Heiress to the New York Shriver's, who owned enormous holdings, here, she was just another little Jewish hippie-chick in tattered bell-bottoms majoring in film production.

"Really?"

"Yeah, they've occupied Van Hise and they've blocked the entrances to Bascom Hall and the Social Sciences building. If we want to go to class, we have to cross the picket line."

"Damn, I've got work to do."

"I don't think it's gonna happen today and maybe not tomorrow or the next day."

"Are you kidding?"

"No, they're trying to shut down the whole university. Word has it that the governor has called up the National Guard."

"Again? Shit, bunch of rednecks playing soldier on weekends."

"Hey, they're just trying to stay out of Vietnam, like the rest of these guys, but, at the same time, they're scared kids with guns and some innocent student's gonna get killed in the process."

"I'm bettin' Professor Shapiro isn't going to cross the line. Maybe we should go check the Union and see if he's sipping coffee in his usual corner in the Rathskeller?"

"Yeah, I'm for that."

They trooped down the steps into a curious Germanic subterranean vault with solid square columns supporting sweeping arches that amplify a whisper into an echo, if one stands in just the right spot. The walls and ceiling were decorated with murals celebrating student life, at the turn of the century, and the benefits of beer and wine. The girls pushed through noisy crowds, effervescing with rumors, to the service line for coffee, then under the 'Rathskeller' sign suspended from the grand archway to find the Professor tucked away in a corner surrounded by a dozen students.

"Ah, now we have a quorum!" laughed Andy Shapiro, as Taylor and Milly pulled up a couple of chairs. "We've all agreed that the entire student body needs to stand together, so it looks like we'll be missing class for a few days."

"We're already behind on our project," sighed Taylor.

"I'll see to it that no one is penalized for honoring the picket line," said Andy, sipping the last drops of coffee from his cup. "On the other hand, I would also be inclined to credit those who take the initiative to make something inspiring out of this situation."

Taylor looked inquiringly, "How?"

"Well, it certainly qualifies as a momentous event in the history of the university and it should be documented, so everyone understands the real story, when all is said and done."

Milly's eyes sparkled with mischief, "And we have access to all the equipment we might need – cameras, film, darkrooms. It could be a multimedia project with film, photos, recordings, interviews, written descriptions and background. This could be amazing!"

"This could be a very powerful project," smiled the Professor.

"So, we have your permission?" asked Taylor.

"I'm afraid there's no way for me to know what's going on in the studios, if I can't cross the picket line, now is there?"

The dozen students cheered and headed up the stairs.

Milly walked up to the chalkboard and reached tippy-toe to begin a list, "Here are the first things we ought to get covered and feel free to add your suggestions, okay?"

The group gathered around.

"Okay, first we need interviews with the folks who started this whole thing. They've taken over Van Hise, so we need a photographer, a film crew, and a couple of good writers to head over there and get the background and find out what they're planning."

"I've got the photos covered," said Joe, "and you oughta

send Hank and Melinda to do the interviews."

"Cool."

"Next, we need a film crew to start building a library of images – crowds, occupied buildings, cops, protest signs, and confrontations...but we need some normal stuff too." She turned around, "This whole thing is going on in the middle of a city that is relatively unaffected by the disruption, so far...so, maybe get a little bit of the 'I didn't even know that was going on' end of it too."

"Yeah, great," said Sebastian Meyers, "We'll form two teams of cameras and sound but I want Jerry shooting stills to compliment what we're doing. He can cover five times the action we can."

"Done."

"So what are you girls going to do?" asked Sally, plugging in battery packs.

"Someone's got to coordinate, so I guess I'm it," said Milly. "When you get what you need, check in here and we'll figure out where to go next. Call, if you run across something that everyone else needs to know."

The phone rang and Milly picked it up, "Production."

"Milly?" inquired Professor Shapiro. "I'm pleased that you made it inside. You might want to tell the crew that they're planning a giant march on the Capitol tomorrow."

"I'll be sure we're well prepared," said the little New Yorker.

"Rumor has it that there'll be nine-hundred National Guard troops on the streets by morning."

"Shit. That's trouble. This whole thing gets heavier by the minute!"

"I'll call you back, if I hear anything new," said the Professor.

She turned to Taylor, "Shit's gonna hit the fan tomorrow. Big march on the Capitol to be escorted by nine-hundred National Guard guys."

"Holy Shit!" said Taylor. "We're going to need to leapfrog

crews up State Street and we ought to find the best vantage points today."

"Good thinkin'," said Milly. "Guess you just found your job for the afternoon. Get out of here and lemme know what you find."

"Great, I'll check back with you later," said Taylor, grabbing her bag.

The initial protest of twelve hundred swelled to thousands as curious and sympathetic students packed Bascom Hill in support. Chants went up, "Black Studies Now!" and placards bounced up and down demanding the downfall of the administration and the university. The strike leaders were giving impassioned speeches outside Van Hise but this crowd had no idea of who was running the protest or the real cause they were supporting.

Taylor could feel the edgy energy of anarchy ready to turn on the cops or people crossing the picket lines or anyone else who might be handy. "This could get out of hand in a hurry," she thought, as her block heels clomped down the steps and past a cordon of police in riot gear.

She pulled the little Ghia into the drive at the lake house and unlocked the back door to dump her bag and coat on the table. She picked up the phone and dialed, waiting impatiently until Bernie's groggy voice finally answered. "Bernie, it's Taylor."

"Hey, Cuz, how'ya doin'?"

"Are you super hung over or what?"

"Hey, I run a bar, remember, and sometimes I actually have to show up. The boss has to mix with the patrons and all that "

"When you're not running all over the world."

"Yeah, in between. So what's cookin'?"

"Don't know whether you've seen the news but a bunch of black students are shutting down the university and there's gonna be trouble tomorrow."

"What with guns or what?"

"No, they're just demanding a Black Studies program, so

they've occupied three buildings, so far, and there's lots of support from the rest of the student body."

"Well, fuck yeah, time off from classes. That's a no-brainer."

"I actually need to get some things finished but I can't, so I'm frustrated."

"You are one ambitious bitch, you know that? Why don't you take a few days off to learn how things work on the street? That's more valuable than a degree in business."

"Yeah, my production class is trying to cover this whole thing with film, photos, sound, interviews, and whatever else fits. Prof wants us to make a film when it's all done."

"There you go," laughed Bernie. "Now you've got a productive purpose."

"Yeah, but there's a problem."

"What's that?"

"Victor's supposed to roll in here tomorrow and I've got a bad feeling that it might be dicey at best. With thousands of protesters, nine-hundred National Guard, and who knows how many cops from everywhere, this could turn into big trouble real quick."

"I think, the last time, you told me it was a police riot, maybe that was a warm-up for this time, if the wrong folk get out front on this."

"You see my point," said Taylor. "Is there anyway to catch him before it's too late."

"I'll get on the horn and see what I can do."

"Thanks. We don't need our shit mixed up in all of this chaos."

"I'll call you back tonight."

"Great. I think I've got plenty to do this afternoon."

~

A faint glow of the sun flared through fast-moving clouds casting long, rippling shadows across a writhing swarm of protesters on Bascom Hill, as Taylor slipped through the service entrance into the production studios. The ranting voice of a passionate speaker, at a makeshift podium on the steps of the Education Building, echoed across the Mall, rousing cheers from the crowd.

Milly looked up from a journal, as Taylor appeared, "How's it goin'?"

"I think I've found good perches for our folks but I noticed a couple of Army Jeeps scouting State Street and I'm bettin' they're going to put guns on top of the buildings."

"Shit, that's like shooting rats in a barrel."

"What do you know about shooting rats in a barrel? Doesn't sound like city sport to me."

Milly laughed, "New York has the biggest, nastiest fucking rats you've ever seen. I used to hunt 'em in the basements of my father's buildings with a twenty-two until someone called the cops."

"Really?"

"Yeah, best part was, when I picked off three in a row, the cops patted me on the head and told me to keep up the good work. Just don't shoot any two legged rats or there'd be trouble."

"You are amazing."

"So, what'd you find?"

"I walked the whole route twice, up and back, and the best options are to start with two film crews at the rally on the Library Mall, then the first trucks along Langdon and up the fire escape to Paul and Davis' apartment above the Pub for a bird's eye view on the beginning of the march, while the second moves to Gorham, where there's a little porch about five steps up on the corner. Then, the first crew jumps to the six-way intersection at Johnson and Henry, before everyone finally ends up on the Capitol steps."

"It would be great to have our guys on the roofs but the cops probably wouldn't appreciate it."

"Kinda what I was thinking," said Taylor.

"Okay, that get's 'em there, what about coming back or if there's a riot with people scattering everywhere."

"Then it's game on," said the tall blond. "You've gotta figure that, if things get out of hand and the march can't make it to the Capitol, the kids are going to congeal around the Mall, so let's have the film crews follow the biggest crowd and the still shooters cut over to Langdon and down University, in case there are some side shows."

"Good."

~

The phone in the kitchen startled Taylor and she ran from the parlor to grab it. "Hello?"

"Taylor, it's Victor."

"Boy, am I glad you called. We're fixin' to have a giant protest tomorrow and probably a riot to go with it."

"Sounds like fun."

"I think this might not be the perfect opportunity."

"Well, I'm kinda stuck on my schedule. I've gotta be someplace else by tomorrow night. Isn't there a back way into town where I could avoid the crazies?"

Taylor gnawed on her knuckle, "Yeah, there is. What time are you coming in?"

"I can be there by mid-morning, assuming the weather holds and the cops don't shut down the freeways."

"I'll meet you at the airport at nine and we'll figure it out from there. I've got to be on campus by eleven."

"I'll meet you at the main entrance."

~

Taylor punched the button for the student station on the radio and Rick's mellow tenor filled the little car, as the Ghia motored up Sherman towards the airport. "Looks like we're going to have a major march up State Street from the Mall to the Capitol steps at high noon under cold, cloudy skies. If you haven't been out and about this morning, almost a thousand National Guard troops moved into town overnight and they're stationed at every major cross street from the campus to the capitol."

"Our brothers are stressing that, and I quote, 'this is a peaceful strike against the administration and clashes with the police or the troops will prove counter-productive to attaining the goals of the campaign…instigating progress in racial empathy and open dialogue'. I was taken with Jesse Jamison's last line, 'The only way two people can empathize with each other is for each to really listen, to silence their internal rhetoric and overcome their prejudices, so they can actually hear what the other is truly expressing. Through centuries of brutal enslavement, our voice has been silenced but, now…Now, we're speaking with the thunder of a thousand voices and we'll keep on striking and rallying and marching, until we see some indication that the administration is listening'."

"They need your support, so get out there and join the march!" His voice settled, "If you're lookin' for trouble, how 'bout waiting until this rally is finished. This is about winning friends and influencing powerful people to support a righteous quest Make some noise, let 'em know we all stand behind the Black Studies strike!"

Taylor noticed several police cars blocking the road into town, as she turned north on Fordham, "This can't be a good sign."

She parked the Ghia in the parking lot and marched to the main entrance just as a long black Cadillac pulled to a stop. Taylor walked around and climbed into the passenger seat. "Did you have any problems getting here?"

"No, drove right through."

"Well, Highway Patrol's got road blocks all over the place.

There's one between here and the house."

"Can we drive around it?"

"I'm sure they've got all of the streets sealed up."

"Then, let's fake our way through. You said Highway Patrol right?" grinned Victor, as he reached into the glove box to retrieve a rumpled ball cap with a rebel flag. He brushed his greasy hair back and pulled the brim of the hat down to his eyebrows. He spun the tuner on the radio to Tammy Wynette singing, 'Take Me to Your World,' on a country station. The Cadillac eased out of the parking lot and he reached to drag Taylor closer, "You wearin' a bra?"

"Yeah."

"Take it off and unbutton your jacket so they can gawk at those gorgeous tits. I'm just a jughead from the East Coast out to see my honey for a few days. Okay?"

She removed her bra, snuggled close, and pulled her sweater tight, "You've got some balls, guy."

He just smiled and maintained the speed limit across Commercial to the blockade at Sherman. They were third in line and he leaned over to snuggle with Taylor, "Might as well make it look good."

A cop banged on the hood, "Hey, you two, break it up! Keep movin'!"

Victor rolled down the window, "What's happenin', Officer?"

"We're just checkin' to see who's heading towards campus, got a big protest going on and we don't need troublemakers sneaking in here to stir things up."

"Who's protesting what?"

"Bunch of niggers demanding a Black Studies program at the university, so, all the hippies are marching around town raising a ruckus."

"What do they study in a Black Studies program?" laughed Victor, lifting his cap to smooth his hair. He tickled Taylor, "I don't see there's much to study, myself."

"I'm with you," said the policeman, leaning into the window to inspect Taylor's tits. "Now where are you two kids headed?"

"Well," said Taylor, feigning a slight southern drawl and looking up at Victor adoringly, "we're going to a little house just down the road a piece and I don't think this guy's gonna have any time or energy to mess around with a bunch of protesters."

The cop took one last obvious glance at her pert nipples under the taut sweater and shook his head. "Tell me, what's a young guy like you doing driving a big ol' hog like this?"

"It's my daddy's," smiled Victor. "I've got a Mustang back in Brooklyn but he makes me drive this beast when I'm on the road. He claims it's safer."

"He's got a point," said the cop, leaning on a fender. "Whatcha got under the hood?"

"Four seventy-two," said Victor.

"Bet she goes."

"Yeah, it takes her a couple of strokes to get up to speed but then it's smooth sailin'."

The cop stared at him for a long moment, "Whatcha carryin'?"

"A suitcase and my sweetie, here."

"Let's open the trunk, if you don't mind."

Victor climbed out, "No problem, I don't mind at all."

He lifted the lid to reveal a single battered suitcase in the plush carpeted trunk. Victor laughed, "I didn't think I'd be needin' a whole bunch of clothes for the next few days, even if it is freezing out here."

The officer snorted and leaned to retrieve a green crumb from a seam in the gray carpeting. He inspected it for a moment, then tossed it on the ground, "Shame to have a single little pebble mar such a clean machine. Now, you be on your way and make sure you're nice to that young lady or I'm gonna come lookin' for ya'."

Victor laughed, "Actually, I'm planning to ask the big question."

"Well, good luck with that."

He got back into the car and slowly pulled away, checking the mirror. The cop reached down and picked up the tiny crumb of hash from the ground and looked at it again. Victor turned onto Sherman and sped away, "Shit, he found a little crumb of hash in the trunk."

Taylor turned around, "Doesn't look like they're following us."

"Let's get this done." He backed into the driveway and parked close to the kitchen door.

Taylor walked around to the front to collect the mail, expecting flashing lights and a herd of officers. The street was empty. She returned to unlock the door, "How much did we get this time?"

"I've got four hundred and eighty for you on this round, half and half."

"That'll keep us going for a couple of weeks."

"They want me out on the coast next week, so I'm guessin' you'll have something new to work with," said Victor, pressing through the door and down the stairs with three boxes.

Taylor carried another and loaded them into the lockers in the basement, "Thanks, sorry it was such a hassle."

"No problem," laughed Victor. "I enjoyed getting to maul you a little."

"I didn't mind a bit," smiled Taylor, kissing him on the cheek.

"Time to go."

"Sure you don't want to hang out until all the craziness is over?"

"Naw, I'd rather get out ahead of it, rather than getting stuck here, if the pigs go crazy."

"Which way you headed?"

"Gotta pass through Chicago."

"Tell you what, go the other way, when you pull outta here, and head across Thorton to East Washington, then north. That's One-Fifty-One and it'll hook you right into the highway. Just watch out for roadblocks. I'm sure they've got them set up all over the city."

"Yeah, let's hope they're looking for people coming in, not going out."

Taylor hugged him at the back door, "Just be careful."

"What about your car?"

"I'll take the bus and grab it."

He leaned over and kissed her on the forehead, "You watch your pretty ass out there."

"You too."

~

The black De Ville turned south on Sherman, as Victor exchanged the rebel cap for a dark green hat with a Jet's insignia, then left onto Thorton, winding along a frozen stream in Tenney Park. Dark shades of drab brown painted the grass and plantings under charcoal trees against a flat gray sky. *"I sure hope those kids don't get roughed up in a police riot. They're pushin' up against some big guns."*

He passed under Johnson and followed the curving road on to the junction at East Washington, where four Jeeps and more than a dozen National Guard troops blocked the intersection.

Two soldiers in full battle gear approached either side of the car as he pulled to a stop. He rolled down the window, "What's happenin'?"

The soldier leaned down, knocking his helmet askew as his head bumped the doorframe, "Where ya' going?"

"Chicago. Why? What's up?"

"Just checking to make sure radicals don't sneak into town

to turn a protest into a riot." The soldier backed away to inspect the car, "That's some machine you got there, what's it got under the hood?"

"Four seventy-two."

The soldier whistled, "What are you doin' driving this yacht?"

"It's my daddy's. I'm drivin' it home for him."

"So, tell me, where you comin' from?"

Victor smiled, clacking a wad of bubble gum, "Well, I picked her up from my ol' man in L.A. last week and he's gonna be pissed if I don't have it back in the City by the weekend."

"What're you doin' in Madison with all this marchin' going on?"

"Spending a few days with my woman. Hell, I didn't even know there was a protest goin' down, if you know what I mean?"

The soldier grinned. His partner said something over the car and he leaned down, "My buddy says you've got a low tire in back. We can help you fix it, man. We've got the gear and nothing to do but stop cars and question people."

Victor smiled, "Hey, your lieutenant'd probably get pissed. There's a station a few blocks up. I'll take care of it, thanks."

He started to pull away and the soldier trotted along, "Sure we can't help you out?"

"Naw, thanks anyway."

Victor eased forward and started to accelerate through the intersection when he heard a loud hiss from the right rear. "Damn it!"

He pulled over, parked, and hopped out.

The two soldiers appeared with a jack and a large tire wrench, "Man, I told ya'."

"Yeah," said Victor, leaning to rub his hands around the tread and, finally, removing a screw impaled under the white sidewall. "Here's the problem! I should have listened to you guys.

Sorry, I'm a dumbass."

"No problem," said the young soldier. "You got a spare?"

"Yeah, I'll get it." He turned to the other youngster with the jack, "There's a plate right under the frame over here, if that works for you?"

"Sure! Is it in park?"

"Yeah, I'll check and grab the spare." He walked to the driver's door and pressed the emergency brake. "We should be good."

Vic popped the trunk and carefully pulled the carpet back to retrieve the wheel without exposing the latches for the side panels. The first soldier walked over just as he pulled the tire from the well and flipped the mat into place. He bounced it a couple of times, "Seems like she's full. I checked it before I hit the road."

The kid grabbed the tire and walked around the side to place it on the axel. The jack hissed as the Caddie dropped to the ground and the kid brought the flat tire around.

Victor tossed it into the trunk and closed the lid, "Thanks, man. Next time I'll pay more attention to good advice."

"No problem" The soldier grinned, "I gotta say, you've got some serious shocks holdin' up the back end of this beast."

"Really?" replied the driver, leaning under the wheel well. "No shit! I'll have to ask the ol' man what that's about."

"You could carry an elephant in this thing and she'd still run straight and level."

"Sounds like you know a whole lot more about cars than I do. I check the fluids and tires, put gas in her, and go on down the highway."

"You probably want to get on down the road right now, before anyone else starts askin' questions, if you get my drift?"

Vic waved to the other soldier, "Thanks for your help, man. Stay out of trouble."

"You too," said the kid, as he dragged the jack back to the

truck.

The Caddie motored slowly for several blocks until he spied a Gulf station and pulled in. A young attendant in a brown uniform, with 'Bruce' on his nametag, bounded out to the pumps, "How can I help?"

Victor climbed out and opened the trunk, "Need to fill her up and I got a flat. Looks like I tore up the tire pretty good. Think you could replace her and balance everything out?"

The kid leaned over to grab the wheel, "Yeah, the sidewall's all torn up but the tread's in good shape. I'm pretty sure we've got these in stock. I'll top off the tank, then you can pull over in front of that bay and I'll get you fixed up?"

"Sure."

By the time he parked in front of the open bay door next to a fence, Bruce had the tattered tire off the rim and was installing a new one. He walked over to watch, "You're fast, kid."

"Ah, actually I'm kinda slow, compared to the rest of my family. We've been dirt track racers for generations and swapping out tires in a hurry is a contest."

"Do you drive?"

"Oh, yeah. My two brothers followed my father and his father before him. I just got my first win up in Oshkosh last week."

"Congratulations! That's far out!"

The boy bounced the tire over to the balancing machine and cranked it up. Before the wheel was up to speed, he whistled, "Man, I'm good. Only gonna need a couple of grams and she'll run straight and smooth."

"Cool. What do I owe you?"

"Twenty-four ninety-five plus five bucks to top off the tank."

"After all the work you put in?"

"Yeah, that's included."

Victor handed him two twenties. "Keep the change kid. I

enjoyed watching someone work, who actually knows what he's doin'."

"Why thanks," he said, grabbing a rolling jack. "I'll have you all set in a minute."

"Hey, is there a pay phone?"

"Yeah, right outside the front door."

Victor strolled around the corner, picked up the phone and dialed Taylor's number. It rang twice before the sirens of two police cars, running flat out with lights blazing, drowned out the tone. He returned the handset to the cradle and collected his dime, thinking, *"They're not friendlies."*

The attendant was leaning against the fender when he got back, "All set. I'll put the spare in the trunk, if you'll pop it."

"Cool. Just drop it in there for the time being and I'll take care of it when I stop."

Bruce grinned, "Someone's done some fine work on your ride, man. My compliments to your bodyman and mechanic."

A sense of car guys' camaraderie curled Victor's lips into a sly smile, "Hey, I'm heading for Chicago. Is there a back way to cut across to the highway"?

"Sure, take the next right and head southeast. You'll have to wiggle around a little bit through the neighborhoods, until you hit Eastwood Drive. Just follow it until you see the signs."

"Thanks a lot man, I appreciate your help." He pulled out the station and turned off East Washington to disappear into suburbia.

～

Taylor parked the little yellow car and raced down Langdon to the mall just as the last fiery speech implored the enormous crowd to march peacefully up State Street to the Capitol. A chant went up, "We shall overcome!"

She ran the half block along Lake Street to get ahead of the crowd, pulling a Nikkormat with a zoom lens from her bag. The strike leaders carried a wide banner imprinted with 'Equal Rights for all Students', followed by a sea of fluttering signs: 'Freedom Now!', 'Black Power', 'Expel the Administration!', 'Peace Now!'. The most inspired bore the inscription, 'Fighting for Peace is like Fucking for Chastity."

She leaned against the pharmacy wall and started shooting. The protesters were loud and boisterous but the vibes were different than the angry confrontations last fall, calmer, more festive. Taylor grinned, *"No wonder, time off from classes to join a big party for a good cause. Who could ask for more?"*

Sebastian and Sally raced up the sidewalk to find their next perch and she fell in behind them, as they past under Milton and Robin, who were hanging out of a window above the Pub. "D'you get anything good?"

"Yeah, good speeches and the beginning of the march," panted Sebastian.

Sally added, "Nice clean audio too."

They slowed as they approached a squad of troops in defensive lines, with bayonets mounted and teargas canisters at the ready, blocking State Street at Gorham. "Holy shit! This is trouble waitin' to happen."

"We've gotta shoot this, then get behind them to catch the crowd," said Sebastian, spreading the legs of the tripod to focus on the fear in the faces of the volunteers.

Taylor knelt to exaggerate the size and length of the column then darted out into the middle of the street to shoot a long shot silhouetting a barrier of helmets and bayonets against a sea of marchers approaching a block away. She checked her depth of field and focused carefully, firing three shots before a lieutenant shoved her towards the sidewalk. He loosened his respirator and snarled, "Stay out of the way, girlie, or we'll kick your sweet ass just like the rest of these commie punks!"

She yelled, "Fascist pig!" and shot four frames of his angry face – click – yelling – click – drawing his baton over his head – click – the grimace, as the baton crashed into her temple - click. Taylor crumpled to the ground, just as the jeering protesters stopped within inches of a double line of blades backed by edgy recruits.

Sally struggled to haul her up next to the building, when two med-students picked her up and dragged the limp body up Gorham and around the corner to safety in the Plaza. Jackson, the tall blond medic yelled, "Hey, we've got someone hurt. Can you help?"

The barmaid grabbed some cushions and fashioned a pad on the floor and brought a washcloth to wipe the blood from Taylor's cheek. "That looks bad, we should call an ambulance."

"I agree."

Taylor murmured and struggled to sit up, "No, I'll be okay in a minute."

Henny, the rusty-haired Irish med-student, gently pushed her shoulder, "No, you stay down. You've probably got a concussion."

She took an icy cloth, offering by the waitress, and pressed it against her head, "Shit, did you get my camera? I've got some great shots on that film."

"This camera?" asked the blond guy, holding up the remnants of the Nikkormat. The lens was mangled but the body appeared intact. "Your film's probably okay but I'm thinkin' today's assignment is shot, if you'll excuse a bad pun."

Taylor rolled to rest on an elbow. The room whirled around in a blur and a crushing pain throbbed above her left ear. She leaned over and vomited on the floor. The barmaid brought a mop and a glass of cold water.

"Take it easy, girlfriend. You don't need to be a repeat casualty today. Where do you live?"

"Out on Lakewood, near the park, but my car's down on Langdon."

"I think, if you refuse to go to the hospital, one of us should go get your car and drive you home."

"Is there anyone there to look after you?" asked the little red-haired doc.

"Naw, I live alone but I can get someone to come hang out."

"Yeah, you definitely don't need to be alone for the next few hours. Don't eat a big meal, don't exert yourself, and don't go to sleep."

Taylor grimaced, "Guess that rules out a sex marathon for the rest of the afternoon."

"Shame," laughed Jackson. "I'd even volunteer to help out but we've gotta look out for other people getting hurt on the street."

He turned to the waitress, "Do you think you could drive her home, if we bring her car up?"

"Yeah, I'd do that. I'm off in fifteen minutes, anyway, and there aren't going to be many customers leavin' tips until this shit's over with."

"Great! Now all we need are keys and a clue where to find it."

Taylor reached into the pocket of her jeans and separated the ignition key on a silver nouveau ring. "It's a yellow Ghia in the parking lot behind Badger House."

"How'd you work that?"

"Oh, a friend, who lives there, let's me use his space sometimes."

"Lucky, you."

She rubbed her temple, "Some days. What's happening outside?"

"Can't you smell the teargas?" asked Jackson.

"Now that you mention it, yeah."

A stocky girl, in a dark blue peacoat with a heavy rainbow scarf, stumbled in from the street, coughing, "The march pushed through the troops but they opened up with gas. Those assholes started dosing us for no reason at all."

"They were waiting for you," said Taylor. "It was a trap from the start."

"Ain't gonna stop the people from having their day on the steps of the Capitol," wheezed the girl, rubbing her eyes with a cold cloth from the bar. "You can't silence the truth."

"Amen to that," said Doris, the waitress, "even if it is a pipedream."

The medics carried Taylor to a booth and propped her up, "Henny's gonna run down and grab your car but I'll hang with you until he gets back."

"Could you do me a favor and call my friend, Sophia, and see if she'll meet me at my house?"

"Sure, what's her number?"

Taylor scribbled it on a napkin. "She's probably the only person on campus who isn't in the march."

"Apolitical or just disinterested?"

"Preoccupied with things that matter more to her at the moment."

"Like what?"

"Like crafting a matched set of wedding rings."

"For who?"

"Her and her future husband."

"Under a deadline?"

"Yeah, kinda. She's trying to organize a ceremony in New Jersey for May, while she's taking eighteen hours this semester…mostly art, so, with studio hours, it's more like twenty-four."

"Sounds driven."

"That's an understatement."

Sophia was waiting at the back door when the little yellow car putted up the drive. Doris jumped out and ran around to open the passenger door, as the tall blond reached in to help Taylor stand. "Shit you're wobbly. Lemme get an arm around you, before you fall down and hurt yourself again."

The girls carried her through the kitchen and deposited her on the couch. Doris looked up, "We tried to get her to go to the hospital but she refused. I'm worried about her."

"Don't worry, I'll look after her. I have five older brothers who were always getting the shit kicked out of themselves. Do you have a ride home?"

"I'm going up to see what's happening at the Capitol, so I'll just truck on down the road."

"Watch out for the cops, sister. They don't care who they hurt."

"I'll avoid 'em."

Taylor reached to take her hand, "Thanks for bringing me home. I owe you one."

"No, you don't. Just pass it on to someone else and it'll go 'round and 'round."

"Cool."

Doris bundled up her coat and headed out the back door, as Sophia brought a pillow and a blanket. "You shouldn't lie flat, so let's prop you up a little, and I brought a blanket in case you're cold. No food but a cup of warm tea might be okay."

"Sure. There's some Earl Grey in the cupboard."

Sophia reappeared with a tray of cups, sugar, lemon, and a steaming pot of tea. She poured two cups, "Sugar or lemon?"

"Both."

She handed over the cup and then a cold compress. "Keep this on that wound, I don't want to give you anything for the pain until we see how this tea settles, okay?"

"Yeah, I do feel kind of woozy."

"Shit, girl, you could be dead."

"Funny, I saw him coming and couldn't stop firing off shots. It was like watching about every fifth frame in a slow motion film."

"I'm dedicated to my art but that's ridiculous. You're gonna be laid up for a couple of days, because you decided to be brazen instead of smart."

"Hindsight...but I can't wait to see what's on my film."

"I can take it to your folks for processing later. Meantime, let's get you stable."

"Fine," said Taylor, savoring the warm golden liquid. "How are the wedding plans coming?"

"That's a fucking nightmare, that's all I can say. Don't ever get married, unless you've got your mom doing the heavy lifting."

"What about your mom?"

"She died three years ago, so it's me and my dad and five brothers. No help there."

"So it's on you?"

"Yeah. Augie told me to organize it through his mother but she's really old school, and I'm fairly sure she's a raging alcoholic, so I'm using her contacts and making my own decisions."

"I know it's going to be beautiful. Is everything okay with you two?"

Sophia smiled, slipping onto the couch to cradle Taylor's head, "Couldn't be better."

"I'm glad. You both seem so happy."

"It is kind of a fairy tale...rich handsome guy's buying a sixty-acre spread next to the ocean for our first home."

"The fact that he's more than a little bit mysterious and deeply into the trade doesn't bother you?"

"Naw, I understand and I can only judge him for the person he is inside. He might be a smartass on the outside but he's generous and kind and caring when we're alone. I see him helping people out all the time. Hell, some neighbors of his are having a hard time, the guy's out of work and his wife's got breast cancer. Augie paid off their mortgage, so they wouldn't have that to worry about."

"That's what wealth should be used for," said Taylor snuggling closer. "Just so you're happy."

Sophia kissed her forehead, "Are you jealous?"

Taylor giggled, "Yeah, a little."

"What about Randy?"

"He could definitely be the one but it's different with you."

"I know, I'm just giving you some shit."

Taylor nestled close and sipped her tea, "I want to buy property out of the country, when we're done."

"Like where?" asked Sophia.

"South America. There are places, like Bolivia, where you can buy thousands of acres for almost nothing. Wouldn't it be a trip to stand on a hilltop and know that everything you can see to the horizon is yours?"

"Back to the country?"

"I could see running a huge farm and ranch someday."

"We could go from distribution to cultivation."

"Gentleperson pot farmers…that doesn't sound like a bad goal to me."

"What gave you this idea?"

"My cousin, the international relations wonk, who speaks like nine languages, is married to a woman from Bolivia. I fell in love with her country just listening to her describe its wonders, from lofty mountains to giant salt flats to dense jungle and mighty rivers."

"Might wanna go see it for yourself before you jump in," laughed Sophia pulling her close.

"Definitely," said Taylor kissing her slowly. "Two more years of this and I might actually be able to afford to go off the deep end."

She reached to fondle Sophia's ample breast, "There's just something safe and soothing when we're together."

"How can you be horny when you've got a concussion?"

"Maybe, I just need the release."

"None of my brothers tried to convince me that a blow-job would cure their pain, when I was nursing their wounds."

Taylor pulled up the blanket and reached under her sweater to tweak her nipples. Sophia pushed her back into the pillow "You don't need to be exerting yourself in any way, girlfriend."

She reached for her teacup, "Okay, I'll just lie back and let you do all the work."

The phone jangled in the kitchen and Sophia trotted through the dining room to grab it, "Hello."

"No, this is Sophia. She got clubbed by a National Guardpig and has a concussion."

"Really. I've got her on the couch and she's not lookin' her best."

She listened without responding for several minutes. "Yeah, I'll tell her."

"What was that all about?"

"Your friend Victor said that, on his way out of town, he got stopped by the National Guard and had a flat. The cadets changed the tire for him but one of them noticed the heavy shocks in the car and told him to get on down the road, before someone started asking questions. He pulled into a gas station about two minutes ahead of a pair of police cars hauling ass down East Washington, in the opposite direction from the Capitol."

"Is he okay?"

"Yeah, he's on the other side of Chicago and not lookin' back."

"He's a good guy and I worry about him being on the road."

"That's the chance he takes to make his dough. We all do it."

"That's true but there's something about being out on the

road that's different than flying around in airplanes delivering suitcases full of cash."

Sophia grinned, "I always come, as soon as I have my briefcase stashed under my seat on the plane, 'cause I know no one's gonna be checking anything once we take off. I guess it's releasing all the anxiety."

"I've still got a worry that could use some attention," said Taylor, pulling the blanket back to reveal her long naked legs. "Think you could help me out?"

"Shit, girl, you might be committing suicide by ecstasy."

"I'd die happy with your tongue on my clit."

Chapter 13

"I'm worried about the guys getting through with the new freighter," said Bernie.

"Bing Watt devised a much better way to keep things water tight. We should be good. Have you got the launches lined up and transportation?"

Bernie nodded, "Yeah, man, we've got four boats that'll meet 'em twenty miles out and offload in Monterey. I'll have four step-vans ready to go."

"Think you can get it all in one night?" asked Ruck.

"Yeah, no problem. This time of year, the town's pretty dead, too cold for tourists."

"I think we've used that marina too often. Let's check out Oregon and all those little islands up north," said Augie.

"Think they won't mind if we just pass through?" chuckled Ruck.

"The research says that things are tight up around Seattle and Vancouver but loose further south."

"I'll look into it after we get this one buttoned up," said Bernie.

"One more series in the spring, then we're gonna shut it down for the summer," said Augie.

"If all this comes through, you're gonna hafta buy a couple more grocery stores," laughed Bernie.

"Already looking into it."

"What's happening with the property on the Jersey shore?" asked Ruck.

"Closing on it next week," smiled Augie. "I've got a construction crew ready to get started on some renovations as soon as it's legal."

"I'm not sure I can hang with a Jersey boy," laughed Bernie. "It's almost like you're going over to the enemy!"

"Naw, I'm a Jets and Mets fan. I just fell in love with the place. It's got everything I want…ocean, beach, forest, a protected bay…and isolation."

"Including a gorgeous Sophia to play hostess," laughed Ruck.

"And a whole lot more," added Bernie.

"Fuck off, you guys. You're just jealous!"

"Well, there's that," said Ruck. "If anyone's gonna catch you, she'd be in my top five."

Augie snickered, "Dream on,"

"Alright," said Ruck, downing the last sip of beer. "The shipment's supposed to be in the day you get back but the crew says that everything's perfectly dry, so, I guess you can hook up with our perverted lush."

Augie shook his head, "He's gotta get paid, if we're going turn this thing one more time, before we shut it down for the summer. He's a sick puppy but even that's been useful."

"Shit, you sound like a fucking preacher absolving the sins of the sinner. The guy's a creep," said Bernie.

"Yeah, he is, and he's dangerous too, but we need his product to complete the supply chain. He's the final piece to the puzzle to connect it all together, until we find a better source."

"Just watch your back, bro. He's a slimeball."

Augie, dressed in a long black leather coat over a gray suit against a damp blustery afternoon, walked into the Grand Hotel, on Prins Hendrikkade just down from Amsterdam Centraal, and inquired for Mr. Stoney Montgomery.

The petite clerk, with luminous green eyes and the complexion of a porcelain doll under a mane of thick black hair, asked his name in perfect English and picked up a telephone. She spoke softly, then listened, nodding, "Yes, I'll send him right up."

She replaced the receiver and said, "He's expecting you. Room Six-Oh-Two. There's a lift just behind you."

"Thank you," said Augie, turning to the elevator.

Stoney opened the door to a corner suite with bloodshot eyes, "Evening, mate. Lovely to have you aboard."

"You're in fine shape."

"Completely fucked up and loving every minute of it," laughed the Brit. "You want a splash of Scotch? I'm drinking gin myself, seems a bit more civilized at this hour."

Augie set a heavy attaché next to a Beretta on an intricately inlaid Louis XIV desk before draped windows overlooking the wharf. "It's a little early for me, thanks. I brought a little something to settle our debts."

"Lovely, I'm sure it's all there," said Stoney, swigging two fingers of gin from a crystal tumbler. "After your imaginative gift, the last time we met, I'm sure past unpleasantries and misunderstandings will soon be forgiven."

"Funny how a suitcase full of cash smoothes ruffled feathers. I want to set up one more shipment, as soon as we can get the Albatross back to Thailand."

"I'll have everything arranged, just make sure you have my payment in hand, when we meet again."

"Can do," smiled Augie, sensing Stoney's suppressed indignation simmering just beneath the inebriated, yet sophisticated, cloak of civility.

"When's the wedding?"

"Sophia's aiming for May 24th, if she can get all the caterers and florists and tailors on the same page as the priest."

"Be glad that you're traveling, mate. Those details will derail a marriage quicker than casual sex with the bridesmaids."

"I'm trying not to screw this up."

"That important, eh? She must be one special chickie," laughed Stoney. "I'm looking forward to meeting her and, if she's hot enough to tame you, you'll have to excuse me drooling all over myself, when the occasion arises."

"You just behave yourself, put on your British airs, and all will be good."

"Have I ever embarrassed you...in public?"

"No, not in public."

"Well, there you go! My mum taught me how to behave myself, when I'm in proper company, even when I'm half-blasted."

"Fine, you're invited. In the meantime, I'll meet you in Pattaya the last week in April and I'll bring along an invitation."

"I'll bring some Chinese brown, just to soothe your nerves."

"Probably not the appropriate occasion, brother. I'll be flyin' low."

"We'll see," laughed the slender Brit. "You've got a long time to consider every alternative before you say those magic words that'll cost you a huge fortune and the rest of your living days. And, besides, I know a couple of young ladies in Bangkok, who would love to get hold of your cock again."

"Yeah, that was then. Now, "til death do us part' has taken on new meaning."

Stoney shuffled over and picked up the Beretta, waving it in the air, "I've got to admit that I'm fairly jealous of your situation, mate. You've got everything working – a beautiful bride, businesses, properties, and that arrogant air of cool. I'm not sure whether to blow you away or myself."

"Hey, man, you've got your world on a string. You're handsome, debonair, at home on every continent, and have plenty of money to indulge your fantasies until your weenie falls off. The only thing I've accomplished that you haven't is finding my soul mate."

"That's a major accomplishment, mate. Next come the kiddies."

Augie smiled, watching the wavering barrel of the gun, as Stoney pointed it at his chest then raised it to his own temple. "The future is what we make it, we can fuck it up or we can make things happen. It's a choice."

"I'm a loner, I've always been on the outside looking in, even at school. Sure, you and Sid and a few other people were kind enough but I was never part of the clique."

"There wasn't any clique, just people hanging out."

"Sure there was and you, the class fuck-up, were at the center of it. Everyone wanted to hang out with you because you were cool and, maybe, some of that might rub off on them."

"I, honestly, never saw that at all."

"How could you? You were at the core and the world revolved around you. Hell, I bet you fucked just about every coed on campus and probably most of the female professors."

Augie blushed, "The funny part is, I just asked them if they wanted to get laid and most of 'em did."

He pointed the gun at Augie's crouch, "Maybe I should just blow your balls off."

"Yeah, that's going to help you feel better."

"It might," mumbled Stoney, as his eyes rolled back into his skull and he tumbled onto a sofa that flipped over backwards in slow motion. A loud crack shattered the momentary hush as the Beretta discharged a bullet that splintered crystals in the chandelier and lodged in the ceiling.

Augie ducked a blizzard of shards, grabbed the gun, and pulled the clip, "You definitely don't need a loaded firearm in your condition."

"What condition?" giggled the Brit. His head rested on the carpet and his legs dangled off the front of the couch in a perfectly normal seated position, were he not facing the ceiling.

He turned to a loud rap and opened the door to find a small man with black hair plastered to his head, a thin moustache, and a spotless black suit with a white carnation in the lapel above a small plaque that read, 'Jean Moreset, Hotelier'. The manager pursed his lips and spoke in English with a French accent, "Monsieur, is there an emergency?"

Augie smiled, "No, my friend dropped his gun and it went off. I'm afraid there was a bit of damage to the chandelier."

The manager stepped into the room, surveying a dusting of glittering crystals on the Persian carpet and Stoney, sprawled across the back of the overturned couch in a tangle. "I will have a maid attend to this. Does Mr. Montgomery need medical assistance?"

"I'm sure he'll sleep it off in time for dinner and I do apologize for the inconvenience."

The little man shook his head, "Hoteliers see some amazing things but it is rather unusual for guests to be discharging firearms in an establishment of this status."

"I agree," said Augie, handing over the empty gun with a folded hundred dollar bill, "and I would appreciate it, if you would be kind enough to lock this up in the safe until my friend checks out."

"As you wish, Monsieur." He turned and marched out of the room, closing the door silently behind him.

~

Augie sauntered past a few workers gathered along the bar to find Fasal, seated at the round table at the back of the tiny pub, and set a large valise under the table, "The sausages smell good."

"They're always good, especially with a Grolsch. Have a seat."

A shapely blond waitress appeared, "Beer?"

"Sure," replied Augie with a smile, "and a couple of Frikanellens with potatoes and apple sauce."

"Fasal?"

"I'll have the same, thanks."

The waitress strolled away. "She's sweet on you."

Fasal blushed, "That's Gretel, she's the boss's daughter and I've known her since she was a little flat-chested teenager."

"She's developed some impressive curves, in case you hadn't noticed, and she's definitely not a teeny-bopper anymore."

Fasal glanced up at the bar to find her smiling seductively. "I'm thinking she's trouble waiting to happen."

Augie cracked up, "What a way to go."

"I see you brought me a present."

"Yeah, full payment for the last load and I was hoping we could go once more in early May."

"I'll make the arrangements."

"I don't know whether Bernie told you, but I'm getting married at the end of May and I hope you'll join us for the wedding."

"I'd be honored, especially if I can pick up a payment while I'm there."

"That can be arranged, for sure."

Gretel brought a tray with steaming sausages, potatoes, and applesauce. Fasal's eyes rose slowly, surveying her full hips, tiny waist, ample breasts, and, finally, her enticing smile. He stammered, "Thank you."

"It is my pleasure," said the blond, swinging her hips as she swept behind the bar.

"You're in deep doo-doo, guy."

"I think you're right."

"Tell me, do you do any banking here?"

"Yeah, the laws are fairly lax but I use Deutsche Bank, because they've got branches all over Europe. You can make a deposit here and withdraw it in Paris or Beirut. Proves handy."

"Where's the bank?"

"I'm heading for the train after we finish here, so I'll be happy to drop you off, if you like?"

"Thanks, I'll take you up on that."

Fasal smiled, "It's a problem we all run into, too much cash. You can't spend it fast enough and, if you make large deposits at home or even here, someone's going to notice and start asking questions."

"Yeah, I need to stash some of it out of the country."

He hesitated, "There are places where you can open a numbered account. No names or personal information. They're happy to use your money. Unfortunately, the price of anonymity is that they pay little or no interest."

Augie grinned, "I'm pretty sure that's not an issue."

Fasal laughed, "I'll give you the names of several contacts in France, Spain, Italy, Portugal, and Switzerland. There's a certain assurance in having your funds stashed in more than one place."

"I appreciate your help."

The taxi cruised along the Boulevard Croisette, above a massive harbor and the glistening waters of the Mediterranean rolling in to the shores of Cannes. Magnificent yachts, ocean liners, and a thicket of splendid sailboats lined the docks and Augie decided to make time to check them out after his appointment. He paid the cabby and walked up to a very narrow building with a single door and a small sign that read, 'Societe Financier'.

Before he could reach for the handle, the door opened and a tall, matronly woman in a gray suit that matched her hair, which was twisted into a tight bun, smiled, "Monsieur La Guerre, I presume?"

Augie nodded and stepped inside a formal lobby, heavy with

dark woods and plush carpeting.

"If you'll follow me, I will show you to the Director's office."

"Thank you."

She walked to the far end of the room and through a long, dimly lit hallway lined with paintings, stopping to knock on a pair of ornately carved doors.

A muffled voice called, "Entrée!"

The tall woman opened the door, stepping back to allow Augie to enter, and closed it without a sound, as a small stout man with white hair, dark horn-rimmed glasses, and thin red lips smiled and reached to shake his hand, "Mr. LaGuerre. I am Pierre de Gaulle, no relation to the General, unfortunately. I am pleased to make your acquaintance. How might I be of service?"

"I'd like to open an account."

"Might I assume that you would be interested in one of our private numbered accounts?"

"That would suit my purposes."

"I'm sure we can make the arrangements. How much would you like to deposit?" asked the banker, eyeing the heavy valise at Augie's side.

"Two million U.S. dollars."

The little man's lips barely twitched, "You will find that we are most discreet."

"You came highly recommended."

"Let me have my secretary bring the necessary paperwork. Could I offer you a glass of wine or something stronger?"

"No, thank you," replied Augie.

"Might I also assume that this deposit will be made in cash?"

He placed the heavy case on the floor. "Yes."

A gentle knock preceded a small woman in a black suit. De Gaulle turned, "Mr. LaGuerre will be opening a new account."

"I'll bring the documents."

"And, would you take this case to the counting room?"
"Certainly."

~

Sophia gunned the engine of the Mercedes, under the circular canopy of the Pan Am Worldport, watching Augie stride across the pavement to climb into the passenger seat. He leaned over to kiss her long and slow, "It sure is nice to come home to you."

"I've missed you, too, and I have to admit that I always worry when you're on the road."

Augie grinned, "Other than being half crippled, it all went pretty well."

"Pretty well?"

He laughed, "Except for our Asian contact firing off a gun that shattered a chandelier in his hotel room."

"Shit! I hope he wasn't aiming at you."

"Well, he was for a while but it went off as he tumbled over backwards in a stupor."

"He wasn't just a little bit fucked up?"

"Just a little."

"And you were a good boy?"

"Absolutely. The hardest drug I had on the whole trip was a few glasses of wine and about a bottle of Excedrin for my back."

"I bet I can make you feel better."

He rubbed his hand up and down her thigh as the little car raced onto the Belt Parkway heading south. "How are the plans coming?"

Sophia shook her head, "I never had any idea of how hard it is to put together a big celebration. The details are driving me crazy and I've still got a bunch of final projects to finish up, before the end of the semester."

"The wedding and your work will be beautiful and I only

have two requests."

"What?"

"First, when we finally get there, you let it roll. I want you to have a good time at your own wedding."

"Fair enough, won't be anything I can change at that point anyway. What else?"

"I want to book Peachtree to play."

"I've got a string quartet lined up for the ceremony and the reception."

"That's great but after our friends get a few drinks under their belts, they're gonna want to party."

"Fine. We'll have soft music through dinner and rock-n-roll after. Fair enough?"

"I'll call Standish tomorrow. We can fly them in for the party on a private plane and ship 'em back the next day."

"So what have you been up to for the past ten days?" asked Sophia, sliding her fingers between his.

"The less you know, the better."

"I know, I know, but...?"

"I paid off some people."

"So, there's more in the pipeline?"

"I'm hoping to turn everyone one more time and start shutting it down by the time we get married."

"Really? Are you saying you want to retire?"

"Well, from all of this."

Sophia smiled, "That's some wedding present."

Augie leaned close, "I want to have a real life with you, a family, and that doesn't fit with what I've been doing."

She looked into his eyes for a long moment, then swerved to avoid rear-ending a truck.

He reached into his pocket and withdrew a small piece of paper. "I want you to memorize these numbers when you have a chance."

She took the scrap in her long graceful fingers and glanced at it. Four letters preceded four twelve-digit sequences. "What's this?"

"Insurance. Just memorize it, okay?"

"Fine, if you say so."

"I'll explain when the time's right."

"You know I'm curious and impatient!"

"Not to change the subject but what ever happened with all the riots in Madison?"

"You mean besides Taylor getting beat up by the pigs? And, she's pretty much back to normal, thank you very much," laughed the beautiful blond. "It took a couple of weeks but the administration finally caved in to all the demands."

"So they're going to admit more blacks?"

"Yeah, and they're hiring more people of color to teach and they're starting a Black Studies program."

"Why didn't they just do that in the beginning? That's too easy," said Augie, as he settled back into the seat with a groan.

"The times, they are a changin'...just too slowly." Sophia zipped through traffic onto the Jersey Turnpike and Augie was sound asleep before they reached the first tollbooth.

The little car purred along the path through the forest and Sophia parked on the newly paved drive in front of the four-car garage. She shook Augie gently and kissed him on the cheek, "We're home."

He rubbed his eyes and gazed around, "Shit, they've got a lot done since I left two weeks ago."

Sophia smiled, "I came down a couple of days ago and they were pretty well finished up on the inside. Wait 'til you see the kitchen!"

"I'm more interested in the bedroom."

"You can wait just a little longer. C'mon, you're gonna love this. They've upgraded everything using natural forms from plants and trees and shells they found on the property. The new master bath is a trip with lots of rustic stone, a huge walk-in shower and a steam sauna."

They climbed out of the car and strolled, arm-in-arm, across the drive to the back door. She led him through the mudroom into the huge log kitchen. Slate countertops surrounded stainless steel sinks, a six-burner cook top with a grill under a copper vent-hood on the island, and an enormous commercial stove with double ovens. New cabinetry, with glass doors and pulls forged from twigs, lined the walls and double refrigerators and dishwashers provided ample capacity for entertaining a houseful of guests or an enormous family.

Sophia hugged him, "Isn't it fabulous?"

Augie looked around, "Yes, I love it and I can't wait to cook in here."

"Good thing I stocked the frig. We've got a couple bottles of Bordeaux, beautiful steaks or salmon, if you like, and potatoes and salad stuff."

"Cool."

"There's something else I want to add to this place."

"What's that?"

"A vegetable garden."

"There isn't any soil, it's mostly sand," said Augie.

"Yeah, I know. So we'll build up beds with real soil. My folks call it French Intensive Gardening, using raised beds for good drainage and planting everything close together to hold down the weeds."

"Sounds like you know what you're doing."

"Yeah, I just need a truckload of good rich soil and about a half-a-load of composted manure and I'll be as happy as a pig in shit."

Augie burst out laughing, "I have trouble envisioning you grimy."

Sophia smirked, "I can get down and dirty, big fella! There's a lot you don't know about me or me about you. That's the fun of it. Whatever happened before is just an experience that we can use to make our relationship grow."

"I love you," said Augie, taking her in his arms, "and I'll trade you a truckload of shit, next week, for a backrub and some ass right now."

"Deal."

Chapter 14

A cold north wind battered the four speedboats as they pulled away from the hulking freighter and turned east. The glow of a full moon oozed through ominous clouds racing south on a roaring gale. Ruck leaned over to his boyhood chum, Donny, and yelled above the din, "We're riding heavy and we're sure as hell not gonna make good time in this chop!"

"We'll get this run finished before daylight," replied Don. "It shouldn't take long to offload the last of this shit and send it on its way."

"Yeah, I know, but I like these things to be clean and tidy. Easy in, easy out, no one gets hassled."

"Bernie said he paid some chick to take the harbormaster out for a nice romantic dinner someplace and make sure he's tied up for the rest of the night."

"I'm guessin' he couldn't pay her enough to screw that ol' codger," said Ruck, "but I still hate crappy weather."

"Ah, relax. We've all been through worse than this."

Ruck laughed, pointing to the plastic wrapped pallets of silver bricks, "Yeah, our first venture got swamped in a storm. We lost a fortune. That's why this load is triple sealed."

"Guess that's how we learn," said Donny, "but I'm glad it was out of your pocket and not mine."

"We had everyone paid in less than ninety days. I couldn't believe we pulled it off."

"That's why you're so careful now."

"I'm just paranoid until everything's finished."

"Somebody's got to keep their shit together."

The little fleet split up, with Ruck and Ashton turning south, while Bernie and Teddy steered north to dilute the radar signature if the Coast Guard was watching. At four-thirty, Ruck guided the Chris-Craft around Pacific Grove and into a wharf at the far end of the marina, where two white step vans were parked on the dock, just behind Ashton.

The first van was loaded and gone, by the time Bernie idled out of the darkness, "Ahoy, matie, have you seen Teddy?"

Ruck grabbed a line and tied it to a cleat on the deck, "No, man. We've already sent the third van on its way. What happened?"

"We crossed paths with a Coast Guard cutter heading south and split up. He headed into open water and I hugged the coast."

"Fuck, is he lost or did he get caught?" asked Ashton. "Either way, it can't be good. We've been through years of weird shit on the water together and he's the best seaman I know. He doesn't fuck up."

"Did you try him on the radio?" asked Donnie.

"Of course," replied Bernie. "His last call was two words, 'Heading south'. That's the last contact I had with him."

"Then let's get this shit into the van and we'll go looking for him," said Ruck.

~

Sophia grabbed the phone in the kitchen, "Hello."

"Sophi', it's Ruck. How ya' doin'?"

"Great. Today's the first time it's actually felt like spring might show up this year. How 'bout you?"

"Tired. Is Augie around?"

"Yeah, hang on and I'll find him."

The line clicked as Augie picked up the receiver, "Hey, bro', what's happenin'?"

"Weird shit, man. Weird shit."

Sophia came back on, "Take care of yourself and come see the new house when you get back!"

"Can do," said Ruck. The receiver clunked as she hung up.

"So, what's up?"

"We got the last three out of four. Bernie and Teddy were headed back with the last of it, when they ran into a Coast Guard cutter. Bernie headed for the coast. Teddy headed out and hasn't been seen since. Don't know whether he went down, got caught, or is sitting on a beach in Mexico."

"Any chatter on the radio about interceptions?"

"Nope. Nothing…and that's not something they'd keep quiet about."

"What'd you do with the other boats?"

"Put 'em up in dry dock under cover," replied Ruck.

"Get Bernie to follow up. He's gotta be out there to keep tabs on this shit anyway and the other guys can head down to hook up with Felix. You head back, we've got other fish to fry."

"Cool. I'll take the redeye and see you in the morning.'

"Safe journey."

The phone went dead and he replaced it on the cradle, "Fuck! Stoney Montgomery's weirdness has fucking jinxed this deal."

The luminous hands on the clock read five after four in the morning, when the phone jangled and Augie untangled himself from Sophie, "Hello."

"Augie, it's Bernie."

"What's up?"

"The Coast Guard got Teddy and turned him over to the FBI in Santa Cruz. They haven't pressed charges yet but they've had lots of time to ask questions without a lawyer."

"That's not good."

"I don't have those connections here, do you?"

"Lemme make some calls and I'll call you back. What's your number?" He scratched the digits on a pad on the night table and hung up. "Fuck."

"What's wrong?" asked Sophie.

"Business. I have to make some calls downstairs. I'll be back in a little while."

He settled on a stool in the kitchen, lit a Marlboro, and dialed Mary.

Her voice was sleepy and cranky and he flashed on waking his little sister, by bouncing on her bed or blowing a horn, just to solicit this reaction, when they were kids. Big brothers are cruel. "What could you possible want at this hour?"

"Mary, it's Augie. I need a favor."

"Can't whatever you need wait until the birds start singing?"

"Teddy's been popped with a load."

"Where?"

"Santa Cruz. FBI's got him and he needs a lawyer."

"That's a bummer, I'll see what I can do."

"Can we arrange to pay the bail and fees through one of the corporations?"

"Yeah, it'll be invisible."

"Good," sighed Augie.

"Augie?"

"Yeah."

"You knew all along that this couldn't last forever. Something's gotta get screwed up sooner or later and it's starting to get a whole lot more dangerous."

Augie laughed, "I thought I took care of the bad karma the first time out."

"C'mon, this is heavy shit, man."

"Actually, I'm working on retiring."

"It can't come soon enough. I worry about you and we both know that you've made enough already."

"Thanks. Lemme know what you find out."

"It probably won't be until after noon, they're three hours behind."

"Whatever you can do to help is much appreciated, I'll be here or over at the office with Chester."

"Oh, I haven't talked with you in a couple of weeks. The two sales went through, so you've got five stores. You're becoming a magnate."

"How 'bout legitimate businessman?"

"Sounds good to me. Oh, and I heard that you're giving Nattie a car for graduation."

"She's earned it."

"That's very generous, big brother."

"I try to help where I can," replied Augie. "Goodnight, Sis, and thanks."

"I owe you, remember?"

~

The Chevy pulled up beneath a neon sign flashing 'Lucky's' as Bernie and Teddy stumbled through a pair of leather doors, embellished with large brass studs outlining a pair of diamonds, and climbed into the car. As Augie pulled away, he looked in the rearview mirror, "Nice to see your smilin' face, asshole."

"Nice to be seen, brother," replied Teddy, slumping back into the rear seat.

"So, what happened?"

"We were heading back in with the final load and Bernie and I turned north to circle around, when we spotted a cutter headin' south. He took off to hug the shore and I killed the runnin' lights and headed out to sea, taking a big arc to end up back at the docks. Except they must have figured there was no other place to pull in most of the way down Big Sur, so they just waited 'til I showed up."

"Then what?"

"Guns, bullhorns, handcuffs, stuff like that," said Teddy. "So, they cuffed me, asked a bunch of questions that I wouldn't answer, and hauled the boat to Santa Cruz, where they handed me over to the FBI. They wanted to know where I got the dope in the boat and I told 'em I found it floating about four miles out. Figurin' this was my lucky day, I hauled the pallet aboard, end of story."

"They bought that shit?" asked Augie.

"That's all I gave 'em, said I wanted a lawyer and, after sitting in an interrogation room forever, one showed up. I gotta thank you guys for getting me outta there, I sure didn't want to have to call my ol' man."

"Yeah, well, you still have to get past the trial."

"I know, but the attorney said he thought he could get me off on some technicality. I'm supposed to call him next week."

"So, they didn't ask where you were planning to sell it?" asked Augie.

"Of course they asked and I told 'em I had absolutely no idea, because I only smoke marijuana once in a while and didn't really hang with that crowd, and I'm from the East Coast and just out here on a little vacation. Besides, I don't know anyone in that part of California."

"Yeah, like they're gonna buy that crap. It definitely isn't tourist season in Monterey," said Bernie.

"Honest, that's when the lawyer showed up."

"They're digging into your background and, pretty soon, they'll know every time you took a dump since you were born! Your family, your friends, your neighbors, everyone you ever hung out with in school…they'll know it all, before they drop the hammer on you," said Augie. "I'm thinkin' you're officially on wavers until we get past all this."

"No shit?" whined Teddy. "I need to work. I need the bucks, man."

"Dumbshit, you should have to put some away, because shit like this is gonna happen and you've gotta have a backup. Bernie's gonna give you a fat bartender's gig, until we know where we stand,

and you're gonna to stay away from the business until then. You got it?"

"Yeah, I got it."

Bernie turned around, "You know anything about mixing drinks?"

"Just what I learned from my ol' man and you."

"That'll be enough for my crowd," smiled Bernie.

Augie spied a woman, wrapped in a red cloak, sitting on the steps of the little house on the water, and Abby stood to wave as the lights of the Mercedes flashed through the trees. He parked the car on the drive and walked over to her, "We can't go on meeting like this, I'm almost a married man."

"I know, asshole. That's why I'm here. You're in the final countdown and I never got an invitation. You're my best friend and I want to be there when you say, 'I do'."

He looked down at her, "I think that could be arranged but only if you agree to behave yourself, act like a lady, and don't get shit-faced until you're ready to go home."

"Fuck, what happened to the 'of course you're invited' part?"

"Because I know you as well as you know me. C'mon inside, let's get warm."

"Fine with me, buster. Spring might be comin' but it sure ain't here yet."

Augie brewed coffee and warmed a couple of bagels in the toaster oven.

Abby plopped down on a stool in the kitchen, "So, you're really goin' through with it?"

Augie grinned, "Yup, I think I'm ready."

"I'd say she's a lucky lady but she probably doesn't know

what an asshole you are."

"I've been behaving myself, ever since you gave me a dose of the clap."

"Serves you right," laughed Abby, taking a steaming cup of coffee.

"No, sorry? Nothin'?"

"Hey, you could've said, 'No'."

"You bitch."

"Now, we're even!" snorted Abby, with a deep belly laugh. "We've known each other too long."

He grinned, "Maybe long enough."

"Hey, asshole, I'll be around, through thick and thin, until one of us is dead."

"That's reassuring."

"Count on it." She looked down at her cup, "This would be better with a shot of bourbon."

"Having a real conversation is more important."

"So, I'm sensing the Augie-covering-up-his-real-thoughts syndrome."

"What do you mean?"

"C'mon, I can read you. What's up?"

"Oh, just business stuff, irritating but not serious."

"Bullshit! Are you still thinking about quitting?"

"Yeah, I'm working on it. Trouble is that, once you're in and things are rolling, it's hard to back out."

"Let alone gracefully."

Augie grinned, "Definitely." He paused, "It's like, in the past couple of years, we grew this giant family that stretches all over the world and everyone is depending on everyone else...and I'm in the middle."

"You like being in the middle of everything, you always have."

"Yeah, I guess you're right, but this is way more intense."

"This is the moment when you can choose to go in a different direction. If you don't grab on and hold tight, you'll end up being hooked up for the rest of your life, like your ol' man, protecting your secrets."

Augie stared at her, "That's it, isn't it. I've always wanted my own triumphs but maybe not at the price he paid."

"Then you've made your decision, haven't you?"

"I guess I have."

~

Augie handed out cold Coors as Ruck and Bernie settled on the coach, "So where do we stand?"

"All current shipments have been delivered and are stashed in the safe houses, en route, or already distributed. By the end of the month, we'll have ten million on the street and another ten scheduled for late April or May," said Ruck. "The first-half of the year's been very profitable. After expenses, we're makin' good money."

"By my calculations," added Bernie, "it's somewhere north of forty-million, since the break last summer."

Augie smiled and held up his beer can, "Salute!"

Bernie and Ruck clinked cans.

"Bernie and I spent some time in a townie bar, while things were coming together in Monterrey, and I got to talkin' with a couple of fishermen. I asked 'em how much they could make on a seven-day run and they said, on a really good trip, they might clear five-grand," said Ruck.

"What if we hired local fisherman to cruise down to Columbia and bring a load back for us instead of fish? We could pay them double or triple their normal profit and avoid putting our own people at risk," added Bernie.

"That's a really creative idea but I think it's time to close this thing down. We've been really lucky, so far, but the business is changing right before our eyes. People see dope as free money and they want a piece of the action. I'm hearing more and more stories about guys on the street getting jammed up by punks with guns, stash houses raided by gangs, and people getting killed over weed. It's only gonna get worse."

"D'you really want to get out?" asked Bernie.

"Yeah, man, I do. Can ya' dig it?"

"No, you're the guy who's holding everything together. How can we walk away from making millions a year?"

"Because, if we don't walk away, they're gonna carry us out in a paddy wagon or a box. Take your pick."

Ruck set his can on the table, "Just for the sake of argument, what if we don't want to get out?"

"That's up to you, you can have all the connections. I'll just disappear."

"Really?"

"Yeah, really," said Augie, "but the one thing I will ask is that both of you really think about this. You're both set-up, you both have businesses that'll earn you another bucket-full of money, if you work at it. It might not be as glamorous or exciting but those gigs won't kill you either."

"I'm gonna have to think about it," said Ruck. "It's just too tempting."

"I know. I'm not making this decision on a whim. I've been thinking about this for a long time."

"Yeah, well, you're getting married and making some big changes in your life, so you've got a good excuse," said Bernie.

"I agree, Sophie's excuse enough!" laughed Ruck.

"How's the new place comin'," asked Bernie.

"The construction work is pretty well finished up and the docks are ready for boats. We're starting to buy some furniture and I'm having this stuff shipped down there next week, you'll have to come down for the weekend."

"Yeah, cool," said Ruck. "What are you doin' with this place."

"You want to take over the payments?"

"Sure, I'd love it," said Ruck, looking around the huge room. "Of course, I'd do something a bit more stylish."

Augie grinned, "Not trendy enough for you?"

Ruck looked around the room, "Shit, there is no style or design period."

"Oh, we got a load of Stoney's weed in last night," said Bernie.

"Have Hank run a couple of bricks over to Ned. I told him I'd save him something special."

"I'll take care of it," said Bernie.

"What's the schedule for the Albatross?"

"She'll be on station in Thailand before the first."

"Great. I'll make a fast trip to get that set up," said Augie.

"You've been on the road a lot lately," said Ruck.

"Just tying up loose ends."

Sophia stashed the heavy satchel in the trunk of the little Mercedes and hopped into the passenger seat. Augie leaned over to kiss her, "I've missed you."

She settled back and held his hand, as the little car wheeled out of LaGuardia, "Me too, but it's your fault, you've been gone a lot."

"How are your projects coming?"

She held up a swirl of slender gold spirals grasping a faceted aquamarine on her middle finger, "I stayed up all night to finish this."

"Wow, that's beautiful. It's really like the stone is floating inside those tiny prongs."

She laughed, "There's a little bit of trickery behind the art."

"Well, I'm impressed. When do I get to see our rings?"

"I'm close but they're not ready yet. Soon."

"Tease!"

She squeezed his hand, "Well, yeah!"

"Listen, we've got to drop the cash off at the shop and then we'll head down the coast."

"That's fine, even if being in the middle of that much desolation gives me the creeps."

Augie grinned, "Funny how the most secure place is where no one would think to look."

He pulled up in front of the door with the golden Puerto Rican flag, "I'll go open up and you drive in."

"Okay, I feel kind of honored. I've never been in your secret hidey-hole."

"It would be better if you forget everything you see as soon as you see it. As far as anyone else is concerned, you were never here." He got out, unlocked the office, and rolled up the door.

Sophia pulled the Mercedes inside and the door rattled closed. She climbed out as two Dobermans approached to lick her hands, "Hey guys, you sure are friendly."

He pulled the bag from the trunk and handed each dog a Milk-Bone, "That's Gretel and Fritz. They're great dogs, as long as one of us is here, but, when we lock up, they're the best security money can buy."

"I was expecting something fortified."

Augie grinned, "Better that it looks like the chopshop it used to be. C'mon." He walked up a short flight of concrete steps to a large steel and concrete cage at the back of the building. "This is security."

He unlocked the gate and tripped a secret lever that heaved a panel of steel bars inward to one side. They stepped inside a cavern lined with cartons from floor to ceiling surrounding a second wall of steel bars encasing an enormous safe.

"Holy shit! That thing's huge."

Augie twisted the dial, "Yeah, barriers inside barriers." He swung the heavy door open and started stacking the cash from the valise. "Problem is, it's full and all the other stash houses are full. Gets to be a problem."

"I've never thought about that side of it."

He handed her the empty briefcase and closed the safe, "Did you memorize those numbers I gave you?"

Sophia smiled, "A – 4 1 5 6 9 2 7 0 6 1 3 3
C – 9 9 9 7 3 6 2 7 5 0 1 7
L – 7 6 0 5 4 1 7 9 2 3 0 3
B – 5 6 2 3 7 0 8 1 9 9 4 9."

"I'm impressed," said Augie. "Let's get out of here."

"So, when do I get to know what your number strings mean?"

"How about I promise to explain it before the wedding?"

"I'm impatient!"

He kissed her gently, "This is about insurance for later, so it doesn't have anything to do with what's happening today."

"Fine, just be that way."

"You'll appreciate it when the time comes."

Augie locked up and they headed south, "I asked Bernie and Ruck to come down this weekend to see the place."

"Cool. Our first guests."

"I stocked up the freezers last week and brought in a bunch of wine and beer, so we just need to pick up veggies and stuff."

"Great. When do I get my load of shit?"

Augie grinned, "There are two huge piles behind the garages, waiting for you to lay out your beds, and I've got a couple of local kids lined up to help with the heavy stuff."

"That's incredible! We'll have our own veggies in six weeks!"

"Just save a little time and energy for me."

She stroked his crouch, "Are you still gonna love me when I'm all sweaty and dirty?"

"I'm gonna love you no matter what."

She leaned over and kissed his cheek, "I'm startin' to believe that we really can build this life we've been dreaming about."

"This is just the first step."

Bernie looked up and shook his head, as Hank wandered up to the bar, "It's two in the afternoon and you were supposed to be here before noon. You look like shit, man."

"You ever get tied up with Julie?"

"No."

"Well, watch out. That girl likes to get fucked-up."

"Too hot to handle?"

"Fuck, started with a couple of downers to mellow things out, then endless lines of coke to brighten things up, some nice hash to smooth it over, and shots of B&B to wash it all down."

"After all that, I couldn't get it up."

"I managed but she's a beast in the sack. I'm gonna have trouble walkin' for a couple of days"

"Well, you survived your own nonsense, once again. I'm still pissed but, at least, you came up with a good story."

"So, what ya' got for me?"

"You sure you can drive?"

"Yeah, man. My dick's sore but the compass still works."

"Okay," said Bernie, holding out a grocery sack. "Two bricks to Ned and don't fuck up."

"Aw, man, you know I'm cool."

"Yeah, right. You're too fucked-up to know how fucked-up you are."

"I'll get the bag and myself to Ned's straight away, no

stops."

"You do that and call me when you're through, so I know you're okay."

Hank grinned and grabbed the bag, peaking inside. "Cool silver packaging, brother, Industrial Modern." He turned and lurched to the door.

The streets were slick with sleet and the MGB's tires spun on the ice as Hank pulled into traffic, turning east down Liberty to jump on the FDR. He rubbed his eyes, cranked up Joe Cocker wailing 'Feelin' Alright' on the radio, and concentrated on the taillights of the Cadillac in front as it slowed for a red light. He stopped a few feet behind the other car, "I'm cool man, I can do this."

The Cadillac pulled away, at the green light, and Hank gunned the engine and let out the clutch but the little car lurched and stalled. A Buick behind him honked impatiently. He smacked the steering wheel and cranked the starter but the engine would not catch. He pumped the gas pedal and tried again. The grinding slowed until the click of the solenoid proved the battery was done. "Fuck."

He untangled his huge frame from the tiny sports car, motioned a honking line of angry drivers around him, and opened the hood. He wiggled the wires on the battery and the starter, checked the connections, and sniffed for gas fumes around the carburetor.

A beat cop, whistle clamped in his mouth, walked over, tooting to direct other cars around the MG, "What's wrong with it?"

"I don't know, it stalled and won't start. I think the battery's cooked."

He policeman looked him over, "You don't look so good, kid. You feelin' alright?"

"Aw, my girlfriend kept me up all night."

"I'll bet she wasn't quoting Shakespeare," laughed the cop. "How 'bout we call you a tow?"

"Sure," said Hank.

"Meantime, why don't you push it around the corner so we can unblock this jam?"

"Yeah, I can do that." He flopped into the driver's seat, disengaged the parking brake, and wiggled the shifter into neutral. He found a grip and heaved the car around the corner next to the curb. As he turned the wheel, he stumbled over a grate in the pavement, and landed facedown on the street as the MGB rolled under the chromed steel bumper of a Pontiac Grand Prix, crinkling the hood.

The hefty cop picked him up by the scruff of his neck and dragged him onto the sidewalk. "Are you sure you're okay? You don't look like you should be driving anyway. I should probably sight you for public intoxication at the very least."

Hank struggled to stand, "Just tired and hung over, Officer."

"You stay right here, while I call from that box over there on the pole."

He slumped against a wall and watched the portly cop waddle across the street. When he turned to open the callbox, Hank grabbed the paper stack from the floorboard and stumbled down the sidewalk.

The policeman yelled, "Hey, where the fuck do you think you're goin'?" He dropped the phone and charged after the inebriated bear with a grocery sack clutched to his chest. The cop was panting hard when he finally reached out to grasp at Hank's sleeve, snagging the bag, spilling silver bricks spinning across the pavement.

Hank reached to collect them and fell flat on the sidewalk. The cop pulled his hands behind his back and cuffed him before grabbing the two bricks. "What do we have here?"

"Industrial art, asshole," shouted Hank.

~

Officer Jenkins shoved Hank into a chair next to Detective Sejnowski's desk. "I brought you a present."

"What's so special about him?"

Jenkins laid the silver bricks in front of the Detective, "Young fella's fairly screwed-up but he had these in a bag in his car."

Sejnowski inspected the packaging, "Fancy wrapper on this, watertight. I'm bettin' they came in by sea."

Hank stared at the floor.

"Where'd you get these, punk?"

"Down in the Village, some dude on the street."

"You don't buy, what, four kilos on the street."

"That's how it happened."

"And you don't happen to remember this dude's name do you?"

"Jesus."

"Are you swearing at me, kid?"

"No, that was his name, Puerto Rican - dark hair and eyes, a little bit taller than I am. I met him at a concert last weekend."

"That's bullshit and you know it."

"I want a lawyer."

Sejnowski slammed a brick on the desk, "You'll get a fucking lawyer when I'm finished with you, punk, and that might be a while. I've got a room full of witnesses, who will swear that we just had a friendly conversation. Do you get my drift, hippie?"

Detective McElroy grabbed the back of the steel chair and dumped Hank on the floor. He leaned over and whispered, "Shame you were so drunk you couldn't even sit in a chair." The Irish cop reared back and kicked him in the ribs. "I'd suggest you cooperate."

Jenkins hauled him back into the chair, "Help yourself out,

kid. These guys ain't screwin' around."

"I told you all I know," said Hank, blood dripping from his mouth. Suddenly, he jumped to his feet and screamed, "I want a lawyer!"

Everyone in the room turned to look but no one moved. Sejnowski whipped a switchblade out of his sock and sliced the silver package. He lifted it to his nose and inhaled deeply, "Nice quality." He pulled a bud from the brick and rubbed it between his fingers, "Very nice. Whoever imported this has my respect for having a quality product but I'm still gonna put his ass behind bars for a long time, when I catch him."

Hank looked down at the detective's red face, "I don't have a clue what you're talking about, man. Charge me and get me a lawyer or let me go. It's your call…and, you're right, there's a roomful of witnesses and I'll make sure that lawyer calls every one of them to the stand."

"You don't scare me, punk. I am the law."

McElroy grabbed the neck of Hank's jacket, "Fine, we can continue this conversation in private, once he's sobered up and through booking."

"Yeah, take him away." He turned to the street cop, "Take these bricks to the lab and have 'em dust them for prints and see if they can figure out where this shit came from. And bring me back a tracking slip, so our best evidence doesn't get lost."

"Can do, Detective," said Jenkins, carefully carrying to two silver packets downstairs to the crime lab.

McElroy appeared, grinning, "That drunk punk tumbled all the way down the stairs. Turns out, he had a condom in his wallet, a wad of cash, and about fifty little slips of paper with phone numbers. I'm having the rookies track 'em all down."

"Great," said Sejnowski, sniffing his fingertips. "You know this is from those guys we've been looking for. It's strong and pungent, double wrapped in plastic and sealed in aluminum. This is first-class and I'll bet it's the same bunch."

McElroy sat back in his chair, folded his hands behind his head, and put his feet up on the desk. "I'm thinkin' that shiny silver packaging is distinctive enough that somebody else in this country has got to have run across it too. Maybe we can add some other pieces to the puzzle."

"Call Customs and the FBI...on both coasts," said Sejnowski.

~

Augie wandered out behind the garage to find Sophia with two stout young men hauling used concrete forms to box in her raised beds. She turned and kissed him on the cheek, "Augie, this is David and Fabio. They're from Sea Bright."

He shook hands with the boys, "We sure appreciate your help."

Fabio grinned, "Hey, man, we really appreciate the work. My grandma has a huge garden and this is how she built her beds thirty or forty years ago and they're still getting better every year."

"Good soil, compost, and manure, it's the perfect combination," added David. "If we can use your tractor, we'll have this done in no time."

"You know how to handle a John Deere?"

"Sure as sh...shootin'! I've been drivin' my Daddy's since before I could stay up on a bicycle," laughed Fabio.

"This is a pretty good set-up, with the beds running north-south and open to the sun, but you're gonna need another water source down at the far end so you don't have to drag hoses back and forth," said David.

"And you could fix that problem?"

"Sure," smiled the kid.

"See," said Sophia, "I'm gonna learn a lot from these guys,"

Augie turned back to the boys, "Hey, I saw in the local paper that a local policeman was gunned down last week."

"He was my uncle," said David. "They still haven't caught the bastard."

"I'm really sorry," said Augie. "Is there anything we could do to help?"

"Well, he didn't have much and didn't leave no insurance for my aunt, so she's probably going to lose her house."

Augie glanced at Sophia, "Tell you what, how 'bout we kill two birds with one stone? We'll have an open house for everyone in town, with food and fireworks over the bay, just to introduce ourselves to our neighbors, and I'll match every dollar you can raise to pay off her house."

"Wow, you'd really do that?"

"Sure, I've got a cousin who puts on big fireworks shows every year and I can guarantee that he's always looking for an excuse to test out his latest explosives."

Sophia squeezed his arm and whispered, "That's why I love you."

"That's mighty kind of you Mr. LaGuerre. We'll spread the word tonight and get back to you tomorrow, if that's okay. When would you want to do this?" asked Fabio.

"How about two weekends from now?" He turned to Sophia, "Can you get away for an extra day?"

"I'm gonna be cuttin' it close on final projects but, yeah, I wouldn't miss it."

"Cool, we can get Uncle Manny to cater it and the Barduccis can set up the fireworks on the dock," said Augie. "This can be a test run for the wedding."

"I'm for that!"

~

Ruck and Bernie pulled up next to the kitchen and climbed out to gawk at the massive log house, as Augie emerged from the back door. "Hey guys."

"Hey, yourself," said Bernie. "This is fucking incredible."

"It's one of a kind. The house was originally built as a hunting lodge up in New Hampshire and they took it apart, log by log, and rebuilt it here." said Augie. "Lemme show you around out here and then we'll get settled inside."

"How much land?" asked Bernie.

"Sixty acres between the beach and the bay, except for Ocean Avenue. The pine forest adds some privacy but we can watch sunrise over the water and sunset over the bay."

Ruck followed Augie down the ramp to a long dock in the bay, "How deep?"

"I had it dredged to eighteen feet," said Augie.

"When ya' bringing the boats down?" asked Bernie.

"We'll probably dock the Lollipop here, over the summer, and I'd like to bring in one of the sailboats, the Sparrow maybe. I've got a buoy going in about twenty yards out where it's deeper."

"Cool. Add a swimming pool and I'm movin' in for the summer," said Ruck.

Augie walked up the hill and around the back of the garage, "Sophia's putting in veggie beds so she can grow our own produce."

"I'll say," said Bernie, scanning a dozen beds lined up like coffins full of rich black soil. "You could feed half the local population out of here."

"This is her deal and I'm stayin' in the background," laughed Augie. "I'm going to add a pool and a tennis court down at the far end, after we get past the wedding and all that."

"Where ya' goin' on your honeymoon?"

"We're sailing out of St. Thomas and heading south."

"Destination unknown?"

"That's the plan," laughed the future groom. "C'mon, I'll show you the house."

"Before we go in," said Bernie.

"Now what?"

"I sent Hank over to Ned's with two of those bricks. He never made it. Evidently, his MG died in traffic and some traffic cop found the dope. He's in lockup and we've got a lawyer doing what he can to get him out."

"This is becoming a bad habit," said Augie. "Call Rudy Feinman, if you need bigger guns, but get his ass out of the slammer before he says something stupid."

"I'll check on it when we get back."

"I've got a phone, you can get on it now. We don't need to leave any loose ends hangin' out in the breeze."

Chapter 15

Augie, in a gray three-piece suit with a burgundy tie and shiny black wingtips, stood hand-in-hand with Sophia, at the bottom of the front steps on the circular drive, welcoming guests arriving in a steady procession. Cars lined the winding path, overflowing along the shoulders of Ocean Avenue where two policemen directed traffic. Sophia leaned close, "This is some turnout, think Uncle Manny can keep up with this crowd?"

"Don't worry about it," smiled Augie, as Mayor Johnson and his wife approached. He reached to shake his hand, "Mr. Mayor, I'm so glad you could be with us tonight, but I wish it was under better circumstances. And who is this lovely young lady on your arm?"

"Allow me to introduce my wife, Betty."

Sophia took her hand, "I'm Sophia and I'm so pleased to meet you."

"We all thank you for pulling everyone together to make something positive out of this tragedy," said the petite woman with a tight gray bun at the back of her head, a knowing kindness in her pale eyes, and the faintest twinge of approval at the corners of her lips. "I must say, that's a lovely dress you're wearing."

"Why thank you," said Sophia, curtsying to show off her slinky emerald gown, matching heals, and a polished piece of pink coral suspended from a slender chain around her neck. Her golden tresses were braided into a thick plait, wrapped with a cluster of tiny salmon roses.

"Won't you come in? There's a bar in the study and we'll be serving dinner outside in the back."

The Mayor escorted his wife up the stairs and disappeared into the crowd.

"How do you know him?" asked Sophia.

"We had to get a variance to do the upgrades on the house and the docks, so we had a little meeting over coffee and I made a generous contribution to his re-election campaign."

"Really?"

"Grease," smiled Augie, as Fabio and David marched up the drive. "Hey guys, you sure know how to turn out a crowd!"

"Yeah, everyone wants to help, they just needed a little push, so it's us who should be thankin' you," said Fabio. "People have contributed five dollars, ten, if they could afford it, and some even pitched in more."

"They're givin' all they can and, after this party, I'm sure we'll get some more but it ain't gonna to be enough," added David.

"You come see me, when you've collected all there is to get, and we'll see what we can work out, okay?"

"Sure!"

David turned, "Here comes my Aunt Hattie now." He walked down the drive and took her arm, "Aunt Hattie, I want you to meet Mr. and, the future, Mrs. LaGuerre. This is Hattie Moran."

A large tear rolled down her cheek, as the stout little woman looked up into Augie's eyes and reached to touch his cheek with a fingertip. "Mr. LaGuerre, I don't know how to thank you for trying to help."

"You've been through one nightmare, you certainly don't deserve to go through another," said Augie, putting an arm around her shoulders, "I'm pleased that we can help."

"I'm embarrassed by my situation."

Sophia hugged her, "I can tell, you're a proud woman who's never going to give up, and your gift is our hope that the rest of us might be half as strong in the face of such tragedy. If you'd care to go in, I'll come find you as soon as we're finished here. The bar's in the study."

The tearful woman looked up at the beautiful blond, "Ya'

got any decent Bourbon?"

Augie chuckled, "I think you'll find several choices to your liking."

"A little snort might make this easier for everyone," said Hattie, climbing the stairs in short determined steps.

Long tables were arranged along the driveway behind the kitchen and Uncle Manny served a dinner of spaghetti with meatballs, Caesar salad, garlic bread, and zuccotto – a savory desert of raspberry cream filled cupcakes frosted with a layer of dark chocolate ganache and a white-chocolate cream cheese.

Augie and Sophia guided Hattie and her family, the Mayor's party, the Chief of Police, Harry Sommers, a genial old-timer with a friendly manner and a keen eye for trouble, and several hundred other guests to a gallery of chairs overlooking the docks. Augie stood at the front, "Ladies and Gentlemen, I and my future wife, Sophia, are very pleased that all of you could be with us tonight to celebrate a life lost too soon. Hattie, I…all of us are here to express love and support for you through this difficult time and to honor the loss of a fine man, a friend to many, and a hero to all."

The crowd applauded.

He turned and pointed to the dock, "As I said, this is a celebration! Let me introduce the pyrotechnics of the Barducci Family!"

The first strains of the Star-Spangled Banner rose from a sound system as the sky burst with sprays and rainbows of red and blue, gold and icy silver.

Chief Sommers leaned over to Augie, "This is mighty kind of you, being new to the area and all."

Augie grinned, "It doesn't matter where people come from, you do what you can to help those who need a hand, that's all."

"Well, you're real popular with the local folk," said Sommers. "Say, what's your business anyway?"

"Groceries."

"Really?"

"Really, I've got five stores in Westfield and Watchung and medium-sized towns that need access to quality products close by."

The Chief gazed around, "The grocery business must be good."

Augie smiled, "I've done well but I think our idea can grow even more."

"Sounds like you've got a plan. I wish you good luck and, again, we all appreciate what you're doin' for Miss Hattie. Sam was a fine man, a good officer, and a humble pillar in our little community. Everyone respected him and we all want justice for his murder."

"Still haven't figured out who did it?"

"We've got suspects and we're chasin' down some leads but it can't happen fast enough, if you know what I mean."

"I think I do," said Augie. "The whole town needs closure."

"That's absolutely right. Closure is a nice way of putting it."

"Keeping a lid on the anger of a tight knit community has got to make your job that much harder."

Chief Sommers scanned the crowd, "These are good people, who lost something precious, and they don't have any way to soothe their rage."

~

Before the Albatross cleared Ko Lan, Stoney settled into a padded settee in the mess with a glass of very cold champagne. He reached into his pocket to withdraw two small glass vials and poured out a pile of pale brown powder and another of white crystals. "It's a bloody shame you insist on my presence until this old tub clears international waters."

"It's insurance both ways. I know that you haven't shared our itinerary with the authorities and you're assured that the shipment is safely on its way to providing your next payment.

Besides, we get to share some quality time together."

The Brit drew out lines with a business card and rolled a hundred dollar bill into a tube, "Well, if we have to waste this time, we might as well enjoy it."

"What are you brewing there?"

"Speedballs! The perfect combination of relaxation and cerebral stimulation, coke and dope!"

"That'll confuse your brain."

"Try it, you'll like it," said Stoney, offering the straw.

"In forty-five minutes, you and I are going to jump on the launch for a short ride back to your vehicles. Four hours from now, I'll be complaining about how bad my back hurts, every time I have to sit in those damned airline chairs."

He snorted half a brown line up his left nostril and half the white up his right. "And you'll be on the hook for two million."

"Deal's a deal."

"You really ought to try this," said Stoney, squinting as he inhaled the remaining lines and settled back with the satisfied smile of a Cheshire cat. "I presume you didn't bring along a tribe of young boys for my amusement on this voyage?"

"Afraid not. This is the last leg of a very fast trip."

"I am most disappointed."

"And rightly so, but at least we've reached a point where the benefits out way the gamesmanship."

"Who's to say we're finished with that entertainment? The future can be whatever we choose it to be."

"I choose to make both of us a lot of money, without anyone getting bent out of shape."

Stoney laid out two more lines, inhaled the dust, and pinched his nostrils to stifle a sneeze, wheezing, "Be a shame to waste fine sacraments."

"I remember you talking about being a chameleon, moving from one personality to another to suit the current persona. I'm thinkin' you might be taking this role a bit too far."

"I'm fine, never better."

"You're not a particularly persuasive liar."

"Well, I do copious amounts of chemicals to dull the pain of my dilemma," said Stoney. "It's like I'm living long chapters out of different novels but, somehow, they're all going to meld together into a stunning finale."

"This doesn't have to be your final endeavor but you might consider moving on to the next escapade. This one's gonna kill you before you've finished your lines. You've gotta have enough stashed away to move on to something else."

"I am a millionaire many times over, if you must know, but it's never quite enough, is it? There's always one more goal, one more milestone to pass before you can stop looking over your shoulder."

"Maybe that's the best reason to consider a change."

"I'll take that as friendly advice, mate," said Stoney, sipping a second glass of champagne, "but there are appearances and reputations that must be sufficiently sullied to warrant an escape into a new venture."

"You can go anyplace you want and you have the smarts to accomplish anything you put your mind to, so focus on what comes next."

"So many choices, so little time," mused the Brit. His glazed eyes focused, "I'll be in Manhattan at my favorite hotel the day before your wedding. How 'bout we settle our accounts before the festivities?"

"I'll look you up."

Chapter 16

Tony settled on a barstool in the Tavern under De Branderij Hostel on Koningsstraat, just around the corner from Amsterdam's Red Light District, where comely girls sat half-naked, like erotic manikins, offering their bodies to the tourists from little storefronts. Maybe, if he got drunk enough, he might try one.

The barkeeper, an aging hippie with a gray beard and ponytail, asked in American English, "What can I get ya'?"

"Cold beer," replied Tony. "Where ya' from?"

"Cleveland," said the bartender. "Grolsch okay, it's what all the locals drink?"

"What no Heineken?"

"If you want to look like a tourist, I'll serve you Heineken in a bottle."

"Naw, Grolsch is fine. Say, I'm Tony from New York. What's your name?"

"Hi, Tony from, I never would have guessed from the accent, New York. I'm Trevor."

"Any good music around tonight?"

"Well, we have little jams here on Fridays and Saturdays." He pointed upstairs, "Most of our guests are musicians roaming around the Continent, so we get some really nice combinations. If you want to get out and about, there are tons of clubs but the Paradiso is the coolest spot in Amsterdam."

"Close by?"

"You'll want to take a cab or you'll never find your way back. Oh, the secret to finding your way is that Amsterdam Centraal is the center of a series of streets and canals that arc around that point. If you can keep track of where the station is, you'll have a vague clue about how to find your way home."

"Dope?"

"Well, I can fix you up with a little something. Pot? Hash?"

"Mmmm…hash…got anything special?"

"Sure, how much d'you wanna spend?"

"How 'bout fifty bucks to start?"

"I'll have it for you in an hour," said Trevor, pulling a small loaded pipe from under the bar. "Here, try a couple of puffs of this but be careful, it burns hot."

Tony took the little pipe and flicked his Zippo, inhaling deeply as the brown rock melted and glowed. He coughed, spewing a cloud of white smoke, "Yeah, but wow!"

Trevor grinned, "Told ya' to be careful."

"What about chicks?"

"Well, prostitution is legal within the district and you can buy whatever weirdness you want but, if you're looking for someone closer to your own age, the Paradiso is a magnet for chicks from all over the world. Pick a country and I'll bet they're represented by their finest."

"I'm definitely going tonight."

"When you go, there's a big club on the first floor, a jazz club in the basement, usually an underground concert going on the second level, and then there's the attic."

"The attic?"

"Yeah, a long hallway lined with Persian carpets and lots of people selling pretty much any kind of drug you could ever want. There are lots of hash-dealers and most of them can hook you up with whatever…acid, psilocybin, speed, downers, junk, coke, you name it, but don't expect a great price. It's like going to a cosmic supermarket where the choices are endless but the prices ain't cheap."

"I'm hip," said Tony, squinting through billowing vapors.

A hippie with long dirty-blond curls and muttonchops sat

down next to Tony, "Hey, Trevor, can I get a beer?"

"Sure, man, comin' right up."

He turned to Tony, "I'm Stephen Shirley."

"Tony. Where ya' from?"

"Baltimore and I'm guessin' you're from New York."

"The accent is a dead giveaway."

"Yeah, I bummed around the Village for a while, played a lot of little clubs but the scene was getting weird last fall, so I took off for a tour of Europe and wound up here."

"Yeah, I've been staying with family on Sicily all winter. I'm ready for a little craziness."

Trevor placed a glass of Grolsch on the bar. "Tony's wantin' to go to Paradiso tonight."

"Really? I'm jammin' with an Irish band called Taste over there, starting at nine. If you pay for the cab, I'll get you in."

"Deal, what time are you going?"

"How about eight o'clock? I've gotta meet up with Rory Gallagher and go over a couple of tunes before we play. You ever heard him?"

"No."

"He's got a great voice and he's an incredible guitarist. You'll dig it."

"Great. I'll meet you here tonight."

Tony paid the cabby and followed Stephen, who was using two guitar cases to plow through a horde of raucous hippies gathered at the entry for the show, into the former church on Weteringshans. They walked through an imposing lobby into the chapel, which had been transformed with a large stage, lights and projection screens, and stacks of speakers.

"This place always makes me feel kinda reverent, only we're

worshipping music instead of religion." He smiled, "Listen, I've gotta head into the back to go over a couple of tunes with Rory. You might want to head upstairs and see who's selling what...and don't buy from the first guy you see, check it out."

"Cool," said Tony. "I'll catch you later."

He trudged up the stairs, past the balcony, to a long narrow room gray with swirls of smoke wafting through the light. Dealers were setting up scales and putting out samples of their wares, joking and laughing with other vendors, as lighters flashed and new strains were shared. Tony walked slowly past one little stall after another, each offering their finest smoke. "I've got Afghani hash," said one. His neighbor laughed, "But I've got Nigerian pot that'll paint the sky purple."

Tony stopped before a slender girl with luminescent blue eyes and coal black hair, who was adjusting an antique balance with golden scales and holding a narrow teak tray with tiny weights lined up in perfect order. The scale sat next to a tall hookah with a brass bowl erupting from a bulbous iridescent glass jug with four braided tubes. He grinned, "What ya' sellin'?"

The girl's French accent was soft and sensuous, "I have some really fine grass and hash. What are you lookin' for?"

Tony smiled, "I'm Tony. Just passin' through on my way home to New York."

"I might have guessed." Her lips barely parted but her eyes slowly scanned his body, "I'm Madeline. You want to try a puff of Lebanese?"

"Sure." He sat down on the plush carpet, as she loaded the bowl of the pipe and offered a stem on the end of a tube. She lit the hash and he inhaled, drawing the smoke bubbling through ice-cold water, and held the toke for a long moment. A rush rolled through his brain and his muscles relaxed. "That's far out."

Madeline grinned, "I only sell the best."

"I'll bet everyone down the line says the same thing."

She scanned up and down the room, "That guy, second from the end, laces his hash with pepper for weight. It tastes like shit. That guy over there dusts shitty grass with PCP and the high is way too intense."

"So, not all hippie dealers are good people."

"It's the same everywhere. Buyer beware," said the French girl.

"How'd you end up selling dope in Amsterdam?" asked Tony.

Madeline giggled, "I followed my true love from my home in France and it didn't end so well. There was nothing to go back to, so I decided to start a new life of my own."

"And how'd that work out?"

"Excellent! I'm emancipated! I don't answer to anyone. I earn enough to pay for everything myself."

"Yeah, you seem to have your shit together," said Tony, eyeing pert little tits outlined against a tight sweater. "Got a boyfriend?"

"I've got lots of boyfriends," said Madeline with a coy smile. "As I said, I'm emancipated. I do what I want with whoever I choose."

"What are you doing when you're finished here?"

"I guess we'll have to see, won't we? What else were you lookin' for?"

Tony took another hit, "I was thinkin' about taking some coke back with me. People back home are gettin' into it but, by the time it hits the streets, the shit's been cut at every step down the line, so, it's just crap. Expensive milk powder."

Madeline laughed, "See, I told you it was the same everywhere."

"Do you deal coke?"

"Yeah, but not here. I can get whatever you want. In quantity, ounces are going for…twelve-hundred, American."

"How 'bout a half-pound?"

"I could get you a better price."

"What kind of quality?"

"Uncut and clean."

"Can I try some?"

"Sure. Meet me here at one o'clock, when we start closing down for the night, and you can check it out." She glanced around, then pulled a little bottle from her pocket and dipped a tiny silver spoon into the white powder. "Here take a hit of this and tell me what you think."

He took two snorts. The first cleared the fog in his head. The second produced a bulge in his pants, as he gazed into her shimmering eyes. "That's really nice. Is this the same stuff?"

"Yeah, I only buy hard drugs from one guy and only because, other than sampling new product, he doesn't get fucked-up."

"A businessman."

"Purely."

"I know one of those," smiled Tony. "Okay, tell you what, gimme a couple of grams of that hash and I'll be back before you close up."

"Cool. You want me to roll your hash into spliffs?"

"Sure."

She licked the gum to fasten three papers into a long fat wrapper, laced it with dark tobacco, weighed and heated the hash, then crumpled it evenly through the mix. She tore a little piece of cardboard from a match pack to make a filter and, with a flip of her fingers and a long lick, formed a tight cone. "Here, that'll keep you going for the evening."

"Thanks, what do I owe you?"

"Twenty dollars American."

He handed her a twenty, "I'll come find you later."

"Cool. I'll see what I can do in the meantime."

The crowd was climbing the stairs as he marched down to the second level, where a bunch of black guys with long matted hair were warming up the audience with a thumping, jumping celebration of life in the Caribbean. Stephen tapped him on the shoulder, "These guys are really good. Don't ask me how they got here from Kingston but they know how to rock a crowd."

"When are you playin'?"

"Second set through the encore. Did you score upstairs?"

"Yeah, man I got a spliff that'll knock your dick in the dirt."

"Light that puppy up, brother."

Tony pulled the joint from his pocket and flicked his Zippo, inhaling deeply. He handed it to Steven, wheezing, "Here, take a couple of hits of that."

"Yeah, man, that's really fine," said the guitarist. "I better take it easy, I've gotta remember all the changes I just learned."

"I'll save some for later."

"You gonna grab anymore?"

"Yeah, I met this French chick, who's gonna hook me up after the show. I'll let you know what she wants to do."

Steven smiled, "I'm guessin' I can find my own way home."

"I should be so lucky."

"In this joint, it's pretty hard not to score."

"Especially if you're a hot guitar player on the main stage," laughed Tony, damping out the spliff.

"That does help. Hey, I gotta go get ready. See you after."

"I'll be watchin'," said Tony as he wandered over to the bar for a beer.

He entered the main hall just as Rory was introducing Stephen, "Ladies and gentlemen, allow me to introduce an old friend and ace guitar picker, Stephen Shirley!"

The crowd applauded and the band launched into 'Blister the Moon'. He found a spot right in front of the mixing board but behind a half-dozen drunken Germans, who were singing along at full throttle, if not in key. Steven acted and played as if he'd been jammin' with these guys forever, singing harmonies and taking off on blazing solos.

After several pitchers of beer, the German chorus got out of hand, and Tony moved to the side for a better view. Madeline pressed against his back, "These guys are really good."

"Yeah, the guitar player with the blond curls is a new friend of mine."

"Stephen Shirley. I've seen him play a couple of times and he's starting to get a following," said the French girl, producing another spliff. "Got a light?"

"Sure," smiled Tony, flicking his Zippo. "Are you finished upstairs?"

"Yeah, I close down a little before everyone else. I might lose a little profit but, by the end of the night, the customers are all fucked-up and I'd rather not deal with their trips."

"Good business."

"Speaking of which, I talked to my friend and he said that, if you want to discuss the transaction, we could stop by his place when we leave here."

"That was fast."

"Hey, if you're serious, I can make it happen."

"Cool."

"I've got all my stuff packed, so we can go after the band's finished," said Madeline through a cloud of sweet pungent smoke.

After a steaming encore, Tony found Stephen backstage and left the remainder of the spliff. He followed Madeline out onto the street, as she marched to the tiniest car he had ever seen and climbed into the driver's seat. Tony hopped in the other side, "What is this car? It's so dinky."

"It's a Fiat and I only have to fill up the tank about every two months. It's perfect for what I need."

"I can dig that."

She slammed the little car into gear and tore down the street, swerving to avoid drunken pedestrians, "He doesn't live too far from here."

"What's going down tonight?"

"Just an introduction, so you can meet each other, sample the product, and make arrangements, if you're cool with the scene."

"I'm game," said Tony, grabbing the handle of the door as she squealed around a corner, "if we make it that far."

"Relax. Everyone drives fast in this city and the people on foot know to get out of the way."

The little car bumped up on the curb in front of a drab concrete apartment building and she got out, "C'mon."

He followed her into a dank fluorescent green lobby, up three flights of stairs, and along a hallway to a corner apartment. She knocked three times and the eyehole darkened for a moment, before the door cracked open. A deep male voice asked, "Is this the cat you told me about?"

"Oui, c'est Tony. Tony meet Walter."

"Pleased to meet you, come inside," said Walter, closing the door behind them. He was broad and thick, with short-cropped blond hair, a bushy moustache, and German accent. "Can I offer you something to drink?"

Tony glanced at Madeline, "No, thanks, I think we're fine." He looked around the austere white room with sleek Scandinavian furniture and bold splashy paintings lit with ceiling cans. "No one would ever guess that something this cool was inside this building."

Walter chuckled and motioned for them to sit on a red leather sofa, "It's better to hide yourself in plain sight. You can still maintain a certain level of luxury while remaining fairly anonymous. Most of my neighbors are from diverse parts of the world and many would rather remain invisible."

"Makes sense," said Tony.

"Tony's looking for a half-pound of righteous coke. Can you

help him out?" asked Madeline.

"That I can do, if you're serious."

"I am."

"Do you have the money?"

"Not on me but I can have it available within a couple of hours," said Tony.

"How are you going to get it back into the States?" asked the dealer.

"I haven't quite figured that out yet. I took some hash back in the bottom of a shaving cream can, once."

"I think I can be of assistance. I stashed a pound of heroin inside the lining of a Samsonite for a client recently and, the retrofit was so perfect, he made it right through customs."

"Think you could do that with a half-pound of coke?"

"Certainly. When are you leaving?"

"Thursday," replied Tony.

"Fine," said the German. "I'll have the case ready on Wednesday afternoon. Madeline can bring you by when you've got the cash together."

"How much and what quality?"

"Oh, forgive me," said Walter, producing a hand mirror, in a nouveau silver frame, covered with slender lines of white powder. He handed Tony a rolled note, "This is the product that I'm selling. Be careful, it hasn't been cut, so it's probably more pure than what you get on the street."

Tony snorted a line and grinned, "That's very smooth."

"Pure cocaine is silky, the bite in your nose is the other toxins that have been mixed in with it."

"How much do you want for the half-pound?"

"For a friend of Madeline's, eight-thousand American cash."

"I'll have it covered," said Tony, as he handed the rolled bill to Madeline.

~

McElroy bounded through the door into the station and marched down the aisle to Sejnowski's desk. The fat detective looked up, "What are you smiling about?"

"I think we've finally made the first connection."

"With what?"

"The aluminum pot."

He sat up and leaned his elbows on the desk, "Okay, hit me."

"I've just come from a meeting with Harrison, over at the FBI, and, it turns out, our metallic packaging has turned up before." The Irishman paused and grinned, "A month ago, a Coast Guard cutter intercepted a speedboat carrying a half-ton of primo pot wrapped and sealed in a heavy aluminum foil near Monterey, California."

"Now you've peaked my interest."

"It gets better. Turns out, the kid who was driving the boat is from New York City. His name is Theodore Parsons, as in William Parsons."

"The tycoon?"

"Son of the same," said McElroy. "And...he attended the same high school as Henry Maltinado. Seems they're boyhood chums."

"What school?"

"Sebastian Academy, mostly Italian Catholic kids, and it's private, so tuition's gotta be steep."

"So, we might deduce that they're from prominent families and I'll bet their cronies are poor little rich kids too," said Sejnowski, leaning back in his chair. "We need to poke around to find out about their connections. Dig into their friends, where they hang out, all that stuff. We'll get both of them in here and start asking questions. Somewhere in there, we're gonna find the guy we've been lookin' for or someone close to him."

~

Augie drove the little Mercedes down Park Avenue, "We could live here."

Sophia laughed, "Yeah, like either of us fit in with this crowd. I love the cabin, the setting, and I have every intention of raising a family there."

"Guess that's settled. Just like you needing to make sure that my tux meets your expectations."

"You might even get used to it."

"If that's the biggest hassle we ever have, I'm cool."

Sophia's lips curled into a smile, "Would you be cool with becoming a father?"

Augie glanced at her, "Are you...?"

"Pregnant? Yes!"

He pulled to the curb and kissed her, "I can't believe it. When?"

"We're about six weeks along and mother and child are both doing very well, thank you."

Augie was dazed, "Shit. I'm going to be a father."

"And a fine one at that," said Sophia, placing his hand on her tummy. "You can't feel it yet but, pretty soon, we'll be able feel him moving around."

A taxi honked and the driver leaned out the window, "Hey, buddy, can't you read. You're blockin' up a taxi zone!"

Augie waved and pulled into traffic. "This changes everything."

"What do you mean?"

"I feel like I just got hit by a tidal wave, a sudden flash into the future."

"One's not going to be enough. We both come from big families, so we're going to have more."

Augie grinned, "Okay, now seems the time to talk about something else."

"What?"

"Those numbers that I made you memorize."

"You want me to recite them?"

"No, I want to you to change the letters to places. 'A' is for Amsterdam, 'C' is for Cannes, 'L' is for Lisbon, and 'B' is for Barcelona."

"And?"

"I'll give you the name of a contact at a bank in each city. We have numbered accounts in each of them."

"No shit?"

"The access number is the same for each."

"Your birthday."

"How'd you know that," asked Augie with that little grin.

"You're too easy. 07-04-41."

"My ol' man claims he saw the war comin' and wanted a son before he signed up."

"That's family planning," laughed Sophia.

Augie grinned, as the car slowed for a light, "There's more than eighteen million in those accounts, so you know you're secure, if something happens."

"What's going to happen? You're quitting, right?"

"Yeah, but I won't be completely clear for seven years."

"Can we start counting two days from now, after we say our vows?"

"I've got some things to finish up, in the next month or so, but I won't be involved in any more shipments. Almost everything has been delivered and distributed, so, I guess I'll be done when the final payments come in."

"That's close enough."

He squeezed her hand, "You're meeting up with my mom, after we get done with this, right?"

"Yeah, we're going to check with the florist and then I have my final fitting at three. You're picking up Tony at Kennedy, right?"

"I've got something else I've got to do before he gets in. I'll meet you at my parent's tonight."

"Cool."

Augie turned to gaze at her, "I can't believe how much I love you."

"I can't wait to start building our family together."

Chapter 17

The sun broke through low-hanging clouds and Augie felt a bounce in his step as he walked into the Waldorf-Astoria. The clerk at the long reception desk looked up, "How may I help you?"

"Stoney Montgomery, please."

The clerk dialed the phone and spoke for a moment. She replaced the receiver and said, "He's expecting you. Room 3904. The elevators are just to the left."

Stoney opened the door before he could knock, "Come in, old man. It's good to see you."

Augie stepped inside and placed a large briefcase next to an onyx letter opener and a long pair of scissors with red stones inlaid in the handle on an ornate Louis XV table, supported by four golden maidens clutching bouquets of flowers. Stoney walked over to the bar, "I assume that's payment in full. Could I offer you a splash?"

"No, it's a bit early in the day. I have to pick up my brother at the airport and have dinner with the family."

"If it was my family, I'd definitely be blottoed before I showed."

Augie laughed, "There have been times. Trouble is that my ol' man could probably still beat the shit out of both of us, if he had half a mind."

Stoney lifted a snifter of B&B, "Here's to peace within the family."

Augie flipped the latches on the case to reveal thick stacks of hundred dollar bills. "It's all here, two million."

The Brit smiled broadly, "Pleasure doing business with you, mate. When do you want to go again?"

"We'll see what happens over the summer," said Augie. "I'm taking a long honeymoon."

"Where ya' goin'?"

"Picking up a sailboat in St. Thomas and heading south."

"Destination unknown? How romantic!" roared Stoney, as a young brown boy emerged from the bedroom wearing a sheer silk robe. "Oh, how embarrassing!"

Augie shook his head, "You are a pig."

"I can afford my fantasies," smiled Stoney. "Hell, I've even helped you fulfill a few of yours."

"And now, we're business associates."

Stoney broke up, "You don't know what you missing!"

"I've gotta go or I'm gonna be late at the airport. I'll see you at the wedding on Saturday."

"I wouldn't miss this for anything!" said Stoney, as he followed Augie to the door.

~

Tony trudged up the corridor, exhausted from the long flight and Madeline keeping him up all night with lines of cocaine and rough sex. He waited impatiently at the carousel for the white Samsonite to emerge from the chute and sauntered up to a line of customs stations, glancing up at the gallery to wave at Augie, who was leaning against the rail.

He chose the youngest agent and presented his passport. The inspector took the book, glanced at the picture, then at Tony, and flipped through the pages of stamps from various European countries. "Looks like you had quite a trip."

"I was staying with family in Italy over the winter and took a short tour of the major cities on my way back. I've gotta say, it's nice to be home."

"I see your last stop was Amsterdam."

Tony grinned, "Good beer, the Rijksmuseum, and lots of

beautiful women. What more could anyone ask for?"

"Anything to declare?"

Tony handed over a list of small gifts and their values, "Just gifts for my family."

"That's fine. Put your suitcase up here on the counter."

He lifted the bag and flipped the latches.

"This is brand new. What happened to the one you carried over?"

Tony smiled, "Got ripped-off in a hostel. I had to buy a new one."

The agent opened the suitcase and pawed through a pile of dirty clothes. "It seems they weren't interested in your clothes."

He ran his fingers around the inside of the rim and frowned. The inspector dumped the contents on the counter and pawed around the entire surface before pulling out a small razor-knife to slit the fabric. White powder flowed out and his eyes glinted quizzically, "What have we here?"

Tony glanced up at the gallery but Augie was gone.

Sophia rolled over to Augie, who was staring at the ceiling. "You're worried about Tony, aren't you?"

"Yeah. I called Rudy Feinman and he'll get him out."

"There's more to it than that."

"Of course," sighed Augie, pausing, "I have to admit that I don't trust him to keep his mouth shut. He's still a stupid kid, who spooks easy, and he's facing an automatic seven years in Rikers Island."

The phone rang and Augie picked up the receiver, "Hello."

Ruck sounded hung-over, "Any word on Tony?"

"No, I called Rudy yesterday."

"I'm sorry, man, let's hope he's smart enough to stay cool."

"I have my doubts," said Augie, squeezing Sophia's hand.

"Not to change the subject but have you seen this morning's paper?"

"No, why?"

"Our ol' buddy got his due. Go get your Times, front page."

"I'll call you back," said Augie, hanging up the phone.

"What's up," asked Sophia.

"Ruck said there's something interesting on the front page of the New York Times."

He grabbed a pair of jeans and a flannel shirt, padded down the stairs and out onto the drive to collect the paper. The headline touted the Apollo Ten's journey to orbit the moon and test the lander but a heading on a smaller article read, 'Brit Murdered in Luxury Suite.'

The article opened, 'British citizen and Hong Kong businessman, Stoney Montgomery was found murdered in his suite at the Waldorf-Astoria. Privileged sources told this reporter that Hotel Security entered Mr. Montgomery's room, on reports of screaming, to find the subject's nude body, sprawled on a bed covered with millions of dollars in cash, with a pair of scissors impaled in his groin. A young boy was escorted from the scene by authorities. Further details are forthcoming.'

Augie reread the article twice, "That's kharma coming back to bite you."

He walked back into the kitchen and handed the paper to Sophia, who was pouring coffee. "What's this?"

"This pervert was our Asian supplier."

"Oh, my god, how awful. That poor boy."

"He was definitely off his rocker, in a very kinky way, but he had good product."

She sat down next to him, "It's time to get out."

Augie sighed, "I hope...this doesn't drag everyone down. There are a lot of good people who could get hurt."

"Including you," said Sophia, kissing him on the cheek. "We have to get through tomorrow and then we'll sail away to peace in the tropics for a few weeks."

"I can't wait to run away with you."

"If Tony can't be your best man, you'd better make a second choice."

"I've gotta call Ruck back. We'll see if he'll volunteer."

Sophia and Taylor settled into the nook with sandwiches and iced tea as a crew of caterers hauled crates of food into the huge kitchen and set up to prepare a sumptuous meal for two-hundred and fifty guests, who would start arriving within a few hours.

Taylor smirked, "This is like a fairytale."

"I've been afraid to open my eyes every morning for weeks, thinking that it was all just a dream."

"It is a dream. I can see how much Augie adores you, every time he looks at you, plus, you get to live in a rustic mansion on the beach. What more could you ask?"

"That I won't wake up!" laughed Sophia. "I'm just glad I've got you to help me get through this."

"I wouldn't be anyplace else."

Fabio and David maneuvered through the bustling kitchen, "Hey, we're settin' up the tables on the drive but there's a big truck here with gear for the band. What do you want them to do with it?"

"Have them unload over by the stage. Their plane was due in before noon, so, I'm sure they'll be showing up within the hour."

"Can do," said David. The boys danced through the caterers and disappeared.

"How are things with Randy?"

Taylor laughed, "I wouldn't have believed it, if someone told me that I'd be sharing a man with another woman and feeling absolutely comfortable with the arrangement."

"You don't have any problem with Sunny?"

"No, not at all."

"Good, 'cause I really like her," said Sophia. "She fits right into our little girl's club."

"I've got a secret."

"What's that?"

Taylor grinned, "I think I'm pregnant."

"I can't believe it, so am I!"

Taylor hugged her, "Really?"

"Yup, seven weeks."

"I'm really late but I haven't told Randy yet. I was hopin' this might be the right occasion."

"Do you want to keep it?"

She patted her tummy and blushed, "I think I do."

"Then we'll have to make sure our kids grow up together, like cousins."

Taylor glanced up at the clock, "You better start thinkin' about getting dressed. You're gonna be beautiful."

"Everything seems to be running on its own, so come help me with my dress and makeup."

~

Taylor fastened a pearl choker around Sophia's neck and kissed her gently on the cheek, "You are a beautiful bride."

Sophia kissed her back, "I hope nothing ever comes between us."

"It won't."

A knock at the door interrupted and Taylor skipped across the bedroom to find Sunny, dressed in a slinky yellow dress embroidered with delicate flowers. She looked up, tears streaming down her face, her lips quivering, "They...didn't make it."

Taylor took the little blond in her arms, "What are you saying?"

"I just talked with Mallory and she said, the Pennsylvania Police called to say that the band's plane had engine trouble and went down in a storm in the mountains north of Scranton last night."

Taylor pulled back, "And?"

"There were no survivors. They're all dead!" screamed Sunshine.

"Oh, my God! Noooo!"

Sophia wrapped them in a giant hug and they wept together, their tears splashing down the bodice of her wedding gown.

Finally, Sunny pulled away, "There's less than half-an-hour before the ceremony and the guests are already being seated."

"You have to go through with it," said Taylor.

"But...how can I celebrate my love for Augie when both of you have lost yours?"

"I think we should save the announcement until everyone gathers for food and drink," sniffled Sunny.

"I agree," said Taylor, wiping her tears with a tissue. "Let us rejoice, first, and then we can mourn."

Sophia sniffled, "I sure am lucky to have best friends like you."

The girls crowded together in front of the mirror to repair their makeup.

~

Augie and Ruck waited with Father Malloy on the dock, beneath an arch of white lilies. Garlands of deep pink roses wrapped the pilings and hundreds of votive candles meandered along the pathways between planters overflowing with bleeding heart sprouting from mounds of white impatience. A squadron of pelicans flew through rolling reflections of orange glittering across the bay, as a string quartet struck the opening chords of the grand march. Augie scanned the faces of family and friends and noticed Stanton Tosh sitting with his head bowed, talking quietly with Sunny, who was dabbing her eyes with a handkerchief, as Margo, Penny, and a downcast Taylor were escorted to the altar by Ashton Lambert, Chester Walsh, and Bernie.

Sophia's white dress glowed in the golden gleam of the setting sun, as her father guided her down the long path. Augie took her hand and they turned to face Father Malloy. He looked inquiringly into her sad, puffy eyes and whispered, "I love you."

The priest began, "Dearly beloved, we are gathered here to join Sophia Daniella DeRosa and Augustus Constantine LaGuerre in Holy matrimony..."

The words blurred into a murmur, until Sophia nudged Augie, who was staring, bewildered, into her eyes. He glanced up at the priest, who wore a small impatient smile, and said, "I do."

"I now pronounce you man and wife."

The crowd cheered and applauded, as he took her in his arms and kissed her passionately.

A Barducci missile erupted into a brilliant red heart framed by glittering explosions of gold and silver shimmering against the last glow of sunset. Father Malloy bellowed, "Ladies and gentlemen, may I present Mr. and Mrs. Augie LaGuerre!"

She looked up at him with a sad smile and took his arm, as they strode across the little bridge and up the path to the house.

They passed her father and brothers, who were clapping and cheering. Augie's father nodded approvingly, with a little grin and wink, while his mother clutched his arm, dabbing at her eyes with a lace hanky that was surely blessed by the Pope, surrounded by his sobbing sisters. He spotted Sidney and Fasal, among rows of applauding relatives and friends, and Abby bawling in the back row, before he glanced up the path and noticed Chief Sommers standing at the top of the hill with several men in dark suits.

As the couple stepped onto the pavement, the Police Chief said, "I'm terribly sorry for the insensitive timing but these gentlemen have a warrant for your arrest."

The photographer's flash fired as Sophia smacked the Chief across the face with her bouquet. "Insensitive? What the fuck is the matter with you people?"

Detective Sejnowski stepped forward to present a certified warrant, "We've been waiting a long time to make your acquaintance. With the cooperation of your brother and your buddies, you're gonna be spending a long time in Federal lockup for conspiracy to import and distribute narcotics."

McElroy produced a pair of handcuffs and leaned up to Augie's ear as he latched them tight, "Was it worth it, trading a few years of wealth and power for the rest of your life?"

"Much as we'd like to take you back to the precinct for a private conversation, Federal charges take precedent, so you'll be escorted back into the city by Agent Harrison and his associates," said Sejnowski. "But we'll have lots of questions for you."

Augie looked down at Sophia, as the detective rambled through a list of rights, "I'm so sorry."

"We'll get you out, don't worry," wailed the new bride, as they led him away to a black Ford parked next to unopened crates of musical equipment. "Remember, I'm your wife."

Curious family and guests gathered to console Sophia, who collapsed on the driveway, a wilted blossom of silk and lace, sobbing with Taylor and Sunny.

Chapter 18

The guard closed and latched the steel door as Sophia stepped into a small white windowless room with a table and two chairs under flickering fluorescents. Augie stood and took her in his arms, "I'm so sorry for everything."

"Me too," wept Sophia.

They sat at the table and she reached to caress a brutal bruise around his left eye. "What happened?"

He winced, "Spic wanted me to join his gang. I declined."

"How bad is it?"

"Worse than you can imagine but I'll survive."

"I talked to Rudy and he said that he'd try to figure out some way to appeal the appeal but he didn't seem very confident."

"Maybe they'll give me credit for good behavior."

"I want little Augie to know his father."

"You and he will keep me going."

"Before all this happened, I dreamed of our life together. Now I can't see beyond today."

Augie took her hands, "We're only going to get to see each other once in a while and no one knows how long they'll keep me or where. If the judge had his way, he'd have me locked up in maximum security with the baddest of the bad forever. I'm the example for future drug dealers." He paused and looked into her eyes, "I want you to start a life of your own."

"You want me to walk away?"

"No, I want you to raise our son someplace safe and sane. I don't want him growing up in this madness and I don't want him to know me like this, until he's old enough to understand."

Sophia started crying again, "But...?"

"Take your time, figure out what you want out of life. When you're ready, you'll have enough to cover the dream."

"That's yours not mine."

Augie grinned, "I don't think I'll be wracking up many expenses in here. I asked you to memorize those numbers for our security. Now it's become your future. Go build it and, maybe someday, I'll get to share it with you."

"They've seized the property and everything in it, all the boats and cars and bank accounts. I'm surprised they didn't try to take my wedding dress."

"They took your husband instead," laughed Augie. "Listen, I'm serious. I want you to think about this and then act on it. No but's. I trust you to do the right thing for our son."

She leaned across the table and kissed him tenderly, "I want to do it with you."

"We can't, so it's up to you, and you'll have to be very careful about how you go about it. They'll be watching."

The door clanked open and the guard stepped inside, "I'm sorry, Miss, but time's up."

Sophia hugged Augie, "I love you."

"I love you too. Now go."

Sophia dabbed the tears spilling down her cheeks with a handkerchief, as she walked out of the Correctional Center and flagged a taxi. She climbed into the back and said, "Grand Central, please."

"Si, Senorita," said the Puerto Rican cabbie, glancing in the rearview mirror. "Are you okay?"

Sophia straightened up, "It's Senora and I'm fine, thank you. Drive."

She paid the driver, marched into the magnificent lobby, and slipped into a phone booth. A blue-green ring lamp in the ceiling flooded the tiny space as the door closed. She cracked it open to douse the light and buried her face in her hands.

Finally, she collected herself, inserted four quarters, and dialed.

Taylor answered, "Hello."

Sophia sputtered, "We lost the appeal."

"Shit!"

"He got forty years with no chance for parole...Forty Years!"

"I'm so sorry. That's a lifetime."

"They're going to ship him off to a federal penitentiary someplace, so I'll only get to see him about once every six months, and Rudy said they move inmates from one facility to another, to cut down on gangs." She paused to wipe her eyes, "I don't want to live here anymore."

"What do you mean?"

"Remember that dream you used to talk about?"

"Yeah."

"I'm in, if you are."

"Are you kidding?"

"No, I'm not and, between us, I think we can pull it off."

"I'd love to get Sunny involved but she's still mourning."

"See if she's interested. I've got something I have to do, to get things settled, but I'm up for a scouting mission next month."

"What about little Augie?"

"His grandparents would love to look after him for a few weeks. What about Andrea?"

"I can get my parents to help out."

"Are you and Sunny cool with having kids by the same father?"

"You mean the same dead father? Yeah, I think it's just one more thing that binds us together. We both loved Randy and, even though it's a weird coincidence that we both went off the pill at the same time, I wouldn't change anything."

"Okay. I'll call you when I've got my stuff together."

"What about…all this cash I'm sittin' on?"

"There's no one left to collect, so just put it away and make sure it's safe. Ruck and Bernie disappeared right after Augie was arrested and haven't been heard from since."

"Can't blame 'em."

Sophia started crying, "No, I can't but it sure would have helped to have some support."

"You've got me."

"That's why we're talking. You get in touch with Sunny. I'll call you back in a few weeks."

~

Sophia paid the taxi fare and walked up to a tall pair of doors, on a very narrow building, next to the small, restrained sign that read, 'Societe Financier'.

Before she could reach for the handle, the door opened and a tall, matronly woman in a gray suit that matched her hair, which was pulled into a tight twist fastened with a tortoiseshell comb, smiled, "Madame La Guerre, I presume?"

Sophia nodded and the woman said, "If you will follow me, the Director is expecting you."

She knocked softly and opened the door to allow Sophia to enter, "Madame LaGuerre, allow me to introduce Pierre de Gaulle."

She backed out and closed the door, as the short portly gentleman peered through dark horn-rimmed glasses, smiled, and reached to shake her hand. "Madame LaGuerre, I am Pierre de Gaulle, no relation to the General, unfortunately. I had several meetings with your husband, so I am pleased to make your acquaintance. Might I offer some coffee or tea or something more substantial?"

He held the back of a black leather chair and motioned for her to sit.

"No, thank you."

"I read in the newspapers that your husband had some legal difficulties. I do hope that those matters have been resolved."

"Unfortunately, that is not the case," said Sophia, dabbing a lacy handkerchief to her eyes.

"I am terribly sorry. How might I be of service?"

"It's regarding account number: 9 9 9 7 3 6 2 7 5 0 1 7."

"Do you have the password?" inquired the Director with a raised eyebrow.

"Oh-seven, oh-four, forty-one."

"You husband added you to the account, the last time he was here, so, how may I be of service?"

"What is the balance of the account?"

De Gaulle pulled a thick black ledger from the second drawer in his desk and flipped through the pages. "Ah, here it is. Let me see, the balance at closing last night was five-million, three-hundred thousand, and sixty-eight dollars, American."

"I would like to withdraw two million dollars."

"That can be arranged. How would you like to receive this sum?"

"Cashier's check."

"If I might see your papers, I will have it drawn immediately," said the old banker.

~

After a long dusty ride along mountainous ridgelines and dense jungle, the old pickup slowed to a stop at the foot of the front steps of an immense yellow farmhouse. Wide white shutters flanked large windows and a shiny cinnabar door behind a broad porch that might have overlooked the plains in the Midwest, rather than the Rio Grande in the Cochabamba Mountains in Southen Bolivia.

Pedro, the driver, smiled and pointed, "Senora."

Sunny piled out and fell into Sophia's arms, "I thought we'd never get here."

Sophia laughed, "It's only taken two years to get your cute little ass down here. Once you spend a few days, you'll never want to leave."

A little girl hopped out of the cab of the truck and ran over to hide behind Sunny's long skirt, "Mummy, is this your friend?"

"Yes, dear, this is Sophia. Sophia, this is Carly."

The tall blond knelt down to shake hands, "I'm pleased to meet you. How old are you? No, let me guess. You're just three."

"How'd you know?" asked the little girl.

"Because I was pregnant at the same time as your mommy and I have a little boy, named Augie, who's just about the same age as you. Here he comes now."

A tiny boy, with huge brown eyes under a mop of auburn curls, trotted down the steps to Carly, followed by a little blond girl and Taylor. The boy said, "Hi, I'm Augie and this is your sister, Andrea."

Carly stared at the little blond girl for a long moment, hardly her twin but the eyes were the same and the smile. She walked over to hug her, "I'm Carly and my mommy told me I had a sister who lived far away. I'm glad we're together now."

Taylor hugged Sunny, "I'm so glad you're here."

"Me too."

"I'll have to take you over to the school after lunch."

"School?"

Sophia laughed, "Yeah, this is Taylor's dream and part of it has always been to educate the kids, all the kids. We built a school and brought in a couple of really cool bi-lingual teachers. We've got forty children from kindergarten through middle school and more signing up every day."

"That's incredible."

"No, that's the way it should be. That's what this place is all about, using our illicit gains for the benefit of the community," said Taylor. She walked over to the truck, "Hey, Pedro, would you give us a lift up to the lookout?"

"Si, Senora."

"C'mon, we'll give you the bird's eye view."

The girls piled the children into the bed of the old truck and Pedro drove slowly up a long winding gravel cart path to a precipice overlooking a wide valley, terraced with patches of green and gold, rising above a meandering river.

Sophia's finger swept across the horizon, "We own everything you can see."

"Really?"

Taylor smiled, "We've got horses, cattle, pigs, goats, sheep, llamas, chickens, and geese, as well as dogs and cats and all sorts of other pet critters. The fields produce corn, potatoes, rice, coffee, sugar, cotton, coca, and, of course, pot. Plus we've got huge vegetable gardens up by the house. The local authorities are so happy to have our help providing jobs and making improvements in the village, they look the other way. We passed breakeven in our first year."

"What do you call it?

"Adonis Manor," said Taylor, "because all of this sprang to life, when we lost our men."

"Birth, death, rebirth," mused Sunny.

"A gorgeous male god for women," laughed Taylor.

"Augie told me to start a new life somewhere, in a place where I could build the dream we shared," said Sophia.

"Funny, Randy and I talked about owning land," said Sunny

Taylor's lips curled into a sad smile, "Us too."

"What are you leavin' behind?" asked Sophia.

"Just my mom. My dad died years ago and we're pretty much all she has."

"Think she'd consider becoming a nanny to this brood?" asked Taylor.

Sophia added, "You better know that runnin' this place is a full time job, before you sign on. No one gets to sit on her ass, 'cause there's too much that needs doin'."

Sunny knelt to hug the children, "What would you guys think, if we all lived together?"

The children cheered.

Sophia wrapped a slender arm around Sunny's shoulders and kissed her cheek, "This is our new beginning and I'm planning to stay for a very long time. With you here, it feels complete."

Watch for
Peachtree
Companion and backstory to
Dealer
Coming soon

Characters

Augustus Constantine LaGuerre – entrepreneur

Julius LaGuerre – father

Maria Santini LaGuerre – mother, deeply religious

Mary LaGuerre – sister, law student

Julia LaGuerre – middle sister

Natalia LaGuerre – youngest sister

Antonio LaGuerre – little brother

Ruck – best friend, dapper, dark hair and eyes, clotheshorse, stylish, organized

Bernie Summers – Jewish - short, fair, slender, with waves of sandy hair and green eyes. Studious.

Abby – Augie's high school girlfriend

Ashton Lambert – son of Wall Street banker

Teddy Parsons – son of real estate mogul

Henry (Hank) Maltinado – high school friend

Donny Jameson – high school chum – delivery

Jesus – street kid guarding Bronx warehouse

Mitchell O'Brien - Tony's classmate at Sebastian Academy, white Corvette

Manny Romano – Augie's uncle – Romano's Italian restaurant – a rotund, balding man with a smile to match his girth

Chester Walsh – grocery manager, fat, stubby cigar, savvy businessman and marketer

Rudy Feinman – family lawyer

Stanton Tosh – NY booking agent

Silas Sejnowski & Jimmy McElroy – detectives

Harrison – FBI

Maurie Giles – surfer, boat salesman in San Diego

Whisper – Pacific based sailboat running to Columbia

Lollipop – Julius LaGuerre's family cruiser

Jamaica
Wilfred & Nell – Jamaican suppliers

Columbia
Felix Hernandez – supplier
Juanita – hostess at the Ritz Hotel and Restaurant
Giermo and Padeo – Hernandez' New York relatives

Hong Kong / Thailand
Sidney Chui – Thai beauty – Augie's classmate from graduate school
    – heir to import/export business in addition to her own
    'Chui Antiques'
Beabea – Sidney's aunt and second mother in Hong Kong, tiny
    matriarch
Bing Watt – Thai shipbuilder
Maple Dragon – first little freighter.
Albatross – second freighter
Stoney Montgomery – Hong Kong native, former grad school nerd
Sarah Fine – Stoney's secretary

Amsterdam
Fasal Mohammed – Lebanese supplier – Bernie's college roommate
Sasha – Fasal's ex-girlfriend from Sweden
Jean Moreset – hotelier
Trevor – bartender at De Branderij Hostel in Amsterdam
Madeline – Amsterdam dealer
Walter – German coke dealer
Stephen Shirley – roaming American guitar player

Cannes
Pierre de Gaulle – banker

Madison

Taylor Jones – Bernie's cousin, Randy's girlfriend
Fat Freddy Reid – Madison dealer
David Davison – 'Dave-Dave' – partners with Freddy
Corey Timmons – 'Fleetfeet' – partners with Freddy
Billy Mintor – 'Magichands' – partners with Freddy
Transport girls: Margo, Penny, Patsy, Linda, and
Sophia Daniella DeRosa – surfer from California, art student
Andy Shapiro – Communications professor
Milly Shriver – NY Jewish heiress from Taylor's production class
Davis Richardson – law student
Paul Warner – Davis' roommate, law student
Henny and Jackson – medical students
Doris – waitress at the Plaza

Peachtree

Danny Harrison – guitar / vocals
Ethan Frost – flute, harmonica, violin, guitar, vocals
Tanner Steele – keyboards / guitar / vocals
Randy Macklyn – bass
Ronnie M. Davis – drums
Travis McGee – manager
Chaz – roadie, artist
Jason James – black roadie from Chicago
Terry – roadie
Mallory – Terry's girlfriend
Sunshine – Randy's girlfriend in Georgia
Tera – Ronnie's girlfriend
Jimmy Flanigan – photographer / stage lighting
Hal Nelson – producer the fledgling label 'Momentum'
Jacob Schreiber – drummer / dealer in Fort Lauderdale

Seabright

Fabio & David – teenagers
Hattie Moran – David's aunt, husband murdered at a traffic stop
Mayor Johnson & his wife, Betty
Harry Sommers – police chief
Barducci Brothers – fireworks

About the Author

In addition to his writing accomplishments, Eric T. Stiller, Jr. (Rick) is a renowned commercial photographer, a Master Gardener overseeing expansive gardens with his wife at the House of the Four Seasons, and an innovative musician. He has received rave reviews for the first four volumes in the <u>Morgan's</u> <u>Knot</u> serial fantasy.

Other titles by the author available on Amazon

The Morgan's Knot Serial Fantasy
Morgan's Knot (Vol. 1)
The Island of the Children (Vol. 2)
Ice Island (Vol. 3)
Islands of Glass and Steel (Vol. 4)

Visit – www.rickstiller.com